About Nine Volt Heart

He said, "I love you." She said, "You don't even know the real me." He said, "Great title for a song. Key of G? Can you sing the high parts? Close harmony?"

Two musicians meet by accident in Seattle: Jason, the now infamous singer-songwriter, and Susi, a music teacher whose previous life came off the rails. Quickly their separate worlds and professional desires become entwined in unexpected ways.

Nine Volt Heart takes you on a roller-coaster ride through the back-streets of Seattle, where tourists never go. Where both karma and sunshine can be so unpredictable in April.

> "My back pages, as real as it gets!"
> — Jason Taylor, *Woman at the Well*

> "For the reader who seeks verisimilitude in literature, and enjoys laughing as other people squirm through life."
> — Susanna Neville, *Personal Liner Notes*

※

Real people are saying ...

"Get some sleep aids before you start reading *Nine Volt Heart*, Annie Pearson's riveting, rock music romance about unlikely lovers and a cyber-stalker in Seattle's indie music scene."
> — Emily Warn, *Shadow Architect*

By Annie Pearson

Rain City Incidents:
Artemis in the Desert
Nine Volt Heart
The Grrrl of Limberlost
The Pirate King

The Accidental Heretics Adventure Series:
(as E.A. Stewart)
The Blue Door
Bone-mend and Salt
Trebuchets in the Garden
Crux Lunata
Song of Valerós
The Mad Woman of La Catalane

www.anniepearson.com

9 volt Heart

ANNIE PEARSON

JŪGUM PRESS

First edition, August 2013
Updated version, May 2014
ISBN: 978-1-939423-19-1

Published by Jugum Press
505 Broadway East #237
Seattle, Washington
Find ebook editions at
www.jugumpress.net
Contact: JugumPress@outlook.com

For Chip,
who likes the same music,
likes the same books

Contents

ONE: ALLEGRO

1
"Lonesome Whistle"
Jason

SEATTLE LURKED JUST OUTSIDE the doors of my perception, waiting to beat me with a stick.

In better times, flying into Seattle felt like stepping into a safe haven to escape a storm. To start, to escape jet lag, I always run from Leschi to Seward Park, taking the dirt path by the water. After that, my compadre Ian drags me out to play music in that Fremont after-hours basement club, and then we scarf down huevos rancheros at The 5 Point Cafe with wasted loners left from the night before and baristas preparing for their morning shifts. Then I read while rain pings the windows.

"Mr. Taylor?" The flight attendant had a London accent, fluting two notes above Middle C. "I hate to wake you, but we're about to land."

I wasn't sleeping, just listening to Hank Williams with my eyes closed. *Gotta feelin' called the blu-ues—*

"Thanks, Shannon. I appreciate it."

"How did you know my name?" Her head tilted in inquiry as I opened my eyes.

"You were kind to me when I flew the other direction last fall."

She smiled, a genuine rather than professional smile. "I remember that you had a frightful head cold then, and we were short of vegetarian meals." She gestured for me to return my seat to the fully upright and locked position. "Do you require an escort at the gate?"

"No, I don't need anything special. I'm meeting a driver at baggage pickup. Thank you, though."

"Of course, Mr. Taylor." She hesitated. "We used to come hear Stoneway play when I was an exchange student. It was the best of times."

"Really? Nice." I ran the math in my head. Seven years ago? Nine? "It was the best of times for me, too."

As I flipped open the window shade to see how close we were to SeaTac, she blurted, "I don't believe what they say," and then covered her mouth, embarrassed.

I whispered, "Thank you. It isn't true."

We swooped over the patchwork of cozy homes built for Boeing engineers, Pony League ball fields, and miniature glacier-carved lakes littered with rowboats and sailboards, the plane's wing flaps unfolded. I felt my stomach knot. Alder and cottonwood trees waved fingers of fresh green, either beckoning or scolding. Puget Sound glittered in the west, reflecting the afternoon April sun. When I'd left this town, big-leaf maples were shedding dead leaves on muddied side-streets and the Sound sloshed like molten lead between Elliott Bay and the Kitsap Peninsula. As BA0049 touched down, the air whistled and screamed, resisting the plane's entry. Gotta feelin' called trepidation, weighing down deep in my soul.

Seattle, karma lurking, waited to beat on me, body and mind.

Tail winds deposited us at SeaTac twenty minutes early and, for what must be the first time in the twenty-first century, we taxied directly to the gate, as if the plane couldn't wait to toss me out.

Then I couldn't raise anyone by phone to find my ride. I loitered on the airfield side of the security gates.

Can't find my own way back home.

"Um, hi, do you mind signing this? My mom is a big fan."

—buying peanuts to tide me till dinner—

"Are you Jason Taylor? I bet my buddy twenty bucks it's you."

—brushing my teeth in the john—

"Asshole!"

—having aural hallucinations, perhaps.

Too bad coming back here won't be like meeting that baritone folkie in a Dublin pub, the one who played Celtic punk on a cittern. He declared I was the very likeness of his lost brother and made his city home for us during the week that Ian and I performed there. Or the luthier in London with a shop near my Pimlico hotel, who let me watch him work for three days, talking up a storm about tonewoods and fretboards, and who showed me how to do abalone inlays and then invited me home to eat bangers-and-mash with his wife (who went to a great deal of trouble with an apple-betty when she discovered I couldn't eat the sausages).

Here, in the town where I was born, if your friends don't like you anymore, they won't pretend they do.

2
"Un Bel Di"
Susi

"MISS NEVILLE! MISS NEVILLE!"

Someone called my name as bags crashed down the carrel, flapping bar-coded tags for NWA33 (Schiphol, if I recall) and BA0049 (from Heathrow, I was certain). One suitcase flaunted a tag from a previous flight to FNO. Rome Fiumicino Airport. In former times, I rushed through SeaTac, excited because I'd be walking into FNO fifteen hours later. Now—

The only woman in the line, I stood amidst a phalanx of limo drivers, each a foot taller and double my weight, all of us holding placards to find strangers. They were doing a job. I was seeking my best friend's cousin. I needed him to come change the course of my life.

While there was still time.

"Miss Neville!"

Craning to peek around the flank of fullback chauffeurs surrounding me, I spied a blond girl waving on the in-coming escalator.

Ashley, a second soprano from fourth-period choir. Her mother had insisted that I was forcing her daughter to sing alto just because the choir had too many sopranos. She believed in her heart that

3

Ashley was born a soprano. I failed to convince the woman that I hadn't compromised artistic values, only done what was right for Ashley. Then the principal summoned me, and I failed to prevent bureaucratic compromises. So Ashley sings second soprano, out of her register. Now choir isn't fun for her; it's just work at which she cannot excel. Fortunately, Ashley wants to be an actress, not a singer. Or maybe an attorney working for social justice. Or the corporate art agent for Microsoft.

"There's tons of time to find my calling and pursue my dreams," she said in our midterm counseling session.

Tons of time for some people, I thought, but did not say.

As other people's baggage creaked along the conveyor, Ashley breathlessly described spring break in Amsterdam. Out of the last eight days, she'd spent thirty hours on planes and in airports.

"Schiphol is so far out!" she said, her speaking voice in appropriate range. It took me a second to realize that she was not referring to how far the airport is from the city. "It's like shopping heaven. I could live there. You can find everything that's on Kalverstraat without tripping on those wobbly cobblestone streets."

Ashley's parents appeared, and I thrust the placard with Jason's name behind my back while we shook hands. Ashley's parents also towered over me, but I'm five-foot-four, so I'm used to that. They were too engaged in fetching their child to attend to her choir teacher, which was fine. At the school where I teach, people have money.

I don't, but I'm used to that. Now.

As much as I've learned to love teaching in the past year, I need to be doing more: reaching deeper, extending instruction and opportunity beyond the confines of a high school curriculum, even beyond what I can do at Prescott, the liberal arts academy where I teach.

Drivers were beginning to depart with their charges. The two nearest to me resumed their discussion of the Mariner lineup. It was April, after all, so hope springs once more.

"Will the Mariners ever again go one sixteen and forty-six for the season?" I asked the driver standing next to me, just to be friendly.

"How old were you that season? Five?" another driver asked, teasing.

"That's blatant ageism. There ought to be a law," I said, which made him laugh. His guess was almost in the ballpark, and I look uncommonly young for my age if viewed under poor light. Up close though, people can see the damage done. If I'd never kidded myself into believing I was in love, that damage would not have occurred. I wouldn't be standing here, stuck in Seattle. I'd be headed for FNO and another adventure.

My chauffeur-companions all departed, faring better than me, and a new battalion of drivers appeared, like a changing of the guard. I shifted from foot to foot, after an eon of waiting for the archmagus to appear who would help usher in a new era.

I'm Susi Neville, I would say. *My life is in your hands.*

No, I was feeling too nervous about meeting him and needing his help, and I'm too shy to say things like that these days. Maybe I'd just smile and say *how do you do,* as one is taught in deportment classes. I'd had good teachers, and I believe in the value of solid teaching. Everything I needed to know to succeed, I'd learned in school or from strong tutors.

Up until that bad break, two years ago.

With time and boredom, my nervousness receded and I sank into daydreams as people greeted each other and hauled away their baggage. I'd spent spring break in my garden and working on the new curriculum, so I felt happy—happier than any time in the last couple of years. The weather was good, so I'd sifted rocks out of a new patch of soil and turned over the compost pile. I took my father to see *Tartuffe* at Seattle U and watched him laugh till he cried. I'd polished the curriculum outline and grant request to be sent to that arts foundation. In my mind, the proposal was now burnished so that it shined like a semiprecious stone—say, aventurine, the stone that's supposed to calm a troubled spirit.

3
"We Can Talk"
Jason

"WE'LL DO OUR BEST, Mr. Taylor. Ninety-nine percent of the time, we deliver straying luggage within twenty-four hours."

Since my bags resisted returning to Seattle, there was nothing to do while waiting but get back to business, so I again tried to call Toby. He picked up on the third ring, and I plunged right into begging.

"Come back to Seattle, Toby. Stoneway needs your mandolin."

"Jason, I can't hear you. Are you on a cell phone in a tube station again?"

"I'm at SeaTac Lost Baggage. They made me check that National Steel guitar of Uncle Beau's. Then they lost it."

"You're calling me to complain?"

"No, Toby. We need to talk about our recording schedule."

"Call back later when it's more private."

"What's private anymore, Toby? In the next hour you can check the Internet to learn what I ate and how many times I used the john on the flight from London. I've been hit on four times since the plane landed."

"Why don't you just stay out of public like I do?"

"That's what I tried to do all winter."

"You went to the Grammy Awards with your ex-wife. Why the hell would you want to be caught on camera accepting an award for *Woman at the Well*?"

"My attorney thought I should go, to limit what Dominique says about me in interviews."

"Karl makes you date your own personal Jezebel?"

"Mostly I don't date at all. Contrary to the gossip on the Internet, I'm the indie American Morrissey. Celibate as a stone."

"Our fans don't care about Dominique's lies. They, like me, can't tolerate country schmaltz like *Woman at the Well*, especially if it's supposed to be Stoneway's music. Too bad your own personal Yoko Ono had to screw up our music."

"It was good music when we first recorded it." I looked over at the baggage clerk, who appeared to be absorbed in studying her computer screen rather than listening to Toby chastise me.

Toby's voice crackled over the cell connection. "Thing is, Yoko never jilted John for George Martin."

"Dominique wanted to cross over to mainstream, and she used Ephraim Vance to do it." That didn't hurt my feelings. She had already finished using me. "A country diva needs a producer more than she needs a guitarist." I prepared to admit what bugged me most. "'I never should have been in love.'"

"The wake-up call came when Dominique started whining that our music is too 'alternative.'"

"Thanks for the beating, Toby. I get the same poke in the eye with a sharp stick every time I'm online."

"Crap, man, it burns my ass that she assaulted your soul and battered the band along the way. Have you seen her new video? Lap-dancing to your solo guitar in expensive panties."

"Listen, Toby. Ian and I worked together all winter. You'll join us again—right, amigo? Hold on, I have to give them Ian's address so they can send my bags over. If they ever find them."

"Jason, hang up and call me back."

"No, Toby. I've been calling you for two weeks. Will you be in Seattle by Monday?"

"Are you asking me or the lady at Lost Baggage?"

"Come on, Toby. Our contract requires one more album. If we don't have it by early June, we'll all pay through the nose."

"My name will not appear on another album with Dominique. Get one of those Nashville studio guys to play and let her smother it with boring vocals in the final production."

"She won't be there, Toby. Karl fixed it so we just lay down tracks and send them to Ephraim. We can do what we want once we deliver these tracks. When Ian and I played in Europe this winter, something new happened. You'll like it. We need you back."

"Ian is closer to you than your own shadow. He'll always do what you want. Did you add back the twang and buzz? Who's counting beats?"

"We have buzz. And volume. But you are the twang, Toby. I'm checking out a possible drummer tonight."

"No Hollywood strings with Phil Specter wannabes? Don't let Ephraim drown our music with the Dragon Lady's crappy computer-enhanced vocals until it sucks so bad it blows."

"We will produce ourselves, like we used to."

"No divas with egos bigger than the Mississippi at flood time?"

"Karl promises to keep her away, Toby."

"And you—no falling for divas who play you for a sucker later?"

"My uncle Beau said every man fucks himself at least once."

The woman at Lost Bags raised her eyebrows. I stepped further away.

Toby said, "Beau was stating common wisdom, not suggesting your next action."

"I'm not the only guy in the world who found out he didn't know the person he married. I woke up one morning and she was someone else. Angry all the time, unpredictable. Hating my work, hating me."

"Jason, you have never been with a woman who could work at your level. No divas this time, OK?"

"If you check the fan blogs, my level is judged to be pretty low. Toby, I got us into this nightmare. I'll get us out. My attorney—"

"Screw that, man. Karl can't save you out in the wild. Where are we recording? Temple Bell?"

"Yes, and rehearsing at Ian and Cynthia's house. I'll be sleeping in their basement for the duration."

"Not at your place on the water?"

"That's still tied up in court like everything else—except my guitars, which the effing Port of Seattle is holding hostage."

"OK, I'll see you on Monday. But if you can't deliver twang and buzz, I'm heading right back to Mendocino."

"I owe you, Toby. Thanks for giving me another chance."

"Could never have done otherwise. I love you like a brother. Me and Ian, we'll keep you safe. Just call us if you start thinking you're in love."

"I'm not going anywhere but the studio and Ian's basement. What trouble can I possibly get into?"

4
"Where Shall I Go?"
Susi

FRUSTRATED, I SWIPED MY card in the slot in the phone booth and punched the number for that hotel in New York. "It's Susi Neville," I said to the voice that answered in Angelia's room.

Reflected in the phone's chrome plating, my face seemed pale and doleful. I hate looking pathetic.

"*Pronto.*" Angelia always says this, though she's never lived in Italy.

"I can't find Jason."

"Where are you calling from, Susi?"

"A phone booth at SeaTac. I had him paged six times in the last two hours. How am I supposed to find him?"

"Meet him at that club on Capitol Hill where he's going. It's called Neumo's. He's planning to find someone there tonight. I sent him email, so he knows you're taking care of him while I'm out of town. If you'd carry a cell phone, it would much easier for people to connect with you."

"I wish you were here, Angelia."

"It's just until Monday. The reunion of the Elgar Consort at the New York Chamber Festival is a perfect opportunity for us, Susi. I can hit up every one of my old partners for money to match our grant application."

"All your stories make me nervous about meeting Jason. I need his help. Other than that, your cousin and I have nothing in common."

"He loves old-time music like you do. And he says he reformed after being dumped by his wife. It's years since he's been in the company of an intelligent, decent woman. That's you, Susi."

"So I'm a lamb sent out to greet the wolf?"

"His first wife told me that he's unbelievably gentle for being such a testosterone bomb. The best bad boy ever, she said. You need an adventure like that."

"What I need is an advocate who appreciates the folk tradition and who can also give us decent business advice. I don't need another spoiled rich boy wreaking havoc with my life."

"Jason is not that rich, Susi. Or that bad."

"From every story you've told about him, 'wreaking havoc' is a probability, not just a possibility. I'd prefer to read a good book."

"Lord help me, I continue to believe that my friend Susi is perpetrating an act of self-deception that's bound to fail sometime. Soon, I hope."

5
"Send Lawyers, Guns, and Money"
Jason

HERE'S JASON TAYLOR TAKING care of business, poking at the screen on my cell. There's little use now in keeping the number of that Indian restaurant on Vauxhall Road at the top of my call list. Here in Seattle, someone on Karl's support team—I think it was Warren—answered my next call and patched me through instantly.

"Hi, Karl. I'm back in the good old USA. How's the lawyer business?"

"Jason? *Que pasa?* What's all that noise?"

"I'm at the airport. They lost my uncle's guitar."

"You missed the meeting today."

"I couldn't get an earlier flight."

"You missed the meeting on purpose." Karl wasn't happy with me.

"It's what I pay you for, Karl, to talk to people I don't want to speak with."

"Will you be here Monday? C'mon, Jason, I can hear you fidgeting over the phone."

"We start rehearsal Monday. If it's bad news, tell me now."

"Dominique wants shared rights as co-author for songs you wrote while you were together."

"She never co-authored anything in her life."

"Her chief claim is prior art for 'Rhianna's Song.'"

"Sheesh." I clapped my cell phone closer to my ear, to keep my head from exploding. "She made a comment while reading *USA Today*, and I used it in a song. That isn't co-authoring."

"So I take it I'm supposed to say no?"

"Yes, say no. Does she claim anything I wrote after we separated?"

"No. We excluded your new work from community property."

"Then screw how long it takes to close this. She can have all the money she wants, but not the rights to any of my music. Not when all I got was eight months of singing with the devil in disguise. We didn't even sleep together after—"

"Don't tell me more than I need to know, Jason."

"I'm sorry. I try not to say or think bad things about her. So tell me what we get for giving up rights to a song about my mother, whom she never met."

"She'll let you have the Leschi condo and all your personal effects."

"That's it? She crucifies me in public and I get to keep the shirt I had on when she first stalked me?"

"What else do you want? All winter, you never helped once when I tried to make counter-offers."

"An apology. I want a public acknowledgment that all those rumors aren't true. And that B.S. in her interviews—what is it she says?"

"'I know in my heart he just needs time to recover from grief and the problems in his life.'"

"Great imitation, Karl. She makes it sound like I've been in the Betty Ford Clinic instead of playing music in Europe. What does it mean?"

"She's implying that you took your uncle's death hard."

"I did. Beau was more father to me than—"

"You don't have to say it, Jason. I know."

"Dominique hated Beau so much that she can't say his name out loud. Why does she keep lying? How many times has she said 'I know he'll come back to me' in interviews? She's the one who ran off to sleep with half of Nashville and most of L.A."

"As a country, diva, she needs to protect her wholesome image."

"Then why is she dancing on TV in her underwear? I want an apology."

"All right, Jason. I'll add that to the negotiations. You need to be here for the meeting on Monday."

"Sure. Did you get the email list of benefit shows I agreed to?"

"All the paperwork is done and ready for you to sign. There are other proposals here, including a benefit in mid-May against landmines. Dominique already turned it down."

"Then say yes for me. Say no to everyone else who just wants money."

"You need to pursue the foundation idea I suggested, Jason."

"Yeah, yeah. Ian said Cynthia set up the details with a cousin of hers. You and Cynthia can figure it out."

"Get involved, Jason. You don't have dependents or significant property. Be prudent, or taxes will take everything Dominique doesn't get."

"Like I care about the money."

"I do, since I'm paid to be the adult. You care, too. To be independent of the labels, you need to pay strict attention to business. It's called 'indie,' not 'flakey.'"

"Email the details and I'll read it later. Right now I need food. The vegetarian meals on British Airways didn't stick with me."

"If you'd eat a burger once in a while you wouldn't be so hungry all the time. Jason, can I give you some legal advice?"

"It's what I pay you for."

"Don't get involved with a woman again without written agreements, since Washington is a community property state. When I see a chick buying *Woman at the Well*, I want to ask for my fee up front."

"Be respectful of your income source."

"You are such a nice guy. Why does Dominique hate you so much?"

"It beats me, Karl. Dominique stood on my back to make herself a star. And I didn't stop her from leaving with the next sucker she chose. I don't know why she's so teed off."

"She'll take everything if you don't help. What are you hiding from?"

"Being blind-sided by a soul-sucking vampire? I can't trust anyone."

"Hence my caution about getting legal agreements up front."

"Karl, I have to go before you chill my fearless heart."

"OK. See you Monday? Talk to that cousin about the foundation?"

"Sure, sure. Can't hardly wait."

6
"Call Him Up and Tell Him What You Want"
Susi

"STEVEN? IT'S SUSI. I WON'T make it to dinner tonight after all."

"It's me, sis. Not voicemail. I was about to call you. I have to go out of town, so Damien and I can't make the concert tomorrow."

"Oh drat. I need you with me."

"You don't need your brother along on a double date."

"It's not a date. I'm just escorting Angelia's cousin around. It's Randolph who's the problem."

"Still trying to get you to marry him? Yet you want Randolph to think of you only as a music teacher? Good luck with that, Susi."

"That's all I am, and he's just the vice principal at school and the fundraiser for our foundation."

"You never should have taken the job when you found out Randolph worked there. I told you that he'd interpret it as an invitation to intimacy."

"Yuck. I do not like hearing the word 'intimacy' much anyway, but definitely not in the context of Randolph's name."

"He's a handsome, educated person. A bit too heterosexual for my tastes, but that shouldn't affect your opinion."

"Don't make jokes. Before my accident, Randolph was practically a stalker—and I was married then, for Pete's sake. Now it's like I'm taking a bath in pity whenever I'm around him."

"Where are you anyway? That sounds like an ambulance."

"On Capitol Hill. I missed my connection with Angelia's cousin so now I have to chase him down. Perhaps I should ask Dad to go to the concert."

"No, leave Dad alone. You don't need a chaperone. And by the way, he doesn't need you dropping by every night to check on him."

"Is this the monthly 'get a life' lecture?"

"You have spent most nights alone or camped out with Dad since he moved to assisted living."

"I'm better off alone than lonely, like I was when I was married to Logan. I won't do that again."

"Not all guys are asshats like Logan or Randolph. I'll call you when I'm back in town, Susi. If the sun shines this weekend, go work in your garden."

"I can't. I'm in grant meetings or fundraising visits all weekend."

"Then please tell Randolph hello for me and that I think he has a very cute ass."

"You can amuse yourself thinking I might just do that."

7
"She's About a Mover"
Jason

AFTER WAITING TWO HOURS for my lost baggage and then not finding Cynthia's cousin, I submitted to the mandated extortionist prices for a cab ride into town. The cab dropped me at Neumo's, where I wanted to check out a drummer playing a show that night. We lost our last drummer, Hakeem, to hearth-and-home when his wife had a second child. If I don't find a replacement, we'll be paying a session man. That just isn't us.

I arrived late in the set, but heard enough to know that this drummer wasn't the guy we needed. The barmaid recognized me and gave me a Jagermeister that I didn't want, since I don't drink. After ten hours across eight time zones, I didn't even want coffee. I accepted her gift though and hung around for a few minutes more.

First, I had to reassure myself that the world hadn't changed, so I looked around for the archetypal inhabitants of any club scene. The world's oldest skinhead—replete in Doc Martens boots and red suspenders—had his usual place pogoing up by the stage, although the band's current number was in three-quarter time. Frodo the bootlegging hobbit fidgeted by the sound board, recording the show to post online later, having failed to talk the sound technician into letting him patch into the board.

As the music ended, "That Guy" who appears in every club in North America (we've played most of them) made his perpetually lame attempt to hustle a group of women who just wanted to be left in peace. T.G. said, "What are you ladies doing here alone? Let me buy you all a drink. Good-looking ladies like yourselves shouldn't be alone." Et cetera.

Quentin Henderson leaned against the wall near the back—a real person, not an archetype, even if Quentin sounds like an alias. He appears everywhere I go. I've known him since jazz band in high school, where his father taught sterilized jazz. However, I achieved with Quentin what I tried to do for the others in jazz band, turning him on to a much wider range of music. If old Hector Henderson hasn't kicked the bucket, I bet he is still ticked at me for luring Quentin over to the dark side.

Now Quentin has a job with a Seattle news weekly as music critic and cultural scribe, with high hopes of going further, and he still follows me, as if I could dispense a rock-and-roll elixir that will carry him to fame. In our last interview, I tried to explain that fame isn't a drink worth taking. That particular interview had occurred earlier this same day, when trapped together on the flight from London, I told him the story he wanted about coming to Seattle to record and the new directions Stoneway is pursuing. He won't ask about personal stuff, because that's not what he wants to sell in his career. Months before, he managed to peddle an interview with me to *Rolling Stone*.

Yet here he was following me to a club because he knew I'd be here. At least he had a woman with him, though it was someone who was uncomfortable in this venue and who wasn't listening to the music. All her body language indicated that her date bored her. Quentin himself dressed conservatively in a Nine Inch Nails t-shirt and black jeans, complementing his long, scruffy hair. Mine is just as long, but I keep telling him that you have to spend money and time if you want to look tidy with long hair. Yet Ian, who I trust, says I'm too obsessive about personal grooming.

When Quentin glanced my way, I nodded and toasted him with my unsipped Jagermeister. To tell the truth, I wished he would publish a good word about the band, so I could fool myself into thinking it's possible to live and work in Seattle again.

"Jason!"

I turned when someone called my name, but so did the dude next to me, who looked more salesman than head-banger, dressed in Dockers and a golf shirt. He laughed when he saw me turn.

"The second most common name in America for an entire decade. What were our mothers thinking?"

It was his friend, not mine, who had called our name, and after they shook hands, that Jason and his friend departed into the night. Among the heads that turned when the name "Jason" was called were several other people I know. When you live in the same town all your life, you'll see all sorts of people you know everywhere. If you travel for business as much as I do, that feels good. It anchors you in reality, when you have to spend so much time in other towns while touring. I wanted real people to greet me in Seattle again.

Warren, the admin from Karl's office, seemed shy about returning my wave. He writes the checks for my bills and tracks my business when I'm out of town. P.J. Jones, a piano man from a trio that traveled with us about five years ago, came over to say hi. He had been the coolest road companion, always finding the bright side of rubber eggs and acid coffee after a too-short night in a mosquito-infested motel amid the tumble weeds of Idaho. He had a great repertoire of Mac Rebennack-style piano blues.

"Where are you playing these days?" I asked.

"Nowhere. Home. I have a couple of kids now."

"Nice."

"It is. But I had to remodel my approach to life. I'm working for a monolithic software corporation."

I'd heard this kind of story before, and know better than to express my dismay at another musician lost to the pressures of domestic economy.

"Two kids, P.J.? Girls? Boys? One of each?"

"Boys. The oldest is three, and he's at the keyboard already."

"Lord, is it that long since I've seen you?"

"I'd invite you over, Jason, but I'm sure you're booked."

"No way. I'd dig that. Seriously. Let me give you my cell number. I haven't got a place to live yet, but call me."

Call me. He wouldn't. He doesn't want his old road life mixed up with his new family life. As nice as he is, I could see it on his face. Another voice was calling my name.

"Mr. Taylor? It's good to see you." It was the owner of a Portland roadhouse where we played often, maybe seven years ago. "Your friend told me you'd be here tonight."

He pointed across the way to where Ian's cousin Arlo stood. I shook hands with the promoter but went deaf to what he said as I watched with foreboding while Arlo weaved through the crowd toward me.

"You know, Mr. Taylor, I'd like to book Stoneway again, though I don't have space big enough for you now."

"Give me your card. We haven't finished booking for the summer yet, and we want to play smaller places again."

While I said goodbye to the guy, Arlo began to close in. I saw Warren nearby and took four steps to stand by him.

"Hey, friend, save me from Arlo."

Warren looked up, surprised.

"Gosh, Mr. Taylor. Sure."

Warren is a straight-arrow guy who dresses in the same mode as I do, as if he could afford to do his laundry and iron his clothes. Like me, Warren knows how to comb his hair. In comparison, Arlo, while a bipedal hominid, isn't part of the *Homo sapiens sapiens* line of evolution. It's another branch altogether. He is Ian's cousin, but I know every single person Ian is related to, so I suspect Arlo was switched at birth. Or dropped on his head. He doesn't so much walk upright as scuttle. He keeps his hair long because someone told him he looked like Tom Petty, so he works to maintain an iconic presence of the musician he worships, but the pointy nose and stringy hair also require a certain charisma. My animus started in junior high. I should be over it by now, but he keeps stepping out of bounds.

"Ian said I might see you here tonight, bro."

Arlo grasped my hand like a hippie, trying to get a thumb dance out of me. His palms are always damp, and I covertly rubbed mine on my jeans when he let go.

"Back in town and looking for poontang, huh?" Arlo's voice has a peculiar pitch on a twelve-tone scale that gets under your skin and then rakes along the thinner bones inside your skull. "Didn't you get enough tail in Europe?"

"Actually, I'm looking for a drummer." I gestured to the stage.

"Have you seen fucking Ian since you got back?" Arlo hit a note that exists in an imaginary place between D-sharp and E-flat. "He shaved his fucking head so no one would recognize him. Cynthia is so pissed. Said she'd shave his fucking balls for him."

"Thanks for sharing that, Arlo."

"So tell me about Europe, amigo."

Before I could answer, Warren reached over and shook Arlo's hand.

"Hi, I'm Warren. We've met before—last year at Karl Schwann's barbeque? You know, a girl was just asking Jason about you, Arlo." He stammered slightly, being very shy, and I realized that the favor I asked caused him pain to perform.

"No shit? Where?"

"She went into the girls' can. I think her name was Rachel. Or maybe it was Rebecca."

Arlo scuttled back toward the johns, to wait for an imaginary Rachel or Rebecca.

"Thanks, Warren. You are a true friend. He has been a pain for years. Always hanging around, saying he's with the band."

"I know. He told me last summer that he got a girl to do him at the Winthrop Rhythm and Blues Festival when she found out he was Ian's cousin and traveled with Jason Taylor and Stoneway."

My worst nightmare—other people using our band's name to take advantage of women.

"Thanks again, Warren. I should split before he comes back. See you around, my friend."

"Is there anything else I can do for you, Mr. Taylor? Give you a ride?"

"No, thanks. I prefer walking after the airplane."

That's how Karl's entire staff is, all nice, helpful people. I was hitching up my pack to hoof it over to Ian's house when I spied this woman scanning the crowd. I can't say why I looked twice. She was just this slender soul in an over-starched Brooks Brothers shirt and pressed jeans, a short shock of blond hair in a boy's cut, not even glancing my way.

A dude came by, wanting my autograph on a beer coaster and hoping to commiserate over ball-breaking witches that screw up your life. I used the line I always do when strangers presume to talk about my personal business, "Love stinks—but heartbreak makes great rock-and-roll," while watching this cute woman over the guy's shoulder. I gave him back the coaster along with the unwanted Jagermeister and started to follow the cute woman, only to be blocked by Quentin and Dating Woman.

"Hi, Jason. Righteous band, huh?"

"Hello, Quentin. Imagine seeing you here."

He too wanted to do the hippie handshake thing as he said, "Jason Taylor, this is Laura Stanley. She's a big fan of yours."

Laura looked like maybe she was a big fan of herself. Quentin needed a boost by association.

"Hi, Laura. Pleased to meet you."

"The pleasure is mine." She wasn't convincing. "But it wouldn't be honest to say I'm a fan. Your last album had a couple of cuts that seemed almost interesting." She named the two tracks that had received the worst butchery at the hands of our producer. "I prefer hip hop. Modern country doesn't speak to me."

It doesn't speak to me either. We don't play modern country. However, I smiled, since I'm now used to people taking every chance to insult my music. Including women who move toward me in a suggestive way as they denigrate my work. Heck, I had married the queen of sexually aggressive music criticism.

I said, "Our head-banger's hoe-down isn't for everyone. That's what Quentin says." He didn't. I made that up. "He is always urging me to seek much broader influences. His past recommendations were Phosphorescence and Mwahaha. What do you recommend for my edification?"

"The Lumineers. The Cave Singers." She suggested other good West Coast bands, and I nodded, commenting on the musicianship of their members. Then she named a couple of label-manufactured synth-pop bands and went on to offer me advice.

"No one wants to hear that twangy stuff since rockabilly died in the Eighties," she said. "Except dinosaurs living in trailers in Duvall."

"I appreciate your insights. Though you can still find trailer trash like us inside the Seattle city limits."

Quentin stepped up, needing to claim whatever victory he could with Dating Woman.

"I'll be seeing you, Jason. It would be righteous to do an on-the-job interview while you are recording. Call me?"

"Sure, Quentin. Let's count on it."

※

I looked over Dating Woman's shoulder at the cute woman, who saw me and broke into this indescribable smile that seemed to promise it would never rain again in Seattle. As I moved away from Quentin, she came over, extending her hand to shake like you do in business meetings.

"Are you Jason?" she asked as her hand grasped mine, her voice as clear as a mission bell over the noise of the tavern. "I'm Susi."

"Guilty," I said, since I might as well get on with my life and admit to being me. Her voice compelled truth.

"You look exactly as I expected. Though your hair is longer."

I murmured whatever it is you say when someone has an unfair smile and a voice that sounds like Emmylou singing Billie Holiday covers. If she spoke much, I was doomed.

"I hoped I'd find you here. I'm sorry I missed you at the airport," Susi said. "Did you like this band as much as you thought you would?"

"Not at all." It dawned on me that this person was supposed to have picked me up at the airport, since no one but Ian and Cynthia knew I was coming here. Oh, and Arlo.

"Then why don't we get out of here? The air is destroying my throat." She took my hand and pulled me toward the door. "How was your flight from London? Where did you leave the rest of your luggage? Did you stop by her house?"

"The airlines lost it. They promised to send it to the house by courier when they found it."

"Doesn't that always happen? I spent a week in Milan once, living off what I could purchase in the hotel gift shop. Do you have enough in your carry-on for the night? Should we stop at a drug store?"

By this time, she had pulled me to the street, where she looked up at me with a shy version of her heart-stopping smile. She must practice to be so deadly. Behind her, the same denizens of the neighborhood and their hard-rocking brothers sat in the Comet

Tavern as when I was last in Seattle, and the time before that, clear back to my father's generation, trading stories that might or might not be true.

She said, "You must be jetlagged. Do you want me to take you home? Or do you use that trick of staying up through the first night?"

"I made the mistake of sleeping on the airplane."

"Why don't we take a walk then? You must want to stretch out after the flight. No, don't let's go that way. There are too many street people out at night. Let's just walk up Twelfth toward Volunteer Park."

As we headed up Pike toward Twelfth, I found myself chattering like a fool, having not spoken to anyone other than gallery guards, hotel clerks, and flight attendants for more than a week. She questioned me about the avant-garde show at the Victoria and Albert and then what I saw at the Tate Britain.

"I confess," I said, though I had been up so long, I would confess anything, "I went to the Tate only to see the Turners this time. I have this cross-sensory experience whenever I stare at what he does with light."

"You mean synesthesia?"

"Exactly. I'm looking into the light and seeing the image behind it, but then I hear sounds that I also feel in my fingertips. Do you know what I'm talking about?"

"I can taste certain music."

"Yeah, some songs leave a bad taste in my mouth, but I make it a rule never to name names." I was trying to be clever, but she was serious.

"I mean that certain parts of my mouth respond, like when you get lemon juice on the sour receptors or salt on that part of your mouth. The sound. High C tastes like—oh, never mind. It doesn't anymore. Did you see any of the current shows?" she asked.

"Dames Maggie and Judi together in the West End."

"You are so lucky. I haven't been out of the country since—" Her voice trailed off, and she didn't finish the thought.

"What do you do with yourself most days?" I asked, thinking perhaps I should know her, but jetlag kept me from remembering whether Cynthia had ever mentioned her cousin Susi.

"Oh, my job and music. That's about all. I tried to teach myself to paint this winter, but I ended up back with just music." She shrugged in this charming way, gesturing with both her hands as she talked. My jetlagged mind wanted to read more warmth in those gestures than such a sweet-sounding woman could intend for a man she just met. In my scrambled state I hoped it was real. She said, "In addition to teaching at the school, I have a dozen private students, but I put that on pause while we work on the new curriculum and the foundation grant."

"Teaching is nice," I said, because I'm a feather-brained idiot and I just wanted to keep hearing her voice.

"I'm in awe of what you do," she said, "and I've heard stories—"

"Not a single one is true, Susi. Let's pretend I'm a guitarist you picked up in a bar."

She laughed and the sound of that music nearly brought me to my knees to beg her to stay with me forever, hoping she'd laughed like that again. However, I knew it was jetlag.

"Seattle has changed since I was here last," I said, thinking I could make a real conversation. "Designer pizza has taken over the storefront where I got my first tattoo. The same guys I knew in high school or their first cousins were still standing near the bar, listening to a band with their hands in their pockets."

"Did you want to stay and listen to music? We can go back"

"Not at all, since I'm in your company. Do you want me to show you the tattoo?"

Foolishly, I had embarrassed her, for a rosy flush showed on her neck under the streetlamp.

"I meant it as a joke, Susi."

"Oh. I'm so gullible. My brother loves to tease me because he knows I fall for it every time."

"As a gentleman, I promise not to take advantage of that confession. Though you are the one who took a risk, picking up a guitarist in a bar."

"Right," Susi said, laughing again. The sound of her laughter could slay me outright rather than killing me softly. "She warned me that you tease. I'll be on my guard."

"'You're leading me down a one-way street.'" I hadn't meant to say that out loud.

"I'm sorry?"

"It's a line from Tim O'Brien."

"Hmm. I don't remember that line. I haven't been reading him lately. I'm not afraid of the challenge, but I have to be brave when I read him. The last couple of books—"

"I mean Tim O'Brien the bluegrass musician. *Odd Man In?*"

"Right. Of course. My father and I heard him perform once. He has a lovely tenor voice."

Two people in hoodies and jeans passed us, doing a double-take when they recognized me. But, hey, this was Seattle. People are cool. If Mark Lanegan or Ben Gibbard can buy Cheerios at the Wallingford QFC, I can walk down the street unmolested.

However, Seattle is a small town. It happens that a lot of people live here, but otherwise it has all the other problems of a small town—like, everyone knows your business. You can't escape the people you don't want to see. For example, Ephraim Vance, my estranged A&R man and former producer at Albion Records, sat in the window of a bistro where Crave used to be on Twelfth Avenue, holding hands with Dominique, who had been my wife in a previous incarnation. I did an about-face so fast that I almost knocked Susi over.

I said, "Let's go. I'm bushed. I can't sleep yet, but I don't feel like prowling the streets."

"Do you want to come to my house? We can talk and I could show you the plan we're presenting tomorrow."

"Where do you live?"

"The same place in Leschi. My car is parked over on Pine Street."

It gave me pause, making me wonder if I'd met her before and forgotten it. But I don't forget. I'm a far better man than my father.

8
"Tickin' Bomb"
Jason

JUST BEFORE DOMINIQUE MANAGED to get me to marry her, I had planned to break up because, among other things, she is a slob, dropping every single thing right where she is done with it, expecting others to pick up after her. Needs a maid to clean a five-room condo, and makes fun of me because I hang up the towels in a hotel room.

So I was nervous about this woman Susi, who was as friendly as a pen pal or a best friend's cousin. In spite of her smile and warmth and wit, I wasn't ready to be in her actual house, brought down to the reality of dust kittens and dishes in the sink, or teddy bears and lace. Having lost most of my will earlier in the day, along with my baggage, I agreed to go to her house and got in her car. Classical KING-FM played Berlioz when the engine turned over, but the radio was the sole luxury in her little economy car, which was as soulless as a rental that gets vacuumed by the lot boy every day. No crystal or dreamcatcher hanging from the mirror. No take-out wrappers on the floor. No detritus clutter in the backseat. In the dark, driving to her house, I shivered whenever she spoke, her voice plucking at the strings of my soul, each individual tone harmonious and rich beyond kenning, as Ian's Scottish grandmother would say, yet fractured, letting the luminescence of her soul shine through amidst the jagged edges.

When Susi switched on the light inside her house and smiled, damn if I could tell which action illuminated the room. She was cute but not all the way to beautiful. Whatever else you want to say about Dominique, she is movie-star beautiful. However, if I were dying of thirst and had to choose between water and Susi's smile, it would be hard to choose, very hard.

In the light, I could see that it wasn't a blush of embarrassment, but a burn scar running the long length of her neck. A matching scar ran up her hand and disappeared into the sleeve of her starched shirt. All of which made me take a deep look at her. The burn on her face had been repaired, but a trace of the damage could be seen in the stiffness along one side and small unrepaired scars on her lips. To cover the remains, she had taken great care to apply makeup that looked like no makeup at all. Amid the natural asymmetry of her face, one beautiful brow escaped in an arch of perpetual surprise or pleas-ure, while almond-shaped grey eyes gazed at me in friendly interest. I tried to imagine the pain that she had endured from those burns. Yet she could still offer that beguiling smile.

"Can I make you something to eat?" she said.

Oh god, I wanted to say no. I loathe hurting people's feelings, but home cooking usually turns out bad for me. She saw my hesitancy before I could even begin to stammer and decline the invitation.

"Vegetarian, right?" she said. "I just don't know the depths of your persuasion. Ovo-lacto? Vegan? Please don't be afraid to say."

"Eggs and dairy. Though I will eat a fish once in a while if I don't have to see its head or fins."

"That's what I thought. I just couldn't remember for certain."

"How did you know?" I don't proselytize my diet or carry on a moral crusade. I learned it from my uncle as a way to stay healthy while living on the road. It is nothing more than that.

"Common knowledge," she said, laughing. "How about an omelet?"

It seemed the safest choice that a stranger could propose, and I had already peeked past her shoulder to see that her kitchen was immaculate, with utensils in tidy order on a wall rail, spotless pans hanging from a rack near the range. When I nodded, she washed her hands in the kitchen sink, then pulled an omelet pan down from the rack, though she is small enough that she had to stand on her toes and stretch to reach it.

"You can put on music if you like," she said.

Ah, permission from the owner to prowl her premises. A butcher-block island separated the kitchen from the living area. A baby grand piano stood at the far end of the room, and a large Mission-style sofa and two chairs filled the middle of the room. No TV in sight. Glass-enclosed oak bookcases lined the walls. Three of the larger cabinets held CDs and vinyl records. A couple hundred DVDs were alphabetized and labeled, apparently having been converted from reel-to-reel. The whole lot was worth a modest fortune on eBay. I was longing to see what a cultured pick-up artist keeps in her library, but my goal was to select music.

Very little in her collection had been composed later than the middle of the last century. Plenty of the recordings were newer, but the composers had all died, save for a few like John Adams. An eclectic but deep set of classical CDs stood alongside a collection of Americana artifacts and British and Celtic folk music that I would pawn Toby to own. My hands shook with both challenge and desire:

I needed to choose what to play while repressing an impulse to drown in the liner notes of the CDs. It would take days to work through it all. I had intended to judge her taste, but looking at this awesome collection, it occurred to me that I would be judged by what I selected, and the performance anxiety unnerved me. It had to be something I knew well, so I could pay attention to her and not the music. Shaking from the overstimulation, I went for a CD collection of early recordings by the Maddox Brothers and Rose.

With the West Coast hillbilly boogie turned down low, I forced myself not to examine her books as I passed. Yet I couldn't help seeing the shelves of opera folios and musicology books, the kind you can read only in the reference room of a university library.

"So, you're a musical snob?" I said, trying to joke. "I see you aren't afraid of what Puccini will do to you. You have it all. *Madama Butterfly. The Girl of the Golden West. Turandot.*" I almost selected the homemade CD of *Turandot* from the cabinet to play, but we had Rose Maddox for now.

Susi looked up from preparing the food and smiled again, lighting the room. Dammit. Also, the food smelled wonderful. She said, "I'm not interested in opera anymore. I should have gotten rid of all that before now."

"Would you marry me so I could stay here and listen to your music and read your books?"

She laughed as she turned the omelet out onto a plate. The toast popped up at the same moment. "I thought you'd like it. Oh, I know you don't care for the classical part. The rest is a blessed collection, isn't it? Most of it came from my father when he moved last fall. Do you want butter or jam for your toast?"

She set a plate of golden food before me.

"Dry, please. Why would you think I don't care for classical?"

"I heard you were wild about Lou Harrison and Terry Riley and all those just intonation and open-tuning people who consider the masters too pedestrian for the post-modern world."

The tea kettle whistled just then, and she reached on a shelf behind the sink to take down a tea caddy, while I considered what else she would have learned about me if she'd spent enough time searching on Google to find my open-tuning explorations.

She said, "Earl Grey or Lapsang Souchung? It's Murchie's, so the Earl Grey isn't over-perfumed."

"Lapsang Souchung, even though it smells like bong water. A person can appreciate both Terry Riley and David Diamond. Do I come across as an uneducated heathen?" I had felt the intellectual pull of open tuning, but Dominique hated what she called atonal nonsense and banned it from the condo—and she considered headphones an insult to intimacy—so I hadn't experimented on my own for quite a while.

"Of course not," Susi said. "It's just—I'm not being considerate. You can't find it pleasant, people talking about you when you aren't there. I know I hate it when my brother and friends have talked too much about me. It is unnerving when you meet people who have these preconceived notions about you. We should both try to forget what people have already said and pretend we're two strangers."

My head was swimming, drowning on London time. And the omelet had its origins near the district where the gates of heaven open. Greek olives and chunks of fresh tomatoes, after I'd spent weeks eating those pitiful grilled faux things they serve in Britain. Plus some other flavor.

"Cream cheese," she said. "I didn't have any feta."

I looked up in surprise, not knowing I had spoken aloud.

"Cream cheese," I repeated, and then laughed like an idiot.

"What's funny?" she asked, as if suspicious that I was laughing at her.

"Susi and cream cheese. Like Frank Zappa. *Susi. Susi Creamcheese.*"

"Who is Frank Zappa?"

At that moment I realized that I'd slipped into a time warp between boarding that British Airways jet and disembarking in this woman's living space. Like in those novels you find in airports. Except there were no Scottish warriors or oatcakes, just real food and music created before 1955. Where but in a world that exists in another dimension can you find a woman who picks you up in a bar, knows your tastes in music and food, and yet never heard of Frank Zappa?

Pondering it must have put me into another jet-lagged spin. I discovered that I'd inhaled the food and held the cup of tea in my shaking hands. The kitchen had mysteriously been restored to its former pristine order. As I tried to string words together that made sense, she looked at me curiously and then shook her head.

I was holding her hand, and I don't know how it happened. I snatched my hand back and buried it in my lap, feeling as sheepish as a schoolboy.

"You must be done in, Jason. We were having so much fun talking, I forgot about your jetlag. Now it's late. Do you want me to drive you home? I know it's clear across town, but that's not a problem."

Thinking about what happens when I walk into Cynthia and Ian's house after midnight, I shook my head. "It's too late. I'll get a cab to a hotel."

"That's silly. Don't waste your money. Just stay here."

She popped into the bedroom before I could stop her, to make her understand that I don't sleep with groupies, however much research they do ahead of time, and I don't eat food in other people's houses, and I don't go home with strangers. My attorney Karl would kill me, if my conscience didn't get me first. She emerged with a pillow, blanket, and sheet, which she used to make up a bed on the Mission sofa.

"This is your last chance for the bathroom, because there is only one and I'm locking my door, since your reputation precedes you."

"My reputation is grossly exaggerated," I said, which was true.

"No matter. My brother says that this is the perfect house for peeing off the deck in the dead of night." She pointed to the deck out back, which ran in front of the big picture window, both of which looked onto tall trees. "No one can see you."

I touched the rich oak of the sofa's arm. "This is the kind of couch a man would choose," I said, apropos of nothing in this world. I sank down on it, really, really wanting to sleep.

"It was my father's, like everything else. Nothing fits in the care facility, and we weren't ready to let go of these old things. Anyway, goodnight. We can talk about the plan tomorrow morning."

She shut her bedroom door just as Rose Maddox finished singing.

I stretched out on the man-sized Mission sofa and sank into the kind of physical comfort that you can find only when you are transported into another dimension.

9
"Shame on the Moon"
Susi

I CLOSED THE DOOR on my new friend, hoping to escape into sleep myself, but I made the foolish mistake of playing my telephone messages.

> *"Susi, it's me. We have to talk. I want to spend time with you. We need to get closure over what happened."*

My ex. Logan Childs. Importuning on my time and attention. He's been leaving messages lately, though it's two years past the time that I would ever consider returning his call. Or allowing him in the same room with me. Just twenty seconds of phone messages was enough to destroy any possibility of sleep. Trapped in my bedroom, too anxious to either sleep or read, I felt desperate for diversion. Yet it was far too late to call my dad to chat, and both Angelia and my brother Steven had left town.

When I had to spend that ridiculous amount of time and money on counseling, one therapist had me keep a diary. It is trendy these days, as I understand it, to keep a journal to process life experiences, but I undertook the assignment like every other prescription at the time. Pain pills every four hours, not to exceed. Stretching exercises to tone what would never look natural again. Antidepressants together with morning meditations, until the brain-fogging was no longer pleasant. Sixty minutes of vigorous exercise, minimum. I could fill the diary with just a record of what I had been sentenced to endure in time-released tonics, plus physical therapy every Tuesday and Thursday at eleven.

I sound bitter, but I no longer want any remnants of that unhappiness around me. Anyway, with both insomnia and Jason in my house, I pulled the diary from the nightstand. There is no one I can tell about what I'm thinking. Angelia would want to be titillated, but it feels too perverse to share; my brother Steven would worry or judge; Dad would listen and say wise words, but I could give him even fewer details than I could Steven.

My guest is funny, bright, and intriguing, but disturbing, because I had found myself comparing Jason to Logan all evening. Comparing a near-stranger to my ex-husband felt as if I were rating Jason as a potential partner, which would be a ridiculous way to think.

In these notes I'm writing, I want to avoid thinking about Logan—though I seldom think of Logan anymore except as a symbol of my faulty judgment and poor powers of observation.

So in this diary, I intend to assess my new acquaintance in a rational way, without dredging up the unpleasant past.

First, Jason is too good looking, which must be at the heart of what Angelia describes as his fatal flaw in relation to women. I've known other absurdly good-looking men before—at university; when I performed; in everyday life. Their sense of entitlement is oppressive. If I don't want to think about Logan, then Randolph serves as a prime example. However, this is to be a rational assessment, and therefore my logic appears to be this: extremely handsome men I've known turned out to be self-absorbed jerks; Jason is handsome; ergo, Jason is a self-absorbed jerk. He just hasn't yet demonstrated what kind of a jerk he is. This judgment, however, may be open to criticism and re-examination, for the logic may be faulty.

This assessment is also incomplete in that I haven't performed an inventory of what makes Jason handsome—another part of this analysis that I can't share with Angelia, Steven, or my dad. He is tall and dark. I would think black Irish if I didn't know that Angelia's family came from Barcelona. He has a narrow jaw and high cheekbones. Long lashes and dark eyes, perhaps indicating a propensity for brooding, even if he is quick-witted. A flashing smile and even teeth. Of course, he makes enough money at what he does that he can buy a perfect smile. Given that, it is kind of him to share that smile so often. I don't want to focus too much on it, as a simple act of self-preservation.

Second in this rational assessment, he is immaculately dressed, even after fifteen hours of travel, his shirt starched and bleached to shimmering whiteness, tucked into pressed jeans. His hands are manicured—so few men bother, except musicians and vain rich men. Because most men under forty in Seattle wear shirts hanging over jeans or khakis, I can't say there's anything overtly sexual about how he dresses. However, there's a fringe of dark hair that extends beyond the cuff of his shirt along his wrist, and another fringe that appears where he has left the top two buttons of his shirt undone. When I found him, he hadn't shaved since early morning. A dark shadow traced his jaw line, emphasizing his cheekbones. The shadow of a mustache framed and drew unwanted attention to his lips.

Third, his hips are narrow and he has muscles. It is trite of me to have noticed, but I know what he does for a living, and it doesn't promote the kind of runner's build he has. In addition to being well-formed, everything about him is too long. It creates an unfair advantage, so that I have to look up to him when we stand close. He has a long torso (he must struggle to keep his shirts tucked unless, as I suspect, he has them tailor made) and also has long legs (whose shape shows through denim too well).

Fourth, and the worst of it, he has the long fingers of an artist. He wrapped them around a mug of tea when I fed him, and I worried he'd notice that I couldn't quit staring. I came close to grabbing his hand, to trace the sinews and webbing of the most beautiful hands I had ever seen. He touched me at one point and—well, it startled me, though the details about how I felt about being touched aren't relevant to a rational discussion.

Fifth, he wears a silver buckle, like rodeo riders do. His long torso directs attention to the belt buckle above his narrow hips, and the gathered effect is to make one want to unbuckle it, proving what Angelia has said about him: he is a bad boy. I swore after wasting those years with Logan not to ever again glance a second time at handsome Peter Pans who want to be bad boys when they grow up.

Another distracting attribute is Jason's voice. Mr. Eckhart, my first voice teacher, would love to have gotten his hooks into him. Of course, Mr. Eckhart would proceed to wipe out that smoky quality, to make Jason more of a pure tenor.

Why should I think about any of this? All I want from Jason is advice about our grant proposal and a not-too-unpleasant time while I have to entertain him. I want him to save my professional life, but I do not want anything else from him. The rational mind turns away in disgrace from any other consideration.

10
"My Old Friend the Blues"
Jason

THE SUN SHONE FULL on my face when I woke, making me sneeze. I thought the airplane seat had grown strangely comfortable, until I realized it was Mission leather and sunshine that seemed strange. After spending the winter in Europe, I hadn't seen much of the sun.

I sneezed myself into clear-witted awareness. First, I was sleeping in a strange woman's house. Second, I had to pee. Third, I was naked under the sheet, though I couldn't remember taking off my clothes. The instructions the previous evening had been to pee off the deck, but she meant that for the dead of night. The door that led to the bathroom was open, so I considered making a run for it, but just as I launched myself, I stubbed my toe in the devil's worst way and then barked my shin on the coffee table.

Where I found my clothes, laundered, pressed, and folded. I grabbed them and lurched for the bathroom.

The house was tiny, so by the time I made it safely to the bathroom, it seemed clear that I was alone. A razor, wash cloth, and towel were laid out, and I lost myself in the bliss of a shower. I found everything as generic and sparse as her car: fragrance-free shampoo, soap, and deodorant.

To be straightforward about it: I did not snoop in her desk and bedroom. The one time I read a woman's diary, I was nineteen (my excuse for moral lapse). I learned that I snore when I have a cold and I scream like a girl when someone puts icy feet on my balls. I also found out that the person I had been sleeping with didn't know how to spell and couldn't wait to tell her freinds [sic] how many times she came the night before. So I learned my lesson about that sin.

The one time I snooped in a woman's bedroom—I mastered that lesson quite young and have never needed a refresher.

In the kitchen, a plate with a croissant and a slice of Welsh cheddar sat on the counter beside a note promising her return shortly, when we could talk about her proposal.

Being both quick-minded and prudent, I determined the best strategy was to call a cab and be gone. In the cold light of day, I knew Karl would consider it imprudent to marry her for her music collection. However, in spite of thinking myself an intelligent man, I'm also a weak man. I caved to temptation, taking the croissant and cheese with me to the music cabinet, just for one more look. Then I pulled my laptop out of the pack, plugged it in to recharge the battery, and took quick notes on the titles. I could prowl used-CD shops for ten years—in fact, I had been—without discovering the gold in this woman's oak cabinets.

When I plugged in my phone to recharge it, it rang, which meant it was Ian or Karl, since no one else has my number.

"Jason Taylor's answer service."

"It's Ephraim. We need to talk."

"How the hell did you get this number?"

"Your phone bill still comes to the condo. I tried to get the address changed, but gave up and just forward it to Karl every month. You should watch your business more closely. The details matter."

"What do you want?"

"I want to make sure you don't cause trouble for yourself. Or anything close to trouble for Dominique."

"Ephraim, I have never said one bad word about her in public. If you feel you have to warn me about anything, talk to my attorney."

"I talk to Karl every single day. I talk to him more than I talk to my own mother. This isn't about your bad publicity. You are supposed to deliver a new album. June is just around the corner, and Albion Records needs new CDs in brick stores and tracks in online stores. You and I have a professional relationship. So let's discuss your work."

"Get your witch of a girlfriend to quit lying about me, Ephraim. Then you can talk to me about work."

"As you know, she doesn't take direction well. She will do whatever she wants. You and I, however, have business to attend to."

"Karl does all my business."

"That's one thing we need to talk about. You need more than Karl. You need a real manager again. I should do that for you. You named me as a key man in your recording contract, and we had almost gotten to the business manager stage when you split."

"You sleep with my wife. How can I do business with you? Are you on another planet?"

"The only co-respondent in your divorce is music. You married her for music, and you left her for music. And music—not Dominique—is where you and I have a common business interest."

"I left her? That's your concept of what happened? She left because the grass was greener elsewhere."

"Let's save that conversation for Karl's office. I want to hear about what you've been doing and how you plan to meet your obligations. When can we get together to talk business?"

"On the last day it rains in Seattle."

I turned the damned cell phone off, fuming, and buried my attention in the lower shelf of leather-bound graduate theses, trying to keep my thoughts in check while I leafed through those volumes. That woman Susi must have picked these up from some professor's estate sale. She had more than a dozen texts on the folk tradition in North America (and I do not mean the Chad Mitchell Trio and Judy Collins), including a brilliant piece that mapped tonal shifts between twentieth century Cajun music and Breton traditional music, which I wish I had the good fortune to write. Determined to take advantage of this opportunity, I began to type notes as though my brain was on fire.

How could Ephraim Vance have the gall to ask what I've been doing?

※

I have been doing what a man could do in the situation I am in: playing music. Everywhere I could. A couple of my friends in Nashville felt sorry for me and invited me to do session work with them. That was good, but former friends and fans, whether confused or pissed off, crossed the street to avoid me. New fans who bought *Woman at the Well* because they liked Dominique's voice, and who followed the entertainment papers, wanted to spit on me. Or they were groupies who like to chase bad-boy guitarists.

And the word on the Internet is that Jason Taylor is the bad boy of indie music. Or indie singer-songwriters. No one can decide the appropriate label for our music—the portmanteau of cowboy grunge, "Americana" (whatever that is). That I ended up sorted into the bad-boy bin is the most ironic of the year's events, even more ironic than women asking for my autograph in airports. Most choir boys dabble in greater evil than I do. Our band—Stoneway, named for the street near where Ian has lived since we were skater boys in junior high—may have torn up the clubs where we played. Our lyrics and aggressive use of stomp pedal and kick drum may give the impression that we thrash elsewhere. But Stoneway doesn't tear up hotel rooms. We couldn't even afford hotel rooms until a couple of years ago. I haven't ended the night with my head in a toilet due to either drink or drugs since I was twenty-one. It is not that I don't know how; I just don't see why. I have never awakened either beside the road or beside a woman not knowing how I got there. It's not that I'm a sanctimonious folkie. I don't care, for example, what people in the band do, as long as they are sober in rehearsal and on stage.

Believe me, I have plenty of character faults, which Dominique loved to point out, though I already knew that I'm judgmental and self-absorbed. She wasn't the first woman to say that I'm so fastidious in my personal habits that it gives people the creeps. Karl complains that I'm both compulsive and impulsive, but the only evidence I've seen of the latter was finding myself at the gates of hell with Dominique.

Cynthia, Ian's wife, says I'm just an ordinary everyday asshole. She knows me well, and I find her simple assessment soothing.

Let's be clear: I did *not* hit Dominique. Or any other woman. Ever.

I cannot say aloud what the truth is: that she is a nut case. She has never told the plain truth about why we broke up, because she can't tell the tabloids that while I mourned my Uncle Beau, she screwed our producer while he screwed up our music, dampening the instruments to accentuate her voice and, worst of all, using computerized vocal tuning after I had refused to do that for her. It's embarrassing to acknowledge that she laughed when I found out she was sleeping around, trying to find a faster ride to fame.

How I got myself here: I was standing on the red carpet with Sean Wentworth when he won an Emmy for his Impious Aeneas miniseries (mixed media animation). Sean invited me along, since three Stoneway songs had significant play in the series. We were sipping water, getting ready for the next set of journalists and talking about a headline from that day's news. I said—quite rationally—that since Afghanistan was about the same size as Texas, all hell would break loose if Texas had five hundred drone bombings in one year.

A reporter from one of those Internet gawking sites overheard, and when his story went live after the interview, the headline was, "Want to Know Jason Taylor's Real Politics?" It's not like my politics are a secret or that I said anything outrageous, but the Internet hate machine picked it up as proof that all entertainers are Lefty-Communists who hate America. Then the extreme haters dug around in the Internet way-back machine and found a blog post from my favorite Internet stalker:

If it was me with that witch Dominique, I'd have hit her too.

I know how the Internet works, so I'm not claiming to be a victim of perfidy. However.

Dominique could have told the truth right then and ended half of the Internet catastrophe that my reputation quickly became.

I didn't hit her, or even consider it. I do not believe I am capable of it. However, one night I did stand on the street like a damned fool and scream at her to unlock the door to my house until the cops came. The second time in my life I got arrested.

I wasn't the first man in the world to learn he was a fool, so I shouldn't have taken it all so hard, except the grief of losing Beau distorted everything else. At the time, I was too miserable to notice what I had done to the rest of the band. Then I woke up one morning in Amsterdam and saw that I, too, had betrayed the band. I let Ephraim produce that album so that I could slip out of the marriage without any more acrimony. But Ephraim-the-cuckolder turned my music into the grandest mainstream pap as ever won a Grammy nomination. I betrayed the band after years of working together, playing ten and fifteen hours a day, touring, living so close to each other in that huffing van that we all smelled the same. All our money went into the van and amps and strings. We ate bar food wherever we played to avoid the cost of at least one meal a day, and we didn't care because we were too busy becoming the best in the world. No compromises. *No surrender,* just like The Boss said.

Until I let this long-legged rich girl talk me into handing her our nuts on a platter. Not our nuts exactly, just the digitized original tracks, but it was the same thing.

While otherwise shelling out bongo bucks for a publicist to stomp out forest fires on the Internet, I went to Europe. Emmylou let me open for her the first month. By then I already knew what it was like to be booed on a stage, since I'd done a couple of festival fundraisers in the U.S. after the rumor wildfires began raging across the World Wide Web. So, for fun, Emmylou introduced me as a Russian phenomenon she'd met in St. Petersburg, and I wore a Yankees cap that a songwriter friend gave me because he pitied my poor ass. I didn't speak between numbers, just did acoustic versions of the sad songs I'd been writing. At least I could hear whether those songs had any potential (seven survived the cut).

Then Ian and Cynthia joined me—oh god, what a friend he is, and Cynthia always hated Dominique, so she never believed the stories, which caused her to get into a shouting match outside Barrowlands in Glasgow. By that time I was looking for my lost sense of humor. (I misplaced it while waiting at the bus stop in the rain at five-thirty in the morning, too stubborn to accept a ride from my attorney after he bailed me out of jail.) We got Rocky from the Hell Cats to play drums, plus Cynthia on tambourine—she looks like great rock-and-roll even though she can't sing a note. The four of us tore up every little hall Cynthia could book us into between Galway and Barcelona. We called ourselves the Lost Sonsabitches, said we were from Wisconsin, owed everything we knew to the Blasters and the BoDeans, and never admitted it when we were accused of being ourselves.

That felt good—the playing, I mean, not the lying or hiding behind a full beard. Besides doing a host of loud, fuzzed-out covers of Stoneway and Lost Sons rarities, we turned my seven acoustic songs into scorchers, then added a half dozen more, with enough distortion to peel your eyeballs. I mean, if I'm going to waste my life writing sad songs, we might as well make everyone in the hall scream, too. We have recordings of those shows, and last week I saw bootlegs of fans' recordings being traded online and posting video on YouTube, after that constable in Manchester outed us. Stopped us on the street at three in the morning, demanding to see our passports, and then revealed our real names to his best buddy, who worked at *The Guardian*. By then parts of Europe had decided we could be allowed to walk the earth upright, instead of crawling on our bellies for selling out to the mainstream.

Yet I was still spending half of each day convincing myself that I had more value than pond scum and the other half drowning my sorrow in music. At least people trade our bootlegs again, instead of just plain giving us the boot. Also, I can make jokes in front of a crowd again, though it is still a little hard in front of a mirror.

It had been an amazing couple of years of self-discovery. You just haven't plumbed the possible depths of self-loathing until you've been married to someone you can't trust and who doesn't like you.

"Why Dominique?" Cynthia wanted to know. "How could you fall in love with someone like that?"

I began to stutter.

"How could you even believe anyone named Dominique was sincere from the beginning?" she said.

I protested to Cynthia that she was being unfair to the many worthy Dominiques of the world, because I'm still an optimist, and nothing she did made me think less of other women. I could also have protested that she wasn't actually a Dominique; she was a Jennifer who thought the world had enough Jennifer stars among millions of commonplace Jennifers. I guess in the end that's all we had in common—two of the most common first names of our generation. However, I can live with my ordinary name, but hers didn't sparkle enough to suit her delusions of future grandeur.

Though at least temporarily, it isn't delusional. Dominique has spent the past year higher on the charts than any Jennifers or other wannabes. She chose Dominique as her name because of that disgusting pop song by the French singing nun—it was the singing one, right? Not the flying one? I tried to tell her that the song was rotten, since it was about the Albigensian Crusade, and light-hearted pop songs about holocausts and inquisitions aren't appealing. Why

I didn't see from the start that I was involved with the wrong woman, I can't tell you now.

"'She said she loved me (but she lied).'"

That's how I answered Cynthia's question, but it left me miserable, for truthfully, I wasn't in love with Dominique, which makes me as much of a charlatan as my never-lovin' wife. I don't believe I have ever been in love, though I spent a great deal of time thinking about it, walking the streets of cities like Oslo and Amsterdam late at night after a show. The former viscount of the indie love song doesn't know a blessed thing about love. What a liar I am.

Went to bed with a poor little rich girl, just like my father did. Dominique seemed to believe that, like in a romance novel, outrageous sex would make me fall in love and marry her. I didn't really fall in love. For a moment, I thought *maybe*. Then Dominique blinked and looked away.

What I fell for was having a far-too-beautiful woman sing with me and sigh in the night that she loved me. Sure, she came on to me like any of the sweet, lusting women at the edge of the stage, wanting to take a guitarist home with them when the show is over. Yet Dominique didn't have any reason to want that. At first, I thought she was slumming. She chased after me, begging to sing with me. She had a little scene going in L.A., singing Patsy Cline torch songs. It was a cute act, but it was just that: an act. I'm from a working-class neighborhood—hell, I spent half my boyhood in effing Ballard and the other half in a rickety apartment in lower Wallingford, if you want to know—but I learned enough in that *artiste* high school they sent me to that I know the very rich are indeed not like you and me. So, to rephrase what Bruce said, what was a woman like Dominique doing with a guy like me?

She was looking in my eyes, whispering that I was everything she dreamed of. After a short while, she was telling me I could be so much more if I'd start making the business work for me instead of always working against it. Stop being so self-destructive, she said.

You can go with a big label and take the money without letting them take your soul. You have what it takes. The whole world should know you instead of just your quirky, indie-loving fans in little towns where the sun never shines. Let me help you be everything you can be.

ANNIE PEARSON

I recognize this now, from literature. It's called the siren's song. You plug your ears to avoid being shipwrecked in the straits. The next time I hear "be all you can be," I'm joining the effing army.

Of all the bad-boy things my father did, he never spent a night in jail while the police tried to figure out what the woman meant when she said, "He has abused me awfully." The cops realized that it was only drama on her part, and I hope someday she will tell the world the truth. However, I don't think it's possible for Dominique to speak the truth. Oh geez, I have to stop obsessing about it or all that dramatic self-pity will come out in my music, and I'll sink to my father's depths.

That is what my father did, made himself famous for musically beautiful and grandiose self-pity, veering more to the Hank Williams side of the Lost Highway than the Gram Parsons side. When Jesse Rufus recorded that Neil Young cover, singing "'Better to burn out than fade away,'" he must have thought that meant "better to wrap your brother's car around a telephone pole than get sober and do what a man is supposed to."

He never acknowledged me. If he had done so, he'd have had to do it for God-alone-knows how many other bastards he left behind. Seems like every town I played in America in the last year, a drunk has come up and claimed he is my lost half-brother. Thanks to Dominique, that stupid bust with my uncle left everyone in the world knowing whose son I was. Before then, I had done as fine a job of covering it as my father ever did. I remember sitting on one of those NPR talk shows—the one with the brilliant woman who always asks the leading questions no one else thinks of—and of course she started probing influences.

"Anyone listening to your music for the first time will notice how much you sound like Jesse Rufus. And your guitar style reminds me of the Lost Sons."

Why in hell that had to be the name of my father's band, I can't say.

"There is a heavy Celtic influence in my work, though more Waterboys than the Pogues," I answered as I always used to, intending to throw snoopers off the scent. "Otherwise, I listen to everything. Yes, Beau Rufus plays bass in my band now, but he's so versatile, I don't think he has imported the Lost Sons into our music."

40

My Uncle Beau was part of the Rufus family, one of the original Lost Sons, the only one who acknowledged me. When my mother's wealthy family disowned her, Uncle Beau made sure she had what we needed, took care of me on those frequent occasions when she was too ill to deal with a boy, and then helped me on my way after she died. Uncle Beau gave me a guitar when I was eight and an amp when I was twelve. Uncle Beau went back to my mother's father when I wanted to drop out of high school to play music, and he teamed with that old man to get me into an arts-centered high school. The old man wrote letters pleading for them to enroll me, wrote checks for my tuition, and made a monster-sized donation.

My dear grandfather didn't believe he got his money's worth, and I never saw him again, after I got booted out two weeks before graduation. I'd been playing in two bands for cash—my grandfather paid tuition and Uncle Beau paid the rent, but neither was around often, and I had to bear the cost of my recorded-music habit and instruments to feed the jones I had for music. One of the two bands I played in got good enough that we had a chance to tour in Europe. Yeah, it was like how Ian and I played over this winter, where you commute on a EuroPass, serve as your own roadie, sleep on a promoter's sofa, wash your underwear in the sink of an Airbnb walkup when no one has a spare room to volunteer. The roots music fans in Europe liked us. That was when Ian, Toby, and I first played together, high just from playing music fifteen hours a day. The slight downer was that I got kicked out of school for not showing up for two months.

My grandfather didn't get around to forgiving me for that before he died. At least he isn't around now to ask me, like Cynthia and Uncle Beau did, "Why Dominique? Why fall in love with her?"

Rich girl pushes poor boy to the top. Rich girl takes the poor boy's guitar licks and his best friends' sweat and desire, and escorts them through, as Gram and Chris said, *the gold-plated door on the thirty-first floor.* OK, yes, she can sing. But not like a red-dirt girl. No, the rich girl can just sustain a note for a freakishly long time like every other pop diva. She just can't inject emotion into her voice, because Dominique doesn't have any emotions, other than a vacillating surge between pleasure and irritation.

Then, after she sampled a few other opportunities for getting farther than I might take her, the poor little rich girl took up with Ephraim Vance, the knob-twiddling producer who is the son of the label's president and who made us all rich before the storm subsided. Rich, and hated by our former friends.

11
"I Lost It"
Jason

ALTHOUGH MY CELL CONNECTION seemed pokey, I wanted to upload my notes to the various blogs I keep, especially the notes about the books on Susi's shelves that I wanted to find in a library to read later. I looked at these other notes—the ones I'm writing here—which would have been part of the blog except it's the kind of personal writing that only embarrasses other people when they read it. So I just emailed this file to myself so I could determine later how much goes on the blog.

In the middle of the upload, I clicked a link I hadn't meant to and found myself staring at the new list of bootleg trades and guitar tabs for Stoneway. Someone was offering the tabulations and lyrics from one of the new songs that Ian and I had discarded. We played that song once, one night in Bergen. Some Norse berserker had transcribed every word. My irrational, perfectionist self wanted to reply with a correction to the guitar tabs and the last revision we made to the chorus. My latent inner business manager went into a frenzy, wondering if I had registered that song before performing it, or if the words and music were now out on the Internet without me claiming prior art. Of course I had. I always did. Even Karl trusted me to take care of business at least that well.

As soon as I clicked through to read the message, I had chills. That guy—Ian calls him my own creepy stalker fan—had either been in Bergen or had a contact there. I looked for the alias he was using this time—JessesBoy. It was him. If he didn't use an alias like LostSon2 or BadBro, then he left one of his favorite lines in every message. "This week my brother is in..." or "The fortunate son has now..."

I could ignore the bizarre expression of fraternal rivalry. What bugged me was that he delivered news to fan sites as if he were behind me, looking at my plane ticket, listening from the next table, tapped into my phone. I was at the Family Wash in Nashville, talking to the Pete at the bar. Pete said, "This is The Wash. This is the yin to the yang part of your life. And there's no grey in yin/yang, right? There isn't, is there?" Then the yang part of life returned when my stalker posted a minute-by-minute report on a woman I met at The Wash that night, including her name and phone number and what we talked about (that night's Carpetbaggers Local 615 show with Jamie, Pete, and Reeves). Most of what he posted was fictitious, but Karl had to harass the Internet service provider to remove all traces of her personal information, and then he had to arrange for her to get a new phone and paid her expenses for all the bother that dating an infamous bad boy had caused.

The same stalker who posted, "I would have hit her too," and spawned the last year's nightmares. The "too" part that was a lie.

The detailed news about my business started after I was busted with Uncle Beau, when Dominique began outing me as the son of my famous father. I accused her of leaking my life to the Internet, but then details appeared that she couldn't know, unless she paid someone to follow me. She wasn't interested in me enough to bother to do that. The morning after Dominique called the police on me—which resulted in them threatening to charge her if she ever lied again—I wasn't out of jail long enough to log on before my stalker reported to the world what she screamed at me when the police showed up. Therefore, technically I can't blame her for how the rumor started, aside from the fact that she created the foundation circumstance. Still, she hasn't done anything to counter the stories from my cyber stalker. When the tabloids picked up the so-called news from fan sites, Dominique should have denied it. Between my wife and my stalker, they couldn't have done a better job if they'd worked together to invent the story of Jesse Rufus's son, wife beater.

JessesBoy: The new songs show how much happier my brother Jason is now that he's free of the Dragon Woman. When Jason is doing well, I'm happy too. We were pretty miserable for a while. But when you hear the new boots, you will hear how much better we are doing.

This time, I did what I shouldn't have done. I replied while logged on under my lurker alias.

> Sebastian: I was in Bergen, too, and this song isn't one of Jason Taylor's better efforts. It's not in the set list for other shows for good reason.

Right then I vowed to myself that I'd revise the song, change the words, and take a different tack on the music, just to prove my stalker wrong.

In my own email box—which only a handful of people use, together with my special spam friends who want to help me get out of credit card debt and also get a bigger penis—was a short note from one of my Americana friends. I refer to the kind of Americana that needs disambiguation on Wikipedia. I started a forum under my lurker alias on No Depression years ago. Then I moved it to a blog, where the discussion threads have been a haven since life went sour. My lurker-alias blog is obscure enough that it attracts only the most serious about exploration of roots music, like people writing graduate theses. Nothing gets posted without the site manager's approval, which I know makes me a censor of sorts, but I always post everything received that isn't spam or ads. The etiquette of the blog is that we just freeze out obnoxious posters by not responding. Through the blog I met a few old musicology codgers who had been batting around issues since John Lomax first published and who liked preserving their arguments on the Internet. A few of them have become personal friends of mine.

This morning, it was Chas1933@jugum.com, whom I consider a good friend, though we've never met in person. I learn something interesting whenever he writes to me.

> Chas1933: Your help with more recent influences has been invaluable. I've about chased that Gram Parsons thread to its end. Call me an old fart, but it seems most of his influence centered on who he spent time drinking with.

> Sebastian: That's too cynical. The real influence was his insistence on going back to roots and being true to that, instead of listening to the derivative sound that got radio play in those days.

Chas1933: I can hear that in his music. I confess I just wanted to yank your chain since you always insist on going back to roots. Want to help me with the next thread I'm following? Got time to waste on an old man?

Sebastian: It's never a waste. I owe you far more from what you've sent my way in the last couple of years. What's your next project?

Chas1933: The Lost Sons. No one has done much research into the work those boys did. I see it called Hillbilly Bebop, and one guy calls Jesse Rufus the son of Charlie Mingus and Hank Williams. But I don't think old Hank was AC/DC.

Sebastian: The traditional list of influences starts with the Delmore Brothers, because of the close harmony. Though I believe for Jesse it was the Sons of the Pioneers. The Bakersfield country-western work from the Fifties and Sixties. Gram Parson and Neil Young. And the Beatles.

Chas1933: I can hear all that. You have an opinion on everything. What do you hear in Jesse Rufus? You must have given his work a listen.

I had listened to every line and every note Jesse Rufus recorded, over and over, hoping for hidden messages, the way kids in the Sixties listened to *Sergeant Pepper* and *Sympathy for the Devil.* I spent the eighth, ninth, and tenth grades trying to learn every chord, imitating how Jesse Rufus bent notes with his voice, transcribing chords and words, looking for acrostics or coded clues, any indication that he knew I existed. I have never longed for a lover the way I longed to find out that he knew I was in lower Wallingford, wishing he would come be my real father.

Sebastian: Too much tequila, coke, and speed. I can't hear anything else in the music. It's a crying shame.

12
"Wild Card"
Jason

WHILE I WAS IN MID-CONVERSATION with Chas, Susi returned, dressed in running shorts and a long-sleeved athletic shirt. Though she had cooled down enough that she wasn't breathing hard, her legs were blotched red from exertion in the cold morning air, and her skin glistened with perspiration. In a damp t-shirt, more than just her erect posture showed through. She had the build of a swimmer, strong shoulders and great lung capacity. Fortunately, she didn't have breasts to speak of, and she was small, which has never been a type I'm attracted to. Otherwise, the pure physicality of her strong body and that pert—impertinent—way she had of staring deep into a person's eyes almost had me crawling on the floor and begging.

I crumpled up the note that said *thanks for the laundry, see you around* and jammed it into my pocket.

"Oh good, you found everything I left for you." She smiled. Dammit. I can't take much of that. "I'll make breakfast after I shower. Then I want to show you the notes and we can talk."

The woman had an agenda, with an assumption that I shared it.

OK, I should have split the moment she went to shower. That made two lost chances to just grab my bag and scoot. I did make the effort. I unplugged my laptop and wrapped up the cord, then I finished making the last set of notes from the CD and DVD labels, and I stuck it all in my pack. Except there was a sheet of handwritten music on the piano, and it distracted me for several heartbeats. I couldn't stop myself from playing it several times, struck by both the melody and the golden tone of the piano. She was by my side, taking away the music, hiding it, and saying, "I'm embarrassed that you saw this." Her voice had the same timbre as the piano.

"It was rude to leave you here alone, but I needed exercise," she said. "After meetings all day yesterday, I needed to take a run before everything we have to do today."

Dressed for business, she wore a suit jacket that accented her erect posture and the tidy, efficient movement of her hands, showing off a sophisticated, Katharine Hepburn-beating-up-Spencer Tracey charm. That stiffness where she covered up the injury to her face reinforced the impression that she was a serious woman, not to be trifled with.

"Susi, I don't know if I can help you."

She looked up from where she was manufacturing a breakfast sandwich in a tidy flurry, her brow raised in faint consternation. "You know about the plans for the Troubadours Institute, right? You received the advance draft of the proposal?"

"No, I don't know anything about it."

She sighed as she slipped the sandwich into a pan on the stove. "I knew we shouldn't have trusted email, but she insisted. I just want you to look at the money. Our fundraiser Randolph keeps assuring me, but I don't trust him to tend to business correctly. I will relax when you tell me the pro forma looks like what you'd expect to see if you were giving us money."

The sun went behind an April cloud. It was disappointing to hear, I do admit. She didn't want my body, she wanted my money.

I said, "I'd like to help, but like Bruce said, 'I left my wallet back home in my working pants.'"

She laughed as if I were joking, and then asked, "Who's Bruce?"

"How about later?"

"She said you would keep putting it off. You have to help us." She was busy scrubbing pots while shaking me down. "We are looking for a great deal more money than either of us knows how to manage. We need you to prove that we have a team member who knows this business."

"Susi, I don't think I'm your man." However, I was still seeking to explore the territory and see what I could say yes to, before I had to say no.

"You committed, Jason. When we called, your partner or your attorney friend, whatever he is, promised he'd get the information to you and get it on your schedule."

"Oh, yeah." Damn if I could remember what Karl said the day before. Something about a foundation? I remember saying yes, but thought then that I still had a chance to dodge it.

"I'm asking for a half a day today and tomorrow, Jason. It's only a few hours of your time, but it's my whole life."

"That is a bit dramatic. I'm not used to being the rescuing hero."

Susi said, "She warned me that you'd be like this—putting it off, as if you were lazy and got where you are through family privilege. Which we both know isn't true."

She put a folder in my hands, and I began leafing through it.

"I got where I am through my own hard work, thank you." I tried not to sound too tetchy, but failed.

"So did I. Now I want to get further. This isn't just for summer fun—play with some kids, put on a show, and then forget it. This summer is my chance to prove we can do it. I want to turn this into a permanent project. I know I'm good at teaching, but I don't want to stay at that school where I'm working now. I can't find work in the public schools, because there's no money left for performance arts. If we can do this, then we'll create a place to nourish kids who love music but aren't wealthy enough to go to a school like Prescott. I know how to work with those kids, and I think I can get others to contribute."

"You did your research well, Susi."

"You haven't finished reading the proposal yet."

"I mean your research into my background. This is a perfect concept if you are trying to make me fall in love with you."

She flushed and came close to stammering, but then she focused on the sandwich she was toasting and didn't look at me. Spencer Tracey 1, Katharine Hepburn 0.

"I'm teasing, Susi."

"The numbers start on page thirty."

"Let me finish reading the curriculum part."

"All right. We wanted you to tell us whether the numbers look right, from a funder's perspective. She said to make you look at it closely, because otherwise you will avoid it just to tease."

Since Susi insisted, I stared at the lists of numbers, which I more-or-less understood, but I suspect that Karl wouldn't trust me to have an actual "funder's perspective." She set the grilled sandwich before me. As I read, I ate tomato, cheese, and avocado on what looked like homemade bread, dipped in egg like French toast and then grilled.

"It looks great." I can check the math fine, but I don't know pro forma from Prokofiev.

"You approve?"

"Yes." I shrugged. I approve the fax of the credit-card bills that Karl's admin forwards every month and that is about as deep as my financial wisdom extends. Bought five CDs in Soho, stayed ten nights in a hotel near Chelsea, tickets to three shows at Shepherd's Bush Empire, one hundred pounds from an ATM near Charing Cross Station, sixty-five pounds worth of books at the Tate Britain gift shop. Approved for payment.

She sighed, which I would have liked to have provoked in a different way. "What a relief. I worry that Randolph is sleazing on something."

"The part I don't understand is why you are fundraising in Seattle for a roots music project. Why aren't you hitting people in Nashville and Memphis? Or the Carolinas and Texas. Or even Chicago. Places where they care more about roots music."

"The program will be here. We don't know people there," she said.

"I should introduce you. That's how I could best contribute."

"Great, then let's go."

"Today? Right now?"

"I need to get these people to commit today. The trustees of the school are looking forward to meeting you. The grant has to be submitted by April 15, or we are out of the running for this year's money. If we don't get our funding this year—"

"Then you will have to spend the summer at the beach instead of teaching boys with zits how to play twelve-bar blues."

"No, it's—look, you admired my father's collection last night. Dad hasn't many years left. He's still eager to keep teaching. I want to create the opportunity for him to have at least one more season of lectures. I know he's not a genius. He spent his life teaching music in little schools, too, but he has something to offer."

I was just about to open her curriculum vitae when she took the folder away from me.

"Look at the schools you went to, Susi. All your training is in classical music. What are you doing down in the dirt with hillbillies?"

"My father is a fan of roots music and he made me listen too, starting with the first wax cylinder recordings of the early twentieth century, up through the great bluesmen in Mississippi and Memphis.

I came to be intrigued with American mountain music and the folk traditions of the British Isles."

"Then you were magically transported from 1955 to this brave new world, where you adopted a disguise as a gentle school teacher with the business style of a killer shark."

"So you will help us?" She smiled.

I was doomed.

"Let me call my friends to tell them I won't be around this afternoon."

I couldn't calculate yet how much I was willing to have this adventure cost me, or how I would explain it to Karl when he saw the size of the check I'd be asking him to cut. I sat at the counter to eat the sandwich (oh god, it was indeed homemade bread from an alternate universe), hungriest of all to hear her speak, but not looking at her because I was afraid she would smile.

"You can use my phone," she said. "It's in the bedroom."

"I'll use my cell," I said, and ducked onto the deck to call Ian while I finished the sandwich. I retained access to enough of my native intelligence to know that this woman's bedroom was the last place on earth I should dare to enter.

※

"Speak."

"That drummer won't work, Ian. We need a rhythm master, and he doesn't have it."

"Jason, buddy, where are you? Your bags showed up here last night without you. Had to tip the driver big time for wrangling all four guitars. What is in the box that weighs a ton?"

"Books. I went to the museums after you and Cynthia left."

"Where are you? You didn't stay at a hotel, did you? You get introspective and weird when you hole up alone. You need to be home with family. I'm stuck here by myself. Cynthia is out of town."

"I met this woman."

"Oh crap. Where are you? I'll be right there."

"No, I don't mean like that."

"What other way is there when you don't come home at night?"

"We're just talking. I met her at Neumo's last night."

"Just what are you two talking about?"

"I don't know exactly. She has this unusual voice—"

"Shit, man. Shit. Shit. Step out on the street. What neighborhood are you in? I can be there in a minute."

"Madrona, I think. Or maybe Leschi. You don't need to get me. She'll drop me off later. We have business to take care of."

"Oh shit, man. She doesn't want to sing with you, does she? I don't like the sound of this."

"I don't know if she sings at all. She didn't say. It's just how she talks that gets me."

"Are you jetlagged, man? You don't sound right."

"I'm fine. You can read about it on my blog. It's no big deal. I'll talk to you at dinner."

I hung up, realizing as I did that I hadn't put Susi in my blog.

13
"Mama's Opry"
Susi

I SHALL NOW CREATE a separate record of my sins of both omission and commission and of the embarrassing moments from the first full day of my acquaintance with Jason.

To begin with the first sin, I did his laundry.

It was a considerate, humane action that I would have done for any houseguest stranded without luggage. It takes only a minute to iron a shirt. There shouldn't be social stigma attached to friendly actions between people, just because one is a man and the other is a woman, and the subject is the man's laundry. It is true that I used to do Logan's laundry, but only because he'd let it sit longer than I could stand. So I washed Logan's for my own sake, and I stopped when we could afford household help. This later occurrence was a one-time event for a guest.

(The belt buckle is silver-plated nickel with the figure of an old-fashioned motorcycle. He doesn't keep anything in his pockets other than his wallet, and I did *not* look in it.)

Next, I tried hard to show that I have a sense of humor. I wanted Jason to think that helping us would be fun. This attempt was not a sin on my part. It's merely embarrassing, because I'm so bad at it. I'm far better at giving him the opportunity to laugh at me than I am at rendering true humor. As we got into my car to go to the meeting, he started teasing. Now, after a few mistakes, I can tell when he is teasing from the first two notes of his voice as he speaks.

He said, "I intend to force a confession from you. All the evidence indicates that you are a time traveler from—what? 1955? Or farther back? 1935? What do you like best in your collection, Susi? Hank Williams and his friends on the Lost Highway, or Leadbelly and his field-holler friends?"

"I would prefer whatever Hank Williams' mother sang to him. I can appreciate the significance of the works of Huddie Ledbetter and the others that the Lomaxes recorded. Only a few of them strike an emotional response in me—that's why others appreciate the blues, right? Because of the emotions aroused?"

"Yes. It's also why lots of other people do not like it. What strikes a note for you, Susi?"

"Skip James. Every note he sings makes me want to weep. Little Milton. The others are too masculine for my tastes."

"Too much testosterone for your dainty sensibilities?"

It is clear in retrospect how I get myself into these situations, but I can never see it at the time.

After Jason had entertained himself by making me uncomfortable, he turned serious again and began what would be a theme for the day: asking questions that either exposed a raw nerve or drove straight to my heart.

"And Billie Holiday? Big Mama Thornton? Or Mabel Mercer? Which of them makes you weep, Susi?"

I couldn't answer. As he said Billie Holiday's name, a ball of emotion choked up in my throat so that the most graceful sound I could make was a false "Hmm." How could he understand? I spent hours listening, trying to understand where that sound came from, how she could live with that organ of feeling in her body. I have tried imitating her, may the forces of the universe save me from anyone ever knowing. I will never achieve what Billie Holiday did, and thinking about it plunges me into a personal abyss where I cannot confront my failures.

"I can't see you and Patsy Cline together," he said. "Or Wanda Jackson. Oh, wait, Wanda is later than when you traveled to our own century."

"I know Patsy Cline's music. However, I simply don't understand the Slave-to-Romance theme."

He didn't bother to hide that he was laughing at me.

"All right, Susi. We will move closer to the time you came from in the last century. The Carter Family? Do you like a good mountain hymn?"

"I appreciate their achievement, but I prefer the women from the Appalachian hills. Hazel Dickens and Alice Gerrard, Wilma Lee Cooper. Patsy Montana for cowboy music."

"Because you like pure natural religion?" He was teasing.

"Just the pure and natural part."

Because I can sing it—though I couldn't tell him that. That had been the most exciting discovery in the past winter, changing the entire color of my life. It was more than the intellectual excitement of plunging into my father's old research that brought me to invent this musical curriculum.

When we parked at the school, Jason stood in the parking lot, his hands jammed in his jeans pockets, staring up at the ivy-covered building.

"Why did I let you walk me down memory lane?" he said.

"The trustees are especially interested in your helping us, since you went to school here."

He laughed, as if in disbelief. When we entered, he held the door for me, wrinkling his nose in distaste.

"I hate the smell of this place. It hasn't changed in a dozen years. Creeps me out. Tell me, Susi, is old Hector Henderson still teaching here?"

"Yes."

"He is such a character-disorder guy. It's a wonder he's allowed among children—even his own biological offspring. Still, I suppose everyone has their level. His is just below sea level."

"Don't be mean."

"Me? I'm the nicest guy you will ever meet."

14

"Frying Pan"
Susi

"JASON DOESN'T NEED AN introduction," Gwyneth Lukas said when we sat down for the meeting, after I had introduced him to the three trustees and Randolph. "Your reputation precedes you. As well as your record here at the school."

"I'm not as bad as I'm made out to be," Jason said.

Gwyneth laughed (I try not to let that fluty tone bother me, but it is difficult), and so Rafe Joseph and Talbot Sheldon chuckled too in their gentlemanly, business-like way. Randolph, however, had determined that a competition existed with Jason; guarded hostility was the highest response he offered throughout the day. Why do men sniff each other and growl? For Randolph's part, I knew it was because of me, which made the situation faintly humorous. If there were a competition, Randolph would not be in the running.

I have to render a confession which, even if no one reads this but me, remains difficult to reveal. After the first few skirmishes with the trustees, I let Jason save me, and I was glad of it. I have never had a man rescue me from anything in my life. (My dad's help when I was recovering cannot be considered a rescue.)

It was Gwyneth in her mink vest and limited-edition Italian jeans that my knight-errant saved me from. The other two trustees had supported the idea of the music institute when Angelia and I first presented it. The same men had treated me with kid-gloves when they interviewed me for the teaching position, each saying that he knew my history and—oh god—felt sorry for me. Gwyneth just didn't get the idea of the Lost Troubadours Institute, or even the basic idea of music education.

"I don't understand what British and Scottish folk music has to do with—what do you call it? 'Music Theory and Popular Song'?"

Before I could begin, Jason used Copland's *Appalachian Spring* to explain. He held her flighty attention with a beautiful interpretation of how old hymns and songs are used in that symphony. She stared into his eyes while he spoke, but she apparently understood when he segued into a discussion of a collaboration by Yo-Yo Ma, Edgar Meyer, and Mark O'Connor.

She said, "My husband got me that CD for Christmas last year, because James Taylor is a favorite of mine."

I don't know what orchestra Mr. James Taylor plays with, but his name rang a bell for Gwyneth. She nodded her head as Jason explained the heroic role the institute would play for music education.

We performed the same give-and-take for every other sortie. I presented the idea, Gwyneth attacked, and then Jason neutralized her. By the time we began eating our catered box lunches while completing a line-by-line review of the grant application, Gwyneth had attached herself to Jason like a limpet on a rock. He used every opportunity to show his erudition. If she wasn't impressed, I was. In spite of what I knew about his background, and his chosen profession, he had an encyclopedic knowledge of arts and music, and an uncanny ability to express ideas in a way that even Gwyneth could understand.

For my next sin, as is obvious from how I write about it here, I was as bad as Randolph, though I hope that I didn't physically manifest the scorn I felt for Gwyneth's flirting with Jason. I forgive people their foibles. I look the other way and don't even comment to myself. Still, I wanted to break her little finger.

At the next stop on the road to hell, I enjoyed it when Jason pointed out a typo and a math error in Randolph's pro forma.

"Let's just fix this as we go," Jason said, taking his laptop out of his pack. "Who has the original file?"

Randolph went to fetch the file from his own computer, hunched in hatred. Since it was only a typo, my inflated sense of triumph weighed in on the side of sin.

Then right at the doors of Hades, when it was possible to feel the flickering flames of damnation, I stepped brazenly over the threshold.

I gave Jason my lunch.

There was just one vegetarian box lunch, which Randolph had ordered for me. I gave it to Jason, so he had roasted peppers and hummus on Tuscan bread. I tossed out the ham from another box to create a Swiss-and-lettuce sandwich. Even though I was too keyed up over the grant to swallow even half a sandwich, the symbolism would be obvious to the most casual observer: If this were a relationship (which, of course, it isn't), we had gotten off to the worst of starts, with me playing subservient wench delivering laundry, lunch, and self-sacrifice. All human feeling revolts at the thought.

Whatever my sins and weaknesses, we won the day, if not wholly on the strength of the institute's grand ideals, then on the basis of Jason's easy erudition and great business management. The trustees conferred, and Gwyneth announced that they were granting us the boon we needed: use of school facilities for the summer as an in-kind contribution to the institute's total costs. Having pronounced this as if it were her personal gift to the arts, Gwyneth rose, claiming an appointment, though we had worked through the entire business agenda two hours faster than we planned. "Will we see the two of you for luncheon tomorrow?"

"Yes," I said, though watching Jason, I could see him blanch.

He said, "We will be there with bells on."

With Gwyneth departing, everyone else rose, even Randolph, who (I'm guessing) would have preferred to stay behind and stab Jason to death with his gold Cross pen.

Randolph said, "So will I see you tonight, Susanna?"

Staring at the computer screen, Jason didn't look up, his nostrils flaring.

I said, "It will just be me. Jason has other plans. Please tell your grandparents that I'm looking forward to joining you."

"I have changed my plans," Jason said. "I will be joining you, too, if the invitation is still open."

The invitation had occurred before Jason flew in from London, and Randolph would have loved to snatch it back, but he avowed that he looked forward to the evening.

Once everyone had left, Jason said, "Susi, you can't put your fate in that woman's hands. Where the hell are we going tonight with your friend Randolph?"

"You don't have to come. He invited us to a concert with his grandparents. They are wealthy as Croesus and need one last social exchange to convince them to support the institute. That is the rest of my work for the weekend, to reel in the last of the donors for the grant's matching money."

"You aren't going alone. I committed to this, and I'm coming along."

"That's kind of you."

"It isn't kindness. You sold me on the idea, and I'm going to do what you ask, to make sure the business is handled correctly. Look here, on the page that lists the faculty. You can't use this guy, Susi."

"They say he is well known on the West Coast. He did a seminar for the students one day on the influence of Mississippi blues on British pop. They loved it."

"He's a drunk. You don't want to risk wasting your time with him. And kids don't need to be around that."

"How do you know?"

"You asked me to give you my professional expertise, and that's part of it. I won't tell stories on the guy, but you don't want him."

"Who can I get to replace him this late? He's one of the most famous names I had to show on the grant request."

"Me, since I'm not going anywhere this summer. How much time will it take?"

"Four hours a day, but—"

"Schedule me in the morning, then I can balance it against other work."

"You are insane. You're going to neglect your work to teach music?" After hearing his erudition at the meeting, I couldn't argue that he wasn't as good as a trained professional.

"I'm not leaving my other work. I want to stretch, to do more."

"However, I think I should use the name I have for the grant and make changes later."

He popped the disk out of his computer and handed it to me.

"Let's get out of here, Susi, before I have a flashback and you are forced to place me in a mental institution. I was allergic to this place years ago, and meeting these people didn't help at all. This place gives me hives."

"Let me put these papers away in the office."

"Fine. I have to make phone calls."

The cell phone is his only noticeable vice.

I suppose he can't help the testosterone part.

15
"Devil in Disguise"
Jason

"IAN, I'LL BE LATE tonight. I'm going out to hear music."

"She called here, man."

"Who?"

"Your witch of an ex-wife. She's going to be in the studio with us, isn't she? You promised—"

"No, she's not. What did she want?"

"She wanted you, jerk-face," Ian said, "I didn't get into a discourse with her. She wants to come by and see you tonight."

"I won't be there."

"Neither will I. Jason, life is too short to spend time breathing air with Dominique. I'm headed out to catch a band at the Showbox."

"Then I guess I'll see you in the morning."

When I tapped the End button, the phone rang almost immediately, so I figured it was Ian calling back. Which makes two bad guesses that day about Ian calling me.

"Hello, Jason. Ephraim said you were in town. We need to talk, honey."

"No, we don't, Dominique. Talk to Karl."

"I saw your song list for the new album. Those are songs you rejected for the last album."

"I rejected them because they were too mainstream, but that's what you want, Dominique."

"You want to ruin this album just to spite me."

"The irony in that statement sends me reeling. We'll be in the studio on Monday and playing music. As you know, no one in my band is capable of doing less than his best work."

"These songs aren't appropriate for me." Her voice hurt my ears.

"Perhaps you'll have to practice. The sole freedom I retained in that recording contract you talked me into is that I choose the music. Perhaps if you bothered to spend time rehearsing, you could sing those songs."

"You're being mean, Jason."

"Me? How can you accuse me, Dominique? I do not deserve even half of what you did. You damaged friendships that I cherish.

You lied to the police, and you never helped stop those lies about me on the Internet."

"You hurt me awfully."

"Telling you the truth isn't the same as wife-beating. Why won't you answer a straight question in interviews? Do you know what this has done to me?"

"You got your own meanness back."

"OK, whatever it is you think I did to you, I got my own back. Doubled. Now tell the truth. I didn't hit you or otherwise abuse you. And I didn't steal songs from you."

"Honey, you know I wrote 'Rhianna's Song' with you. 'How can a mother bear to witness the death of her dreams'—that was my line."

"You read it in the paper, which is not like writing a song together."

"We will just have to agree to disagree about that, Jason. Listen, I'm doing a benefit tomorrow for a homeless shelter. Ephraim says you should sit in with me. Ephraim says we would get good press if we perform together in public. It didn't do you any harm to come to the Grammys."

"Actually, it gave me a nearly fatal pain in the ass. Don't call me, Dominique. Talk to Karl."

16
"Something About What Happens When We Talk"
Susi

THE NEXT SIN I MUST record in this journal, as a prelude to describing my wicked spring-vacation beach fling: when we stopped at my house so that I could change before we took a walk, I gave Jason my brother's sweatshirt, which was again just a kindness, since he had nothing but that repellent Yankees ball cap and the thin leather jacket he wore on the flight from London to Seattle.

Except, in addition to that act of consideration, I also made sure that Jason understood it was *my brother's* sweatshirt, so he wouldn't think a man left clothes at my house.

We went north of the Ship Canal to walk at Golden Gardens on Puget Sound, where golden oaks sprawl up the steep hillside. There's a sandy beach for shell hunting, a volleyball court where narcissists can show off their tattoos and muscles, a long strand for walking out along the Sound, and a circular drive for cars to cruise in summer.

As we began walking toward the beach, Jason remained silent for many yards, as he had on the drive over. Then he seemed to rouse himself and moved over to walk close by me just at the moment when we had the divine luck to be in the culvert under the railroad tracks as a train passed overhead, making my bones vibrate from the rumble of steel wheels on the track. It made me smile with joy, first remembering all the times I had come here with my brother and father, and then I smiled just because Jason was grinning. He held my hand against his chest while he matched the tone of the train with his voice, so I couldn't distinguish the train from the vibrating tone under my hand.

As the train grumbled away, we jumped through the broken glass and puddles to ramble down to the beach. As we hit the soft sand, he stumbled into me, putting his arm lightly around my shoulders to steady himself.

He glanced sideways at me as we walked.

"'Who are you really and what were you before, and what did you do and what did you think?' *Casablanca* is from your era, isn't it, Susi? Or did you travel here from before the Second World War?"

"'We said no questions.'"

"No fair, Susi. We've already known each other for seventeen hours. By now I should get a free pass to ask questions, and you should entrust me with honest answers."

"I was married to the second trombone in the village band."

"And his name was Nanki Poo? The son of our Mikado?"

"No, Logan Childs. The son of a druggist."

"You will get uptight if I make jokes about his name, won't you?"

"Hmm. I don't usually laugh when I think about him."

"He's a fool and a sinner, and there is nothing you should blame yourself for, Susi."

"How can you say that? Did she tell you—"

"I'm just making logical deductions. He is not with you now, and that proves he's a fool for letting you get away. Clearly he's a sinner, for he appears to have hurt you."

He touched my face, the problem side, and I had to draw away.

"Your turn," I said. "Same questions and honest answers required."

"You know the story too well."

"Tell it from your point of view."

"My friend Toby says I married the Wicked Witch of the West. But I just married a woman who wanted me to be someone else. She went where she wanted to go, leaving me to find where I should go next. I stayed married to the wrong person too long, because I thought that you're supposed to stay married, no matter what."

"Most people don't think that anymore."

"It's one of the rules carved on the millstone I tied around my neck, daring myself to be a better man than my father. How about you, Susi? How long did that fool hang on before he lost you?"

"Seven years."

"Ouch."

"Excellent choice of words for the ending, if not the rest of the time."

"What would be the word for that, Susi?"

"Boring. Like this conversation. Let's climb up the bank and walk on the train tracks."

It was cold enough on the beach that we couldn't idle around. At the end of the sand spit, I led him up through the rocks to the train tracks. At one point, he slipped and nearly collided with me before grabbing a branch to stop himself. His knee touched me, however. As we walked along the railroad tracks, he took a harmonica from his pocket and played, bending notes like the old blues gentlemen on my father's recordings.

"You play a song," he said, handing me the harmonica.

"Oh, I couldn't."

"You're a music teacher. Of course you can. You're just lazy."

I didn't want to put my mouth where his had been. He thrust it on me. All I could think of was a cowboy song my father taught me years ago. Something I could play automatically, while I removed my mind from the wetness where he had—

Oh damn. I so don't want to think that way about him.

He followed me up the track, balancing as we walked along one rail. A quarter-mile along, we could feel the vibration of a north-bound train.

"Jason, there's a train coming."

"We have lots of time." He grabbed my hand, pulling me alongside him as he hopped the ties.

"No, we don't."

He delayed as much as possible, teasing me. Since I have a brother, I knew that showing impatience or fear would only make him tease more. As the train approached, we were far too close for my comfort.

"I will save you," he said, leaping off the tracks with me in his arms, dragging us both into a pile of boulders and holding me much too close while the train thundered past, so close that my ear against his chest heard the rattle of the train as if it were his heartbeat. He kept us there while the echo of the train faded as it made its way to Canada or Montana or wherever it was headed.

When I stirred, pressing against his chest so I could stand up, he pressed back, holding me down briefly. Then he released me. When I stood and dusted my jeans, I stumbled on a rock, falling against him. His hands lingered as he righted me, steadying me with his arms, breathing in my ear, the sound a rasp that vibrated with the last echoes of the departing train.

We clambered down the boulders to the beach, kicking at the flotsam along the tide line, picking up limpet shells.

"What used to be important, Susi? What's important now?"

"Music, as an answer to both. Only then it was classical. Amer-icana and older influences are new to me."

"Why does it not surprise me that what's old is new to you? What dragged you away from Schubert and Puccini?"

"My dad needed me to help go through his things when he moved to assisted living—he's older and has arthritis. While I worked, he dragged me through graduate-level studies in folk music. He taught me guitar, though he couldn't make more of me than a Sixties folkie with a five-chord repertoire. I used his impromptu lectures while creating the new curriculum for this year's classes. And for the Institute."

However, my father's greatest success was to apply roots music as therapy, moving my mental focus away from grief. When I think about it, I can feel Dad's hand guiding mine, wrapped around the neck of that old guitar to show me the fingerings. That's what I understand about "healing touch." I know it must have cost him, as much as arthritis pains him, to have showed me how to feel music in your fingers, after the old ways of feeling music were lost.

"Susi absorbs music through her fingers as well as her ears. That's a good thing," Jason said.

We found the sandy beach deserted and, without discussing it, hunkered down in a driftwood shelter and listened to the water and another train echoing across the Sound.

"The wind in the sea grass," he murmured near my ear, making an inventory of everything we could hear. Surf birds. A murder of crows descending in late afternoon into the trees in the hills above the beach.

Then he said, "How long, Susi?"

"Since when?"

"Since you sat beside a man like this?"

"More than two years."

"That's a long time."

"I was unhappy. It's better to finish that kind of business alone."

"Are you still unhappy, Susi?"

"No. I didn't realize it until a little while ago, but no, I'm not unhappy anymore. I rather like my life now."

"Still staying alone? Though that's the same tack I took. I've been trying to get over feeling betrayed—you must know that about me, Susi."

"I don't actually. We agreed that we're strangers, right?"

He grinned, and we listened to echoes across the Sound until he began singing that song from *Anchor's Away*.

"'If you knew Susie, like I know Susie, oh, oh—'"

"Only my brother can sing that song to me. You must stop now."

"I was planning to." He tossed pebbles toward the water. "I want to stop doing what I did all last year. I intend to follow my own ideas about music, wherever it takes me."

"Give up your current work?"

"I have to. Last year's work just left me feeling like I had sold out to the corporations and prostituted myself."

"How will you live?"

"I can afford to do what I want, if I'm careful about it."

"That must be nice." I hoped my voice didn't hold any bitterness.

"I have to be immersed in creative work, or I get so depressed that you have to scrape me off the floor," he said. "Now I know exactly what music I want to make."

"What's it like?"

"If it were a painting, it would be by Caravaggio."

"Dark and violent?"

"No. Why is that what everyone thinks? I mean illuminating common people, so they become like gods. Animated, so you see movement, even in the shadows."

As he spoke, his fingers lingered along the lines of my face, brushing my cheek with his fingertips.

"I wish you would let me kiss you, Susi."

I don't believe that my longing carried me out to sea. I'm certain that I gave him a secret sign of assent when I felt his hand hovering over mine, as if the energy from his palms would levitate me like a magician's assistant. He was so near that I could smell that scent of man caught amid the web of hairs at his throat. It might be that the irresistible pull of my own longing is what drew his face closer to mine. Yet it was he who kissed me. So lightly at first that it felt the same as his breath on my lips, a ghost, an echo that carried across the water from far away. He traced the edges of my lips with his own and lingered over my eyelids. Then he nipped at my lower lip, urging my mouth open and his tongue slipped inside, the hard point of it pressing against the tip of mine, as he brought me closer, wrapping me in an embrace. I could feel the heat radiating from his hands, even with my shirt between his hot palm and my skin.

We kissed for a thousand years, while nations rose, struggled, and fell again, and we came to live in a more philosophical era, where sin faded from concern, and we forgot about remorse and caution. With each new breath, I slid down from the driftwood bench, into the cold sand with his hip against mine. I had a singular longing, to feel his weight on top of me, as if it would answer the riddle of why we are here on this earth and what it all means.

He whispered, and the rasp of his breath fell on my ear like music, or affection. "Susi, you are the most incredible creature on God's earth."

Then he shifted us both in the sand, settling his weight against me. Through both his layer of denim and mine, I could feel him throbbing, leading me to wiggle against him. He moved his hand up under my shirt, responding to my unspoken wishes, and his hand cupped my breast, gently pressing.

"This feels like it wants to be more," he murmured, "but you have to say so. Tell me you want me to touch you."

The rational world clattered down around me, like the claxon of a boat's horn, shattering across the water. He was asking me to say aloud what I wanted. However, it was desire like this that led to the destruction of my old world.

"Please," I said. I took two breaths, to say what I must. "No. Please don't. Please stop."

He rolled off me and sat back against our driftwood shelter, shaking his hair, as if to clear his head. I sat up beside him, trying to breathe, feeling a hideous need to explain myself.

"I got married for the wrong reasons. I still don't trust my judgment."

He didn't answer. I felt a hideous need to fill the silence.

"Can we pretend this didn't happen?"

"All right, Susi. We'll pretend I'm a frog, and whenever you're ready, you can kiss me."

"I've heard what you're like, Jason, and I don't want that."

"My reputation is vastly exaggerated."

"I want your friendship much more than I want—that."

"My friendship?"

"It will be embarrassing when we see each other later if we just go on in the way they say you do. We're having a good time together. Can't we continue as friends?"

"I can if you can." He stood up. "I'm hungry. Can we get food before we go to this concert?"

And that is the story of my sinful beach fling at the end of spring break.

17
"I Ain't Ever Satisfied"
Jason

"STOP AT FRED MEYERS, SUSI, so I can get clothes for tonight. I can't wear these everywhere. Your rich friends will think I'm a loser."

"I'm going to wait in the car."

The cashier and three young women in the store recognized me, but this was Fremont, and everyone was nice about it. I signed for one of the women who wanted my autograph—it was a receipt for a Fleet Foxes CD, so I'm not sure what she will tell her kids twenty years from now.

When I joined Susi again, Shostakovich played on the car radio for spring time cheer, and she didn't have anything to say on the ride back to her house, where she made yakisoba with tofu, snowpeas, and shiitake mushrooms while I changed. Then she left me to eat my noodles alone while she changed.

I went to the trouble of getting a tie when I was in Fred's, ripping black jeans and a black shirt off the hangers and sprinting for the cashier, thinking I would look respectable enough for Seattle, though I wasn't sure what would make me look respectable enough to be seen with Susi. I had met the two versions of the Brooks Brothers girl, the one in jeans and the one dressed for success, and I had seen the compact athlete in damp t-shirt. Now I met the artist that her classical training had created, wearing a long black sheath with a high turtleneck. The sole ornament she affected was a wide cinch belt, so it looked like I was escorting the second violinist or the harpist.

By this time, I was getting used to Susi taking me wherever she wanted me to go—to Benaroya Hall for Mozart's *Requiem* in this case, where we swapped roles and I could forget all the paranoia I have about being recognized. When we came into the hall, everyone knew Susi, starting with the gentlemen taking tickets at the door. The woman selling annual subscriptions called Susi's name and came over to speak with her. Same story with the ponytailed guy tending the wine bar beneath the giant Rauschenberg mural. Susi refused my offer to buy her a glass of wine, and I don't drink, so we both had seltzer water and walked up to the second-tier gallery to wait for Randolph. An older woman dressed in dark green linen came over, giving Susi a hug and kissing her cheek.

"I saw your father just the other day, Susi. He said you were doing so much better. It's so nice to see you out and about again."

Susi had the knack some people do of turning a conversation around on the spot, and in a flash she had the woman talking about her dog and her grandchildren. When the woman drifted away, Susi said, "I have something in my eye. Wait for me here," and she handed me her drink and departed down the hall.

"Cute girl," a voice breathed in my ear. "Does she sing?"

"Ephraim."

He looks like Bruno Ganz as the angel in *Wings of Desire*, in black silk and leather trench coat, his hair pulled into a tight ponytail. He's ten years older than me and likes to lord the extra years as being meaningful.

"The same. This gives us a great opportunity to chat, Jason."

"No, it just proves my luck still sucks. Every time I turn around I run into you or hear from you."

"It's because our fates are bound together."

"Is Dominique here?"

"She's in the women's room with your girlfriend."

"Oh geez. Say what you want, Ephraim. You will, no matter how I try to dodge it. It can't be good, or Karl would have already told me."

"All I want from you, Jason, is a small set of reassurances."

"I can offer a profound assurance that I'm still pissed off about what you did to my music."

"I won't forget that. The situation will not occur again if you stay and complete the work yourself this time. You were supposed to deliver last month. I pulled every trick I could to delay and still get a new album in stores this summer."

"Thank you. You are such a great friend."

"Jason, reassure me that you are professionally committed. Otherwise, there is no use holding an expensive charade. I will just work in a friendly way with Karl on how you pay your way out of the contract. And I will make sure no major label ever gambles on you again."

"I'm here to do the work, and I'm committed to deliver what I owe, as quickly as possible."

"Beautiful. And you will do all the work necessary to make this next album as successful as the last."

I wanted to curl into a ball and rock like a child until I felt safe.

"Jason, you need to do the interviews, make the videos, and appear in public. Sixty or eighty minutes of tracks aren't much better than dead air if you won't promote it."

"You have the beautiful Dominique to do that. She loves it. Point a camera or a microphone in her direction, and she'll get you all the publicity you could want from an artist."

"For true success, you need to do the same, Jason."

"Her last video was quite popular."

"That isn't the video that first sold people on *Woman at the Well*. It was the earlier concert videos that you did—both your soulful acoustic number and that rocking piece with the whole band. Best live-action video of the year."

"Second place only."

"You're quite photogenic, Jason. The camera loves you, and women of all ages appreciate it. At least women over seventeen. Younger girls find you too masculine, but our market studies show that men aren't put off by your brand of masculinity. Albion Records couldn't hope for a product that tests better in both markets."

"You did a market study on my effing face? I'm a product?"

"You've been in the business too long to be naïve about this."

"OK. Your request for small assurances is proving to be a real bundle. Let's see if I have it: turn in a marketable album."

"On time. Finished tracks no later than the second of June."

"I can do that."

"You are one of the few in the industry who could turn tracks around that fast, Jason. I've got production and distribution lined up to get to market in support of your effort."

"Do radio, TV, and video, with my best side turned toward the camera."

"With your face, you don't have to worry about the best side."

"I can tell where the rest of this is headed. Tour. I have to play on stage with Dominique."

"Even you have to admit that logic is inescapable. The first date is June 27 in L.A. I gave Karl a list of all dates yesterday."

"Escaping Dominique is all I care about, Ephraim. You can't force me back into everyday life with her."

"After you finish rehearsing for the road, you'll see her only a couple of hours every second or third day. The monitors and rest of the stage gear should help you keep a distance."

"What else, Ephraim? If you're going to wrap your hands around my balls and squeeze, let's get done with it."

"Sign another contract to record with me."

"Are you insane? After I get Dominique to let go of me, I won't come near either of you."

"Not with Dominique. She needs to find her own band. It is too hard to adapt your material to her voice. Just you. I want you and whatever musicians are working with you. Ian, I assume, will never go away. I hope Toby will stay. Who else have you gathered?"

"I can't believe your effing gall, Ephraim. I spent the winter approving more than a million dollars in charge-backs from your recording company. I had to pay for half of Dominique's tits-and-ass video and all the publicist's fees. What was that about? I could have Cynthia and her cousin do publicity and booking, like we always did before, and not pay a quarter of a million bucks for it."

"You never sold three million CDs with Cynthia doing your publicity."

"So you want the rights to all my future work, in addition to walking off with my wife."

"You didn't want her by the time she went walking with me."

"I don't know what you see in her. It makes me think less of you."

"Because you were glad to see her go, you believe that she's worthless to others?"

"She interviewed three replacements before she chose you, Ephraim. They were all richer and more famous than either of us. Whatever else you think, you have to acknowledge that Dominique is an accomplished liar. You saw for yourself how ugly she could be in the studio before you got involved with her."

"She's beautiful. I like her voice."

"You are joking."

"Different people have different tastes. Perhaps my tastes are more plebian than yours."

"But the lies, Ephraim, the lies."

"It's a way she covers for weakness. I like to think she feels safer with me, less threatened. She has less need to lie to me."

"I never threatened her."

"There are many ways to make people feel unsafe, Jason."

"I promise to wish you luck when I don't feel so threatened myself."

"You know, Stanley Donan and Gene Kelly worked together for years after Kelly took Donan's wife. Tell me, if you're so unhappy with her now, what did you once see in her?"

"She came after me like I was God's own child. It wasn't until later that I realized I was God's own foot stool."

"Dominique is young—what was she when you first found her, Jason? Twenty-two?"

"She found me, Ephraim. I didn't go looking for her."

"No one ever taught her how to behave. She was a spoiled rich girl at the start, and not much better when you left. But she's learning. I like to think that she needs an older, steadying influence. I rather enjoy the job."

The two women came up the hallway on a parallel path, unaware of each other. One tall, in a long red leather coat and high-heeled boots, attracting everyone's attention, the other as anonymous as lilies in the field, her pale face luminous in the hall's dim light.

"Keep her away from me, Ephraim. And watch your phone bills. Check your back every now and again, to be sure she hasn't knifed you."

I turned away, toward the light.

18

"The Night's Too Long"
Jason

SUSI TOUCHED MY ARM and said my name as she came up. Lord help me, when I turned around I wanted to just put my arms around her and run from the building, to have her to myself, to finish what we had started in the afternoon, to flee from the world. She led me as if I were half-blind to join the playboy vice-principal from our earlier meeting where he stood with an older couple, a stooped giant of a gentleman and a tiny grand dame with immense dignity.

God alone knows how I made it through that part of the evening, shaking hands with people I had never met and would never see again. Feeling that I needed to protect Susi from something, but not seeing what. Wanting to poke Randolph in the nose, just for the pleasure of it. Smiling the whole while, charming the grandmother who seemed to be my assigned seat partner. Randolph worked out the arrangements, so Susi sat as far from me as possible. While I conquered the adrenalin rush from not being close enough to protect her, the grandmother chatted about Schubert and dying young being such a tragedy.

Then, just as the lights dimmed and we applauded the concert master, everyone stirred and Susi took the seat beside me because, the grandmother said, Susi couldn't sit by someone wearing too much perfume.

I had almost calmed down by the time the orchestra made it through the Schubert piece, knowing I was sublimating the residue of feelings from speaking with Ephraim, and projecting all my flight-of-fear emotions onto Susi, who was about as safe as a person could be, with the grandfather chatting in her ear as soon as the lights came up. The sole threat to her well-being was the overchilled air from the HVAC system. I saw the tiny frisson of a shiver shimmying up her spine and, without even considering another alternative, I draped my jacket around her shoulders as Randolph and his kin huddled beside her during the break, longing for her attention. Everyone is in love with Susi.

When the lights dimmed again and the chorale took their seats for the *Requiem*, she murmured a thank-you to me as she drew the jacket close and fixed her gaze on the stage.

Thirty seconds into the Kyrie, I glanced over and found her subvocalizing the words.

I missed the entire rest of the program, seeing the director's hands occasionally while trying to understand what Susi saw from her seat, finally realizing—like an effing fool—that this was the career she had been forced to leave behind. Yet from her speaking voice, she could never have had the proper range for it. A poor teacher had led her down a garden path, telling her she was capable when it wasn't right for her.

During the applause, I had to stand up, for we were sitting so close to the stage that it would be rude not to stand while everyone applauded the performers. Susi stood beside me, gently swaying. I put my hand at the small of her back to steady her. The grandfather noticed too.

"My goodness, child, are you well?"

"I'm fine," she said. Tears glistened in her eyes. "The music is just so very beautiful."

Then Randolph was at her side, having aced out his grandfather in the role of solicitous Randolph kin.

"Susi, I never should have brought you here."

"You didn't bring me, Randolph. I came on my own."

"This was a poor choice. Let me take you home."

"I'm fine. I have my own car here and a guest to take care of."

"Susi, I should insist."

"Please don't, Randolph. I'm fine. However, I must decline your kind offer of a late dinner."

The admonishments continued, until I could get her out of there.

On the street, I was steaming.

"Didn't his mother teach him how to act right? Why wouldn't he leave you alone when you asked him to?"

As we walked to the parking lot, musicians fleeing the building called out to her, and she greeted them in return, her voice sounding warm and golden, but her expression strained. At the car, she handed me the keys.

"Could you drive, please?" she asked.

"No, actually."

"Why not?"

"I don't know how." For the first time, it felt like admitting a weakness.

She managed the thinnest smile, shaking her head.

On the ride home, I commandeered the radio, finding the Blues Time Machine on KPLU, thinking we had endured enough classical depression for the night. Susi was silent, and Alice Stuart soothed us on the trip up Yesler Way and across the neighborhoods to her house. In her carport, Susi grabbed the keys out of the ignition and ran into the house, closing herself into her bedroom, so I had to satisfy myself with washing my hands and brushing my teeth in the kitchen sink, though I wanted another shower.

I sat up late into the night writing and listening to her music through headphones. My friend Chas launched an instant-messaging conversation about guitar steels, which diverted me from brooding.

Chas1933: You play music, right? I'm researching the equipment the old blues guys used, especially the rural musicians who first developed the bottleneck sound.

Sebastian: How many of them used real bottlenecks?

Chas1933: Don't know. The notes I've found say some of the old guys often used a comb or a pocket knife. What do you think?

Sebastian: I'm clueless. I'm also spoiled. I use commercial steels.

Chas1933: Look, I'm old as shoe leather and I can't play anymore. Can you tell me what it's like, playing with a comb or a pocket knife? In those days, it would have been a steel comb.

Sebastian: Yeah, you made me curious. I'll try it. Can't do it tonight though.

Chas1933: I'm in no rush. At my age, I'm going nowhere fast.

Sebastian: You sure have talked me into some weird experiments in the past year. Do you suppose that they used the pocket knife with the blade open or closed?

Chas1933: You're pulling my ancient leg now. You plan to experiment both ways? You don't want to use guitar strings for the tourniquet.

Late in the night I uploaded the last of my notes from London onto a couple of different blogs on the Internet, but I still couldn't tell what to do with the last two days' notes, so I mailed those to myself again. When that was done, I began pillaging Susi's library. For most of the time, she sobbed her heart out behind the closed bedroom door.

It was like being married again, but without the guilt and remorse.

19
"Chains of This Town"
Susi

LORD, I DIDN'T WANT to leave my room on Sunday morning. It couldn't offer anything more than another opportunity to humiliate myself.

So I sneaked out for a run, rising early. Jason lay sprawled on the sofa and didn't move, though he was dressed this time, thank the gods, since I do not like the idea of him being in my house naked. The run helped pound my thoughts in place, after falling apart the night before.

I live on the hillside above Leschi, which was a vacation village a few generations ago. Now it's expensive water-view property, but a few of the old fishermen's shacks like mine are still nestled into the hillside, surrounded by Douglas fir, cedar, and madrona trees, offering a false sense of woodsy isolation amid the postmodern villas and remodeled Craftsman bungalows. When I came back here, when my father took me in after the accident, Leschi felt like home. I could walk the steep, meandering streets under the trees, admire others' gardens, or run along the lake. Men still come out to fish from the wooden piers in the morning mist, the old woman down the block still walks her Pug at seven a.m., and kids still ride bikes through blackberry-lined alleys, just as I did twenty years ago.

After the accident, when I was well again physically, all that remained was music and long walks in Leschi. I took this job teaching before I had finished mourning my lost life—Angelia led me to it, since she was also making a career shift. What saved me from drowning in grief was creating a curriculum I was proud of and working with kids who love music.

I've come to see the past as just one kind of a life, where I had inappropriately loaded all my hopes. Yes, it was a grander world than the simple one I live in now, but I never fit anyway. Maybe I would have pushed myself to the next level, but maybe that last wonderful year was a fluke and I would have had to make a career out of being third on the left in the chorus. I never planned to teach, because I had only the Juilliard model as a reference, and I'd never have fit in that world either. I don't think I'm afraid of competition at the university level. In my former life, I scrapped hard to end up where I did. Those aspirations have been replaced by helping others to find how music fits in their lives.

What I miss: the singing. And the applause.

That is what made me cry for the first time in months, when the audience shouted "Bravo!" for the chorus. Through the whole program, I felt happy enough to be sitting in the audience. I witnessed it in the same mode as one would listen to a CD, letting the music carry me away. I was fine. After the intermission, I even lost the sense of that man sitting so close that I could hear him breathe and feel the heat from his body. It was my first venture hearing live music, other than what my students perform, and I enjoyed it. I let the music rule my response and sensibilities.

Then the applause came, like I will never hear again. Grieving for lost worlds, I fell apart again as Randolph's grandfather patted my shoulder.

I'd rationalized all of it by the time I came back to the house from my morning run, though I dreaded facing Jason, since he must have heard me the night before. Though, bless him, he hadn't said a word or tried to comfort me. Good god, but I hate it when people try to comfort me. Arms around me feel like steel bands.

Whispered condolences feel like they want to suck what is left of the breath from my lungs.

※

When I came in after my run, Jason was cooking breakfast, as if he lived there. Sons of the Pioneers played on the stereo, and he was singing along, matching the harmony, as if he lived there, too.

I finished my shower and joined him. He turned down the volume on the stereo, but still sang "Rye Whiskey" while he served up French toast and coffee. He continued his teasing banter, as if neither the concert nor the debacle on the beach had occurred, which was comforting.

"Who are we begging today, Susi, besides our luncheon with that barracuda from the board of trustees?"

"There is a teacher at Cornish who says he remembers you from Prescott. He represents a collective of teachers and musicians who promised to contribute. Then there's the luncheon. Late in the afternoon there's a benefit concert our students are putting on. You can skip that."

"I wouldn't miss it. I said I'd help, didn't I?"

He kept me rapt in conversation over the curriculum, which he spread out on the kitchen counter, asking me questions about the directions in each segment, making me explain choices against alternatives he presented, as if this were my master's thesis and he was the committee against which I had to defend it.

"Susi, it's like you stopped at Haydn when considering influences on modern symphonic music. You ignore certain folk traditions, and you have nothing from the Northwest except songs Woody Guthrie maybe wrote here during the Depression."

"Like what?"

"Local folk music. The Sonics. The Wailers. The Screaming Trees. Isaac Scott. Jo Miller and Ranch Romance. The Melvins. Bing Crosby."

"Bing Crosby?"

"He's from Tacoma. Went to Gonzaga. You can hear the influences when Eddie Vedder does mellow stuff."

"Who is Eddie Vedder?"

"Never mind. I was exaggerating."

"Someone else will teach that part."

"You already convinced me to do it, Susi. I won't back out now."

There wasn't time in that discussion to be distracted by anything, except he hadn't shaved, so by the end of our friendly discourse, I couldn't look at his mouth without thinking about testosterone.

20
"Get Rhythm"
Jason

PAUL HARRIS. I COULDN'T believe it when Susi drove us over to the Cornish campus, parked in a back alley, and dragged me into the gamelan shed. Paul looked up when we entered, flashing as much surprise as I felt.

"Jason." He grabbed my forearm in one of those grown-up versions of a hippie handshake. Susi retreated to the sidelines, where she sat with a notebook, oblivious to everything else while we talked. "I misunderstood what Susi was asking me. She is the sort of person you have to give whatever she asks, so perhaps I didn't listen closely. I thought it was just about money. But I'm pleased to see you."

"Thank you, Mr. Harris."

"It's Paul. I'm not your teacher now. Hardly was at the time, was I?"

"Actually, I owe you a great deal. You were one of the few sane voices at the time. And you had plenty to teach me."

"Do you want to sit in with us this morning?"

"May I? You know percussion wasn't my strong point."

"Your weakest points beat most everyone else's finest. Sit by Jane and just feel through the first round," Paul said. "Here's the notation, so you can follow along. We will play the whole set over when it's your turn to take up the mallet."

A gamelan is an orchestra of instruments invented in Bali and Java. The notation for gamelan looks like space writing, like Mr.

Spock's annotations in the ship's log. Yet after ten minutes of listening and watching, I think I got it. I could join them only in the most humble way, but the ringing of the gong and the joyousness of Balinese gamelan drew me in, irresistibly.

What can I say? I lost three hours in the gamelan shed, and the only intrusion of so-called reality was seeing Susi on the sidelines with her notebook. And hearing the rain pound on the roof. Otherwise, we were lost to rhythm and tone and that finest of all sensations, finding music with your whole body in the midst of an orchestra of other musicians. I was drenched and exhilarated when Susi came up during a pause in our playing.

"We have to go. You have to shower and change before our luncheon at Gwyneth's."

I said goodbye to Paul, intending to return when I could, and followed Susi to the car. The thought of breaking bread with Gwyneth—who secretly longed to savage Susi for being more beautiful—would have been a damper, but I was far too high from the music.

"That made up for the sex I didn't get last night." I blurt these things to her and, Lord help me, she must think I do it on purpose.

"All the more reason to shower," she said.

Which was the actual moment when I gave up and decided to go ahead and be in love with her.

She said, "When I asked to bring you around, Paul was rather vague about remembering you, but you seem like old friends."

"It's more than ten years. I feel like I could work with him as an equal now. Except the gamelan part. That will take me another ten years. I suppose he'll be ten more years ahead of me by then."

The trip to Susi's house proved too short to shake the sensations cascading over me like rain. I felt like a runner who had been made to stop before cooling off. Isn't that how people have heart attacks? I was on the verge of at least a minor coronary, but she insisted that I shower as soon as we came into her house.

Maybe my life could be reborn in Seattle, mixing with people like Susi and Paul. It felt like moving to a town I had never visited. I shaved and dressed as the man in black again, including the necktie. Susi didn't give me a second glance when she brushed past to close herself up in the bedroom and dress.

While waiting, I turned on my laptop to make notes. I wanted to share what I was feeling with a real person, so I logged on line and went in search of my instant-messenger friends.

Chas1933@jugum.com was right there for me.

Sebastian: Ever play in a gamelan orchestra?

Chas1933: That's what I like about you. I can be sitting here, minding my business. Then you show up and knock me around a bit. I never had the pleasure. Pentatonic scale, isn't it?

Sebastian: Not all are, but I played in one this morning that used the five-tone scale.

Chas1933: You always come up with something that makes me wish I was young and roaming again. I've heard recordings but never seen one live.

Sebastian: There's a set of instruments that carries this interwoven melodic line, with brass keys suspended over resonating bamboo tubes. You strike a key with a mallet and then dampen it as you strike the next key.

Chas1933: Like a xylophone?

Sebastian: You could say, but only because there's nothing else like it in a Western orchestra. Another instrument is made up of a series of small gongs mounted on string carriages. That takes two or four players, which is more cooperation than I could manage as a rank beginner playing with strangers.

Chas1933: Now I'm going to Google for pictures, because I'm seeing jingle bells in my mind, and that can't be right.

Sebastian: Nope, not right. The gamelan also has a set of gongs with amazing, pure tones plus several pairs of pitched drums and cymbals.

Chas1933: OK, I know you play guitar. Did you pick up playing in the gamelan quickly?

Sebastian: That interwoven melody means a faster line of music than one man or woman alone can create, so I had to learn what everyone else was doing simultaneously. The result brought them a lot of amusement. Though they were too polite to laugh out loud.

Chas1933: Like trying to learn a new language as soon as you step off the plane in another country?

Sebastian: Maybe that's a good analogy. I had to think in a different scale, a different rhythm, unusual manipulation of the instruments and musical notation in Bali. It stretched way beyond patting your head and rubbing your stomach while learning to blow bubbles and jump rope—on a five-tone scale.

Chas1933: Man, I got to see this. Take pictures and record it next time.

That's the world I want to inhabit, where people trade ideas and learn new things. Rather than the brave new world I live in, where people step up uninvited and insert themselves into your personal life. The exchange with Chas calmed me down a little, reminding me that I have friends in the world, and all is well. And also reminding me that I needed to let my best friend know what the heck had happened to me. I hit call-back on my phone to raise Ian.

"Ephraim Vance."

"Shoot."

"Jason? I'm glad you called."

"It was a mistake."

"Don't hang up."

"I have made enough mistakes in this life already."

"That's what we need to talk about, Jason. Dominique says she couldn't persuade you to change the song list."

"I'm never persuaded to choose songs based on whether Dominique wants to sing them."

"However, I want to persuade you to make a successful record. I want at least three-quarters of the album to be new songs from you. No covers. I want you to do the production."

"You have the songs. She can effing learn to sing them. I won't have that woman standing over my shoulder again."

"It is far more peaceful if we just pull in studio musicians to work with her, or else have her sing against taped tracks. I learned how to get more from her by doing things you never would."

"Like what?"

"Coddling her. Telling her she's good before asking more from her. She's cooperative when she knows how much it costs her to horse around."

"So you have had her in the studio alone?"

"I couldn't trust that you'd show up, Jason. She needs to have a new record out to keep up momentum."

"What songs?"

"None of yours."

"What then?"

"Cover songs. Works in the public domain."

"That's why you don't want us doing cover songs on this album."

"It's just business. Original music was always in your contract. Let's be professional, Jason."

"Your profession is to suck musicians' souls, and mine is to play real music. Where does that leave us, as professionals?"

"You signed the contract, Jason. It's your business to write and record songs. It's my business to make sure that your choices earn as much money as possible for all of us."

"Thank you for your concern."

"And?" Ephraim fished for more from me.

"Nothing else."

"Come on, Jason. You always want the last bitter word."

"Hang up and leave me alone."

"What did you mean last night when you said to watch the phone bills?"

"That's how I learned she was shopping herself around, in search of better players."

"You don't even check your own phone bills."

"She turned them in to the accountant as business deductions, along with her hotel receipts and plane tickets." I'm too chicken to cheat on my taxes, so the accountant watches everything. "Karl called to ask why she was entertaining at expensive hotels while supposedly visiting her sister."

"I see."

"I always like it when my attorney calls to give me good news, don't you, Ephraim?"

"You didn't want to keep her."

"I didn't mind her leaving. What got to me was all the destruction she felt compelled to wreak on her way out. Watch your back."

21
"Money Honey"
Jason

TYPING FURIOUSLY TO CAPTURE new notes from the library, I worked to forget Ephraim and recapture sensations from the morning in the gamelan shed. The rhythm of typing got me rushing again over those feelings until I had to just put the laptop away and use that sheaf of music manuscript paper from my pack to write down what I'd heard. As I pondered what the notation should be for a particular sound that makes one's wrist bones go into a harmonious vibration, she came out of the bedroom.

More than my wrist bones were vibrating.

"You look like an Italian opera star. Maria Callas going to a tea party."

She seemed startled, but what else could I say? People in Seattle don't dress that way. She wore a spring-flowered dress that must be worth as much on eBay as everything else in her house together. Silky and substantial at the same time, it had a flared skirt and tight shimmery green bodice that showed all her swimmer's power. She wore a drama-inducing bra, rather than none, as she had at the beach. Although the high-collared bodice covered her neck and arms, that covering made the body under it even more enticing than uncovering it.

I'm focusing on the dress, because the total effect created an image that I could hardly stand. I mean, I was once married to a beautiful woman and maybe that altered my susceptibility, but this is the first time I had looked at a woman and had this particular visceral response. The sole thought I could form was, *This is way out of your reach, beyond anything you can have.* Her boyish blond hair was moussed into place, and she had done her makeup to enhance her eyes. She wore strappy high heels and still moved with a fluid ease that I was becoming familiar with. Katherine Hepburn for the trustees meeting, Audrey Hepburn for Sunday luncheon.

"We're late," she said, grabbing her keys and bag.

In the car, she kicked off her high heels to drive, where I noticed she was barefoot and her toenails were painted. I couldn't shake off the sensations she created, even as intimidated as I felt.

"So this is for Gwyneth, right?" I said. "You're dressed like that so she can't out-do you."

"No, it's for her father-in-law. He considers himself a patron of the arts, and I intend to get everything I can from him. I know how he likes to be titillated, and I intend to please him today."

"I can't believe you would prostitute yourself, Susi."

"I'm not going to catch any diseases flirting with a seventy-five-year-old man. Do you know what? I want this institute so bad I will do anything for it. Within the bounds of human decency."

"Dressing so an old man can leer at you, that's decent?"

"What's wrong with it? Women do it all the time."

"You seem pretty comfortable in that."

"When a dress costs this much, it's comfortable."

That wasn't what I meant.

"So how far would you go, Susi? Would you sleep with a rich man to get his money?"

"That is a definite no."

"Would you change your curriculum for a generous donor?"

"Add something, perhaps. For my work, it would have to be an idea that deepened what I'm trying to do."

"Would you sell the rights to your project just to get the teaching part of the gig?"

"I don't know." She bit her lip, thinking. "It depends on what I lost and what I gained."

We were in the driveway of a house on Capitol Hill. It wasn't particularly ostentatious on the outside, except that the surrounding grounds took up half a city block.

"This is a bad idea, Susi. I'll just give you all the money you need."

"That's a kind thought, but you saw how much I need from the financials we reviewed."

Actually I only had enough spare change for the first year of her plan. I figured I could find more money after that. I need to save my capital in order to gamble with my own business.

"I'll prostitute myself, Susi. Better me than you. I'm used to it."

"Jason, I hope you're being kind, and not teasing."

"I don't like you having to do this."

"Not relevant. I can take care of my own business. It's no different than wearing a suit to a board meeting and observing common conventions of business etiquette. It's how this kind of work is done."

"You asked me to help you—"

"But not to tell me how to behave or what to do, Jason."

I am old enough not to seethe and pout like a jealous fourteen-year-old. Only just barely. I grabbed a leather strip from my pack and tied my hair back, and then took a different earring from my wallet.

"What are you doing, Jason?"

"If I have to pimp someone, it's going to be me. Our hostess bumped into me enough yesterday that I'm sure she's in the market."

22
"Slippin' and Slidin'"
Susi

GWYNETH TOUCHED HIS BOTTOM when she greeted us at the door, giving Jason one of those New Age hugs and then resting her hand right on his tight rear end while introducing him to Freeman Lukas.

"You look like the divine incarnation of a pop star," she said, gazing up at him with her seven-thousand-dollar, capped-tooth smile. She was wearing Prada casual pajamas, and her midriff peeked through whenever she moved. Like when she put her hand on Jason's bottom.

"I hear that's why I make big money, because of my looks," he said. She pretended that he was witty. With her hand still on his bottom.

While she chatted him up, Jason nodded. That silly dangling silver cross he had in his ear shook, so that I scarcely heard Freeman greeting me.

"Oh, you darling girl," he said. "You are looking so well, one could hardly know."

He had his arm around me as he led me over to sit by him on the sofa in the living room. The western wall, all glass, opened out to let in the light and view from the backyard woodlands. A dogwood with just the tips of its branches turning a dusty pink served as the focal point in the view, with cherry trees glimmering white among cedars and magnolias in the background. Freeman patted my knee through the skirts of my dress, consoling me as if I were still struggling with recovery. I was trying to convince him that things were fine now, truly, when Gwyneth and Jason joined us from the hallway. She had her finger in the belt-loop of his jeans.

She chirped—well, that's what it sounded like to me when she spoke, and I'm disappointed in myself for thinking the things about her that I did—saying, "The Simmones canceled. They are so sorry not to see you again, Susi, but his father is ill. And Bill is at a conference in San Diego." Bill is her husband, whom I have never met and who could be a fictitious person, although I have seen his picture in the paper occasionally. "So it's just us, but that's cozy, don't you think?"

She got all cozy with Jason on the other sofa, so that I had to see them in a tête-à-tête any time I looked up to glance out the window. Whatever he was saying, she listened with wide-eyed, breathless attention, crossing her legs so that her calf rested against his. He asked about the collection of ethnic music instruments decorating her walls, wanting to take one down and play it, but she thought he was joking.

Freeman wanted to hear about what we had come there to discuss, but he wanted my personal narrative. I did what I came to do, focusing all my attention on Freeman, telling him about teaching music theory with a twist on folk and Americana. After my story about how much I enjoy teaching teenagers, Freeman was again shaking his head and patting my knee.

"You have a brave heart, my girl. I know whatever you put your head to, it will succeed. I'd be proud to help you in any way I can."

He was saying what I wanted to hear. "I would want to help you no matter what, because I feel so sorry for you."

Which I have so hated hearing. However, that's what I was prostituting myself to, a pity party to raise funds for music education.

After the single most important chat of the day dwindled to a trite discussion of how music could lead to world peace, Gwyneth invited us to the table. I excused myself to wash my hands.

In the hallway, before I could open the powder room door, Jason's arm came around me from behind, blocking the way, and he leaned over me. Heat emanated from his body, which I sensed as cloying as perfume. I couldn't possibly smell him. He had showered only an hour before. Yet I had the distinct sensation of being trapped by a large animal.

"What are we doing here, Susi?"

"We're raising funds for music education."

"I mean what are we doing, you and me? Don't give me that bullshit line you did yesterday. When I stand this close to you, when you look over at me, it's as if—" Jason stopped mid-sentence. "I'm sorry. My imagination ran away with me. I'm famous for it."

"They're waiting for us."

"I hate sucking up to the rich and powerful."

"I thought you did it for a living, Jason."

"Touché. For a nice girl, you know how to cut deep. But that guy treats you like an invalid or a child who needs coddling."

"He's giving me a half million dollars this year and a promise for more later. What will you get from Gwyneth?"

"If I follow her lead, herpes and late-night, teary phone calls. Maybe a public remonstrance about my unfaithful heart. You win, Susi. You are much better at this than I am." He traced his hand down my cheek and lifted my chin. "Still, it would be worth a million bucks not to see that guy's hand on your knee."

Gwyneth chirped from the other room. "Are you lost?"

"In more ways than one," Jason called back to her.

I turned away, and Jason whispered after me.

"I hate your effing ex-husband. This is all his fault."

※

Shamelessly, I used the telephone in the powder room to dial long distance, hoping that Angelia had her cell phone turned on, even if they are the invention of the devil. Wherever I found her, it was noisy with the clatter of china and dinnerware and multiple voices.

"Angelia, did you tell Jason about Logan?"

"He knows you were married once."

"You know what I mean. Did you tell him?"

Her silence was telling.

"Angelia, how could you?"

"May I ask what is happening that it matters?"

"Nothing is happening. We are talking to donors and raising funds."

"Then why do you sound like Lady Macbeth after the murders?"

"He just walked away saying it was all Logan's fault."

"It was Logan's fault."

"I don't want Jason to feel sorry for me. I wish he didn't know about Logan. It's so humiliating."

"Are you sure it's Jason we are talking about?"

"Definitely. He has Gwyneth wrapped around his artistic fingers, just as you predicted. Though she hasn't volunteered her own money yet. However, because Jason is so persuasive, she and the trustees agreed to let us use the school this summer."

"If that's all my cousin does for us, it's plenty. Did he make his big move on you yet?"

"We decided that this isn't a good time for either of us to pursue anything personal."

"Oh brother. I hope you're lying."

"What I'm not doing, Angelia, is telling him any of your secrets the way you told mine."

"I don't have secrets. Life will go more smoothly if you stop thinking that you do. None of it was your fault."

※

After the accident, I blamed myself for a long time. Before the accident, I was hardly ever home, since the way I earned opportunities to perform was to be in the cities where any production wanted me. My career rose faster than Logan's. I tried to be sympathetic about how he felt, but we both knew that I was more talented. I suspect that I'm smarter, but my judgment remains clouded. While we were together, I thought it was smarter to have finished school as I did, rather than leaving a year short as Logan did, taking the first orchestra position offered him.

Long before the accident, I had talked myself into being satisfied with my handsome Peter Pan husband. Just before the accident, I was blaming myself for how distant and uncaring we had become with each other. When the accident happened, and I had to face certain truths, I assumed it was my fault. I didn't listen to what my father said, or what my friends told me, and I couldn't understand what the paid counselors were saying. When the health insurance money ran out, I was at bottom and went to an Al-Anon meeting for junkies' partners. Maybe going to that meeting was the step I had to take, but at last I heard what everyone was saying: Logan was just a junkie. It wasn't my fault.

He wasn't the second trombone in the village band. He was second trumpet in a reputable civic symphony. He wasn't ever going to be first chair, and I'm not going to bother to understand at this late date whether that had anything to do with being a junkie. Back then, before the accident, I thought like most everyone else with a comfortable home and a good job, that junkies are those other people who live on the margin. Bikers and public-housing rejects, street people and pop singers, and super models without sufficient brains to know better. Not the guy wearing a five-hundred-dollar dinner jacket, sitting at a table with friends in a nice restaurant, stepping into the men's room for a moment and coming back in a different and better mood.

What I still worry about is how I managed to turn a blind eye to what was wrong. Yes, I was hardly ever home, so I wasn't aware of how his personal habits had changed. Besides, the last couple of months when I lived in Seattle, rehearsals took every waking moment.

Then after the accident, there was no opportunity to ask questions and learn what had happened. He was gone—first to rehab, and then to a job in another state. So I'm still arguing with myself over this. It is not my fault he was a junkie, but it was my fault that I didn't notice.

I'm now awakening from that nightmare. I'm not hiding away so much, though I still worry that I don't understand people well enough to be close. I'm not sure how it works with getting to know men, because I never dated before: Logan and I married our sophomore year—yes, I married the first person I had any kind of relationship with. I don't know what it takes to be intimate. It is enough right now to be enjoying life with my old friends and making new friends.

Perhaps I should have left Seattle, left my entire story behind, found a place to work and live where I could be anonymous, where no one would ever come up and ask, "Aren't you Susanna Childs? I'm so sorry for you."

Because it is excruciatingly painful that a new friend should view me with the same pity as my old friends.

At the luncheon table, Freeman served food for me while Gwyneth tempted Jason with morsels of catered designer food, and then her lap dogs came in, pestering at my feet. I neither enjoy dining on animals nor dining with them. Freeman kindly remembered what he knew of me in former years and only put things on my plate that I could eat. Jason's own attendant put a piece of dead chicken on his plate. He smiled when she did, and I could see in that look the practiced predator Angelia described.

"What have you been out to hear of late?" Freeman asked.

"We took in Mozart's *Requiem* just last night," I said.

"Ah. We went on Thursday. People applauded the Chorale as the true stars."

"Indeed."

Gwyneth fluted concern over a missing condiment and left the table for the kitchen. As Freeman bent his head toward mine for a private exchange, Jason's chicken slipped from his plate to the dogs at his feet. At the same moment a clatter of noise arose from below stairs—which would be Zak, her son, practicing his music.

"Oh, that boy!" Gwyneth exclaimed as she returned with more hollandaise. "The worst thing his father ever did was give Zak those drums."

By this time, I knew Jason well enough that I recognized a defining moment. He ceased playing with Gwyneth. In fact, she scarcely got another polite word out of him. After a few moments, he stood.

"Will you excuse me, please?"

A door opened and the sounds from downstairs echoed more loudly in the hallway for a second.

Gwyneth said, "I tell you what, Susi. If you let Zak into your program, and if you can keep him in school until he graduates, I will pitch two hundred thousand into your little plan. His father has been after him about college, but neither of us can get through to that boy."

"I too have been trying," Freeman said. "I made it clear to him what the value of his education will be."

"Zak can't see anything except music," Gwyneth said. "He's so delayed in looking at girls that his father is worried."

"I'll take your offer, Gwyneth. Zak is one of my best students." When he shows up for class. I didn't mention that.

"I'll triple it for next year if you can persuade him to go to college. If anyone can do it, you can, my girl." Freeman squeezed my knee.

23
"Rip It Up"
Jason

I STOOD WATCHING THIS LANKY, long-haired kid in the doorway for ten minutes before he ever looked up to notice anything around him. He worked with his eyes closed, listening with his whole body. I like watching drummers who make it look like their loosely knit bones are part of the overall instrumentation. What I like even more is the amazing moment with kids where you can see the future. You see the man that is about to emerge from the funky shell of a boy. You see a future of hopes and failures, adventures and love affairs, and in some kids, you see a dynamic life about to unfold. This particular kid, doing what he was born for, was so energized and heated that I swear he glowed, the primordial percussionist.

When he saw me, he sat back, folding his arms, drumsticks clenched in his fists.

He recognized me.

"So you're who she's having for lunch? Are you spending the night?"

Brutal.

I shook my head. "I'm vegetarian. And under age."

He laughed, rueful still. "I wanted to break up the party. I need a ride to the show we're doing this afternoon."

"Why not come up and ask?"

"I can't get her attention unless I drive the annoyance level up to a certain point. I was supposed to ride over with our rhythm guitarist, but his grandmother is dying, so he has to hang around the hospital where everyone is crying."

"You don't drive?"

"I was at the wheel one night when the cops stopped us. One of the guys was holding, and my parents' lawyer worked a plea bargain. For doing nothing, I lost my driver's license."

"I can identify with the random karma of being in the wrong place at the wrong time."

He laughed again, ready now to look me in the eye. "I guess so. What do you do about it?"

"Swallow it. Learn not to care about what people think." As he nodded, I said, "Actually, I'm lying. I don't have a clue how to deal with it. What if we give you a ride? I could sit in on rhythm if there's an instrument for me."

"The other guys will shit themselves."

"You're OK with it? It's your show. I don't want to distract."

"As a fellow innocent, falsely accused, I could go with it."

I think for Zak that passed as unbounded enthusiasm.

"What do you play?"

"Lame folk songs we learned in class. Here's the set list."

"Tame." I studied it.

"We, uh, changed up the rhythms. We do 'Tom Dooley' as punk rage and 'Barbara Allen' as reggae."

"So we play like we're Sly and Robbie on a British folk song?"

"We had to do something. It's such a girl's song. I mean, dying for love? Come on."

"What do you do to 'Come All Ye Fair and Tender Ladies'?"

"We skipped the autoharp and treat it sort of like 'Gloria.'"

"It's all acoustic?"

"We'll be miked. You'll have steel strings. What else do you need?"

24

"American Music"
Susi

WHEN WE PREPARED TO leave Gwyneth's house, she didn't have an opportunity to put her hands on Jason, or down his pants, since he made himself busy helping Zak load his drum kit into my much-too-small car. I said goodbye to Freeman, whom I believe cares for my well-being. He promised that he'd appear at the benefit later if his driver returned on time. Gwyneth didn't even offer an excuse for not coming to the benefit.

I fumed in silence all the way to Town Hall, where everyone was preparing for the afternoon performance. Jason lingered behind when Zak hauled in the first load of his drum kit. I peeled off that prima-donna jacket and put on a sweater, still so furious that I buttoned it up wrong.

"Here, let me fix it." Jason put his hands on me again. Actually, on my sweater buttons. "Are you mad at me, Susi?"

"I'm furious with Gwyneth. You see these kids trying to grow up, and the adults who are supposed to help don't do what they should."

"Zak seems fine to me. You're sure this isn't about Gwyneth rubbing her leg on mine all afternoon?"

I ignored the comment. "Zak wants to drop out of school. His mother can't be bothered to come hear him do what he loves most in the world."

"Susi, the rhythm guitarist isn't here. I'm going to sit in with them. You don't mind?"

"Not if Zak doesn't. Do you know how good they are?"

"Didn't you hear him in the basement?"

Then Jason disappeared.

After I had greeted parents and siblings, I sat in the back to write notes about what each of the kids did best in their performance. After the first few acts, I was dragged to the parking lot by one of my student's parents, who wanted a serious discussion about whether their little girl should accept an offer to a school like Julliard. The question befuddled me, but I applied my most zealous efforts to convince them, with the result that we were still talking and the parents were still shaking their heads when the program ended. As I came back, just in time to hear the chords of a last unidentifiable song, the kids in the audience all yelled and whistled and clapped, which wasn't how I thought audiences received folk music.

"Let's get out of this noise," Randolph said, grabbing my hand and tugging me up the aisle and back outside.

The sound system buzzed and shrieked, and the young people in the audience shrieked back.

"You seem to allow your guest every privilege," Randolph said.

"Not particularly. Zak needed a stand-in. How is your grandfather? I regret missing dinner with you last night."

"Really?" Randolph said, like a drowning man grabbing thin straws.

No, but it's the sort of thing that one is supposed to say. "I enjoy his company a great deal."

"Come out to dinner with us tomorrow night. As a rain check."

"All right. But please don't make dinner mean more than it should, Randolph."

"Is that what you tell your houseguest?"

"Don't be petty. It's unbecoming to you."

"Susi, what would it take? Other women find me attractive. I'm educated. We enjoy the same music, books, and films. It's just going to take more time, isn't it, Susi? I have to be patient."

"No, I think the time already passed. I don't want the intimacy and demands of marriage."

Parents and children streamed out of Town Hall, everyone animated from the performance. So I fetched my car and brought it to the loading dock, then waited quite a while before Zak and Jason appeared to once again fit the disassembled drum kit into my little car, with Zak cramming gear in the trunk and Jason fitting the tom-tom to ride in the back seat.

※

Back at Zak's, the house was deserted and dark. He and Jason talked about music, none of which I recognized, each speaking as fast as the other, while Zak made peanut butter sandwiches and poured milk. It was a more enjoyable supper than the luncheon we had suffered through.

While they chewed their sandwiches, Zak and Jason started a series of one-word exchanges with each other. Most of the words seemed to be in English or were people's names. I kept looking at the clock, trying to judge the time and whether I should leave Jason here. However, then I would be leaving him at Gwyneth's house, which didn't seem acceptable.

"Too derivative," Zak said, licking peanut butter off his fingers.

"I don't know how you can say that," Jason said.

"Watch my lips. Too. De-ri-va-tive."

"Yikes, I would hate to find out what you think of Stoneway."

Zak didn't say anything for a moment.

"Shoot, man. That bad." Jason laughed.

"What period? Before the Yoko Ono effect or after? Though I have to say, I dig on what the real Yoko is doing these days."

Jason said, "It's the same thing she was doing in earlier days, if you had a memory that went back that far."

"Don't pull the shit on me, man. Like, 'you will understand when you get older.' I can listen to any MP3 on the Internet, and the music is happening right this moment. It doesn't matter when it was first made."

"Zak, music happens on a space-time continuum, in a social context." Jason caught a drop of jam as it fell from his sandwich and paused to lick it from his finger. "So what if you discover Shostakovich's Fifth this year, and it affects your thinking? It's the song that plays everywhere when you fall in love that anchors you in a special emotional world, the same way certain smells always make you think about Christmas. It creates a shared meaning of that time in history. You and I can understand musically what Lennon and McCartney were doing by playing a CD alone in your room. But we can't understand what it meant for kids suffering through high school who heard that music for the first time."

"I don't think music has meaning," Zak said. "It's just feeling."

"Lord, that is the saddest thing I ever heard. You are saying that just to jerk me around."

"So what does 'White City Blues' mean from your work last year?"

"I can't explain it without a guitar, pedal steel, and penny whistle."

"Then tell me what the rules are, if you don't do secret meanings."

"Stoneway has always had the same rules: no samples, no house music. Know your instrument. Get tight and stay there."

"I can't deny you the goodness of that. It's similar to my personal taste."

"Gee, Zak. Thanks for condescending so far."

He shoved Zak's shoulder with his open hand, and Zak responded by bumping back with his shoulder, causing Jason to spill milk on both their shoes. They laughed and kept shoving each other.

Then Jason caught my eye, like he just woke up.

"Susi, I'm sorry. We're ignoring you."

They mopped up the kitchen and whisked away the remains of our sandwich frenzy. While they were horsing around, experimenting with the acoustics of kitchen implements on granite versus butcher block, I took a deep breath and decided that I would bring Jason with me. It felt like I could trust him to keep personal secrets.

25
"Everyone's in Love with You"
Jason

WHERE SHE TOOK ME next was to church. I am not joking.

We walked up a street on Capitol Hill and into a Presbyterian church. The narthex rang with a bluegrass twang the moment she opened the door. The sanctuary was deserted except for six musicians standing or seated in a circle below the altar, instruments and cases scattered around them. The tallest of them saw us come in and hailed Susi.

"Baby, you always show up after the whole congregation has left and the preacher has taken off his collar."

"I just don't get organized in time, Dan. I apologize. You aren't headed home already, are you?"

"We're still playing a little longer, baby. Hope you came to join us and not just to break our hearts."

"I brought a friend. Jason, this is Dan, Roy, Pete, Aaron, Bobby, Gene." She ticked off their names around the circle. "It's Pete's congregation that lets these boys play here."

"Gentlemen." I nodded to all. Pete made a point of shaking my hand. My fingers itched to join in, but I managed to mind my company manners and only sang along on the first song they played.

Most of them were hippies who never gave it up—grey beards, hair tied in a ponytail, comfortable belly above low-slung jeans, silver and turquoise on their wrists. A couple of the guys looked straight from Sunday school, matching the surroundings where they played. What they all shared was excellence: precise, well-practiced, and personal guitar and mandolin licks; voices cracked from experience and controlled with practice.

Bluegrass is difficult. The musicians are technically precise; singing close harmony is extremely demanding. It's where certain kinds of elite musicians like Toby go for the satisfaction of hard, precise work. I don't mean "elite" as a pejorative. Good bluegrass musicians deserve great respect, and there were six truly good men in that sanctuary.

However humbled I felt in this roomful of virtuosos, I begged for an instrument after one song. It didn't feel right to sing with empty hands.

Susi hadn't joined in the singing, but Dan urged her. "Come on, baby. 'I'll Fly Away.' I know your daddy taught it to you."

"All right," she said. "In G?"

Then I heard what I had longed for.

She had a voice that pierces the veil, so we can see God face to face.

This wasn't my personal prejudice, because I was already in love with her. You could see it on the face of every man in the room. That little swimmer's body produced huge sounds, but the emotion she projected into the music made you want to stop breathing and just pray that she'd go on. She had perfect pitch, which made playing difficult music nearly impossible, for it was tempting to just stop in awe. After Dan had coaxed a second song from her, she balked at a third.

"It's me standing here singing by myself," she said. "I can do that in the shower. What are the rest of you doing? Dan? Jason?"

Dammit, if that wasn't the bravest thing I've done in years, though I'd never been afraid to sing before in my life.

Dan said, "What do you know, Jason? What shall we play?"

"'Shake My Mother's Hand'?"

They nodded. I started the lead, and it went fine, though pinpricks of adrenalin shot through my fingers when she came in on the high harmony counter-point in the chorus.

We were singing together.

Lord, I still don't know how we made it through such an emotional song while learning to work together, in front of all those strangers, to find the right pitch and rhythm. Yet as in the sweetest of dreams, we matched. We fit together like when you listen to those old family bands, when they have sung together around the dinner table for so many years that they knew each other's voices and choices as well as their own.

Dan and Pete coaxed more from her—"Life's Railway to Heaven," "Take Me in Your Lifeboat," "Farther Along," "Angel Band."

"Give her a rest, boys," Jimmy the banjo player said. "Jason, seems like you're holding back. Did God give you any special talent you can share while Susi gets her breath?"

"I can yodel," I said. "Though I don't know any yodeling hymns." And I never do it in public. The two times I have, someone came up after to tell me how much I sound like Jesse Rufus, and both times occurred before Dominique let the world know all about my parentage.

Pete suggested a Hank Williams or a Lost Sons song. I chose Hank, and the guys kindly helped me through "Long Gone Lonesome Blues."

Then Susi begged to sing again, and Pete said only one more, because his wife was waiting at home, so we did "I Am a Pilgrim," with Susi asking for a key so that she could sing a tone lower, getting that same warm sunshine into her voice as Maybelle Carter.

In the end, they sang "Goodnight, Irene," with their arms around each other's shoulders. The guys who angled themselves into position with their arms around Susi's waist made her laugh and made love to her with each chorus. After, Dan was talking to Susi about her father's health and maybe getting together with him. I returned the borrowed guitar to Pete.

"I hope you won't mind," Pete said, offering me a sheet of music ledger paper and a pen. "My son isn't going to believe I was playing with you if I don't bring home proof. Would you be so kind as to sign this?"

I scratched notation for the first line of the Lost Sons song Pete had suggested earlier that I sing.

"Will you be back to play again?" he said.

"I'd be honored if you'd have me."

"It'll be fun, Jason. You are almost a match for Susi. Few of us dare try."

"Scared the heck out of me. I hadn't heard her sing before tonight."

"You don't need to be modest. You sound just like your father on the high notes. Takes me back thirty years, when listening to the Lost Sons got me started playing roots music."

We shook hands again, and I went to join Susi. I almost slipped my arm around her waist, a possessive gesture I have never made toward a woman in my life. I clasped my hands behind my own back, nervous again.

Dan said, "We are going up to the Hopvine for a beer, those of us who can stay out late. You coming, Susi? Jason?"

She looked to me for an answer, but then spoke before I could.

"Not this time," she said. "I have to be at work in the morning."

I tried not to gloat about getting her to myself again as we got into the car. She stopped before turning on the engine and turned to me.

"Don't tell anyone about this, Jason. I don't want others to know."

"You don't want your friends to know that you got hillbilly religion?"

"It's not the religion. It's the singing. I want this to be a private experience, outside the rest of my life. You must appreciate what I feel."

"It will be all over the Internet before tomorrow," I said. "Bootleg tapes of Susi in concert. They will trade them on eBay. Someone will open a whole new forum to trade Susi's collected works."

"What do you mean?" She sounded terrified.

"It was a joke, Susi. Do you know about bootleg concert recordings?"

"Yes, of course."

"And you know people trade them on the Internet?"

"I suppose. Yes, I do. But what did you mean?"

"I didn't mean anything. Do I have to explain the entire twenty-first century for time travelers, so you can understand my jokes? Or am I simply not funny?"

From the look on her face, the answer was clear: I'm not funny.

"Susi, the world should hear you. You are—"

She wasn't listening to me.

26
"Carry That Weight"
Susi

"I HAVEN'T SUNG IN PUBLIC since the accident."

After what had happened, singing with Jason, I felt I had to be honest.

"I need to hear what my voice can do before people see my face, and—oh, I can't consider it."

"Sure you can, Susi. We could do it together. I can help you keep from feeling nervous."

"Nervous? That's not it. Terrified in the pit of my soul is more like it."

"Are you afraid people won't like it? Or they won't like you? Neither is possible."

"I'm more afraid of pity."

"Pity? Yes, that's worse," he said. "I know what you mean."

"You can't possibly. It is not a mental exercise. It's a feeling down deep in my stomach."

"Do you know how much I value what you did tonight, Susi? Letting me hear you and sing with you?"

"It's funny—I was afraid to do it, since I consider it private. But then, it felt so natural to trust you."

He leaned back and yodeled, which made me laugh.

"You brought me along because you trust me? Is that true, Susi?"

"It's true. Yes, I trust you. And you? Do you trust me?"

"I could put my life in your hands, Susi. Like today. You could not have made a better day if the gods in heaven gave you the agenda."

"You enjoyed yourself?"

"Except for lunch. Playing with Zak made up for that."

"When you're playing music, you're another person. Like—"

I stopped. The look was like a man making love. I'd seen him several times that day with an expression of pure ecstasy, lost to everything else in the world. "Jason, you said your ex-wife led you in the wrong direction. To me it's obvious what your career should be. I'm sorry I doubted you when we talked on the beach. Clearly, music would come out your pores if you didn't play."

By then we were at the door to my house, and I was fumbling with the key. Fumbling, because we would be alone there, together.

"Lord, I'm starving," I said. "Are you hungry, too? We missed dinner, except for the peanut butter."

As we stepped inside the house, he put his arm around me, tipping my head up so that he could kiss me. Not wild and wet like at the beach. Just profoundly, as deeply as I have ever been kissed. The only way he touched me was to stroke my face with the calloused tip of his finger.

"I would trust you with the keeping of my soul," he whispered in my ear. "And yes, I'm starving."

27
"That's Why God Made You"
Jason

"SUSI, COME HERE A MINUTE."

She had been pretending to be busy tidying the kitchen after our meal. Though I had already done most of the dishes, she was straining to find yet another chore. When I asked, she sat down beside me, stiff and distant, but I put my arm around her. Gently, lightly, not wanting to spook her. She accepted it like a child being admonished.

"Don't we want to sleep together?"

She sighed—no, there has to be another word for the sharp intake and release of breath, as if startled but then not afraid after all. When I looked closely, her eyes shifted warily, but when I took her hand, she lost focus and I could feel her first stiffen and then relax as I held her lightly.

"I want to pretend that sigh was a wishful yes. So why don't we? That's not a romantic way to say it, and I don't mean to sound so practical. You must know I'm falling in love with you."

"I'm not ready to be in a relationship. It's too soon—"

"Susi, people in 'relationships' don't meet like this. Talk like this. Feel this way. When it's this good, it's not a relationship. You can't get ready for it. It's here, right now. Let's admit what's happening between us."

"I admit something is happening and—"

"What?"

"I'm not ready."

"Me either. You can't get ready for a freight train to run over you."

"I don't know what to do."

"Make love to me, Susi. Trust me. Everything you heard about me is wrong. I have never hurt a woman in my life. I couldn't ever hurt you."

"I don't sleep with people."

"I'm not people. I'm the man you are supposed to be with."

She kissed me. She let me start again what she'd stopped on the beach, though now I knew to go slow, to restrain the need to touch her bare skin.

"It is not romantic, but I have to ask sooner rather than later. What do you have for protection?"

"I still have an IUD. My husband didn't want children."

"And the other kind?'

"What?"

"I know that in 1955, or wherever you come from, hip young women understood 'protection' meant birth control. In my century, we also worry about STD."

She flushed. "Of course. I know that. I don't have condoms. I didn't have a plan to sleep with anyone."

"Due to what my uncle taught me, I always have a couple with me. We can get more tomorrow—I mean, if it turns out you like me."

"What if I don't like you?"

"You can put me on the curb in the morning with the recycling. Isn't Seattle famous for recycling what it discards?"

"Are you going to make me laugh the whole night?"

"I was thinking more that I wanted to make you sigh, and maybe shriek. Laughing is OK at first. Can you take this dress off? It's scary and I'm afraid to touch it."

"How can you be scared of a dress?"

"I'm just plain scared, Susi."

"That's not reassuring. Why?"

"Because it's been so long. I'll come too soon and embarrass myself."

"You can come too soon if I can cry the first time. I'm sure that's how I'll embarrass myself."

"Maybe you could cry when I come too soon, and we could get all that done and over with right away."

28
"Ring of Fire"
Susi

HE FOLDS HIS CLOTHES when he takes them off.

He has long toes as well as long fingers.

He has that line from the Andrew Marvell poem—*Had we but world enough, and time*—tattooed in a circle around his left bicep and *No Surrender* tattooed in uncial lettering on his right forearm.

The hair on his clavicle tickles my lips, especially after the coarseness of his beard rubbed my lips raw. In bed, he turns his head the same way he does when he is singing, savoring every moment as if it were ecstasy.

It's cool and damp amid the fine hairs at the base of his spine, which you can feel when he stops moving.

What else do you want to know?

29
"Wake Up, Little Susi"
Jason

"SUSI."

I whispered her name when the rain began to pour at dawn, and she slithered her leg over me, wrapping her arms around me and then sitting on my groin.

"I love you," I said. "Let's stay together."

Half-lidded, her eyes lost focus as I moved, and she moaned softly, her lips parting.

"Don't tease," she said, barely able to voice the words.

"You like this, don't you?" I touched her in the way that caused such a cataclysm the night before, and it worked as instantly in the morning light. "Is this how you always are?"

"I don't know. I've only ever been with my husband. I don't remember anything like this."

The near-exclusivity thrilled me in a way that should be embarrassing for a hip young man such as myself.

Her face glowed, the makeup worn away after our hard night, so that she appeared luminous, like a golden dawn before the sun rises. The stiffness and web of scarring that she worked to hide seemed like a tissue-thin mask, tenuously covering the ardor that wanted to break loose. She incarnated two beings at the same time, an assured and controlled person wrapped around the most passionate woman I had ever touched.

"I mean it," I said, understanding for the first time in my life that this was where I was supposed to be and this was who I was supposed to be with. "Let's stay together."

"I can't go away with you. I have my work and—"

"You don't have to change anything, Susi. I'm staying here. There is nothing else I want to do but play music and be with you."

"Don't be foolish."

"I have been foolish before, and it didn't feel like this."

She scarcely listened. Her eyes fluttered in a way that I hoped would become familiar and that I lusted for as much as I did for her body and soul.

"How can you get out of bed at a time like this, Susi? You are heartless."

"Believe me, I'm feeling far from that."

"I read in a magazine that I found at the airport that most women want to cuddle and linger in the afterglow. So why do you have to jump up and bruise my heart?"

"You should have come to Seattle last week. It was spring break and I could have lazed around with you all day. As it is, I have a job and I have to go to it."

"Will you marry me, Susi? We could sing together every night. Have children. We could get an old Ford pickup and roam from town to town with our family band."

"Are you insane?"

"Being in love with you is the sanest I have ever been."

"Marry a guitarist in a bar band?" She was teasing, and I loved that she had relaxed enough with me that she could do it with that particular smile on her face.

"I make a living. I don't have a car or a place to live at the moment, but I can support you in the style to which you are accustomed."

"I'm not accustomed to being supported, Jason. I don't need a rich boy bugging me to marry him out of pity, or whatever it is."

"Pity you? What sort of fool am I competing with? Because he might as well learn that he won't win."

"No one could compete with you, Jason."

"That Randolph guy can't be rich enough to buy a clue, if he's the competition. Anyway, if we start now, do you think we'd we have our first child by Christmas?" I counted on my fingers. "Shoot, it's April already isn't it?"

"Will you stop teasing?"

"OK. Let's set more immediate goals. Call in sick and come back to bed with me."

"You have a unique style, but I'm not persuaded, Jason. I have certain responsibilities."

In the shower she sang "Angel Band," her voice even more open than it had been the night before, and I flattered myself that I had helped her relax. I longed to record it. I wanted my laptop, so I could capture the previous day's sensations. Yet I found a modicum of self-restraint, pulled on my jeans, and went to start the coffee.

I could taste her on my lips and smell her on my fingers over the burnt odor of coffee. My fingers and toes still throbbed faintly, where twenty minutes before I hadn't been able to distinguish her pulse from my own.

One important piece of business demanded attention early in the day.

※

"Hey guy. What's up? Dominique and her attorney are coming at ten. Will you be here?"

"No. I want you to finish it, Karl. Get me out as fast as you can. Let her have the stupid condo. Give her everything she wants, as long as it doesn't hurt the band. Let her share rights to the songs I wrote when we were together, if that's what's keeping the whole thing from ending."

"From the fax they sent this morning, I think Dominique wants to take the band name."

"No, she doesn't. She just wants to burn me. Give her the songs and tell her how deeply she has hurt me, and she will let it go. Listen, I'm with someone. Finish the business with Dominique as soon as possible."

"Is this one taking you for another ride to the tabloids? Excuse me for playing skeptic. You let one woman screw you up, but it was a royal screw."

"No, this woman is falling in love with me."

"They all do. It's the three-and-a-half million copies of a single album. Plus the Grammy nomination is a real babe magnet."

"No, she is falling in love with the real me."

"The real you has a pocket full of money. Get her to sign—"

"She's going to marry me, not sue me."

"Call me a romantic fool, Jason, but I'm going to work on the pre-nups, for when she sues you later."

"Geez, Karl, you're jaded."

"I made too much money off your first mistake. I don't know if it's the last. Perhaps I should plan to add a couple of rooms to my house now that you are dating again."

"Oh, stuff it, man. I will bet double your retainer that she marries me, and the only work for you is re-drafting my will. You might as well start on that now."

"OK, I'll get right on that. What's her name?"

"Susi."

"I mean her whole name."

"Shoot."

"Seriously?"

"Shoot, I don't know her last name. I didn't ask. She told me her husband's name, but it was something ridiculous that I forgot."

"I'm calling my architect. Why settle for two rooms when I could add a whole wing? Even if I'm never home to enjoy it."

※

I was picking notes on her daddy's Martin guitar, trying to hear whether the sounds racing around my brain made up a melody, when Susi came into the kitchen. She was dressed for work in a pleated skirt and starched shirt, singing "Take Me in Your Lifeboat." In her work clothes, she looked like Audrey Hepburn as Eliza—dancing with the professor, I mean, not selling violets in Covent Gardens.

"Someone tried to take a bite out of this guitar, Susi."

"That was me. I was three. I suppose I wanted attention, because I sure got it."

"It's charming. It might even add to the tone. Is it hereditary? Will our children try to eat my guitars? I'm rather tetchy about them."

She was grilling toast and scrambling tofu with roasted peppers, and I was in love with how my teasing caused her to bend her head when she smiled, trying to keep me from seeing it and failing every time. She set plates out for us and poured coffee, and I set aside the Martin to join her, catching her hand to kiss her fingers.

"Here's jam for your toast. It's the last of the blackberries from summer. There's only honey until the strawberries are ripe."

"I already know your honey is sweet, Susi. I just want another spoonful. Did you make this jam back in 1955 when women still did that, and then brought it with you into the future?"

"It's from that mass of vines in the alley. If you're here in July, you can help pick berries for next year's jam."

"Why wouldn't I be here in July?"

"You will be back at work and—"

"I'll be working here. And I'll be teaching in your institute, remember?"

"Jason, stop teasing for a minute."

"I'm not teasing. I'm enjoying myself immensely. I intend to be here in July, eating breakfast and picking berries with you. However, if we're going to have a serious relationship, you need a good Internet connection."

"That borders on more commitment than I can consider."

"You'll have to chase me off with a stick if you don't want me around, Susi. But you do want me, or you wouldn't curl around my hand and purr like that when I touch you. I have to tell the office to forward my mail to heaven, since that's where I am."

She sobered, looking at me seriously.

"Jason, don't tell your cousin about this yet. I know you tell her everything, but please wait until we understand what's happening between us."

Before I could answer, her phone rang and she disappeared into the bedroom to answer it.

The only other man she's ever known was her ex. Yet she didn't know me either.

I don't have a cousin.

Two: Adagio

30
"I Gotta Know"
Susi

"WHAT THE HELL HAPPENED at my house, Susi? I leave you with my cousin, and it's destroyed. The neighbors called the police twice about the noise. I can't believe this of you."

"We've only been at my house, Angelia, not your apartment."

"Your crotchless underwear is hanging in my bathroom."

"We were here every night. Jason is playing my dad's old Martin in the living room."

"No, he's here, passed out on my bed. Where he committed who knows what travesties in my absence."

"Then who's here with me?"

"Well, it isn't my jerk of a cousin. I'm throwing cold water on him and tossing him the hell out of here. You failed to keep him from wrecking himself again."

31
"I Must Be Somebody Else You've Known"
Jason

SHE CAME BACK SHAKING, looking pale under her carefully constructed makeup.

"You aren't Angelia's cousin."

"Who is Angelia?"

"Oh my god. You aren't Jason Ferran."

"Angelia sounds like someone in a song. Maybe by Dave Alvin or Marty Robbins? One Raul Malo sings?"

"Sweet lord, I went to bed with a stranger."

"That is not what happened, Susi. We spent a year together over the last two days."

"What else can you call it?"

"Two people found each other, discovered that they were two flames burning as one, and fell in love as Heaven intended."

"I picked up a stranger in a bar and slept with him. Lord, if my father ever finds out—"

"That is not how we are going to explain it. We'll tell him the part about singing together and two flames as one, and—"

"You knew I mistook you for someone else."

"Not until just now. I was about to tell you that I don't have a cousin."

"Then you thought this whole time—oh god—you think I pick up strangers and go to bed with them."

"Susi, sweetheart, I mistook you for my friend's cousin. It was a long, long time between the bar and bed."

"This is humiliating. What's your name?"

"You're hyperventilating, Susi. Take a deep breath and hold it."

"What's your name?"

"Jason."

"I mean Jason *what*?"

"Jason Taylor."

"But you went to Prescott? Paul Harris knew you."

"Yes, I went to Prescott, though they threw me out when I went to Europe with my band."

"Then that nonsense about playing in a bar band? I thought you were teasing. That's real? You really are a musician?"

"Yes, and I really am in love with you."

"I don't know anything about you. You could be a psycho-killer or—"

"I'm a good guy, Susi. Guitarists are never psycho-killers. We could search it on Google, and I'm sure it will show that even bad guitarists are never dangerous. I'm fairly good."

"And you don't have a place to live? Or a car? You weren't joking?"

"It's true about no car. I've never owned one because I can't drive. Not having a home is temporary. Anyway, what does Jason Ferran have that I don't?"

"He's a private banker in London."

"So he tells rich old ladies how to make more money? I always thought that was a cover for high-priced gigolos. Susi, you aren't marrying him. I won't stand for it."

"I have never met Jason Ferran. Oh god. How did this happen? You sat in that trustees meeting. I took you to Gwyneth's house. Randolph's family met you, believing that—"

"Come on, Susi. Let's cuddle up and calm down. This isn't a true catastrophe. It's heaven. Or it was until your friend called. If the phone rings again, please don't answer."

"Don't touch me. I'm not someone who does that with strangers."

"If you could let Jason Ferran touch you, why can't Jason Taylor? I know you far better than he does. Also, I'm in love with you. He's probably a cad who will string you along and then hurt you."

"Stop teasing."

"Laughing is the only way through this. Years from now, our children will ask for the story over and over, so everyone can laugh. 'Daddy, tell us about when Mama picked you up at a bar and'—oh Susi, don't cry."

"Please let go of me. I can't remember what I said to you. I assumed Angelia told you all about me. She said—oh god, you don't know anything about me."

"Let's just start over, Susi."

"What do you mean?"

"Let's take a walk and get to know each other. Or let's just go back to bed. We were fine until we got out of bed."

"I'm late for work. Most people have jobs, you know. You have to leave. Right now."

"You didn't make me leave on the other days. I'm still the same Jason. You can't—"

"I can't even think about it. And I can't be late for school."

"When is class out at lunchtime? I'll meet you at school."

"I have appointments until late tonight. You can't come to the school."

"I'll be here when you get home tonight."

"You can't stay here. I don't know who you are. You have to go."

"OK, Susi, I'll call you at work."

"Don't you dare. Get your pack so I can lock the door."

"You're just going to throw me out to the wolves here in the wilderness? I haven't even showered. Dogs will follow me around all day, as funky as I am. Hell, I'll follow myself around."

"Get in the car. I'll leave you at the bus stop on Thirty-fourth. You can take a bus or call a cab."

32
"The Cause of It All"
Susi

AT THE BUS STOP, HE touched me, which sent shards of fear through me, leaving my fingers tingling, like an electrical shock. He rubbed the back of his hand against my cheek, letting that dark hair at his wrist tickle my face.

My heart was racing from an adrenalin surge, my insides so flooded with flight hormones that I could scarcely think.

He smiled, far too handsome for anyone's good.

33
"Fearless Heart"
Jason

"LOOK, SUSI, I THOUGHT IAN and Cynthia sent you, and you thought I was your friend's cousin. So let's invite them over tonight. Ian will vouch for me being a good guy, and your friend can protect you if Ian and I turn out to be psycho-killers. *Qu'est-ce que c'est?*"

"Please get out of the car so I can go to work. I can't think right now."

"OK. But it'll be St. Patrick's Day before we have our first child if you waste time fretting about a simple misunderstanding. I love you."

My sole regret was that this momentary disturbance in the field left her flustered. I was so confident she'd be back—since no one in the world could run away from what had happened in the last two days—that on the bus ride I took out manuscript paper and wrote music, not lyrics. Just the sounds that had been haunting me, first since the gamelan shed and then after the twangy hymns in the Presbyters' chapel.

It was five hours until our studio time started. I took the bus across town instead of a taxi, switching on Twenty-third Avenue to take the long ride on the number 48 bus to the U district, so I could switch buses to get to Ian's house. I sat writing, blissed out. If I licked my lips, my skin still tasted salty. If I rubbed my nose while thinking, my fingers still smelled of her. When the bus went over the grated bridge at Montlake, where the tires kick up harmonic distortion on the metal grid so you can feel the vibration in your teeth, I realized she still didn't know who I am.

Who's Frank Zappa? Who's Bruce? Who's Eddie Vetter? Who is Jason effing Taylor?

OK, my name looks pretentious in that context. However, she didn't know who I was the whole time we spent together. She still didn't know when I told her my name. She thinks I'm a guitarist in a bar band.

Well, I am. Or I was for years. Life would be much simpler if I still were.

She went out with me, she walked on the beach with me, she trusted me to hear her sing, she went to bed the night before thinking it was just me. Not Jason Taylor the infamous indie songwriter who sold-out so he could run with the big dogs. But who just went to the dogs instead.

Two possibilities presented themselves.

First, she should sing with us. It was as important that she sing with me again as go to bed with me. Maybe more important, because if she would sing with me, she would trust me, which was all I wanted. Or needed.

Second, she was in love with me. Me. In the couple of days it would take her to get over the mix-up, I could enjoy that it was me she wanted, the real me. While she was getting used to the idea of *musician* instead of *banker*—how the hell could anyone think I was a banker?—she didn't have to also be thinking he's rich, he's famous, his fruitcake ex-wife says he—

Shoot. I'd have to tell her that part.

I'd have to tell her things I assumed she already knew, but I didn't have to start with the trash that accumulated as a consequence of the last couple of years' bad decisions. Susi had already recognized the essentials about me: music is more important than food or sex. (Although she knew how to do things in both the kitchen and in bed that would never occur to me.) I can't stop myself from spending all my time writing, playing, and thinking about music. (I pondered what I had written that might impress her, but I'd have to write a song especially for her.) She won't be asking about things I don't want to talk about, in the same way that I'd never ask her to discuss gruesome details of her accident or what caused her to spend Saturday night weeping. We understood the essence of each other. The details were tawdry and irrelevant.

The thrilling, fundamental truth was this: she hadn't picked me up in order to sleep by a famous body, and she didn't drag me through those meetings because she wanted my money.

"She likes me," I said when I walked into Ian's house.

He and his cousin Arlo sat watching a dieselpunk web video with the sound off while Ian dinked with a Stratocaster. He looked better with a shaved head than when he pissed Dominique off by cutting a Mohawk just before we filmed that concert video last year.

"Jason, my man! We gave you up for lost."

"I am."

I pitched myself down the stairs to the basement where Ian had piled my bags from British Airways, and then I showered and changed. Yodeling sounds good in the shower. Maybe the steam helps. Regrettably, my hands smelled only of soap afterward.

Ian was sitting on the bed when I came out.

"Let's go over to the studio now, Ian. I am so stoked and ready. Wait till you see what I've been working on. And Toby's going to groove on what we did this winter."

"You missed curfew, buddy."

"I was playing last night. I met these bluegrass dudes, and they let me sit in with them."

"Then one of them took you home, made hot cocoa, and tucked you in?"

"Of course not. I was with Susi. She made polenta and goat cheese."

Ian closed his eyes. "And the last thing said this morning was what?"

I thought closely. "'Please get out of the car so I can go to work,' and 'I love you.' I'm pretty sure that was it."

"What the hey? Nobody says 'I love you' on a first date. She's a lunatic and you should run."

"What do you know about it, Ian? You've been married since you turned twenty-one. Anyway, she didn't say it. I did."

"Shit, man. You haven't been back in the country forty-eight hours."

"Sixty-six. I was with her for sixty-four of them."

"So a little groupie picks you up right after you step out of the cab, like some hick come to the big city. She polishes your wanker, and you fall over the edge."

"It is not like that. When you meet her, you'll see. As soon as you hear her sing—"

"Oh crap. She sings. You found another diva."

"She is so far from diva-ville. You'll laugh out loud at the idea when you meet her, Ian."

34
"Right in Time"
Susi

THE FANTASTIC THING ABOUT approaching obstacles as a professional is that there are trained skills to fall back on, such as deep breathing exercises.

I'm trying to be rational about this. I made it through the events of the past rough time by keeping a rational mind. When my great-aunt on my mother's side prescribed faith healing and my father's cousin claimed that Bag Balm and tobacco juice are the best remedies, and even my brother tried to talk me into Chinese herbs and acupuncture, I found that following my own advice—to stay rational—was the key to salvation. That, and music. To me, music is just another kind of rational thought. I just can't explain to others how that is true.

To approach this situation rationally, I had to breathe in order to calm down enough to think. I took up my journal to write, trying to turn down the volume of my own voice saying oh god oh god over and over again. Since I don't believe that sort of prayer is anything other than an invocation for despair.

And I don't believe in despair.

Fine. First foundation truth that I have to accept and live with: I slept with a complete stranger.

As I write that statement and sit back and examine it, it is false. I knew him to a degree. The correct statement should be: I slept with someone who was someone else.

No, the truth is: I went to bed with a man because after singing with him, I thought I knew him. In retrospect, I didn't have the correct name in my possession, but I was sure I knew who he was last night, and that I could trust him with my life.

Oh god. I did that.

I trusted him in ways I wouldn't trust anyone else in the world. I never trusted Logan in all the years I knew him to surrender myself completely (thank heaven).

Then, after I trusted this man completely, he—

I suppose the logical conclusion is that Jason didn't cause the misunderstanding.

However, he did laugh about it.

And he touched my face.

I could still smell sex on his hands. He had used a condom—more than one—so I must have smelled myself. Oh god.

※

Half-way through music theory, I couldn't stand it any longer and left the kids with an in-class rote assignment to transpose a piece of music from one scale to another, while I tore into the library. It took a minute, both to discard Nancy the librarian's insistence on offering help and to determine which years that man might have been at Prescott, but I finally found the right yearbooks.

I sank to the depths of sneaking books out of the library and back to my desk, where I spent the next two periods, stealing time from my students to look through them. Over the two years he attended, his name appeared multiple times in the index of the first yearbook: orchestra, debate club, chorale, drama club, track, honor society, jazz ensemble. Though in most instances, the caption included the tag, "Not pictured: Jason Taylor." Or, as in the case of the track pictures, distance, movement, and crowds occluded any real study of his face. In the few pictures where he appeared, it was the same person I had met. Thinner, with that gawky awkwardness of a too-tall, too-fast-growing adolescent, and even longer hair than now. The later year, his senior portrait was missing, and there were far fewer entries. No track, no debate or drama club. No picture in the orchestra later than Christmas. In neither book could I discern what instrument he played, though he seemed to be in the back with the larger woodwinds, fooling around instead of looking at the camera.

Two days' intimate acquaintance with a man and I had become a liar, sneak, and library thief, in addition to having participated in certain activities that I couldn't quit thinking about. With no sleep and an adrenalin-laden sense of fear crowding me, making me feel that I needed to flee danger, I performed my duties for the day no better than a simple-minded twit. When I did try to pay attention to business, my body kept interrupting my thoughts, as if the aftershocks of an earthquake continued to ripple through me. This did not bode well.

During my prep period, when I was not engaged in preparing for anything except despair, Angelia came into my classroom.

"Susi, what the hell happened?"

"I found the wrong Jason at that music club."

"Then kept him all weekend? You took him to the trustee meeting and—oh lord, you took him to the symphony with Randolph's grandparents. And to lunch with Freeman Lukas."

"He's a musician. He fit in with everything. People liked him—that is, everyone but Randolph."

"Did you sleep with him? Oh god, you did."

"I don't know how it happened. We were singing together. Then—"

"You sang with him? You went to bed? What else does this guy have going? Can he walk on water?"

"No, but he is talented. Paul Harris knew him from when he went to school here. Look at this yearbook. It's his junior class picture."

"He looks young for you."

"This was twelve years ago."

"That's his name? Did you ask Rosemary or the career counselor for his file?"

"Angelia, I couldn't do that. It would be prying."

"I could. I'll go ask now. You should Google him on the Internet."

"Stop it. He wants to bring a friend over tonight, to convince me that he is not a psycho-killer."

"He is at least a master of the six degrees of separation. Can I drop by for a peek at what it takes to get you into the sack after all this time?"

"It is not going to happen again."

"He wasn't any good in bed? Too bad. He seems cute, but those can be the worst."

"It was the most incredible night of my life. Yet I don't trust what happened. It went from dream to nightmare in a heartbeat."

"So he was good in bed? From this track-meet picture, it looks like he has long fingers. We both know what that means."

"Angelia—"

Rosemary, the school secretary, knocked and came in with a sheaf of papers in her hands.

"Susi, Randolph asked me to print out your grant application and mail it. Everything seems to be in order, but there are three pages that need signing. And I need a copy of the 501-C-3 information for your institute."

"Show me where to sign."

"Here and here. This other page is the request for background checks for you and Angelia and one of the instructors. You each have to sign."

"The other instructor isn't in town this week. He said he would sign, but I don't know how to find him."

Angelia said, "I'll sign it. I wonder why the check they did on us when we started teaching isn't enough."

"You can't sign, Angelia."

"Susi, Rosemary, you two close your eyes and don't look. Rosemary sees so many forged signatures every morning when the excuse slips come in, she won't mind turning a blind eye to one more."

I did manage to pull myself together to call my friend Andrew at Berklee to beg him once again about Zak's admission.

"You didn't get my phone message?"

"Andrew, you know I'm bad about the telephone."

"Yeah, and you can't do email. I should have used Pony Express. The admission office sent a letter to the boy's house this morning. He's in."

"Thank heavens. You don't know what this means to me."

"I won't be so crude to ask if it makes a difference in our friendship."

"You are such a sweetheart, Andrew. Now I have to go call Joseph at Juilliard for that girl I told you about."

"The soprano?"

"Yes. She got all of her paperwork in on time. All of her recommendations and her audition were stellar. She still needs to be convinced she can do it. She's eighteen, but you'd think she was thirteen. She's too sheltered at home, and they haven't prepared her to let go."

"Maybe tossing her into the deep end of the pool wouldn't be right for her. I can't believe you spend your time this way, Susi. Come back East again and play with us big boys."

"It turns out that I like working with kids. You heard what I'm up to?"

"Yes, and I hope it works for you. However, you of all people can swim in the big pond."

"That was before. I'm better off here. I need to be in Seattle, because of my father, if nothing else."

"How is he?"

"He's as active as ever, however hard it is for him to get around. I just wish he could have stayed at home."

"It's trite to say, but it's part of growing up; seeing your parents grow old."

"I've had enough lessons in growing up for a while. I'd like a reprieve. Thank you so much for your help, Andrew. Will I see you out here soon?"

"Next fall when we do auditions."

"I will be right here, trying to find the best for you ahead of time."

"I still love you, Susi."

"Save it for your wife, Andrew. You know better."

"I don't much like being grown up, either."

35
"You and Me and the Sea between Us"
Jason

"JASON, BUDDY, I'VE BEEN trying to reach you all day."

"Hi, Karl. I switched off my phone when we went into the studio."

"You also told the chick who answers the phone not to put me through because you're too busy."

"She's a woman, not a chick. Are you in the office early tomorrow, Karl? I want to come talk about the foundation thing. Do you have time?"

"If it's before eight-thirty. Can you be here that early? How did work go today?"

"Early is easy. Work is outstanding. Toby and Ian got tight on the new material right away. We should be able to wrap up this little task quickly. Look, I want to get on to the next thing right now. The studio is open mornings until July, so I reserved it and said you'd work out the details. Can you? And can you get me a temp like we had last year? Can you find that same woman, Martha Cooper? She was excellent."

"She works full-time in my office now. I need—"

"Lend her to me for a couple of months. If she can't start today, tell her tomorrow is fine. I need her no later than eight every morning. Can you have your guys arrange to get the masters in the vault duplicated? I want to spend a little studio time packaging live material from the past years. Then I need—"

"Jason, slow down. Contract for studio and masters, yes. Admin, OK, if Martha wants to do it. Otherwise, I'll have her find and train a temp."

"How do I hire someone under eighteen? Can you take care of that? I remember having to sign something when I first worked, but that was for playing in bars, and I don't need that. Martha should arrange the food right away. Lunch was inedible. There is other stuff I need and several people I have to contact, so I'll email that list to her, OK?"

"Fantastic. Say, Jason, what are you doing this summer? Are you going on the road after all?"

"Yes, of course we'll be on the road. Except part of the time I'm staying here and teaching guitar."

"Ephraim Vance would like to talk to you. You need to come in so you can meet while I'm here with you."

"I saw Ephraim Saturday. What more does he have to say?"

"He wants to help work out the final problem with Dominique. Do you want to talk about it now or wait till tomorrow?"

"I was in a good mood but it's gone now. So you might as well tell me."

"She claims a stake in the band name, because of the recording contracts you signed while you were married to her. The record company has already booked a tour for Stoneway this summer, and you need to come along. Otherwise, she will take the name to tour and—"

"Twist the shiv when you stick it in, Karl. Where did she get this idea?"

"Ian and Toby have already agreed to give up their rights if she's part of Stoneway. Of course, Hakeem signed off interest when he left last year."

"So what's she going to do? Go to Disneyland and pick boys off the performance stage?"

"The contract says that Stoneway does a tour this summer, so—"

"Frickin' hell, Karl. I spent the last dozen years building that band's reputation. How can Ian and Toby just walk away? They didn't say a word today. Good god, she cannot take the band's name, and she cannot come on the road with us."

"Actually, looking at your contract, she can. Stop breathing like that into the phone. Do you want to talk about it now or tomorrow?"

"Tomorrow. The break is over. We want to work more before we go across town."

"Did you think again about what I said this morning, Jason? About getting legal agreements?"

"Forget that. Just concentrate on getting me out from under the frickin' circus with Dominique."

"Did you at least get little Sheila's last name?"

"It's Susi. No, I forgot to ask. We got off track when it turned out she doesn't know who I am."

"Oh shit and firecrackers, Jason. How could she not know? She's just not admitting it."

"She mistook me for a friend's cousin, and she doesn't know Jason Taylor from Adam—Ant, Faith, or Duritz. Or Ryan, for that matter. She doesn't know anyone living in this century, except half the Seattle Symphony and all the rich old men on Capitol Hill. I think she's a time traveler from another dimension."

"You have to explain your situation to her."

"I'm going to wait for a day or two. She likes me for who I really am. You can't imagine the thrill."

"Who you are turns out to be a target for vituperative women."

"One woman. Though I still don't know what Dominique has to vituperate over. She's the one who damaged me."

"Tell your little Susi what's up with you. As your attorney, I'm advising you, it doesn't work out like Ernest Lubitsch comedies."

"Two days. Maybe three. I want to enjoy this. Just for a moment."

"Please tell me you used a jacket, Jason. At least tell me that. As your attorney, I—"

"You were a lot more fun before you passed the bar exam, Karl. When you used to sit in with us and play music all night. Why don't you come play with us again?"

"Perhaps. Someone, however, has to be the grownup. I need to call my architect right now and tell him the budget for my house is larger than I thought. I can make it big enough that my wife won't even have to see me when I'm there. That should make her happy."

"I'm going to audition a new singer with Ian and Toby. I'll see you tomorrow morning."

"Who's the singer?"

"Susi, of course."

36
"I'm Gonna Sit on the Porch and Pick on My Old Guitar"
Susi

IT WAS ALMOST EIGHT when I got home, though with the spring-time switch to daylight savings time, the sky still held a vague pale glow. Randolph had taken me to dinner in Leschi with his grandparents, to finish the discussion aborted by my ridiculous emotionalism on Saturday evening. His grandfather was gracious about it, though Randolph was less so.

Over dinner, Randolph's grandmother kept commenting on that nice young man, while, Randolph looked like he had blood pressure problems. Since I'd gotten no sleep the night before, all I could think about was foregoing consciousness in the comfort of my bed.

However, Paul Harris sat on my front porch with Zak Lukas, their voices drifting out through the trees in the dusky light. Zak appeared to be beating on the railing with mallets. Paul greeted me with a hug and a kiss on each of my temples.

"I misunderstood who you were bringing by yesterday, Susi."

Zak said, "Jason called and asked me to come over. My mom said I had to, because she wants me to do your school thing this summer. Is it true that Jason will be working with your program? I'd jump for the chance to work with him."

"Susi!"

Jason hailed me from the road below, where he had emerged from a minivan and was walking up to my door with two men.

"This is my friend Ian," he said, pointing to the taller of the two men, who had a shaved head and looked vaguely Finnish. Or Scots.

"Cynthia is in Minneapolis until the end of the week," Ian said, nodding rather than shaking hands because he was loaded down with instrument cases. He had a piercing look, as if he mistrusted me. "Otherwise, she would love to meet you."

"Ian brought along his friend Les Paul," Jason said. "Plus a twelve-string Martin and my National Steel guitar. Oh, and this is Toby." He pointed to his smaller, bearded friend.

"Pleased to meet you both, and your instruments."

I opened the front door wide, and they all came inside from the porch and found places to set down their bevy of instrument cases.

"Can I offer you all a drink? I have beer. Or wine. Or sparkling water."

As a trio, none of them answered. Ian was examining the music on my shelves, and Toby began tuning his mandolin against the piano. Ian was tall and thin in an angular way, with a pointy nose, a shaved head, and a translucent complexion; every time he looked my way, I thought his icy blue eyes might bore a hole through me. Toby was a head shorter than Jason and slightly round. He had sparkly, impish eyes and deep dimples in both cheeks, made more charming by a well-trimmed Vandyke beard, in dark Vandyke brown. He was dressed in the t-shirt and jeans that the three of them seemed to wear as a uniform.

Jason just stood and grinned at me. He looked over his shoulder at his friends and then followed me to the kitchen, whispering.

"Toby doesn't believe a man should sleep with a woman who doesn't keep her piano in tune, so he's satisfied now that all is well.

Ian will call Cynthia when he gets home, and then she'll send me email to let me know whether it's OK to keep seeing you. They all wanted to break us up before they even met you."

"They can't break us up," I said. I assumed they'd want beer, so I fetched bottles from the back of the refrigerator.

"That's what I said." He smiled.

"They can't break us up because we aren't going together."

"It is true we aren't going anywhere. We're staying here, right?"

"Jason, I don't know you."

"Yes, you do. What you don't know, I'll tell. Anything you want to ask. My secrets can be your secrets."

"It's confusing. I don't want to trade secrets. Please don't touch me."

"Susi, neither one of us is guilty of anything."

"Please."

"I won't touch you, but don't make me leave. How can you not believe that fate brought us together?"

"I can't afford to believe in fate. It leads to despair."

"Can't we start again as friends, Susi?" He stopped, pointing to the beer in my hand. "Unless Paul wants one, you should put those back. We don't drink while we work. Just water and coffee. I'll make coffee."

"Working?"

"We're playing music. They want to hear you sing."

"Jason, I asked you not to tell people."

"You said you wanted to keep it a private experience outside your regular life. We're outside your regular life. I didn't tell my cousin."

"You said that you don't have a cousin."

"Yes, but if I did, I wouldn't tell her that you sneak out at night to sing."

In retrospect, I can't explain how I lost control of my house that night. I could blame it on being so tired, but that wouldn't explain how I ended up singing, not just in front of Jason and his friends, but in front of Paul and Zak, too. Paul came with a small selection of woodwinds, including a penny whistle. Zak had come with an electronic trap set, which was as much as he could carry on the bus over to my neighborhood.

Jason made everyone play. That's how it happened. He wasn't bossy, but whatever he thought was a good idea, everyone went along with it. Ian and Toby seemed willing to consider anything he proposed, each making suggestions only for songs or keys or rhythms that we might try. At midnight, Paul left, offering Zak a ride back to Capitol Hill. Jason talked them into hauling the unused instruments out to the car as they left.

By two in the morning, we were singing quiet songs, and I had abandoned posture and breathing, having already sung enough that I saw that sweet indigo blue spot between my eyes for more than an hour. I fell asleep with my head on Jason's shoulder where we sat on the sofa.

When I woke in the morning, they were gone, and all traces of our philharmonic orgy had been tidied up, with Zak's electronic trap as the only reminder they had been there.

I was an hour late for work. It didn't seem that I could offer "too much time in the key of G" as a medical excuse.

37
"Shop It Around"
Jason

"GEEZ, KARL. I DON'T KNOW what to do."

"Hello to you too, Jason. You have Martha. She can handle whatever it is. Are you out of clean socks? Do you need a new bus pass? A glass of water for your wife when she chokes while explaining what a heel you are?"

"Very funny."

"Martha did that yesterday for Dominique. Very professional of her, for I don't think Martha likes your Lady D."

"I need you to go after someone."

"Estoppels against the blog where your starfucker SusiQ brags about her conquest?"

"I'm effing serious, Karl. That stalker hacked into one of my blogs and listed every move I made after leaving London. Now that National Steel guitar my uncle gave me is missing. My stalker friend stole it while we were loading or unloading instruments this morning at the studio."

"Stalker?"

"This guy has been haunting the Internet, says he's my brother. Puts notes on fan sites, pretending like he knows me and knows my business. He's the same one who jammed me for all time over Dominique."

Karl knew the story: When I got busted for screaming at my wife, this guy had news on the Internet before I even got out of jail. It was his blog postings that made people believe I'm a scum wife-beater. He wrote (I quote): "Dominique screamed, 'You hurt me, you bastard.' I can't say I blame him. If it was me with that witch Dominque, I'd of hit her too. Then she called the cops to take my brother away." End quote. It's the "too" that's wrong, and the "brother" part. Both weren't true.

"The same guy's still bugging you?" Karl said.

"It's like he is always lurking nearby. He's who posted lyrics and guitar tabs on the Internet from our show in Bergen. He started trouble for that woman in Nashville whose only sin was going on a date with me. He posted the news that I'm recording in Seattle before I got off the plane. What can you do?"

"Not a hell of a lot. Have Martha report the theft. If this guy doesn't threaten you overtly, there is nothing the law can do. How is he posting?"

"The webmasters don't know how to trace him. They just pull his stuff off the pages, after it's already too late."

"Is he one of those guys claiming to be your brother? I'm still battling with a few who filed claims when your uncle died."

"I told you to let them have whatever they want."

"As your attorney, I'm not letting you give away the farm. These guys all have ruthless ambulance chasers for lawyers, while I am just a calm, noble-minded protector of your interests. Maybe we can find out if one of them is your close buddy."

"Something vile gets spit on me every time he shows up. He could be standing by me or in the bushes watching right now. And holding onto Beau's steel guitar."

"Have Martha call the police about the guitar."

"I know enough to call the police, Karl. I want all the pawn shops checked in case it isn't my friend the stalker. I want to put out a reward."

"I do contracts, Jason. Ask the cops to give you advice when you file the theft report. Please have Martha fax me a copy of the report so I can prepare an insurance claim."

"What does insurance pay for the sole family heirloom I have?"

"Replacement cost."

38
"Way Over Yonder in the Minor Key"
Susi

THAT AFTERNOON, ON TUESDAY, I came home right after work, graded papers, and worked my kitchen over. Baking bread, making lasagna, roasting peppers, starting a pot of soup—it all helped me to feel like I could manage a sane life again. I was too tired to think and the repetitive work of cooking felt soothing. I thought that I'd have a little of the soup and then just go to bed.

Then Angelia showed up. She ate soup and tried to make me talk to her. We sat out on the back deck, getting the last of the April light, and when I had nothing to say, Angelia had no trouble filling in the silence.

"Musicians are bums, Susi, at least when it comes to love. Being a musician, I know. They can't talk about their feelings, and they forget about you if they have to decide between playing and love. Playing will win. Lord help me, I will never get tangled up with a musician again. Nope. I'm looking for a lawyer or an accountant or an engineer. If you have to sleep with someone who can't talk about his feelings, it might as well be someone who will be there the next time you look."

Then everyone arrived again, except Paul. Jason was standing at the door to the deck and likely heard us.

"This is my friend Angelia," I said.

128

"My long lost cousin!" Jason hugged her. "I missed the last family picnic. You'll have to give me the dirt on all our other cousins and aunties."

"What in the world? What's going on?" Angelia backed up from him, seeming serious. He smiled and shook his head.

"'All we do is sit out on the porch and play our songs,' just as Uncle Tupelo says."

"Do you really have an uncle named Tupelo?" I asked. Angelia rolled her eyes and shook her head.

"See?" Jason said to Ian and Toby. "I told you. She's like a character in *The Man Who Mistook His Wife for a Hat*. She's neurologically blind to pop culture. Angelia, this is Ian Griffith and Toby Beaumont, who are my brothers as much as you are my cousin."

Angelia didn't wait a heartbeat before she had her violin out of its case, and we were playing Celtic and Cajun songs. They ate my food and played music late into the night. Talking during a break, Toby shyly asked Angelia about her background, his dimples growing deeper as they talked.

"Your classical roots are so obvious—I mean that as a good thing—but how did you come to be slumming in Cajun territory?"

Angelia said, "I wanted to play the violin because of my mother's Fairport Convention records, not because of Itzhak Perlman. In my fantasies, I'm Mark O'Connor in reverse. He went from being the world's greatest fiddle player to recording with Yo-Yo Ma. I could go the opposite direction."

While Toby struggled to keep the conversation alive, not realizing that Angelia had already fallen in love with him, I found out that Ian is a bait fisherman. We traded stories about places our fathers had taken us, and it turned out that he spent his honeymoon hiking a trail off Highway 2 that my dad used to love. After we talked steelhead, Ian taught me a song I hadn't heard before called "Fishin' Blues." It was fun to sing, except I had to sing it with Ian, because Jason couldn't sing it without laughing.

"'Bet your life, your sweet wife, Catch more fish than you.'"

Jason had taken that leather string he wore in his hair on Sunday and braided it around his wrist. I talked to his friends in order to keep from looking at his hands.

39
"I Ain't Broken but I'm Badly Bent"
Jason

"PRESCOTT PREPARATORY SCHOOL."

"This is Angelia Ferran's cousin, Jason. Can you help me get through to her by phone?"

"She's teaching in the music lab right now. May I take a message?"

"I want her to send me a copy of her grant application. Perhaps you can ask her to send it to me by email. The teachers have email, don't they?"

"Yes, though not everyone uses it. I think that Miss Ferran uses hers."

"Let me leave my address and phone with you, in case she doesn't have them."

"Do you want me to send you a copy of the grant, Mr. Ferran? I have the file on my hard disk."

"That would be kind. Please have Angelia call me, too."

OK, I lied, though I did have familial feelings for Angelia when we played together the night before. She's quite good. I thought it beneficent that we were almost related, because otherwise it wouldn't have occurred to me to look for a classically trained musician who could play bluegrass and both Cape Breton and Cajun fiddle styles. Hey, I'm from Seattle. Cajun fiddle players aren't standing on the corner looking for a gig. You have to know their booking agent. Or pick up her agent by accident in Neumo's.

※

Although I said before that Seattle is a small town, it's so tiny that there are only about thirty-four people and they are all vibrating in a tight, intense orbit. When the police came—the day after we called —one was Officer Lee Page, the cop who cuffed me when Dominique called the police last year. He's big as a linebacker, but has a baby face and a quick smile that his job hasn't burned down yet.

"I'm sorry for your loss, Mr. Taylor," he said when I showed him a picture of the National Steel from my wallet. I am not, by the way, a weirdo with a guitar fetish. The picture was of Uncle Beau, who originally owned the guitar. Officer Lee was writing down the details as we talked, remaining politely restrained about dealing with me.

"I got to be a real fan after I met you, Mr. Taylor. My wife loves the new album, so I hear it all the time. Reminds me whenever I hear it how you didn't get a fair shake. When women get mad like that, it's always best to just get your distance."

I explained about the stalker, but Officer Page and his partner didn't have much to help me.

"Make sure you have good locks. Get an alarm if you don't have one already. If it gets to be a problem, you can consider private security."

"Like bodyguards?" This was way too much for me.

"Just protection. My brother-in-law is in the business. I can give you his number." Office Page said. "You know, I was a big Lost Sons fan in high school. So I like your earlier stuff better than the new album."

He left the card with Martha.

That morning, I spent my time working over some live recordings, which took only a certain kind of attention, so I applied visualization techniques while I worked: seeing myself surrounded by the football players who beat me up in junior high but who would keep me safe now, and seeing my guitar come back through the door. Hard to say which image was the most unrealistic fantasy. Before lunch I went for a run, where I settled for my usual visualization of the way Susi's brow arches up so that she always looks curious and surprised. When I ran, I had an urge in my fingers to provoke that surprise, the same way my fingers want to feel out a melody that isn't actually playing anywhere.

Chas1933: Did you hear Greg Vandy on KEXP last week? He did a short Lost Sons retrospective.

Sebastián: No I was working that night.

Chas1933: Well, did you see that post on the Lost Sons site today? Looks like the Rufus estate is about to settle. I'm going to find the attorney and get access to the papers. I'm betting no other archivist has tackled that trail. I heard that Jesse Rufus's papers have been sealed up for a dozen years.

Sebastian: I've been avoiding the Internet the last couple of days. So I don't know. There are a lot of liars out there. No reason that anyone should know more about it than you or I.

Chas1933: It isn't going to do me a lick of harm to waste time writing to some attorney who has a box full of musical history sitting in his vault and isn't doing squat with it.

Sebastian: Go for it.

Chas1933: Want to hear my other good idea? I'm going to poke around for song rights that have been abandoned by record labels and publishers. I bet I could buy some old lost gems, and maybe find a new publisher.

Sebastian: Where are you going to look? People aren't posting them on eBay.

Chas1933: I don't know. But I'm going to find out. Shoot, I got nothing but time on my hands.

※

"Karl, can't you answer my texts, so I don't have to stop what I'm doing to call you?"

"It is bad enough with phone calls, Jason. When you're in town, I have your voice in my head all the time. Like that girl on your fan site who says your songs cause her to have auditory hallucinations."

"You were looking at the fan sites? I thought you used the Internet only for Lexis searches."

"I have an assistant to do that. I have an assistant to do almost everything, and managing them drives me cuckoo. However, I wanted to see for myself what your stalker was up to. I wonder how he knew I filed to close Beau's estate? It was just a couple of days ago."

"Maybe he works for you. Do you have anyone on your staff that looks like Anthony Perkins in *Psycho*?"

"Everyone who works for me had a background check, is bonded, and has too much to do just to keep track of your business.

I looked at the stuff this guy posts about you. Even though he uses different names, I think I can see which ones belong to him. This guy is wacko. Listen to what he said this morning."

"I think maybe I don't want to."

"He wrote, 'Since my brother came back home, he's romancing an angel. She sings like one. She looks like one. After taking us all to hell with the devil he married, now my brother is going to take us all to heaven. Does that sound—"

"Yikes. How could he know without following me everywhere?"

"I think you should get personal protection."

"Walk around with goons all the time, like Dylan or something? I don't think so."

"OK, you won't listen to my unsolicited advice. Did you call for a purpose? What am I supposed to tell Dominique about the band name?"

"Tell her to take a flying leap. There's a friend of mine who wants research access to Jesse Rufus's papers. When he contacts you, say yes."

"What is his name?"

"Chas."

"Chas what?"

"I don't know."

"How in hell can he be your friend if you don't know his name? You know Quentin Henderson, and you made me tell him no when he asked for access."

"I met Chas through one of my blogs."

"Where you pretend to be someone else?"

"Where I pretend to be myself, using my middle name."

"That's not being yourself. Who you are is in fact someone famous—both good and bad kinds—and you can't hide from it."

"So write to Chas1933@jugum.com and ask him his name."

"He must be related to your Susi, who also has no last name. Have you got her name yet?"

"Yes, it's Neville. I forwarded you the grant application she submitted, so you can read all about her. Check your email once in a while. Or at least get your staff to."

"Are you still seeing her?"

"We rehearse at her house every night. You should come sit in. It's just your style. We don't hardly even use electricity. We start recording tonight."

"Oh shit and shoepolish. Let me fax you a release for her to sign."

"Lord, Karl. Do I need a note from my attorney to play guitar in the company of friends?"

"Yes, you do. Friends or strangers, it's all the same from my viewpoint."

40
"That High Lonesome Sound"
Susi

ON WEDNESDAY, I HAD TO take a nap in my car during lunch break. I fell asleep at my desk during the notation test in Music Appreciation, but I don't think anyone noticed. Zak was absent again.

When I got home, I just went to bed for a couple of hours and got up feeling much better, just in time to let my new friends in. Toby brought pizza from Pagliacci's, and Ian brought new strings for my dad's Martin. Jason seemed moody and almost unpleasant, but when I asked, he looked at Toby and sighed.

"We want to record the sessions," Toby said.

"But you have to sign something if we do," Jason said. "If a label picks up our work, you need to have agreed to what we're doing."

"That's cute," I said, thinking of what I knew about how easily record labels ignore or break contracts. "So am I in your band now?"

Jason looked at Toby and Ian, who both said, "Yes."

"What's our band's name?"

Toby said, "We will have to think of one."

"I can't sing in bars," I said, as if that'd ever happen, but the whole idea seemed so cute. "The smoke hurts my throat."

"That won't be a problem," Jason said. "Smoking has been banned almost everywhere we play."

After they were so nice as to let me be in their band, they decided that the sound shattered on the glass bookcases, which would have to be muffled while we recorded. So we draped my entire living room in quilts, like building forts on rainy days in the second grade.

When Angelia came later in the evening, she and Toby tuned with each other instead of with the piano.

※

On Thursday, Jason took greater pains than he had before, over every little thing. While we waited for him to position mics and approve everyone's tunings, I asked Toby to go with me on Sunday night to play bluegrass gospel. He's such an excellent musician that I thought he might enjoy it as Jason had. Toby shook his head, saying he didn't do church and he had to finish his laundry and jamming wasn't his style, though I don't know what he thought we'd been doing all week if it wasn't jamming.

Jason fussed more, changing guitars and stopping everyone multiple times in the first song we tried to do together.

Ian said, "Take it out of the bag, man. Or go home."

What Ian meant, it turned out, was that Jason had a new song but felt nervous about wanting us to learn it. It had Celtic influences, so the tonal range and rhythm were easy for me, but we had to work through the whole piece a dozen times to get it the way that he liked. The lyrics were about rusty angels and poems for which rhymes could not be found. On the page, they made no sense, but that's true for half of the history of lyric song in the west, isn't it? Once the layers of music were added, it was rather pretty in a spooky sort of way.

When I was making more coffee and the others went out onto the deck to take a break, Angelia came up behind me.

"I'm not used to musicians who can express themselves, Susi."

"That's what music is about. Communication."

"Horse pucky. You might say that in music appreciation, but you know it isn't true. It's about movement. Getting high. What we're doing here."

"All we're doing is enjoying ourselves with music."

"Excuse me for snorting when I laugh. This is just sex and drugs and rock-and-roll, Susi."

"That's crazy. There's no sex, and certainly no drugs. And we aren't singing rock-and-roll. It's folk music."

"You don't see what's going on? Jason has us all enrolled in a weird sort of foreplay. We are supposed to make sure you get high on music so he can have sex with you."

"We are just singing his pretty little song."

"That song is about you, Susi."

"It is just some images and sounds. It doesn't even have a chorus."

"It is such a come-hither song. I don't know how you can resist him."

After we drank coffee, Jason wanted us to learn another song, but he didn't have lyrics for it yet, so I had to improvise an old-timey version of scat singing. More typically he just looks at his instrument while he's playing, or he keeps an eye on Toby or Angelia. Yet he watched me the entire time we worked over that song with no words.

※

Friday morning, after four nights of playing into the wee hours, Jason and Ian were both asleep in their chairs when I woke. Toby and Angelia had departed. Which had become their usual thing.

I dressed for work and started the coffee for Jason and Ian. It was a borderline possibility, but it seemed like I might get to work on time.

"Hey, Susi," Jason whispered, looking up at me. His whiskery face reminded me of early Monday, which seemed like a year ago, and I reached out and touched his lips without thinking. He caught my hand and kissed my fingers, softly, slowly. "Can we have a date tonight? Go out to dinner?"

"Yes."

"Did you like my song? Will you marry me now?"

"Yes. I'm flattered. But no, I'm not going to marry again."

"Susi, I'm not the kind of guy who has children without marrying their mother first."

"I'm late for work. I have to go."

"Don't you feel anything, Susi? After all of this?"

"I feel like Snow White in reverse."

"Like the touch of your fingers awoke Prince Charming?"

"Like I have to go to the mines while the Seven Dwarves get to sleep in my charming cottage in the woods. Heigh-ho, it's off to work I go."

I'm getting to be a really good liar.

※

The whole time the principal reprimanded me for tardiness, Randolph sat pursing his lips like he was trying to keep from speaking. Don't vice principals have to recuse themselves the same way that judges do when they have a personal investment in the issue under judgment?

Zak was absent from all his afternoon classes. I begged Angelia and his English teacher to ignore it. It's too late in the year to be honest on the attendance rolls.

To cap a bad work day, that bastard Logan left a message with the secretary for me to call him, like the wicked witch leaving a poison apple. I will not bite.

41

"Mean Woman Blues"

Jason

"EVERYONE IS LOOKING AT us, Jason."

"Are you bragging or complaining, Dominique? You're the one who suggested the highest traffic coffee bar in Seattle. Did you get my fax, Ephraim? The song list?"

"Yes. That's why I thought we should all get together. Without any attorneys."

"Are you sure you feel safe being with me, without the protection of the law, Dominique?"

"Jason, that wasn't my fault."

"Karl doesn't allow me to say the word 'fault' when he's not present."

"Knock it off, both of you. This is just business. These are really good songs, Jason."

"Of course they are. For the others that I sent before, I changed the key and reworked the vocal part. I have the notation and lyrics here. We'll have all the rehearsal demos for her to work with by the end of next week. We'll make your June deadline if you can persuade Dominique to spend even five minutes practicing—"

"I practice."

"What? 'Practiced at the art of deception'? You're a star, Dominique."

"You are such a self-righteous prick, Jason. Why don't you bend over and screw yourself?"

"Stop it, you two. The vocal range is fine, Jason. I'm concerned that this might come off as too rockabilly for Dominique's direction. She is aiming for a higher sensibility."

"Too bad she won't be able to hit her target." I sipped tea. She sucked her chai latte.

"I have succeeded at everything I ever tried, you brat. Which is more than you can say, since you haven't—"

"Stop it, Dominique." Ephraim was firm. "I don't want to hear more from either of you. Jason, you know what I'm saying about the music."

"The underlying music will be densely textured, and I'm not asking her to bend notes or add twang in the vocals. I am in all sincerity trying to give you what you want—commercial music that appeals to a wide and undereducated audience."

"I knew you were a smart boy." Ephraim sat back. He seemed satisfied with my song list. Or maybe just with his triple espresso.

"I want out from under both of you. If this is acceptable, then let me off the hook. Let Karl file the papers without any more bullshit."

"There is still the tour to discuss, Jason."

"I'm out of here. We discuss everything only when Karl is present."

Dominique gasped as if in pain. "Damn it, Ephraim. Make him sit down. That bitch-boy writer who trashed me in the *Seattle Buzz* is sitting over there watching us."

"So let him watch. Dominique, you love every column inch you get." I waved at Quentin

"You are just saying that because he took your side, Jason. He wants to go to bed with you himself, the fool."

"I didn't see the story. Quentin has to be radical and rude to keep his job. He trashed my music long before I met you because there's too much melody. He thinks I should revive the post-grunge scene in Seattle. Don't take what he writes personally."

Dominique rapped the table in frustration. "We're supposed to be recording together. He'll start all kinds of stories if he sees us like this."

"Like what?"

"You being all pissy and superior, Jason."

"I left my positive mental attitude in the studio, where it has value."

"Kiss me."

"What?"

"Don't run off without kissing me goodbye."

"Geez, you duplicitous witch. I need anti-venom, quick."

"Ephraim likes it fine."

"He must have got all his shots at the vet. Here, Ephraim. That's the complete notation for all the music. A courier will bring tracks over to your house. Which, please remember, is actually my house."

42
"The Weight"
Jason

PART OF THE TIME, it felt like I was back in high school, trying to make up for skipping too many classes and delaying term projects for too long, cramming a half a year's work into a week or two. However, once I finished the notation for the vocalist, it felt like a weight had been lifted. No, it felt like I had pried Ephraim's foot off my face.

After the first few days back in the studio, I had sorted my thinking into categories, since it felt jumbled the first day we came to plug in. The work at night, when it was possible to play without thinking too much about it, kept me calm enough that by Friday I knew where I was going.

With the music, I mean.

Agitating Ephraim wouldn't get me out from under Dominique or Albion Records. Since I was smart enough to figure that out by lunch on Monday, it didn't take much to plan what would satisfy him as the Albion key man. Then he'd take care of Dominique in relation to the music. As angry as I felt about what had happened between us, I knew to take Ephraim's advice about the business end of the music. He had no motivation except to make money. Once I decided to roll over, the solution lay in how fast I could transcribe the music.

Toby and Ian accepted my argument for what it was, and we'd played together too long for it to take more than a series of afternoons to work out the basic music, since the solution was to pick the obvious answer to every musical question. Toby decided that if he had to do it, he was going to do the best possible job, as long as I promised that the instruments would be heard in the final mix. Ian just did what he always does, elegantly, which is to read my thoughts before I think them.

We had all been having too much fun at night to complain about workingman's blues from noon to seven in the studio.

Mornings, I cleared up the notation work quickly, because I wanted to remix some older live recordings. We were giving Albion Records one last goodbye kiss. Then we'd do what any ambitious band can do if it has sufficient capital and only modest desires for fame: work without a major label; distribute through the Internet. To do this, we needed viable material right off the starting blocks. I'd been playing historical tapes every morning, but it took me until Thursday to recognize how our sound had shifted as soon as Dominique began to sing with us that fateful night in L.A. In the ten months of sound-board tapes from when we had been together (if you can call it that), the sound drifted off. I don't mean it was experimental. I mean we didn't know where we were going.

Me. I didn't know.

A radio talk-show therapist could have diagnosed the early demise of my marriage. The dynamic I'd always had with Toby and Ian leaked away, with no new foundation replacing it. The resulting music, when I struggled to merge Dominique's vocals with our old guitar sounds, was not collaboration. It was more like a shotgun marriage.

So I took a digital knife and cut out Lady D from everything up until I sent the *Woman at the Well* masters to Ephraim so he could make the masters with his new mistress. These made decent instrumentals, though it was unmoored sound seeking anchor. Then I tweaked the recordings Ian and I made on our European anti-valedictory tour. The tectonic shift was profound. You could hear it now when we played at night. Ian and Toby are having fun again. We could bring others in to play with us in the mornings to explore the same vein we mined each evening.

However, the studio time was costing me a personal fortune. We needed to do our work efficiently and get out. We had to build our future on work in three basic piles in the studio. One pile was the older, pre-Dominique work, saleable as classic Stoneway. Another was last year's confused effort, which the Dragon Woman co-owned. She wanted Stoneway's name as the price for my freedom, and I needed to be free to continue with the third pile, our modest recordings from Susi's and Ian's houses.

No one could help me find the straight line through the mess. I can't ask Karl for advice about music. Ian and Toby are waiting for me to tell them what's up. Fundamentally, that's why Ephraim ticked me off so much. I once thought I could trust him; I believed he could help untwist the musical confusion that began when I let Dominique sing with us.

I can't rely on others. I have to figure this out on my own.

43
"Little Honey"
Jason

"MARTHA, DID ANY OF the pawn shops call back about Beau's guitar?"

"You know I'd tell you the minute they did."

"How about any of the bass players you called? Are any available?"

"No, sorry. Do you want me tomorrow, Jason? There's food coming at noon. I left breakfast for you in the refrigerator."

"No, thanks. You've done a spectacular job."

"If I don't come tomorrow, are you going to take care of that girl's breakfast? Should I make sure she doesn't need a doctor? I'm worried about her. I still don't think it's a good idea to let her sleep here."

"What girl?"

"The one your brother sent here. It's hard for me to be quiet about this, Jason. I think he took advantage of that girl just because he's your brother."

"Martha, I don't have a brother. What girl?"

"That one sitting under the tree on the corner. She spent the day hanging around, waiting for him to come. She had a note from you that said, 'Do whatever is necessary.' I didn't want to disturb your work this week."

※

We couldn't get much of a story out of her, except her name was maybe Crystal. Or maybe that is what she used instead of food and she had gotten the two confused. She had that wasted, red-rimmed look in her eyes that meant her skeletal thinness didn't come from suburban anorexia. Clearly under age, she wasn't telling us her name, rank, and serial number because she didn't want to get sent home. So we tried to learn the man's identity, which I needed to know for my own purposes.

"What does the guy look like who sent you here?"

"Like you, but shorter. He's your brother, isn't he? Though you are a lot better looking in real life. I can't believe I'm meeting you."

"What's his name?"

"Is this a joke? He's your brother."

"Crystal, I don't have a brother. Someone played a trick on you."

"I can't believe it. He seemed like a good guy. He was real sweet and kind of shy. He knew everything about you."

"He isn't a good guy."

"But he used a rubber. That's how you tell if he's a good guy."

Even Martha, who solves all problems on the material plane, was at a loss for what to do with her, but we decided to try the YWCA for shelter.

"Where did she get the note?" Martha asked. "I feel so guilty now for not asking more questions."

"It is not your fault, Martha. It's the original note I faxed to Karl from my hotel in London."

"She surely didn't follow you from London?"

"No, but my low-rent doppelganger did. Can you find that card from Officer Page and call tomorrow? I guess we need security, though I don't know who I pay to stop a creep from using my name with street girls. Here, take this money for dinner and the shelter, but don't give her any of it. Stop at that twenty-four-hour clinic on Denny to see if she has anything that needs medical attention. Good god, I shouldn't ask you to do this."

"It's not your fault either, Jason."

"The worst problems seem like they're never my fault. Yet there's such a pattern, it makes me wonder."

Crystal kissed me before Martha took her away, exhaling a sugar-laden, druggie breath and whirling her dirty blond hair across my face when she turned away, which left me feeling like I needed medical attention myself. I went back in the studio and brushed my teeth in the can, twice, trying to resist the impulse to wash with sink cleanser before saying good-night to the remaining crew at Temple Bell.

44
"Tougher Than the Rest"
Susi

BY DRIVING ACROSS TOWN as soon as class ended on Friday, I managed to pick up sheet music on Stone Way by three-thirty. Then I thought I'd take a quick run around Green Lake, even if it is crowded most afternoons. The Wallingford–Green Lake neighborhood is a former working-class mélange of bungalows and post-

Victorian farm houses snuggled up hip to shoulder, remodeled to accommodate small families and urban professionals, the parking strips now plowed into drought-free gardens full of lavender and santolina, oregano, and Pampas grass. Green Lake has been a destination site for the last twenty years for runners, moms teaching their five-year-olds how to ride bikes, and rollerbladers who enjoy skating backwards in a crowd. In spite of how busy the path around the lake can get on the weekend and just after work, it's still a pathway that allows you to see wildlife in the winter and a host of urban life in the spring and summer. If you can find a place to park.

Jason was standing near one corner of that complex, five-way stop on Green Lake Way, kissing a woman.

A tall, gorgeous woman in a long red leather coat looked over his shoulder while he kissed her, as if to see who saw them. She caught me watching. When she broke away from him, he turned and handed something to a man standing with them and then loped up the street. I had no choice but to take my turn to drive through the intersection, just as the beautiful woman pushed away the other man's arm from around her shoulder and stalked into Starbuck's.

The run around Green Lake was relaxing in spite of the people, or perhaps because of them. It was a rare but glorious spring afternoons—we get beautiful weather in February, and then March is schizoid, neither here nor there, and April breaks your heart because the cloud cover descends depressingly, with rain falling like tears, washing away the cherry blossoms before you have a chance to enjoy them. However, on that Friday afternoon the sun glinted on the water so that you had to squint against the glare. The mallards and Canada geese had hatched their babies for this year, and they all thought it a great afternoon to paddle in the lake. The mean-spirited farm geese at the north end of the lake felt too lazy in the sun to chase anyone. It was warm enough to dampen the skin during exercise, and everyone seemed delighted to be wearing t-shirts and sunglasses again and to walk around the lake with their dogs and their children and their boyfriends.

We only play music together. We aren't—going together. I don't have any feelings. I know how to prevent that.

※

Trying to find Ian's house, I got lost between the North and the Northwest street names, and ended up driving the lower Wallingford back streets, looking for the collection of low-rise warehouses that Ian said surrounded his house. There was Jason on the corner of a street again, in one of the four-corner business districts, a remnant of old Wallingford, with a dental office and what had once been a greengrocer and now sold liquor and espresso. Jason was giving money to a thin, severe-looking woman in jeans, who walked away with her arm around a rail-thin waif in a black leather jacket, who resembled a drop-out from the heroin-chic clothing ads of the early Nineties. The waif ran back and kissed Jason, wrapping her arms around his neck and raking her fingers through his hair.

She had a cross tattooed on her cheek. I myself would never think of doing that to attract men.

I am also much better at governing my impulses.

The disturbing sensation came when I turned my head away so that I wouldn't see. It felt like every time I'd turned away to avoid seeing what Logan was doing.

45
"Hey, Mister, That's Me Up on the Jukebox"
Jason

ON THE WALK TO IAN'S house, I remembered a guy I met the first time I went to jail, and began to wonder if he knew anything about creep management. It wasn't a guy I could ask Martha to call for me.

Susi was already waiting for me at Ian's, and there was just enough time to shower and put on a clean shirt. So I forgot about creeps for a while.

She sat primly on Ian's sofa, looking at a trout-fishing book from the table, not even taking the opportunity to prowl the three hundred CDs on the north and east walls of the living room. She always has more self-control than I could ever aspire to.

"Where shall we go?" I sat down beside her and felt her move away, holding herself aloof.

"Did you make a reservation? It's Friday. All the cafés will be full."

Like, did I know not to cross the street against the light? I had not assigned my love life to Martha to take care of as I had everything else, so of course it hadn't occurred to me to make a reservation.

"It's early and I know a place in Belltown," I said, making myself sound like Mr. Savoir-faire, when in fact I'm the guy who has to look around and find his ass in order to save it. Then I could not figure how to start a conversation on the trip downtown, and Susi pretended that she was too busy navigating traffic to help out.

She likes me. I know she does, even though I don't know how to get her to admit it and I don't have any evidence to offer as proof, except she sang with us all week. We walked into a hip restaurant in Belltown, so awkward with each other that people couldn't tell we were fated to be together and had already enjoyed the bliss of consummation. We just didn't know how to talk to each other at the moment.

Johnnie, an acquaintance who played in a nouveau bash&stun band that owed more to John Doe than Dave Grohl, was waiting tables. I stepped back to ask him to seat us where we wouldn't be observed and to keep people away. I gave him a bill for it, which we both knew I didn't need to do, but he plays in a band, and I couldn't ask a favor without returning what I had that he didn't.

"I can put you in my section, Jason. Sit on the north side by the window so the boss lady can't see you. Nadine came down on Dominique's side. I don't know if she'd serve you."

"You know that's all a lie."

"Yeah, but I can't say that to my boss, can I? Nadine is a piranha and swims in the same pool as your wife."

"Ex."

"Are they ever really ex?"

"God only knows. Johnnie, do you have a standing gig?"

"We folded last month. My brother's girlfriend made him get a job, and Michael quit to work in a cover band. I'm auditioning all over."

"Can I borrow you on drums for a couple of weeks for session work?"

"Sure. Where?"

"Temple Bell. Mornings."

He was gracious with Susi, though for such a modest person, she seemed to accept that treatment as natural. When Johnnie left, she leaned over the table.

"Are you independently wealthy? I know it's rude to ask, but I can't help myself. I'm curious."

"No. I've worked for every dollar I ever had. Why?"

"You gave the waiter a hundred-dollar bill. That's not the kind of tipping that I thought bar musicians did."

Busted. I scrambled, trying to make my brain work, because I still wanted to be just Jason Taylor, ordinary guy, in her eyes. "I owed him."

"What for?"

I reached for a lame excuse. "From a card game."

"You gamble?"

"No. Just when we need to kill time on the road." Lying wasn't where I wanted to go and, if I was forced to persist, I would have to end the pleasant interlude of being me without the hype. A crowd of people entered the restaurant, including Quentin Henderson with yet another incarnation of Dating Woman dressed in basic black. Then the hostess seated Ephraim and Dominique behind Susi.

I put on my Yankees hat and sun glasses and hunkered over the menu.

"The polenta sounds good," Susi said.

"Can't be as good as yours. You've ruined me for second best." As I spoke, she looked up at me and I couldn't read her expression, so I took a flying leap. "In more ways than one."

She studied her menu. "Please stop. I don't enjoy being pursued."

Nadine came over to kiss Dominique hello, and I twisted away to study the menu while looking out the window. After Nadine disappeared, the background music switched to *Woman at the Well*, I suppose in Dominique's honor (though the two words form an oxymoron).

Johnnie passed by, and Susi reached out to stop him.

"Can you please turn down the volume on this music?"

He made a helpless gesture with his hands, while avowing that he'd check. By this time Ephraim had seen me and dipped his head into his menu, laughing. Within a moment the volume of the music dropped, then rose even higher. Johnnie was arguing with Nadine at the front.

Susi stood up. "Let's go."

Quentin wanted to grab my attention in mid-departure. I had to put him off in order to catch up with Susi. "I'll call you this week, man."

Outside, Susi hurried down the street, so I had to scramble after her.

"What was that about?"

"Someone sitting by us was wearing too much perfume. And I just can't stand that pop diva trivia that passes for singing. It's like fingernails on a blackboard. In fact, I prefer the blackboard."

"You little snob."

"I am not a snob, Jason." She must have missed the smug satisfaction that settled over me as I listened to her savage my former wife. She protested in earnest. "It's just irritating. You get irritated when anyone fails to keep the beat you want. Can't I be irritated when I have to be subjected in a public place to bad phrasing and poor breath control? Or a wobble that tries to pass itself off as vibrato? What are these women thinking? What kind of exhibitionist would stand up in public and subject the world to that inefficient sound production?"

"Different people have different tastes," I said, thrill-chills running down my spine. I wanted to kiss her, but that was still off limits.

"Even a child could tell they used pitch correction in the recording."

I stopped. "How do you know?"

"Anyone with half an ear can hear it. Oh, don't look at me like that, Jason. I may not know anything about pop music, but I know about vocal recording techniques. They went in with a computer to erase that singer's flubs and paste in corrections, for which they should all be ashamed."

"I wish they were."

"Don't try to appease me when I'm angry. At least my students voted down that song."

"What's wrong with that song?"

"The lyrics are fine, I suppose, though I can't stand to listen closely enough to be sure. I let my students nominate songs to analyze for influences. One student brought that song, but only one other person voted for it. Thank heavens. If it had won, I would have had to listen to that woman's computer-corrected vocal habits a dozen times while we analyzed the influences on the song."

"Hank Williams, the Maddox Brothers and Rose, the White Album."

"Oh, you're good. My father would admire your abilities. One of the kids in my class said one other name. What was it?"

"I'm sure that's all."

"No, it was the vocals. They said the male voice was imitating the Lost Sons, but I don't know their music, and I can't stand listening to that woman enough to hear the other voices. That woman's voice is so cold. It reminds me of *Turandot*."

Beautiful analogy. I wanted to fall at her feet in worship. The opera of the little slave girl whose love saved the secret prince from the cruel death that the ice-princess Turandot consigned him to. Like most listeners, I especially love the solo by the slave girl Liù.

"You're a delightful snob, Susi."

"I am not. However, I wish you wouldn't wear a hat indoors. I know it's what men do now, but I just haven't been able to adapt to the idea." She stopped and turned around. "I'm sorry, Jason, I never should have said that. I let my irritations run wild. Do whatever you want."

She didn't mean that, when she said, "Do whatever I want."

We found dinner at The Shop Agora on Fifteenth Avenue East. Nikos poured white wine for Susi and mineral water for me, and chatted while we chose food, which made up for the difficulties Susi and I had starting a conversation. While we ate fried halloumi and salads, we managed to converse about music—what we'd been singing the past week and where that music was headed. Gradually our exchange was warm and almost intimate. At one point I tricked her into talking about teaching. For a while she dropped her guard and enjoyed herself, but then she touched my hand as she gestured in the middle of a story, and it was if she'd taken a full hit from a stun gun. She stopped talking and folded in on herself—I'd seen her do that before—and no topic would draw her out again.

So we learned that talk is good and touch is bad. If she had only one other experience with a man, and since I knew for a fact that what she enjoyed with me had been good, then the enemy of our mutual happiness was her ex-husband.

She left me at Ian's and went home alone. However, she kissed me on the cheek. A guy can keep hoping.

46
"Give Back the Key to My Heart"
Susi

SATURDAY I SPENT MOST of the day in the garden, turning soil and planting vegetables that didn't require warmer temperatures. Lettuces and peas. Spinach. After half an hour, I realized that I'd foolishly forgotten gloves, but by then, I liked the feel of soil on my bare hands so much that I didn't stop. Because the soil was too rocky, one patch hadn't been planted for years. So after lunch, I listened to Celtic music on the radio playing from the deck while I screened rocks out of the soil. It made for a hypnotic afternoon, shoveling soil onto the screen, rubbing it through to catch out the stones, carting the debris to a pile that I would use to make a path later. For this work I wore gloves, and in fact almost wore them out. Then by midafternoon, I felt worn out.

After a shower, I sat down to tea and grading papers. It took more than a half an hour to repair the damage I'd done to my nails, but that work was calming too. After grocery shopping, I made bread and several containers of food for the coming week's dinners.

Why am I collecting the detritus of daily life in this notebook, like nail parings? It's too excruciating to write what I can't think about.

I couldn't sleep last night. It's my own fault. At times like this, a thinking woman turns to Anthony Trollope to make it through the night, to keep the mind thoroughly engaged without creating enough warmth to lead to the temptation to touch oneself for comfort. Yet Trollope didn't help. I thought I'd developed a higher degree of self-discipline, both for my mind and my body. It turns out I just developed a higher degree of self-deception, the foundation sin for the agony I endured in previous years. My mind tells me to run away, and my body wants me to stay. Isn't that the same dilemma that kept me with Logan, years after I should have gone on my way? The "call me" messages that Logan leaves on my answering machine every other day should be enough to remind me to be scrupulous about my personal associations. No more staying with bad boys because of sex.

What was I thinking last week, to let Jason and his friends invade my home and steal my time? I had resolved to stay away from him, and then spent every night in the throes of ecstasy with him, even if we never went to bed after that first mistake. This is not how a self-aware woman conducts her personal life.

What was I thinking after those chance encounters—I still believe in chance, just not in luck—to have gone on a date with him? It would have been better if we'd just played music on Friday evening, like every other night. He told me what he was: a rock-and-roll musician. So why should I be surprised by women in red leather and street urchins kissing him? Isn't that what young men play in rock-and-roll bands for? To get all the sex they can find?

How could I have acted all week in such an unsuitable fashion, just because I mistook him for a friend and allowed situations to occur where he made me breathe far more deeply than is healthful?

I delayed my dinner and instead went for a long roving run along Lake Washington, hoping that pounding pavement would serve to pound sense back into my brain. It seemed to work, though walking the last leg of the trip up the hill to my house, I found myself singing aloud again.

On my front step, I found Jason.

"Hey, Susi."

"Don't you ever call? You have a phone with you all the time. Can't you use it?"

"I'm sorry. I didn't think of it."

My heart was thumping from my long run, and the walk up the hill made me breathe deeply.

"Are you going to invite me in, Susi?"

I couldn't make the key work, but he just stood there with his pack in his hands, waiting. Even my brother would have tried to take the key away and do it himself, since it took me so long.

"Look what I brought." He started unpacking take-out food from his bag on my kitchen counter. "We ate all your food and didn't contribute anything nobler than a pizza. I don't want you to think I'm an insensitive slob. I'm thoughtful and considerate. If I take a minute to remember."

"I already made my dinner."

"Maybe we can have this for lunch tomorrow. It's getting a bit cool in here with the sunset. Go shower before you catch a chill, Susi."

"Don't sit down. You aren't staying."

"But I don't want to go out. We didn't have any fun last night. I know girls like to go out on Saturday night, but I want to stay home. Please?"

"You aren't staying here. I want you to go."

"Why? I didn't do anything bad."

"I need time to myself, Jason. I haven't been alone since we met. I have papers to grade and lesson plans to finish. I want to finish my chores, clean my house, do my laundry."

"Susi, I have my own business to take care of. I'll just be in the corner with my computer and headphones. I won't say a word. When you're done being alone, you can just take me off pause."

"I need to be alone, without distractions."

"I promise not to be distracting."

"You will be though. If I see you sitting there, I know you'll be thinking about how to get me to go to bed with you. So I won't be alone at all."

"We can just agree now that when you finish being alone, we'll go to bed. So you won't have to worry about what's on my mind."

"Jason, go home."

"I don't have one."

"Maybe that's why you don't understand how I feel. I need to be in my own house, doing things that make me feel stable and sure of myself."

"Then you should understand why I want to be here with you. Also, it will be good practice. When we're married, we'll have to learn how to create solitude while we're together."

"We aren't getting married."

"Why not?"

"I didn't like it last time. There is no reason why I would ever like it."

"You stayed married a long time for not liking it."

"Maybe I managed it because I had plenty of time to be alone."

"Then maybe you retreated too much."

"Maybe that was the problem with your marriage and not mine. Stop quarreling and go home."

"Cynthia is back, so they don't want me there tonight."

"Go stay in a hotel. Or find one of your card-playing friends. I'm not providing free room and board for you."

"OK, I'll go stay at Zak's. He asked me over and his mom said it was fine. Though it will be like being in the eighth grade. We'll have to go to the garage to play music. Can I use your phone to call a taxi? I think my cell phone battery is dead."

"Jason—"

"See, you don't want me at the mercy of Gwyneth. You're jealous. You want me with you, so you can keep your eye on me."

"I have never been jealous in my life."

"You're shivering. You need a hot shower. I'll set the table while you get warmed up and dressed. Then we'll talk about how you can be alone."

He took charge, and I couldn't keep saying that I wanted him to go without telling an outright lie. When we had dinner, he exclaimed over the stuffed grape leaves and made me take the first bite from his fingers when I said that I hadn't yet sampled my own cooking. So thirty minutes after I tried to shoo him away, I was licking garlicky oil from his fingertips.

He chattered the whole time he did the dishes, about how he would give me all the time in the world to grade papers, but didn't we want to play music tonight, too? First it was the guitar, and then piano, which he plays much better than I do. Then he left me alone for ten minutes, when I agreed he could borrow some of the musicology texts from the library. This kept him quiet—he could only stuff a few into his pack—until he unearthed my oboe from the cabinet and began coaxing me to play it.

My entire oboe repertoire consists of pieces from Volume One of the Suzuki books, because after six months, my teacher decided that my talents lay elsewhere and I never returned to the oboe, except for idle recreation. The one Suzuki piece that most lends itself to the oriental tones of the oboe is *Chant Arabe*. I could still play it, but no less pathetically than I had for my last recital.

He took the oboe away, and when he did, he touched me, his long fingers curling around and stroking mine, though he was just being careful of the instrument, so that it wouldn't fall when he took it. He licked his lips and wetted the reed again, where I had just been playing it myself.

Then he played, but he knew the Schumann and a Mozart piece from Volume Two.

"That is almost all I can do," he said. "I never could practice enough because it makes my lips numb. Aren't yours numb, too?"

He brushed his thumb over my lower lip.

47
"Fool's Paradise"
Jason

SHE STARTED IT. I SWEAR. I'm giving her anything she wants, or not giving her anything she doesn't want, because it's worth it to me, no matter what.

I went to put on that copy of *Turandot* I saw on her shelf, because I'd been hearing it in my head ever since she rendered me helpless with admiration on the streets of Belltown the night before. Susi would have none of it. So we agreed on *Madama Butterfly*, though the story of a woman spurned by a cad didn't seem a good candidate for make-out-and-hope-to-get-lucky music. I'd decided when she sang scat on Thursday that I'd wait as long as it took, so I could afford a couple of hours with—what was it Susi called it that first day?—the Slave-to-Romance theme.

She sat beside me when I motioned for her to come, but she left enough distance that we could have been strangers waiting on the same bench in a dental office. I confess that I sprawled a little more than I do at the dentist's, but she touched me first. She's the one who elected to have oversized furniture. If she didn't sit back and get comfortable, she'd have to perch at the edge in that ramrod way she has. At one point I could be comfortable only by stretching my arms across the back of the sofa, and then she let her shoulder and thigh touch me, but it was a long time after that—all the way through *Un bel di*—before my hand slipped down to her shoulder. She did not shrug it off.

Lord help me, I was waiting for the faintest signal to stop, since I wasn't going to end up married to her as quickly as I wished if I failed to notice the traffic signals.

Her shoulders didn't rise up. On the contrary, she moved more closely, and it was all I could do to keep from calling notice to how well we fit together and how much more comfortable her sofa was when she had me to lean on.

So instead I said, "How could a woman be so blind as to spend years lusting after a total cad? That's the tragedy, isn't it? Everyone else can see it, while Madama is walking around blind."

Which seemed to douse any hope-to-get-lucky fires that might have been smoldering. She didn't move away from under my arm, but I could feel her turn small and tight under my touch.

I could have said, "Tell me what happened to you," and would have spent the night trouncing through the gardens of lost love, or maybe she'd have said, "Tell me the same," and I'd have to struggle to invent a more flattering history for myself. At the time I didn't consider either of those alternatives. Instead, I blurted like a fool more than I'd ever told anyone. I murmured that my mother was another Madama, waiting forever for my cad of a father to come back to her, never rebuilding another life or finding another love, for reasons I never knew, because she died before I was old enough or bold enough to ask her to answer all the "whys"—why she abandoned her own career as a singer in favor of typing in a law office, why she never told me anything about my father until my

Uncle Beau showed up and offered to help her, why she sealed up her feelings and let no one else into her life.

"What she couldn't tell me, I had to find out after she was gone. The story of my father's life was a series of Pinkerton-type adventures with one Butterfly after another, or as many at one time as would listen to his story about being a lost and lonely man."

"How did you find this out, Jason?"

"Uncle Beau left me all their papers when he died. I read all I could stand of my father's correspondence and then put the letters away."

She closed her eyes, listening to *Addio fiorito asil*. I blurted, "I think this translates as *I'm a flaming asshole, but it's too late to do anything about it now*." I didn't mean it as autobiography. I just resented what faithless men leave behind for the rest of us to deal with.

She said, "I never understood the unrequited love theme. My lack of understanding makes it impossible for me to listen to *Werther*, for example. I have to forget what the words mean and just listen to the sound."

"Susi," I whispered while Madama Butterfly was getting ready to die. "I spent a lot of time making myself into the man my father wasn't. I want to be that man for you. I want to take care of you. Please love me."

"I don't want you to take care of me, Jason."

"What do you want, Susi? Tell me. I'll give it to you. I'll be that man."

That's when she jumped me. I swear I did not start it.

Her hand went up my shirt, her tongue darted into my mouth. I was still setting my biological programming to the idea that it might take a month or two, or even six, when she stretched me out on her sofa, her pelvis jammed up against mine, her knee pressed against my thigh.

I'm expressing surprise here, but I maintained considerable élan at the moment, and I didn't refuse the advance. When she let my mouth free enough to speak, I asked the question.

"Are you sure this is what you want?"

She thumbed my nipple and twisted her fingers in the hair on my chest, so that it almost hurt, and I assumed that meant I should do what I did, which was to make up for not having kissed her during the past hundred and thirty hours of deprivation. I was making decent progress against that goal—in fact, I was out of my head in bliss—when she unzipped my fly and took me in hand.

"Are you sure this is what you want?" I asked again, though I had already slipped over to the more feeble side of self-control.

There is no use describing the nature of her affirmative reply in detail, but in the midst of all that affirmation, we rolled over so that I was part way on top, trying to figure how I could reach a condom and get out of my jeans without letting go of her, when she said:

"Don't. Please stop."

It took several moments for me to form articulate sounds.

"Stop?"

"Please."

"All right." I could have choked to death, swallowing the words. It took me a moment to catch my breath and achieve any sort of dignified posture. I had to zip up without calling attention to what it took to avoid hurting myself. Then I stood with as much poise as I could manage.

"Where are you going?"

"Susi, the whole evening, you've been touching me while acting like you didn't know you were doing it."

"I don't think so."

"When you let me hold you, I tried to keep the brakes on. But you kept writhing against me, driving me effing nuts. Now your pupils are dilated, your skin is flushed and every other sign indicates an aroused woman. I asked twice—didn't I? Then you tell me to stop, even though you started it. Do I get a medal for valor here?"

"I don't feel ready."

"Masters and Johnson could use you as a textbook example of ready."

"I mean I'm not ready for a relationship like this."

"This is like high school. This is like dating Sunday-school girls."

"Where are you going? Are you mad at me?"

"No, I'm taking myself out of the game. My internal coach is sending me to the showers."

48
"Last Blue Yodel"
Susi

HE DIDN'T ASK PERMISSION. He just went into my bathroom, shut the door, and turned on the shower. I had to assume that he stripped, because first he shrieked and then began singing in the shower. No, he was yodeling.

I was no more comfortable now with him naked in my house than I had been the first time. Also, he was mad at me, even though he denied it. Yet he came out smiling, dressed again, rolling up the cuffs on his shirt, exposing the fine dark hair above his wrists.

I tried to articulate my excuses, so he would understand and not be mad.

"Jason, I explained when we first got to know each other. Teaching and my work to establish the institute matter to me more than anything. I can't let myself by seduced into an inappropriate relationship."

He filled the kettle and began making tea.

"You like Jasmine this late at night, don't you?" he said.

When the water boiled, he measured the correct spoonsful into the teapot, poured the water, and set it to steep. He took two teacups down from the shelf and put my favorite in front of me, dripping the half-teaspoon of honey that I like into the cup before pouring tea over it.

He stroked my hand with his little finger when I reached for the cup.

"If I meet your ex, I'm going to wipe his effing face across the pavement, Susi. I don't need to know what he did, but I'm now over-qualified to punish him for it."

"You're angry with me."

"No, I swear I'm not. Listen, starting tomorrow we're rehearsing at Ian's at night, so we won't be invading your life."

He set down his teacup and picked up his pack.

"I hope like hell you'll still sing with us, Susi. We start at eight every night. Call Ian if you're unsure about coming."

※

I went to sing at Pete's church on Sunday night, alone, which must have sent me off the deep end instead of saving me. Because after that, I went out of the house every night to sing.

THREE: SCHERZO

49
"Box of Rain"
Jason

"SONNY, IT'S JASON TAYLOR. How you doing?"

"Far freaking out, man. Good to hear from you."

"What are you up to?"

"Going to meetings. Working a gig at a motor hotel out on Aurora. The owner pays me to keep the property clean at night, if you know what I mean. Sweep away the solicitors and all that follows in their wake."

"Are you playing music?"

"At home. At church on Sundays. Me and a couple of friends do some weddings here and there."

"I heard you've been playing Luther's part for a Johnny Cash tribute, doing the casino circuit."

"I'm not doing any more club work. There's too much temptation for a fucker like me."

"Have you done session work?"

"Who's going to invite me to a fucking tea party?"

"Are you morally opposed to the idea? Can you work with me afternoons for a few weeks?"

"Sure. What you have that needs cleaning up?"

"I mean that I want you to play bass. We're working at Temple Bell. You know the place?"

"Far freaking out. What do you need? Blues? Nashville boogie? That cowboy shit you were doing a couple of years ago?"

"Yeah, all that. Sonny, I have to ask you another favor."

"What you need, man?"

"There's a creep who's been messing with me on the Internet for a while, but he's started to put himself in my real life."

"Me and my friends can take care of him, Jason."

"I haven't ever seen him to know who it is. It was just annoying, but things have gone missing that I care about."

"You want twenty-four hours of protection?"

"The record company is paying for security inside the studio—though they'll charge me for it later. I want someone to watch for a creep by Ian's house. Nothing outside the law. It's just that your usual rent-a-cop can't watch for this kind of weirdo."

"I can call a few friends."

"Great. When can you start playing music?"

"This afternoon? I can come right now if you want."

It's going to be like *The Little Prince* from high school French class. At least, it will not be *Huis Clos*—I will not be sitting in hell with Jean-Paul Sartre, smoking cigarettes and longing for a mirror to reveal my true self. My true self has resolved to give up self-loathing in favor of true love. Since I'm a quick study, I'll just have to practice patience while waiting for her to catch up with me. I can't force divine revelation. Though it seemed to be at my fingertips to command that one morning, just before she discovered I was the wrong Jason.

However, I am actually the correct Jason.

To prove it, the new music is coming along outrageously well.

Maybe the music will prove it to Susi too.

I tried reasoning through the situation while waiting for everyone to show up at Ian's on Monday night.

"I'm a good guy. I don't drink out of the carton. I put the seat down, even if I'm alone."

"Pussy," Toby said. "You'll never get any if you act like one."

"Toby is right. Maybe you're too nice," Cynthia said. She had spiked her hair again, which she hadn't done for years, but it was a sign that she wasn't in a mood to be trifled with. "Lots of women have a problem with that. I know I would."

"Fortunately, I'm good enough that I don't have to be nice," Ian said.

"Oh please." Cynthia scratched her nail across the stubble on his head, and he responded by Frenching her so deeply one had to look away.

We'd spent five hours getting the living room set up for Monday night's work. Ian still calls it the living room, though Cynthia shakes her head every time. We soundproofed it and prepared it for rehearsal and recording space when they inherited the house from his parents seven years ago. So getting ready meant positioning mics, hanging futons over the windows, and setting up Zak's muffled trap at the far end of the long room. Cynthia had removed anything breakable or reflective.

Even better, Karl had finally sprung my recording equipment free from the condo. All we needed was a vocalist. Angelia came over on Sunday, when we played music without taping. I guess the choir of bluegrass angels kept Susi in church on Sunday. I hoped that was it.

Hope. What an effing stupid, fragile word. It was more like a canker sore than an abstract ideal. Might as well believe in fate.

"I'd forgotten what nice microphones you have," Toby said.

"Yeah, I think I want a couple like these," Ian said.

"I think not," Cynthia said. "You blew the budget on guitars. You need to restrain your impulses."

"There's plenty of money," Ian said, grousing.

"If you continue working in the studio, then yes. If not, then not," she said. "You need to go back on the road."

"We're doing that anyway," Ian said. "We're playing twenty-two cities this summer."

"That's not what Jason said." Cynthia's words turned both Ian and Toby around to stare at me.

"Actually—" I hadn't explained that part yet. "Stoneway has twenty-two cities to play if we want to play with Dominique. Otherwise, she'll play those towns with other musicians dressed in our clothes."

Toby softly picked out the melody to "Wild Horses" on his mandolin. "There are hundreds of cities in America. Not every house is booked up. Some might still need a second act."

"Cynthia has been researching those possibilities. We won't be playing as Stoneway—not unless we play with Dominique."

"There's ten thousand band names that no one thought of yet," Ian said.

"You made your decision." I wasn't asking, since I knew the answer.

Toby nodded. "I won't go on stage with her."

Ian hesitated. "Buddy, I'll go where you do. But shoot, how can we play with Dominique after Susi?"

"How can another singer change the band's direction?" Cynthia said. "Except that Dominique bent your music sideways until it hurt. I thought Jason swore to give up writing songs for a specific woman to sing. Didn't you swear it, Jason?"

Susi was at the door, with Angelia at her side. Toby and Ian both leaped up to unlatch the screen. I almost dropped the mic I was dinking with.

"Oh god," Cynthia breathed beside me. "You fell in the deep end, and you still can't swim."

"It's different this time."

I had sworn that it would be different this time. However, as soon as we started recording, I slipped and started telling Susi what to do, repeating the very action that had destroyed any ability to work with Dominique.

But Susi did it. Everything I asked, without complaints, without sulking. She asked questions back, but only for the sake of ensuring that she performed as I wanted.

She also brought great food for the break.

50
"Cynthia"
Susi

IAN'S WIFE CYNTHIA IS tall and gangly, and she has long, thin, big-knuckled hands that seem to be battered from gardening or similar rough work, though she covers the damage with brightly colored acrylic nails. She is pretty in an ordinary sort of way, but wears full-battle eyeliner as if she made up for the stage, and her hair has been bleached and tortured within an inch of its life.

She scares me.

My first encounter with Cynthia had the same flavor of my first day in high school, when a gang girl caught me in the women's restroom and threatened to cut me with a razor for kissing her boyfriend. After school her gang caught me and pushed me into the dirt, and she stood over me saying, "Sorry, baby doll. Wrong chick," since she realized I was the wrong person. My mother put me in a private school after that. However, in this case, I'll have to learn how to be friends with Cynthia with no outside help.

Cynthia caught me alone in the kitchen.

"So you're a teacher, huh? What do you teach? Where did you go to school?"

"I teach vocal music at Prescott. I went to Oberlin and Juilliard."

"Pretty classy for just a high school teaching certificate."

"I don't have a certificate. Not every teacher needs one at a private school. What do you do?"

"I'm a teacher too. But I only went to the UW. I haven't got kennel papers. Just a teaching certificate."

"Where do you teach?"

"I'm just subbing this year, since things are so crazy in the family. Ian's schedule got all screwed up and our grandparents were ill, so I had to find care for them. And I helped my kid brother transition to decent care. He has cerebral palsy."

"What do you teach?"

"Special Ed. The basket cases and worse, like my brother. I haven't been in the classroom much this year. I mostly tutor. It's been kind of nice to be free. For years I had to be the one to go to work every day so we could pay the bills and have health insurance."

"So you aren't worried about that now?"

She stared at me like I was dog meat.

"Ian won the lottery."

"I didn't know. In fact, I didn't know real people won."

"Me either. It let us we move my brother out of low-rent care and move our grandparents into assisted living. How about you? Did you win the lottery after Juilliard so you can slum at Prescott?"

"I live on my salary. I don't play the lottery, and my brother pays for my father's care. Cynthia, why hate me? You don't even know me."

"It's nothing personal. I just don't like the effect you have on Jason." She poured herself a cup of coffee, though maybe she should consider cutting back on caffeine. "Ian says you fish. We're hiking in the Olympics over Memorial weekend. Want to come along and look for fish to kill? Be warned, we don't do that equality shit in the wild. I don't chop wood, and I don't eat burned pancakes."

"I know how to cook over a campfire."

"Then you should come. If you're still hanging around. What happened to your face?"

"A burn accident."

"If Ian hadn't warned me, I wouldn't have noticed. He didn't see it the first couple of days. You cover it well. That must have been some tough shit to handle."

"There's worse in the world. I like Ian. How long have you two been together?"

"Eight years. Just after I finished school."

"Do you travel with them on the road?"

"Lots. It gets boring though."

"You don't have kids, is that right?"

"Can't. I turned up broken in that department."

"I'm sorry."

"There's worse in the world. Listen, Ian asked me to put in a good word for Jason. Woman to woman."

"I don't know—"

"You must have noticed by now that Jason is no more of an asshole than any other guy. You should give him a chance."

Toby came in for coffee just then, and I felt rescued for a moment.

"Toby says you're a cock tease," Cynthia said.

I looked at Toby, who blushed deep red.

"That wasn't nice of Toby to say."

"I never did. Honest, Susi. I would never even think it." Toby fled, coffee in hand.

Cynthia said, "I figured it out for myself. If you wanted a desperate, crawl-on-his-knees lover, what would you do different?"

"I'm not doing anything."

Cynthia stared at me through her spiky bangs. "You seem nice, but I can tell you have secrets. The kinds of secrets that hurt people. I'm psychic that way."

"I'm sorry? What are you saying to me?"

"Jason has enough hurt to write songs for the next decade. Don't make it worse."

At midnight, when we took another break, Angelia followed me to the upstairs bathroom, the only private place in Cynthia's house.

"Did the foundation find you today, Susi? I spent an hour on the phone at noon."

"Yes. I spent two hours. They seem interested."

"Don't you think I should marry Toby? He's cute. He's smart. He's good in bed."

"Oh god, Angelia. You've only known him for a week."

"Didn't Jason decide to marry you after two days?"

"He isn't serious."

"Fooled me. How did he ask you? On his knees?"

"Just lying in bed. He said, 'Let's stay together.'"

"That isn't asking you to marry him, Susi."

"He keeps talking about having children together by Christmas."

"Oh god, guys never joke about babies. How does that make you feel?"

"Honestly, Angelia? My first reaction is that I want to take off all my clothes and do whatever he wants. It requires every ounce of self-restraint to keep from behaving foolishly."

"What's foolish? He's whacked for you, Susi, and he's a nice guy. Much nicer than my crumb-bum cousin."

"Me with a guitarist from a bar band? It's too comical to consider. Pheromones cannot lead me into another unsuitable entanglement. I don't need it, and I won't let it happen."

"This will be fun to watch."

51
"Playing in the Band"
Susi

TUESDAY, I COULDN'T FIND parking near Ian's and had to leave my car a couple of blocks away. I took the shortcut up the alley to Ian's, where a man stood astride one of those huge, too-loud motorcycles, the kind my brother favored just after college, before he made real money and switched to something German. The bike was silent at the moment, and the man smoked a cigarette, watching me come up the alley. After he flung down and stamped out the end of his smoke, he switched to stroking his beatnik-like goatee while he watched.

He wore the complete distressed denim look of the season, though the stains and tears appeared to come from true distress. The metal and leather appeared to have been buckled and bolted onto him too many years ago—he seemed close to fifty—to be the adoption of a fashion trend. He smiled, first showing several gaps where teeth had gone missing, then closing his lips as a joyous expression sparked his face.

"My, my."

"Good evening,"

"It's getting better."

As I tugged open the gate to Ian's house, the man still watched.

Toby and Ian greeted me as I came into the house. Angelia was playing music alone in the other room. Cynthia and Jason stood in the kitchen arguing with a long-haired, ill-dressed man over whether the soup on the stove was truly vegetarian.

"Susi's here!" Ian called.

"Did she bring food?" Jason asked. "Cynthia and Arlo are trying to poison me. I'm effing starving."

Ian said, "Have some pizza. Quit being such a prima donna and just pick the sausage off."

"There's an odd person in the alley smoking a cigarette and watching the house," I said.

Ian bolted out the back door, and Jason abandoned his argument to harangue me as I unpacked the cornbread and the butternut squash soup I'd brought, with the idea that we would all snack on it later.

"Why did you walk up the alley?" Jason scolded me while he served himself dinner.

"Because it was the closest passage from where I parked my car."

"You shouldn't be walking in alleys."

"Excuse me, this is Wallingford. I have been walking in Seattle alleys since I was five. It's not even dark yet."

Ian came back with the man.

"It's just Sonny," Ian said.

Sonny proved to be quite tall, more than half a head taller than Jason, and he weighed at least seventy-five pounds more. Even ignoring the outlaw attire, his presence was felt in the room, and he seemed uncomfortable, moving awkwardly.

Jason said, "This is our new bass player. Sonny Richards, this is Susi Neville. That's my cousin Angelia Ferran in the other room playing fiddle. You know Cynthia? And Arlo is just leaving now. Right, Arlo?"

Sonny shook my hand. "I'm just a session man."

"No, we don't work that way here at night," Jason said. "You have to be in the band."

"Far freaking out. How cool is that?" Sonny sounded like a kid, even with his bass voice. "What's your band name?"

Ian said, "I vote for Half Way to China."

"Humble Willy," Cynthia said. That night, her nails were fluorescent purple with silver crackles.

"Good lord, Cynthia, how does your mind work?" Ian said. "The other choice is Jason and the Insurgents."

"Too derivative," Zak said as he came in the front door.

"Dare I say it?" Toby asked. "The obvious?"

"What's that?" Jason seemed almost to be sulking.

"The Jason Taylor Band."

"That's what we've always been," Ian said. "Dominique can't take your own name away from you."

Toby whistled. "What if she could? She is so scary."

"Who is Dominique?" I asked.

"Someone we used to know," Ian said, "but don't anymore."

"Shall we start?" Jason said. "We've screwed around enough for tonight. Arlo, no visitors while we're working. Please go now."

When we began playing at Ian's house, Sonny introduced yet another dimension for how the musicians interacted with Jason. Ian and Toby had always exchanged code words with Jason, apparently based on their past work together. Angelia and I had to be coached, so everyone had to stop if either of us needed instruction or correction.

Although he was positioned half-way across the room, practically on the porch, in order to get the sound from each instrument separated properly, Sonny watched Jason constantly. As we began, Jason played a few chords and then Sonny responded, as if asking a question with the notes he played. Almost always Jason nodded, and then the rest of us were invited in. After a couple of nights working together, their guitars asked each other very few questions.

For all the dithering I do in my solitary hours, there is no opportunity for that while we work. Jason owns my attention, in the same way that everyone else focuses on him for direction. The first week at my house, all our work together had been an exercise in exhilaration, just coming to that sweet, high place from hours of singing. At Ian's, we worked hard and Jason served as our task master. Yet he also listened to what others might be doing.

"Ian, what's up, buddy?"

"Sorry, Jason. I know I'm slowing it down. But I hear it another way."

"Then let's stop so I can hear what you do."

"It's like this. Almost a reggae rhythm."

"OK, I get what you have. Let's all try it."

As hard as we labored, it would be impossible to complain about the working conditions. I have been in enough rehearsal halls in enough cities in the western world, under every sort of director, to say that the conditions and the cooperation under Jason was as good or better than could be expected anywhere. Ian, Toby, and Sonny seemed attuned to how this work would proceed. At first I felt unsure, but soon we all responded as if we had been placed in the hands of a more than usually competent director. Jason helped us all see the goal, and what each of us was to bring to it, and the raucous, good-natured friendship in the kitchen disappeared in the living room under a mantel of professionalism.

Jason is polite and congratulatory to each of us while we're working, but he doesn't single out any one of us for special attention, which helped remove all the tension left from Saturday night. For the four or five hours we work each night, the only thing between us now is music. When Ian or Toby signals that it's time for a break, Jason takes a second to come back to himself, but then he becomes his other self again. Every night he wants to keep working far longer than any of us can endure.

I suppose Ian and Toby experienced this before, but I learn something every night. We were playing this mountain-music piece, and it seemed that it helped me to play guitar while singing, perhaps because that's how I'd been practicing it at home. Jason shifted the strap so that I held the instrument higher, which changed my voice. "You don't want to hold it like this all the time," he said. "Just when we're trying to get that high-lonesome mountain sound."

Then he directed me to sing at a lower register for one part that we had practiced much higher for days. The change clicked for everyone. Maybe Ian and Toby aren't immune to how remarkable Jason's influence can be. At one point he requested a series of key changes in a song where we had established parts several nights earlier. In the kitchen over break, Toby remarked, "I would never have thought of that."

Tonight, I found his notations for some pieces we are working on. How do I use English to describe writings in another language? He does just as he described Copland to Gwyneth, quoting other music, but then he drives the borrowed theme in another, different direction with key and tempo changes.

I stole a sheet of his music.

Oh, I'll bring it back tomorrow night, when we rehearse again. I just wanted to look at it, so I could understand that this precise, detailed notation came from the same person who—well, who did all the things we did together many days earlier. He is no longer coming on to me all the time. In fact, he scarcely looks at me except when we're working together, and then it is no different from how he looks at anyone he is trying to get more from in rehearsal.

※

"What's this?" Sonny asked.

Zak was unpacking the bag he brought in. The instrument was from the collection that hung as decorations in Gwyneth's living room.

"It's a Celtic bodhrán. I couldn't quit thinking about this song all day. A muffled tom-tom isn't going to give the effect Jason wants. Listen."

Zak stood, holding the drum, to demonstrate what he intended.

Jason was grinning, which was doubly disturbing because he hadn't shaved all week, and his teeth flashed white amid the dark stubble of beard. "You are brilliant, sir. You incarnate the musician's equivalent of a scholar and a gentleman."

We worked on that one song through the night. Jason had to stop us several times, making everyone else wait while he rehearsed one individual to get what he wanted.

"Yes, Angelia, it's in perfect pitch with the others, but I want it off by a quarter tone. Will you allow me?"

He took Angelia's violin, tuned it the way he wanted, and then played several bars. He handed it back to her, saying, "You get the idea, but you'll do it much better. The effect I want is that the violin is the other voice's memory, so it's at slight odds with the principal melody. I'll tune with you when I sing that line."

To Toby, he said, "Be the virtuoso on the high-lonesome piece. This time, all I want is this Celtic tone in snatches when the main theme comes around. You're going to be the principal voice's memory."

While Toby was playing, Jason touched my hand.

"Susi, I want three tones right here in this range." He pitched his voice with the mandolin. "We don't want the listener to be able to tell at first whether it's passion or grief. Then bend up a half tone so it's keening grief. Here's the rhythm."

He beat it out on the back of the acoustic guitar he held.

I tried to give him those tones.

"If you sound like a Croatian mourner, all to the good. But there's a thin line I want you to tread. Keep the vibrato from sounding like Bedouin ululations. I don't want that thought to occur to anyone who hears this. Then hold this high A until everyone else is done."

Ian said, "You'll have to use a tape loop. No human can hold a note that long."

"Susi can."

Jason touched my shoulder as the cue, though I knew perfectly well when I was supposed to come in.

I should stay away from him.

That's the key to stopping destructive behavior: avoid the situations that spark it. Yet if I avoid him to save myself, I lose the opportunity to sing and condemn myself to the purgatory I inhabited before Jason appeared in Seattle. I could sing in the shower and at Sunday night church, but now that I'd gone past that protected world, I couldn't make myself go back. I could no longer stay home amid the silence every night.

So I go to Ian's to sing, sneaking under Cynthia's radar as it scans for secrets. If I look at his hands, it's to see whether he is marking a new rhythm or wants the voices to increase in volume or change in pitch. I'm not looking at how beautifully tended his hands are, how gracefully his long fingers direct our attention, or how comfortably he cups his hands around his instrument, teasing out the sounds that only he can control.

I'm not looking at that.

We played it over again until Jason was happy. At eleven, Zak called home and left a message on the answer service to say he'd be late.

At midnight Sonny called in to his other job to say he was delayed. At one-thirty we stopped and Jason played back the last version.

No one could speak after, and not because we were so tired that it left one's body vibrating slightly, even after we finished playing.

Toby said, "That's why Dominique wanted to own you, my friend. She effing wanted a magician."

Angelia said, "When you direct, it's like you're making love to each and every one of us at the same time."

Then the others had to depart. Ian and Cynthia gave Zak a ride home. For the first time in a week I was alone with Jason again.

"Toby was crying when you played the tape back."

"That's just to get Angelia to take him home with her. He's passing himself off as a sensitive guy. He thinks she's his soul-mate, and it was the hand of God that made me persuade him to come to Seattle."

"She's been taking him home every night since the first time, Jason."

"Oh. How did I miss that?"

"You seem to be wrapped up in the music."

"Not totally. I'm also studying on why this sensitive-guy stuff works for Toby but not for me. Can you explain it?" He kissed my hand, forcing my fingers to stroke the bristly hairs of his unshaved face. "You can stay here, if you're too tired to drive home."

"No, I had better go."

"I don't think 'better' and 'go' belong in the same sentence, Susi. May I take you out to dinner tomorrow? I promise to get a reservation where it isn't noisy and the people don't wear too much perfume."

"That would be nice."

"Of course. I'm a nice guy, right?"

52
"Take Out Some Insurance"
Jason

"YOU'RE PLANNING TO RETURN to your safe little indie world, aren't you? Jason? I hear you breathing and not speaking, so I'll take that as a yes."

"Goodbye, Ephraim."

"Don't hang up, Jason. Let me talk you out of any numbskull decisions. You'll spend the rest of your life selling t-shirts to cover the cost of touring. You'll get up every morning to stick CDs in bubble-packs for the FedEx guy to deliver to your Internet fans."

"I don't need to get rich, Ephraim. I don't need three million so-called fans screwing up my life. I need to make my own music."

"Jason, after last year's success, you can get your label to let you do that. What you don't need is a reputation for being difficult to work with. You complain that Dominique's a diva, yet you play prima donna. Be professional. Finish this album. Then re-sign with your label."

"You guys put every musician into the packages you know how to sell. You have Dominique, who's dying for that. I never fit the mold, and you know I never will. I don't need the mainstream fans you dug up for me."

"Stop looking down your nose at your new fans. If you get rich, your indie fans will hate you. It has nothing to do with the quality of your music. Listen to yourself, not your bitchy little indie fans. You always know what's best for the music."

"I sold out once. I need to buy my soul back."

"Quit reading about yourself on the blogs, Jason. 'Sell out' means you made money, so people feel jealous. 'Different direction' means you aren't churning out the same sounds people liked a year ago. When you make money, you can buy the opportunity to go in another direction. But, my friend, you need to listen to advice."

"I've had the experience twice now of a studio making my music into something that isn't what I want. Six years ago, the studio made our sound over into retro rockabilly. You made me sound like—oh geez, I don't know. It wasn't what I intended."

"You had a more than reasonable hit six years ago, a less modest one two years ago, and now a big one. You're twenty-eight. No one can afford to get that second opportunity and then let it go by."

"In between I got to write and play what I wanted. That's all I need out of the rest of my life."

"In between you ate happy-hour bar food and brushed your teeth at freeway rest stops."

"We got very good and very tight doing it the way we did. I created a repertoire of songs that will keep me in chicken feed until I die."

"Jason, you can't throw away this kind of opportunity. You won't take advantage of your father's legacy, which I understand. But you can't throw away your own legacy before you have a chance to create it."

"I feel like I'm listening to Satan on the mountain top."

"For the temptation I'm offering, you aren't required to commit any sin. Just compromise a bit."

"There's that word. I knew it was coming."

"It's what adults do, Jason. Damn, it's easier to work with a truckload of self-destructive jerks like your father than it is to work with one self-righteous jerk like you."

"It's self-confidence, not self-righteousness. It gets the work done."

"You're just like your father, aren't you? You'll end up the same way, with a miniscule cult following and no one else remembering you ten years after you die. You'll be sleeping with barmaids just to have a home to go to."

"When I'm alone with myself, I can stand the company, Ephraim. I'm better than my father in that way at least."

"You pathetic bastard. My request stands. Please consider it."

"It's raining in Seattle, Ephraim, so I won't be considering it today."

"I'm an optimist. Perhaps the sun will shine tomorrow. Tell me, where did you find the new vocalist? Is it that woman I've seen you with? Her voice is a fantastic fit with your material. I had to keep Dominique from listening, because I know she won't like it."

"How did you hear? We aren't recording at the studio."

"That cut on your blog. I heard it this morning."

"Oh fuck me. Hang up. I need to call Karl."

53
"If Money Talks"
Jason

"KARL, I NEED—"

"Good god, as clients go, you are the neediest mo'fo' I have the pleasure to bill. I earned my retainer today, my friend. You win the DNA war. It's all yours. One hundred percent. The judge declared it this afternoon."

"Do you mean Beau's estate?"

"Not a single one of those pretenders could prove a DNA case for himself as Jesse's son. Funny that it was all lost sons coming after a piece of it. No lost daughters. By the way, your archivist friend contacted me. Do you know who he is?"

"Give him whatever access he wants. I can't think about it right now. That effing stalker managed to snatch tapes of our rehearsal two nights ago and then hacked a music file onto my blog. I had my site manager take the MP3 down. What else can I do? Come on, Karl. You wasted your time in law school when you could have been our manager. Tell me how to control this creep."

"I'm equipped to do contracts, not criminal law. If you don't know who it is, you can't get a restraining order. I have to think about it. Do you want the security guys to work Ian's house?"

"I already have friends of Sonny's doing that."

"Oh, that's reassuring. Are they watching your little Susi's house, too? I can call her to arrange—"

"No. Do not call her. Let me emphasize. I do not want her to know."

"You haven't told her who you are yet, have you?"

"She knows all about the real me. She doesn't need to know the sordid parts. Do you tell your wife everything?"

"I can't because of attorney-client privilege."

"So, Karl, did you tell your wife about the time you were in Phoenix with us and you—"

"No. She doesn't need any additional proof that I'm a jerk. She finds her own proof every chance she gets."

"I rest my case. I'm trying to get Susi to admit she's in love with me. Of all the attributes I want her to admire, 'pursued by scummy stalker fan' is not one that promises to be an aphrodisiac."

"The Phoenix event consisted mostly of humiliation and vomit. Knowing about it wouldn't help my wife keep herself safe."

"I'm taking care of that."

"Why am I not made easy by that idea, Jason?"

"What's a good vegetarian place to eat in Madison Park? I don't want to go downtown tonight."

I paid a waiter I didn't even know a hundred bucks to keep people away from us. We were at the dead end of Madison, down where the streets are lined with BMWs and Saabs while their drivers enjoy their Friday dinner, and out of deference to Susi's taste in manners, I went hatless. I'd shaved the week's stubble into a goatee.

We were dining on tofu, four-dollar-a-pound wild spring greens, and shiitake mushrooms. Susi became animated and talkative, relaxed to be with me, loving the food and telling me about how she got one of her voice students to agree to a summer session at Julliard in advance of going there this fall, which would be the girl's salvation. I didn't understand the point of the story, but it was clearly important to her, so I was listening closely.

Then some jerk pounded on the window to wave hello to me.

Frickin' hell, do we have to eat in the effing kitchen to be let alone?

Touching Susi's hand because it had startled her, I nodded and smiled at our would-be friend, who fortunately didn't look like the slimy stalker type, just a good ol' boy with no sense and worse manners.

At the same moment, a skanky guy in torn jeans and a work shirt spun our friend around and laid a finger on his chest. The greeter swatted the finger away, and skank-man pushed him again with two fingers.

I had a pretty fair notion that I'd set a bad scene in motion.

"Excuse me." I left Susi to the shiitake mushrooms and waded out into the flotsam and jetsam of my life.

"Hey, friends." I shook the greeter's hand while laying my other hand on my protector's shoulder.

"Shoot, you're Jason Taylor. Man, I used to see you play at the Tractor Tavern ten years ago. I was there the time you opened for Neil Young in Portland."

"How you doing?" I gave him the old hippy grip with my right hand, while feeling my protector hunch up under my left hand. "No offense meant here, but my buddy was trying to help me have a quiet dinner with my lady friend."

"Man, I'm cool with it. My old lady is going to freak when she finds out you were eating right where we had dinner last week. She really digs on your new album."

I let go of my protector and felt in my shirt pocket for a pen. All I had was a bus pass from coming across town to meet Susi, but I signed it, addressing it to the guy's woman friend. He left happy enough, and then I had to turn and make friends with my guardian.

"Thanks for your help," I said, shaking his hand, too.

"I'm Russ. A friend of Sonny's."

"I appreciate what you are doing." I took out my wallet and advanced him the hundred bucks he was supposed to get paid for lurking in the night. "Please go easy on people, though. Better if you call the police than create a scene."

Russ laughed. "Me? Call the cops?"

As if on cue, a police cruiser pulled up to the curb, and the officer on the passenger side stepped out. It was Officer Lee Page from days before, now cruising on the other side of town.

"How are you gentlemen tonight?"

Standing as close as I was to Russ, I felt a fight-or-flight jolt surge through him. He stayed though. We both rode out the officer's request for identification.

"A woman on a cell phone reported an altercation. We were in this neighborhood and happened by."

"She must have misunderstood," I said. "We were just saying hello to an old acquaintance. I'm about to rejoin my friend for dinner."

"Happy to hear it, gentlemen. Mr. Taylor, if we might have a word."

Officer Lee invited me to sit in the patrol car while we chatted. It was far friendlier than the last time I sat in the rear of a patrol car, with the officer commenting on the coincidence of being transferred to this neighborhood and then meeting me here. It wasn't more than half a second, though, before Russ disappeared.

"That gentleman used to sell smack a little farther up the street. Word is, he's clean now, but we wanted to be sure of your well-being."

"He tried to stop someone from harassing me, as a friendly gesture."

"Just so we know you're safe. Did you make any progress on your lost instrument, Mr. Taylor?"

"No. My friends and I took pictures to several pawn shops and promised a reward, and we faxed pictures to a bunch of other stores. Thanks for making that suggestion."

"Wish we could help you solve that problem. If we can help in any other way, please be sure to call."

"I appreciate it."

"You know, my wife about lost it when I told her I met you again."

I didn't have another bus transfer, but he gave me a piece of paper, and I wrote a greeting to his wife, too, with a line from her favorite song. Once again we parted friends.

I could see as I returned to the café that my companion had lost her enthusiasm for the food, her success with young musicians and, apparently, her pleasure in dining out with me.

"We all went to junior high together," I said, like an effing idiot. On the next beat I managed to come up with a lyric line that seemed to salvage the evening. We talked about the music that we'd worked on over the past week. What we heard in Toby's and Angelia's duets. Her amazement at finding a dedicated musician under Sonny's jagged exterior.

"I understand Zak better now," she said. "Paul said Zak had enormous potential in the recommendation he wrote to Berklee. I only understood Zak's enthusiasm before, not what he was struggling to master. Now I know why he prefers the drums when he's so gifted at the piano."

"He certainly has enthusiasm in spades." I didn't know about Zak and the piano. It caused me to lose track of what she was saying for a moment.

"Now, if he would only come to class."

"He's learning plenty at our night school. How about you, Susi?"

"Playing with your friends has felt like a baptism or an initiation into a secret club I didn't know existed."

"Do you enjoy the work?"

"Joy is too small a word for it."

"You can't know how happy that makes me. May I come play music with your bluegrass friends on Sunday night?"

As soon as I asked, I realized that I was impinging where I shouldn't and began back-pedaling.

"Actually, I don't know if I'll be able to. I shouldn't have asked."

"It's OK, Jason. Yes, please come."

"How are your other plans are coming? Have you heard anything about your grant?"

"We had phone calls asking us for more information. I'm still holding my breath."

"Will you let me know if I can help find more money for you?"

She gave me a funny look that I strained to interpret and couldn't. "You've done enough," she said.

When we finished dinner and headed for the door, she said, "Gambling debts again? Is that what you do all day? Play cards?"

"No, that was an old debt. I play music all day."

"What a nice way to spend your time. Who were those men really?"

"Old friends," I said. "Since I've lived in Seattle all my life, I run into people everywhere."

Oh geez, busted again. I can't lie for shit. This wasn't going to work.

She went home. Alone.

I didn't get lucky, though I hadn't begun the evening with much hope. It wasn't as if I thought that I could write a stupid song she liked to sing and then she'd sleep with me again. Back to playing the fox hoping to out-wait the Little Prince. Or was it the other way around?

What kind of joke is it anyway, pretending as if being with her means the same as "getting lucky"? I went to an after-hours club, but there wasn't an invitation to sit in with anyone playing and no magic to the music, compared to what had been happening in Ian's living room. I took the world's longest shower and reduced the pretentious goatee to a soul patch, since a beard didn't prevent a single person from recognizing me. Now I'm sitting here in my own private Internet café—Ian's basement—drinking coffee and listening to music through headphones (because Cynthia came down and reminded me that I'm a self-centered effing asshole with no consideration for others), keyed up because I'm alone. After spending all of last year celebrating that I could finally be alone again at night, glorying in the freedom of solitude, here I am writing another letter to myself—my email box is full of them now—complaining to myself that I'm here instead of where she is.

I'm down to sending email to myself and answering hardly anyone, except a handful of musicology friends like Chas who have nothing to do with my every-day life in Wallingford. I haven't posted anything to any of my blogs in days and days. If anyone else saw how monomaniacal the inside of my mind has become, they would shrink in horror.

I always thought that high-lonesome crap in love songs was made up, just a pose to make girls feel sorry for you.

54
"That's Not the Issue"
Susi

AFTER SPENDING ALL OF Saturday putting my household back in order and grading papers, I went to visit my dad for the evening, then came home and went to bed early. I took a long run on Sunday morning, putting off the chore of my diary. Most of the entries in the past week consisted of writing down lyrics to the new songs to ensure that I remembered them, though I have never failed to learn lyrics after a first trial. I'm trying to create the same notations that I'd seen Jason do for his music.

Every few minutes I think I should call my dad to say what I couldn't make myself tell him last night: "I'm all mixed up over a man. He wants to marry me, and it sounds so logical whenever I see the hair on the back of his wrist. Or if I look at his belt buckle. What do you think?"

Before I can make myself call, I try to think of what Dad would say, and it stops me before I can dial. Soon, I have to tell Dad that I'm singing every night, that I plan my whole day around being with these musicians, that I drive across town like a junkie looking for a fix—and believe me, I do not choose that conceit without considering everything it implies.

I made more notes about the songs we were working on—the kind of "artist's impression of working with greatness" pap that would embarrass any diva trying to flatter a maestro in order to get hired again. Things I'd never consider writing at any time in my life. We are talking about pop music, for heaven's sake.

To prevent embarrassing myself, I stopped writing and spent the rest of the afternoon making bread and wishing it would be evening soon, so I could go sing with Jason, wondering if everyone had played together on Saturday and didn't invite me. How perverse is that? I would say it felt like high school, which is what Jason said when he complained about my indecisiveness, but I didn't remember feeling like this in high school. I remember auditioning for parts that I wanted badly, and holding my breath when the phone rang. This felt like that, except my stomach was tied in knots, instead of just my brain racing and rationalizing.

Hence, when a knock sounded at the door, I leapt up, tipping over my tea. I tried to hear whether a tall person knocked, or was it lower? It couldn't be Angelia, for she never knocked and she was too busy these days to speak to me outside of rehearsal. I mopped up tea with a kitchen towel and then carried it with me, like a brainless idiot, to answer the door.

That Logan stood on the porch shouldn't have surprised me. That it wasn't Jason distracted me, with the result that I invited Logan inside.

Which I had promised myself I would never do.

"Hi, Susi. I've been calling, but never hear back from you. So I stopped by on my way out of town." His skin had that deep hickory color that people get when living in Texas, but when he took off his sunglasses, the skin around his eyes was ashen white, almost grey. He seemed ill under the robust color of his skin. As ever, he dressed at the expensive end, even in casual travel togs.

"You shouldn't have."

"It's no bother. I wanted to see you."

"I mean, you shouldn't have come, Logan. I don't want to see you."

"It smells delicious in here. You must be in one of your high-energy relaxation moods."

"In fact, I'm busy getting ready for the coming week. I have an engagement this evening. What did you want to see me about?"

"Let's sit down and talk. You look fantastic."

"I prefer not to sit. You may stay for a moment, if it pleases you, Logan, but I shall stand."

"Please don't be obstreperous, Susi. This is hard enough for me."

"I wouldn't want things to be difficult for you."

"You didn't used to be sardonic."

"It's funny how people change. What do you want?"

"I want to make amends to you."

"Oh no, you don't."

"Yes, I do." He held out his hands, helpless, whining with a gesture.

"I mean that I won't stand for you coming here and saying that. There is no possible way you can make amends. If you were working your program the way you should, you'd know that, too."

"You can't preach to me about how to work the program."

"I can if you choose to come into my home to indulge in some piety that's supposed to help you but will do nothing for me."

"Susi, we have to get past this."

"I have gotten past everything that it's humanly possible to do. It is not possible for me to allow you to work out your issues at my expense. I have neither patience nor time."

"You have to accept some responsibility, Susi. We were married too long for you not to accept your piece in what happened."

"Is that little speech designed to create a scene you can hash over in your club meeting tomorrow? I had rather a higher opinion of Narcotics Anonymous than I do at this moment."

"I'm not doing NA. I wasn't comfortable with all those junkies. I'm much more at ease at AA meetings. I met a really, warm sweet woman there who has helped me a lot. We have a saying—"

"Yes, I know about your sayings. I have a new acquaintance who stays alive through NA. He has a saying, too. He says, 'A fucker is a fucker. No way around it.'"

"Susi!"

"Listen, you never came to see me once while I was in the hospital. If you want to make amends, spend as much time volunteering in a burn ward as I spent there."

"I was in rehab."

"You were in rehab less than half the time I lay in that ward. Go see what the little children go through. Give something of yourself to someone. Just once in your life."

"I have been hoping you would forgive me."

"You also believed in Santa Claus and the tooth fairy far too long. Just get in your car and drive away, Logan."

"I came in a cab."

"You said you were traveling. You always rent a car.

"Except I can't rent a car without a license."

"You don't have a license?"

"There was a little backsliding episode a few months ago that resulted in a DUI. Because of everything else, I lost my license for ninety days."

"Call another cab. There's the phone."

"Actually, my plane leaves in two hours. You know how slow the cab companies can be. I was hoping you'd be kind enough to give me a ride."

I didn't murder him, for which I hope to receive full credit when final judgment is laid down on all our souls.

"Get in the car, Logan. I have just enough time to take you to the airport and then make a standing date. This does not endear you to me, so I would appreciate silence while we're driving."

"Come on, Susanna. You are being as unreasonable as ever."

"I'm happy to hear that's true. Please don't call me by that name."

55
"Maybe I'm Amazed"
Jason

AFTER IAN AND TOBY begged off working on Sunday afternoon, I put on shorts and a t-shirt, stuffed my pack with jeans and a real shirt, and ran over to Susi's house from Wallingford, which is a clean ten miles. I went around the hills instead of over them, so it wasn't a particular feat, just a pleasant sort of trance work.

As I walked up her alley way, still cooling down from the run, she came out of her house with a man who stuffed his suitcase in the back seat of her car. Then they both got in and drove off down the alley. A blond beach-boy son of a bitch with too much of a sun tan, which indicated he wasn't from around here, or else spent a lot of time away. He was talking a mile a minute, as they so tritely describe it, as they drove away.

I sat on Susi's front steps, checking the time on my cell. Perhaps I'd gotten it wrong, and we were supposed to meet at the church. Or not meet at all. I went around to the back, crawled up on her deck where no one can see, and changed into jeans and a clean shirt. When I sat on the edge of the deck, Sonny slipped in beside me.

"Figured this was where you were headed. I wasn't going to break my ass running after you."

"Hi, Sonny. What are you doing here?"

"I pulled Sunday watch for you. Damn, this lady has a great garden. Her early peas are weeks ahead of mine."

"Do you know who she's with?"

"Someone she didn't want to see. She pushed him out fast, while ragging him to shut up when they drove past me. If you want my guess, it's her ex. You could see him stepping into her space like he thought he had a right, not noticing she didn't want him close anymore."

"Rats. I missed the chance to pound him."

"Want to play music while we wait to see if she's coming back? I have a guitar in my car."

"I have a mouth harp."

So we played. When we paused, Sonny said, "I heard you were Jesse Rufus's kid. I didn't know he had one. You know, we opened for those dudes back in the Seventies. Then I played a few weeks for him myself, right before he croaked himself."

"What was he like?"

"Self-destructive as hell. Even I had to hold my breath sometimes."

"Yes, I guessed that," I said. "I spent a lot of time worrying that I might be like him."

"You have more going on. Your songs are better. Your voice is stronger. Your guitar work—man, you had to be standing in the front of the bus when God handed out talent."

"Thank you for saying so."

"You look and sound like him. I'm guessing you aren't too happy about that situation."

"He was a drunk. He ruined my mom's life. He ruined his own life. He didn't even come into mine. I can't forgive him, Sonny."

"You feel that way about me, too?"

"My business wasn't mixed up with yours in the past. There is nothing between us to either forgive or forget."

"You think my kid should forgive me?"

"I didn't know you had a kid."

"Knocked up his old lady when I was nineteen. That means he's, what, twenty-five now. Almost as old as you."

"Do you talk to him about it?"

"Long hours in the past year. It's unforgivable, the stuff I did." Sonny paused. "But he's talking to me."

"I didn't have that privilege. I just talk to my father in my head. We've been conversing since I was thirteen."

"How's that conversation progressing?"

"He's still a bastard and I'm still one ticked off son of a bastard."

"If you want to talk with my kid, I can ask him to call you."

"No, it wouldn't be the same. He at least knows you."

"Maybe I could answer for Jesse."

"Too weird."

"Nah. One fucker is the same as another. I can make as good a guess as any. What do you say to him in your head, Jason?"

"You had everything going for you, man, and you drank it all away. What's that about?"

"I bet Jesse would say what I'd have to say: 'I honestly don't know.'"

"That doesn't help me much, Sonny."

"Try another question."

"OK. Here's what else I say over and over: Your brother Beau grew up the same as you. He went through the same shit on the road and had a lot of the same problems. Yet he came to see me. Tried to help. Didn't get drunk and kill himself."

"Maybe Beau hurt, too, but we just weren't wired the same."

We sat, keeping quiet, for a while. Sonny poked me with his elbow. "Ask the question you really have. Let me try what Jesse would say."

"How could you screw my mother and not accept the consequences?"

Sonny shook his head. "That's what my son asked. Here's what I told him: 'Can't say I thought about you all the time, but I stayed away because of you. I'm such a complete fucker, I didn't want you to have any of it.'"

"But I wanted my father there."

Sonny laughed, but not because it was funny. "The devil is smoking my tail all the time. I didn't want him getting a chance to light on my kid too."

We had to stop at that one.

"Frickin' hell, Sonny. I guess there isn't much more to say."

"Except that answer only makes sense if he knew about you."

I said, "Beau came around. To me, that says Jesse knew."

"Then, like I told you, a fucker is just a fucker."

"So, want to play music for a while?"

"It's what you pay me for."

※

When the modest afternoon sun disappeared, Sonny gave me a ride to the church on Capitol Hill—said he could take church just fine, but he got enough bluegrass in the studio. I arrived just as the service started and took a place in the back, looking for Susi, even though I remembered from the first time that she often missed the liturgical part. I did a fair job of engaging in the music with the rest of the congregation, though my eyes were on the door and not the altar. When the worshippers left, abandoning me to just the true musicians, I greeted them as friends, which I wished they were, and I didn't make an excuse for Susi's absence.

"She never misses," Dan said. "Hope she's well."

At four o'clock she'd been plenty healthy. Why not at ten o'clock? I didn't ask that question aloud. We played without her, which seemed to create a preference for lonely cowboy songs and enough high-lonesome hymnifying to make my nose bleed, even though my voice is peculiarly suited to that music. I'd spent Saturday and Sunday composing and playing music intended to blast me out of self-pity mode. However, I'd come there to get high singing with her, without being the director or the leader—or imperial dictator, as Dominique calls me—just as her partner. Here I was harmonizing with tenors and baritones.

She didn't show, and at the end I was trading phone numbers with everyone, and the preacher Pete was at me about promises and real intensions that we play together soon, in other venues. I liked the idea of these guys wanting to stand up in public with me, but I was talking to myself too loudly about Susi to hear everything we promised each other.

"There's a little benefit Saturday afternoon," Pete said. "It's just our folkie friends. Why not join us?"

I agreed. There's nothing else to do the whole day long but play music.

Then I walked back across the Madison Valley, up Madrona ridge, and down to her house in Leschi. I should have gone home. I turned a half dozen times to find the bus line, knowing I should go back to Wallingford and crawl under my rock. Instead, I sat on her neighbor's cement wall in the alley, shivering in my shirt.

She came home just before midnight, riding in a BMW with a Johnny Depp-pretty guy, but blond. I hate guys like that, because they are so used to getting by on their faces that you can't trust a damn thing they say. She kept him inside forever, and then he kissed her goodbye at her door. His car's headlights cast my shadow on the cement wall in the alley. The sight of my shadow looming eight-foot tall on rotten concrete caused me to see myself as the stalker I had become.

There was no sign of Sonny anywhere, and it was too late to catch a bus, so I hiked over to a convenience store on Twenty-Third Avenue, the kind that makes its gross sales in malt liquor and cigarettes. I called a cab and waited, talking with the clerk about whether you can legitimately call a woman faithless if she hasn't made any promises.

※

"So I'm not deluded, right, Ian? I have a high tolerance for ambiguity, but this is driving me nuts. She lets me lead when we're rehearse, doesn't she? She never complains."

"Yeah. She never argues or complains. If you ask me, she's not the same species as Dominique. Or the same planet. What's she like in bed?"

"Geez, Ian. I'm not telling you that. Anyway, she won't do anything I want except in rehearsal."

"You are never anywhere but in rehearsal or in bed, man. So you're saying that—"

"I mean in real life. I want to take care of her. I can make all the things happen for her that she wants. Karl could help me find the money she needs for her music institute."

"That idea is too strange—summer camp to teach roots music to kids. Why can't kids today learn music in garages like God intended? That's where rock-and-roll school is, in the garage. You need more than one hundred eighty credit hours to graduate."

"I want her to marry me."

"You're still married to someone else. Meanwhile, she sings like an angel, and she comes every night to sing with you. Why not be satisfied with what you got?"

"Why did she go off with one guy and then come home with yet another man, when she could be singing with me?"

"Why don't you ask her, Jason? I swear this is like high school. 'She looked at this guy by the lockers. What do you think it means?' Call her up and ask. Then maybe we can get some sleep."

"I can't ask her who those men are. She'll think I'm a stalker."

"You are an effing stalker. If you can't sleep, at least shut up and stay downstairs in your cave. I need more sack time than you allow anyone."

NINE VOLT HEART

56
"Price to Pay"
Susi

LOGAN MADE HIS PLANE with time to spare, so he wasted my time trying to kiss me goodbye, complimenting me once again about how nice my face looks. I had gone as far from the airport as the feeder road that goes to I-405 when my car lost power and stopped working.

When you are trying to force a car to the side of the road without power steering you forget everything else you were thinking of, instead just hoping you aren't killed by another vehicle. A roadside hero—an off-duty cop—stopped to help, and then called AAA for me when she couldn't. She waited for the tow truck with me, and only cautioned that a person shouldn't be wandering the highways alone without a cell phone.

The tow driver fished—mostly steelhead, and mostly standing under bridges between Monroe and Carnation, just to watch the river flow.

"Like Bob Dylan says," he joked.

I know who Bob Dylan is, though I don't know that song.

At the repair shop on Stone Way, he left me and waved goodbye. I called my brother Steven for a ride home, all the while trying to not think. I needed to find the same mental and spiritual space I found when I left the burn ward, where I no longer hated Logan with each breath I took.

Ashes. There is nothing left from that fire but the ashes to sweep away. I thought it had all been swept clean, and I didn't like learning that it was still possible for Logan to open the door and let the ashes blow back in. While waiting for my brother, I stood at the edge of the car lot, singing so that I wouldn't waste time thinking about my lost afternoon, and then slipped into singing one of Jason's songs, but turning it into a wail instead of a thoughtful folksong.

I thought of walking over to Ian and Cynthia's house, but I hadn't been invited and changing plans would just create a problem for Steven. It was well past too late to go to the church on Capitol Hill. When Steven appeared, he insisted on taking me to dinner after hearing that I hadn't eaten since noon.

191

"You should never have given him a ride, Susi. You should have called me then. You are tough enough to say no."

"Steven, please don't lecture me."

"You scared the hell out of me when you called and said you'd been with Logan. You aren't letting that snake back into your life, are you?"

"No. I gave him a ride to get rid of him. Twenty minutes to the airport would be faster than thirty minutes waiting for a cab."

"Promise me you aren't thinking of starting up a relationship with him again. Too many people return to destructive relationships."

"Steven, in all honesty, I don't think I was in a relationship with him for the last four years we were married. Something slimy tried to crawl into my house today. I think he's either still using or on the edge of falling back."

"Just so you aren't involved. I don't care if Logan flushes himself down the toilet."

I took a large breath to change the subject from the unbearable to the unreportable.

"I'm sort of involved with someone else."

True to his usual self, Steven didn't probe or beg for more details, but just sat quietly, waiting for me to reveal more.

"He's a musician. I met him by accident, thinking he was Angelia's cousin. One thing led to another and we've been—" I couldn't make myself say it straight out. "Listen, promise you won't tell Dad. This is bound to upset him."

"We must be talking about a different father. Don't tell me what you've been up to if it's too intimate."

"It feels like such a secret, I have to tell you. We sing together."

He took it about as badly as I expected our father would, his spoon clattering on his plate. He grasped his hands together, trying to look cool.

"So, what do you sing?" His voice cracked. His nervousness seemed to have the reverse effect on me, however, and I felt free to speak.

"We started with bluegrass—he has a beautiful, smoky tenor. Then we played traditional music and cowboy material. Old hillbilly swing, like Dad has in his library." I took a breath again. "And songs he writes."

Steven laughed. "Susi the folkie, huh? It goes well with all that bread-baking and gardening you took up."

"You won't be mean about it, Steven? I mean, it's silly of me, but at the same time it's thrilling to sing again."

"What's this resurrecting lover's name?"

"Jason. But we aren't lovers. It's different from that."

"You started out saying you were 'sort of involved.' When does that not mean 'lovers'? Did you fall for him, but he didn't fall for you?"

"No. He wants to marry me. That's what he keeps saying anyway."

"Whoa. We go from 'sort of involved' to getting married? How long has this been going on and you haven't told us?"

"Just a couple of weeks. It seems longer, and more intimate, because of the music. I don't want to marry again, as ideal as Jason makes it sound."

"It's difficult to start a relationship with two opposing ideals."

"That's the problem, Steven. We're too different from each other, and it would never be suitable."

"Meaning that he's a hillbilly slob who sings twangy music?"

"No, we're compatible around music, but we're from two different worlds. You know I grew up in the classics. And that I believe in salvation through hard work."

"You're a presbyterian extremist, it's true."

"He plays and writes pop—sort of twisted rock-and-roll versions of the roots material Dad has."

"What about the hard work part?"

"That I worry about. He has no visible means of support."

"Maybe he's rich and can indulge a hobby. You knew plenty of people like that in your former work."

"He just plays in a bar band. From what I can tell, they never have any engagements, because the whole band is free to rehearse every single night."

"You're rehearsing with a rock-and-roll band?"

"Yes. They like my singing."

"Ask him where his money comes from."

"I can't."

"Of course you can. Just do it."

"If I start asking him questions, then he can ask me questions, too, and I don't want that. I want him to like me for what I am, without having to consider what's missing."

"You don't want to marry him, but you want him to like you. There's an 'and yet' hanging in your voice."

"After seeing Logan today, it's made me conscious of why I worry."

"Do he and his friends use drugs? Drink? They must all smoke."

"Jason doesn't let anyone drink in rehearsal, and no one except the bass player smokes. He lives in his friend's basement and takes the bus everywhere or walks. I see him giving money to odd people on the street and waiters in restaurants—a lot more money than you tip someone. He says it's debts from card playing. Friday night, the police had him in a patrol car for ten minutes. I don't know if it's drugs, but it's not how grown men behave."

"Is he like Logan in any way?"

"No, he's always alert."

"I think I'd like to meet this man. I'm out of town all week. How about Saturday?"

"He'll be at my house when we get home tonight."

"You have a date?"

"We were supposed to meet tonight. So I'm sure he'll come looking for me. Why don't you come to my house for dessert? I'll show you the music we're singing."

When we came home, there were no messages or other sign that Jason had come by. All I had to give Steven was a few of the lemon squares I'd made to take to Ian's. So we ate those and drank tea while we looked at the lyrics and notation I'd made for Jason's songs.

"What does this sound like when you sing it?"

"Perhaps not so interesting when it's a cappella."

"Let me hear."

"All right. Promise you won't tell Dad."

I sang, and Steven listened thoughtfully.

"Susi, you have to tell Dad. It's cheating that he doesn't know you're singing."

"I don't know if it's real yet. It happened so fast. Maybe it'll turn out that I can't sing after all. I don't want to break Dad's heart again."

"You have never broken his heart, Susi. You're projecting your own feelings on him. Anyway, I want to meet your new beau, to see if I can understand what's going on with your mystery man."

We said good-night, and I tried to calm down after taking that risk, singing in front of Steven. I saw the lighted dial on the clock too many times between midnight and three o'clock.

Jason never left a message, but I found the single rose on my doorstep again in the morning.

57
"Dark As a Dungeon"
Susi

AFTER SCHOOL, ANGELIA DISAPPEARED when the bell rang, so I had to beg Randolph to give me a ride to my brother's, who wanted me to use his car while he was out of town. The ride across town with Randolph was not pleasantness to stand on its own, without comparison, and unfortunately my brother chooses to live on the north end of lower Queen Anne, which necessitates driving all over creation to get to his house.

Randolph began harassing me before we left the school parking lot.

"Won't you come for dinner this Friday, Susi? My grandmother has been asking after you."

"Friday? I don't think I can."

"Another night then? Thursday?"

"No, I'm engaged all week."

"Doing what, Susi? You've been unavailable, ever since—"

"Yes?"

"Since Angelia's cousin came to town. Are you having an affair?"

"It's not your concern, but no. I was unavailable before then. You just chose to disregard what I've been saying to you. I'm not interested in being in a relationship."

"That doesn't account for how you are at school. You've missed most of your committee meetings. You haven't been to a faculty meeting since early April. You don't have time at lunch to eat with any of us. It's as if you've abandoned your job."

"That is not true. I don't have time at lunch because I'm meeting with students. The committee meetings are after school, and I don't have time after four o'clock for that right now."

"What's pulling you away? You said you couldn't be with me because teaching was your entire life. Was that just an excuse, like 'I have to wash my hair tonight'?"

This conversation did not end well.

The good things that happened while riding with Randolph was that he was busy changing lanes and navigating through the Mercer Mess, even cursing a driver who cut him off, when we passed Jason on the sidewalk, standing by a police car, talking with two officers, gesticulating while they stood shaking their heads.

Whatever was going on with the police and his other affairs, it caused Jason to lose his natural ebullience. When we started work that night, he listed the songs where he wasn't happy with the results on tape. We began working through each of them, with about as much enthusiasm as any of my students taking a make-up test. Then he sent Angelia and me home early and made the others stay to work harder. Cynthia watched us leave, with an expression that made me think she found us both as interesting as insects looking for a new rock to crawl under.

Angelia and I started down the walkway. Jason's voice followed.

"What is it about the concept of coming in on the upbeat that is so freaking difficult?"

"I guess it's because you're so downbeat, boss."

"Screw you, Ian. Are we playing or jacking around?"

"You tell us. You're the boss."

A thunderous chord rang out before Jason spoke again.

"We are doing this one without twang tonight. Follow Sonny for the rhythm if you get effing lost again. Sonny, start with that skanky bass thing you had on Sunday morning."

I looked at Angelia. "I wonder why Jason is so on edge."
"Yeah, I wonder."

※

Rosemary, the school secretary, showed me again how to read my email, since Andrew at Berklee and two other old colleagues had complained that I've made myself inaccessible to cross-country communications. Andrew's email was easy to find and then answer. The others were harder to identify, but I resolved those. Then I found that my father had amused himself a couple of times, sending me email, but he gave up when I didn't answer.

Then there were a whole string of emails from Jason, who had written to me almost every day since—well, since he turned out to be Jason Taylor, not Jason Ferran.

I confess, reading all of them in a sitting, I felt disappointed. Some of it was like the lyrics in the songs we sang, but the rest seemed to be out-takes from others' poetry, without attribution, or doggerel he had never evolved into songs. I'd seen or sung the lyrics to several of his songs, and as pop music goes, they had far greater literary merit than his email. I should be more romantic, I suppose, but I didn't like reading them, so I stopped, because they made me think less of him.

Then I found my first flame email—that is what they call it, right? This was like the poison-pen letters that girls slipped in others' lockers in high school. I shouldn't have paid it anymore mind than trash of that variety.

> I'm sending you this message for your own good. Jason Taylor wants one thing from a woman. After he captures the essence of your soul for his own work, you will hear nothing more from him except the repeated catalog of your perceived inadequacies.
> If that's what you choose to embrace, do it with foreknowledge. When he's done with your voice, he's done with everything else.

Signed by Dominique.

"Someone we used to know but don't anymore," Ian had said.

Someone who used to sing with the band. Who slept with Jason—for what other relationship could result in a malicious need to slander him? Who therefore was his ex-wife.

I could respond to the email with questions. I could ask Jason, when I ask him to explain his disquieting behaviors (though I had my own disquieting former relationship, about which I did not want to answer questions). I could worry about it, but it didn't seem to warrant any greater concern than the bad poetry in his email. Instead, I would ignore it. I couldn't ask him if he was using me for my voice, because I was using him for the opportunity to sing. The relationship was progressing only as that of director and performer. I'd spent a weekend without seeing him, with no stronger feelings than a sort of existential ennui, fueled by overexposure to testosterone.

Also, seeing Logan extinguished any sense I had of wanting to be intimate with a man. You just had to glance at that embodiment of utter catastrophe to lose any desire to replace it. With a booster shot of revulsion due to Logan, I made it through our brief Monday night rehearsal without rekindling flames of desire for Jason.

When I closed that nasty email, another insipidly titled email from Jason popped in my box. The senior soprano from fourth-period voice class stood at my door, ready for her bi-weekly counseling and cheerleading session, where I'd spend thirty minutes trying to convince her that only a dolt would not go to Juilliard after being accepted.

"Damn it, damn it, damn it."

I let myself have an oral tantrum after that girl left my office, insisting that she wasn't going to summer music camp in Michigan, and she wouldn't go to Juilliard in the fall. She asked, instead, what I could do to get her into Sarah Lawrence at this late date. All of that irrational hysteria on her part had been too telling, and by the end of the conversation, I fear that I showed my profound annoyance at her utter stupidity.

"Are you all right, Miss Neville?"

Zak stood at my office door as if in mid-knock, but I hadn't closed the door completely, so his knock had pushed it open, so who knows who heard my tantrum down the hallway. He held a rose in his hand—my usual morning offering.

"This was outside your door."

"Thanks."

"What's wrong?"

"I have a student who doesn't want to go to college in the fall."

"You think everyone should, huh?"

"Not necessarily. However, talented kids who get a real chance at a great school should at least try it. I'm just dismayed because one of my students chose to not go to school because of her boyfriend."

"You mean old Chastity, because she's in love with Jeremy Simpson?"

"Zak, you know I can't share a confidence with you."

"If it's Chastity, tell her that Jeremy is never going to marry her. In fact, after she said their souls were already married, he signed up for summer school. He's leaving for Sarah Lawrence the day after graduation."

"How do you know this?"

"Jeremy had to tell someone. He already told us that he banged her, after we warned him not to go for Sunday-school virgins. Now she thinks she's in love with him. He's too chicken to break up with her because he has to see her every day so he's just going to sneak out of town at sunset. You'd be doing Chastity a favor if you tell her she hosed herself, telling a guy like Jeremy that she loves him, for crissakes."

"I can't think of how I could do that gracefully."

"Maybe I should help. I could write her a secret letter. Do you think that's a good idea?"

"Of course not. The only message she needs is that she should make her own decisions about her future. It's not good to decide because of what someone else wants. Lord, we shouldn't be talking about this. What did you want, Zak? Can I help you?"

"No, I just wanted to leave that flower here before it got stepped on."

"Will you be in class this afternoon?"

"Class? Oh yeah, sure."

"I have a copy of your Berklee acceptance in my email. You said you didn't get it at home. Do you want me to print it for you?"

"Yeah, sure. Great."

Angelia poked her head in to ask if we were playing music tonight. Zak turned on like an incandescent hundred-watt bulb. "Oh man, yes! Jason has a new song. He showed it to me and I have this idea—but not for the house tonight. At the studio. I believe it needs a Hammond organ instead of drums. Do you think it will blow his mind?"

"Like Billy Preston and the Beatles?" Angelia said.

"Billy who?" Zak and I both said, just as the bell rang for class. Zak left us.

"Rosemary tells me you're doing email now," Angelia said, pointing to the screen behind me. "Is a cell phone just around the corner?"

"Never in this life. I did it to communicate with Andrew at Berklee about Zak. I just printed his acceptance letter."

"Want me to give you Jason's email address?"

"Unfortunately, I have it. He's sent me a host of mails with bad poetry. It's like that rose he sends every day. It's embarrassing. I'm not tempted to keep reading email, though. For some reason, his ex-wife feels compelled to send email to explain that Jason is a terrible person. Look at this one."

"What a venomous witch. This doesn't sound like Jason."

"She strikes me as unbalanced."

Angelia said, "Tell him about it, and ask him to make her stop."

"It's not his fault."

"Men are responsible for their ex's excesses. He should make her stop."

"I'm just not going to read it."

58
"You're Still Standing There"
Jason

WE FINISHED THE NIGHT with nothing new recorded that anyone would be happy with in the morning. Most everyone was pissed at me and went off to find Thai food. I took a cheese sandwich down to the basement and cruised the Internet to relax. My friend Chas is as much of an insomniac as I've become, so he and I traded instant messaging jokes and notes throughout the night.

Sebastian: What do you think most transformed American music in the twentieth century?

Chas1933: It's a toss-up between Rural Electrification and the railroads.

Sebastian: That's about the last answer I expected. Explain please.

Chas1933: The first let everyone hear a wide world of music on the radio, and the second let big bands and other acts tour every town in America. And abetted the migration of the blues to Chicago. The world came to people's doorstep, and everyone got to stir the melting pot of music that resulted.

Sebastian: OK, you convinced me. Rural Electrification also let my hillbilly ancestors plug in their guitars.

Chas had almost repaired my mood when Ephraim called me.

"I heard the rehearsal cuts from the last few days, Jason. Karl says that no one in the band wants his name on the album, yet it didn't seem to stop any of you from doing great work. This material needs you to finish it. You need to sign your name to it."

"You had no problem signing my name to your work on the last album, Ephraim."

"Because you left town and wouldn't speak to anyone. This is just a business proposal. I'm sure your attorney can show you your obligations for this album, so you and I won't discuss that. Let's focus. You need to be the named producer."

"Since I'm not a member of Stoneway anymore, you can do whatever you want, Ephraim."

"I can't produce her again if I want to keep peace in the house and stay professional in the workplace."

"You sleep with your client's wife. What's professional about that?"

"As I understood it then, and do still, you were done with Dominique by the time I met her."

"She was done with me. Though we were still married."

"You still are."

"Dominique keeps dragging it out."

"Because she wants you to apologize, Jason."

"For what?"

"You hurt her feelings."

"Hurt her feelings? I spent five effing days in jail because of her. Now she won't let me out of marriage jail because no offer ever satisfies her."

"You can make this good for both of you. I can get her to cooperate in the studio. Do the production. Make this a good album."

"Is this blackmail, Ephraim?"

"No, I'm considering every possible way to stop you from sabotaging your own career."

"It's not sabotage to want my music played the way I conceived it and performed by people I trust."

"It's definitely sabotage if you don't also figure out how to make money doing what you do. It's not possible for everyone, but it is possible for you, Jason. Work with me."

"We must be living in parallel universes, Ephraim. What does 'no' mean in your universe?"

"That I will have to get up tomorrow and work on yet another way to convince you."

※

Karl met me at Lowell's in the Pike Market, where you can see the ferry coming in; best food with a view downtown. We'd met there at seven in the morning since high school, when we had to pony up enough cash to split a plate of eggs. That morning I pointed to that irony in comparison to our current lives, but Karl was too ready to change the subject back to how fucked up my life is.

"You know what's comical?" Karl said. "You're a rock star who doesn't do drugs, hasn't had sex in a year, and his old fans hate him because the last album doesn't sound like rock-and-roll. Now that's damn funny. Maybe you can sell the options to your life's story as a situation comedy. Then you'd have to stop acting like your life is as much a tragedy as Hamlet's."

"Hamlet was sane until he foreswore doing the sweet thing with Ophelia. That's when he turned into a comic figure."

"Dang, Jason, trust you to have a uniquely contrarian viewpoint, even on Shakespeare."

"Think about it, Karl. One could posit that it wasn't his father's ghost but deprivation that put our buddy Hamlet over the edge."

His father's ghost. That was worth a laugh a minute. I changed the subject. "It reminds me of when Arlo thought there wouldn't be laugh tracks on TV anymore when we read in the paper that the inventor died."

"So is Arlo your stalker?"

"I can't prove it, and he's so disorganized, I don't know how he could pull it off. Maybe he gets Quentin Henderson to ghost-write his blog posts. Can you find a job for Arlo this summer? He needs to be employed, and I won't let him come with us as guitar tech or roadie or anything else."

"Perhaps Arlo can help Cynthia do your booking and publicity." Karl help up his cup to the waitperson, seeking a refill. "How much has she lined up for you so far that doesn't include Dominique? I mean besides the benefit you're playing this weekend. Oh, don't sulk. I'm married. Pouty looks mean nothing to me. Just more Seattle rain running down my neck."

"Maybe that's how I look every morning."

"Ephraim is right. You need a real manager planning ahead for you instead of a part-time attorney sweeping up behind you."

"I have come this far doing business myself."

"No, you haven't. Beau did every lick of your business work, until he was too sick to go on. Ephraim picked up half of it until you—"

"Does Ephraim pay you too, Karl? Every time I turn around, he has my balls in a nutcracker over yet another demand."

"Ian and I are your oldest friends, right? We both think—sit still and listen, OK? Separate out Ephraim and business from whatever the hell is going on in Dominique's mind. He knows the business, and he has your best interests at heart. What he proposes is not a different direction for your music. It's just business science, so that there's an actual direction to your decisions. You can't call your winter of discontent in Europe a career move. It was more like you put yourself in a corner for a timeout."

"I created a lot of new material with Ian last winter. We're giving it strength and body in rehearsal now. We'll make money from my timeout."

"You need to do exactly that. You want to sink money into your girlfriend's nonprofit rat-hole, which as your attorney I do not recommend. You need to pay for the next few years of timeouts and new directions. Ian needs an income-producing partner, not a petulant gambler."

"Petulant? Karl, what the hell?"

"Look, Ian has big bills to pay for years to come. Cynthia's brother's new care is not cheap. Keeping four grandparents on assisted living—how does he pay those bills for God-alone-knows how many years? He set a half-dozen cousins up in business. Yet he won't do studio work for others, because he's so loyal to you. Meanwhile you want to walk away from a record label that's begging to re-sign you. Everyone else is supposed to go diddle themselves while you reinvent your own private reality?"

"OK, I'm an effing asshole. You made your case. Where the hell do I find a business manager? I'm not getting an agent who'll talk me into living a life I don't want, just so he can take a huge percent of the money I make."

"I wish I could do it myself." Karl seemed wistful.

"Why can't you?"

"I'm married. I have a law practice. I have to be an adult."

"This grownup stuff bites a big one."

"Is it true you haven't had sex for a year?"

"I made love with a goddess a couple of weeks ago." I seemed wistful.

"But that girl won't sleep with you again?"

"She's a woman, not a girl, and she's still getting used to me being someone else. Why are you asking me?"

"I was wondering if I gave up law and became your manager, would I get more sex? Because if I quit law, my wife is bound to quit me. If she doesn't quit anyway, which she probably will."

"Karl, you're the great paragon of married bourgeois virtue."

"Except I think my wife hates me. She says I love my work more than I love her."

"Dominique used to say that to me, too. It was flat out true."

"Alas, it's also true for me. My wife thinks that work is just how you get money to buy things. The fact that she doesn't understand how important my work is just leaves me feeling lonely."

"Now that bites worse than being a grownup. Sleeping by someone and feeling lonely."

"Don't write any new songs about it, OK? I feel like you're a sneak thief, stealing scenes from my life. Speaking of sneaks, have you told your girlfriend who you are?"

"She refuses to talk about the past, and I'm not hiding much. She sees all of my everyday life, except for the recent crap that got public attention. That will go away soon enough, once people forget about me."

"What about your money, Jason?"

"She seems about as blind about money as she is about popular culture, except for funding her institute. Are you paying for this bill or am I?"

"Either way, you write the check in the end, because if I pay, it's a business expense. Or rather, Warren writes the check when he pays your bills. Here, I'll pay the bill. Don't leave a separate tip. You tip too much."

"The waitress is in a folk duo that plays house concerts and coffeehouses. She's financing her heart's work by pouring coffee and juggling plates of eggs and hash browns."

"Twenty percent is sufficient. You don't make enough coin to be the goddamn Musicians' Aid Society of Greater Seattle. Worry about Ian and Toby and whoever else you have riding your new band wagon."

59
"Get Rhythm"
Jason

LATE IN THE AFTERNOON, Ian and I took Zak to the gamelan shed and, as expected, it blew Zak's mind. As I'd planned with Paul Harris, we recorded the three hours we spent together, working with members of the gamelan. It's crude to say, but it felt like taping a boy while he learned to make love. As I watched Zak, ecstatic in percussive wonderland, it was as if you could see the fusing of his adolescent bones into a grown man's skeleton. While we'd been rehearsing all those long hours in the past few weeks, he had beaten his way out of his chrysalis and begun shaking his wings, getting ready to fly.

When Ian drove us back across town, I turned the conversation back to business.

"Zak, you should listen to Bob Wills and Hank Williams. We're going honky-tonkin' for the afternoon work. Now I need you in the morning sessions too."

"What about Johnnie?"

"He's playing in another band."

What I didn't say: that Johnnie and I had a long talk that morning about how it wasn't working, though he already knew it and started the conversation himself by saying he wanted to quit. Johnnie was good—four years ago, I would have kept him—but he's not the percussion genius Zak is, who's spoiling me with his excitement. I'd already found Johnnie a gig in another band, having never promised anything more than a couple of weeks in the studio. He knew it himself, but it bummed me, because the band was going exciting new places and Johnnie didn't have what it would take to be invited along. It wasn't as bad as saying, "I found a new lover"; it was worse: you're good, but I choose Zak.

Zak, however, said, "I don't think I can do mornings. My afternoon teachers, like Miss Neville, have been letting me slide, but I don't think my morning teachers will ignore when I skip. I can't do it until mid-June."

"We have to be done by the second of June. I expect to be back on the road soon after."

Zak looked so glum that I realized what a total effing jerk I am.

"Oh geez, Zak. I'm sorry. I did not mean this to be an ultimatum."

"No, it's fine. I'll be there. It is not like I might miss anything at school. What time do you start?"

"Eight," I said. "You'll find me in the studio by seven-thirty."

"OK. I have to take the bus across town. But I'll be there."

"I need you in the morning because I'm trying something that hasn't been done before, so I need a virgin."

"I'm not a virgin," Zak said. Adamant.

"In the recording studio, dummy. Can I ask you a couple of questions?"

"Shoot."

"Why didn't you tell me about the piano?"

Zak shrugged as if it were an irrelevant question: why didn't you tell me about your opposable thumb? "The piano is just another percussion instrument. I'm planning a Hammond B3 surprise for you for the reworked version of 'White City Blues.'"

"Frickin' hell, Zak. You could give me a heart attack with any more of your surprises."

"Next question?"

"How much do you work each day?"

"At least twelve hours. I have to get up by five-thirty though, to get all the practice that I want. School eats too much of the day." He was biting his thumb in agitation. "I could quit school. I turn eighteen next week. What happens if I quit school?"

"Shoot, you're asking me? Talk it over with your folks."

"We've been 'talking it over' all year, though the only talking is them screaming at me about ruining my life. They want me to go to college."

"Is that what you want to do?"

"No, I want to work full time in a band—or two bands, or three, if I have to. I don't know what two more months of high school gets me."

"I think you should ask Susi. She knows about stuff like school."

"Then I might as well quit. She told me yesterday that you should never decide the future because of what someone else wants you to do."

It was my job to apply caution, but I was the last person to know what that might be. Before I could come up with some lame-ass admonishment, Zak asked the hard question.

"Are you taking the band on the road with you? Or going alone?"

From his place in the driver's seat, Ian glanced over at me for what seemed like too long while we barreled up I-5 at sixty-five miles an hour.

"I haven't got any gigs wired for the new band yet," I said. "Except the benefit that we're playing this weekend. I'm behind with that effort. So I can't ask you to tie up your time, waiting for me to find us work."

As Ian turned his attention back to the road, the grinding of his jaw pulled tension lines across his whole shaved head.

Yeah, the Musicians' Aid Society. That's me. Launch your career with me. See if you can make enough spare change gigging for me to get your teeth cleaned and your rent paid for a month. When we run low on cash, I'll share the extra guitar picks that have the band's URL printed on them.

The sole solution I could see was for me to work harder.

This band was getting to be too good not to be heard.

60
"All the Right Reasons"
Jason

"Where is everyone?"

Susi came late, so late that I thought I'd expire from dread. I'd worked myself into a racehorse lather of anxiety combined with an adrenalin rush of hope, so that I had to strip off one shirt and settle for a sleeveless t-shirt in order to pretend to be cool and calm when she arrived. My hands were as damp as Arlo's, and I washed them a half dozen times, grateful that Ian wasn't around to harangue me for being the obsessive jerk that I am. When she came, I could hardly look at her, knowing she'd see the fear in my eyes.

"Everyone had an excuse for taking the night off," I said. If they didn't have an excuse to begin with, I had assigned one to each of them. "It's just us rehearsing new songs tonight. Do you mind?"

"No," she said, stepping back as if I were the Big Bad Wolf instead of the patient Little Prince.

I took a breath and went ahead, as if I were brave.

"Susi, I want you to listen to something."

"More of your music?"

"No, some female vocalists. I burned this CD for you today. I still can't understand how you missed the whole last half of the twentieth century."

"I was busy doing other things."

My parents' whole generation got the idea from rock music that you could beg for love and maybe get it, which must have bred a phalanx of stalkers incapable of believing that no means no. I was hoping I hadn't inherited it, because I was about to beg her for even more than love.

"Never mind. Please just listen, Susi."

I played each song without comment. We listened to Janis giving away another piece of her heart, Lucinda changing the locks on her door, Emmylou saying goodbye on *Wrecking Ball*. By the time Marianne Faithfull was begging to hear it said in broken English, Susi held up her hand, distressed. She started to speak a couple of times and stopped. She fidgeted and twisted her hands, then switched off the music.

"The last one is too painful to bear, Jason."

"Do you have any patience left? I want you to hear some of my music."

"Like what we've been working on? That would be a consolation after hearing this."

"No. This is different. Ian and the others are working with me on this new piece. Here are the lyrics."

I couldn't be more obvious about what I was asking her. I couldn't expose my soul in a more naked way than this, playing an unfinished piece of music for her, when I wanted her to take me for what I am.

When the music ended, and after a roar of silence for a long moment, she said, "You want me to sing this."

"Please consider it."

She stared at the lyrics without looking at me.

Still nervous, I spoke to fill the silence. "This feels like asking someone to try an unusual sexual practice. I'm sorry. I put you on the spot."

"No, I'm not afraid of the challenge. I just don't know how to listen to this music. Can I keep those songs on the other disc? I need to understand better what you want."

"Will you try to sing this? Can we start now?" I couldn't keep either the eagerness or the anxiety from my voice.

"Yes, but could you put your shirt on, please? I'm not used to rehearsing with men clothed in their underwear."

61

"Flesh and Blood"
Susi

IT TAKES ME A MOMENT each night to force myself to not look at that patch of hair he left on his chin. I'm not so divorced from the modern world that I don't know it's in style, but on Jason it seems such a startling declaration. Secondary sex characteristics advertising the presence of that much testosterone interfered with my ability to breathe. When I forced myself to look past that, my mind wandered through a series of speculations about what had happened to the well-groomed man I had first met, who often forgot to shave and now appeared in his undershirt. Then I mastered myself and listened to what he was saying, instead of staring at his chin, trying not to look farther down, at the hair escaping from the top of his t-shirt, trying not to remember the well-defined, taut muscles across his chest and shoulders, along his forearms.

The first voice he forced on me was too deep for me to emulate, others were too southern, and the last singer was in more pain than I could bear to be reminded of. Although I was getting some idea of what he wanted from me, I couldn't render it by emulating any of the samples on that CD.

"Play your music again, Jason. I want to hear the other instruments."

I followed along with the written lyrics this time, trying to hear the empty places that still remained between the different instruments, no longer as distracted as I had been by how he looked in a sleeveless t-shirt, though he hadn't buttoned up his shirt, and he rolled back the cuffs, drawing even more attention to the hair on his arms.

"Again."

This time I sang the words as he'd written them, in the way I thought he wanted a human voice to thread its way among the other instruments' voices.

"Again, please."

He hadn't made any move to correct me, or betrayed any response in his expression, but he always critiqued or corrected when he was unsatisfied, so I believed we were making progress toward what he wanted. As the instruments died away on my third attempt, I hung onto the final A note so it died away like twilight taking forever to fade in St. Petersburg.

He sat with his face in his hands. I wanted to provoke a response, to gauge his reaction, to see if I was giving what he wanted.

"The first time I had to sing in Croatian was easier than this."

He grasped my wrist and kissed my fingers, and then snatched his hand away again, picking up his guitar.

"It will never be a hit. Hits have to be in a major key. We will likely never make a dime off it." He laughed in a rueful sort of way.

"There is more to be had from music than money."

He looked up. "I have to believe that's true. Can we record you this time? Do you want to rehearse more?"

"If you're happy with it, I can repeat what we just did."

"Then let's go."

Perhaps because of my previous work experiences and the last few weeks spent rehearsing with him, whenever I found what he wanted, I could return it to him again a second or third or fourth time as faithfully as he needed. So without the other musicians, he didn't demand repeated attempts while we taped.

"Another go?" I asked.

"That's fine. That is more than fine. Susi, do you have any idea how good you are?"

"So we don't have to do it over and over? Are there other songs we can work on? Or is that the only one I get to sing tonight?"

He had two other songs. One was close in form to the Anglo-Celtic ballads we first played together, with a middle part that churned up passion, and drove to an ending that resembled the pyric release of great opera.

"It's pretentious," he said. It was easy to sing, and we spent no more than an hour making it sound the way he wanted.

The second began like a mountain song—a sort of "Pretty Saro" mourning hymn—but he had planned this long instrumental interlude, and then the song went off in another direction, more like the raging part of deep mourning, where you hate the loved one for ever existing since the result is to be left in so much pain. I said as much, and he nodded.

"My uncle Beau died last year. This is for him."

"You should use the steel guitar for the middle part, Jason. And you need the voice to come back in sooner."

"I don't hear that. The guitar and mandolin need to finish what they have to say."

"If you do it that way, they finish too much of the story. The voice at the end just sounds like a tantrum howling in the night. An after-thought."

"OK. We will do it with just the guitar. Show me what you mean, Susi."

It took two hours to achieve something we were both happy with, pausing in the middle so that Jason could take notes on how he would change the instrumentation in the middle part. Toward the end, when we were both nodding that we had what we wanted, I felt the beginning of that place, where the music in your chest, at your solar plexus, in your head, even in your nose, is in complete harmony—with what? The music of the spheres? With some vibration that you can feel if you exhaust all the usual, human ways to breathe, like a runner getting a second wind. I wanted to go on. I would beg and plead for it, but before I could speak after the end of our final recording, Jason said, "Let's do the first one again, but just you and me, guitar and voice."

He turned on the tape, and we breathed together through that twenty-first century paean to joy that transcends loneliness and loss.

When I could speak again after a few moments of silence, I said, "That final A left me with a twilight blue behind the bridge of my nose, where you can't tell the difference between blue and grey and yellow."

I was standing too close to him and uttering complete nonsense, as if I had hyperventilated myself into hysteria.

He set the guitar on its stand in that methodical way he handles his instruments, and then took my hand in his, tracing the lifeline in my palm.

"Oh god, it's two a.m. I'll be late for work yet again. I have to go."

"Don't go. Please stay, Susi. If you don't want sex, all right. But how can you go after this? How can you not think we belong together?"

He stood so close that "not think" was all I was capable of. His shirt was damp—I suppose mine was, too—from our exertions. I could smell everything I'd been avoiding. Clean sweat. The soap and starch in his now-wilting shirt. Whatever it was that caught in the small hairs across his sternum together with the sensation in my nose that threatened to lure me into hell-fire. He spoke in my ear.

"When I close my eyes, I still see all the colors and the shape and form of your voice. It vibrates on my fingertips like the strings of my guitar."

He touched me, putting his fingers on the side of my face where it tickles, and I couldn't speak to stop him. He turned my face up and kissed me in a rather chaste way, and I know it was me who opened my mouth and responded as if to devour him. Then I managed to stop myself.

"Please keep your distance." I pushed away from him. "You are doing everything to confuse and distract me."

"What? I'm not."

"You have all this hair on your body."

Oh god, I said it out loud.

62
"Go Slow Down"
Jason

SHE STARED AT MY WRIST, and I turned my hand over, trying to see what it was that offended her.

"What can I do about that? Take it all off like a swimmer who—"

Yikes, she had nudged herself so close to me that I could feel her pulse, which felt like a frightened cat. I sat down and pulled her along with me, half holding her on my knee like you do a child. For everything she said about keeping my distance, she didn't resist.

"Susi, I think it's time we tell each other our secrets."

"No. I don't want to hear yours. I don't want to tell mine."

"I think you're punishing me for something your ex did."

"No, I did it myself. I let sex blind me, when that was all there was in the relationship."

"Between us there's so much more than sex. For one, there's music. Or is my ego as big as the moon? Two weeks ago you sang my music for the first time, but things changed tonight, so it's our music now, not just mine."

She dropped her head against my chest. I couldn't tell whether it was surrender or emotion or simple exhaustion from how hard we pushed ourselves working. The sole emotion I had in reserve was the day's last dregs of self-will, the energy I use to propel myself through life. I picked her up and carried her down to my room, moving as gracefully as I could. The most gallant part of the maneuver came in managing not to break her head on the door frame or lose my footing on the steep stairs. I laid her down on my bed and pulled the coverlet over her, then curled up beside her, with one arm as her pillow and the other wrapped around her waist, holding her close to me, feeling her heart beating far too hard. I whispered into her hair.

"I don't need consummation as much as I need comfort. Please let me put my arms around you just for that."

Burrowing up against me, she nestled her head into the crook of my arm, so that I could smell the essence of her and feel her lithe body relax under my hand, until her breathing became even and her heart quit thundering and she fell asleep, lightening in my arms as she did.

Mentally I wanted only comfort. The rest of me wouldn't cooperate. By four in the morning, I'd spent a couple of hours pondering whether I'd most like to murder her ex or Mr. Levi who, if he'd spent two hours in a pair of his jeans with an unrelenting erection, might have modified his design. Or perhaps that's why adolescent boys prefer their jeans four sizes too big; they learned a lesson the rest of us with unfulfilling lovers still have to master. I eased my arm out from under her so as to not disturb her, and then cast off the garment of torture and crawled between the sheets, making myself want nothing more than to watch her sleep.

She had wakened, and grey eyes regarded me under that look of perpetual surprise her eyebrows framed. She smiled at me the way she first did weeks before, the smile she gave more freely to others than to me.

"I have to get to work on time today," she murmured.

I turned over and buried myself under the covers, trying not to show my dismay, trying not to call out, 'What about me?' like a blooming idiot. Other men knew how to turn situations like this to their advantage. Where had I missed the lessons everyone else got? It had to have been a day when I cut Health-Ed class to finish my calculus homework.

Then I felt her slight weight on the bed again and her hand on my arm—where all that offending hair grows—and she curled around my body as I had done with her earlier, but I could feel even through my t-shirt that she was naked, and she put her hand between my thighs instead of around my waist. Everything I had done to ease my discomfort was canceled, and she took matters firmly in hand.

"No teasing," I breathed. "No stopping in the middle and making me go home."

"We're at your house."

"Still. Don't stop, Susi."

"I can't anymore."

The next part I won't post on even the most anonymous blog (I can't post the previous part either, since it doesn't reflect well on my prowess as a lover that, after two hours in bed with the woman I love, all I had achieved was a great deal of discomfort), but she ducked her head under the covers and tended to the part that her hand couldn't attend to while stroking so confidently. In some unfamiliar but artful gesture—for I had no previous experience with her commandeering my body and overruling any choices I might make—she had turned me and thrown off the oppressive weight of the blankets, exposing me so that one hand tenderly cupped and tugged at my balls, while the other grasped the base of my cock as she tasted and tickled the head, tracing the curves and edges with her tongue and lips, and pressing the hard tip of her tongue into the slit.

"Susi—"

"Hmm?" Her hum threatened to send me into delirium, as she stretched the skin around my scrotum more tightly, holding my balls and my life in her palm.

Then, after she pulled it all so tight there was no room to throb, she demonstrated open-throated production of sound. Except I was the only one singing.

"Susi, stop," I whispered. "You'll make me come." I urged her head up, and she looked at me, questioning, blinking.

"So? You can do that more than once in a night."

Then she had both hands working my shaft while holding my balls in her mouth and instead of humming, she moaned, while having doubled herself up to mash the wetness of her vulva against my knee. When there was no possibility for me to hold back any longer, she must have felt it too, for in a heartbeat she had her mouth off my balls and pressed hard with her thumb against the base of my cock while she buried the length of it deep in her throat.

All right, yes, I held her head down, but it was an involuntary reflex, since my hands had become entranced with stroking and pulling her boyish hair. She could have stopped, but she didn't until she made me let go.

My fingers stayed trussed in her hair, even after she let me be and rested her head on my belly, her hand now satisfying itself by twirling in the hair there, making it tickle, making me shiver.

"Oh geez." My brain found itself able to do the work it is supposed to. "We're supposed to use a condom for that too."

"Why? I can't get pregnant from swallowing."

"STD protection."

"Where would either of us get a sexually transmitted disease? I haven't been near anyone since the last time the doctors worked over every cell of my body."

"You do it to protect yourself, Susi."

"Why would I need to protect myself from you? Cynthia said—"

"Cynthia said what?" I flipped her over and pinned her with my knees. "Why are you talking to Cynthia about me?"

"She and Ian are on a crusade to convince me to be in love with you. I think they want their basement back."

"What did Cynthia say?"

"That you haven't been with anyone since you found out your wife was unfaithful. That instead of being broken hearted, you just went to a doctor. She wanted to make sure I didn't think you were unsafe."

"Cynthia doesn't know everything I do."

"Doesn't she?"

"Oh geez, I have such good friends. What does she say to make you be in love with me?"

"That you aren't as much of an asshole as some men."

She wiggled away from under me and tried to get out of bed.

"Where are you going?" I pulled her inelegantly back to me.

"For mouthwash. I read that most men are fastidious about not tasting themselves, and you are more fastidious than most men."

"Not about that. It goes with being less of an asshole than at least some other men."

"That is so romantic. Take off your t-shirt so I can see your body."

We tried romantic kisses then, this time in utter silence, with no ravishing Puccini opera or humping rock music playing in the background, just those sounds almost beyond the range of human hearing—of breath across the hairs on the back of your hand, or under the soft skin at the base of your earlobe, or the rasp of early-morning beard across a lily-smooth belly. With such exquisite pleasure, I couldn't believe it when my brain began interfering, hoping against hope that she could tell how I feel from how I kiss her fingers. That my lips touching the tiny scars on her lips revealed existential mysteries. That my eyelashes fluttering against her small breasts reassured her that pain now lay only in the past and that we could rise from this destroyed bed as partners. My sentimental brain won out over animal instinct just before she again took me in hand, coaxing me more erect and guiding me toward her innermost secrets. I'd like to have strangled both reason and emotion, but they won out and my tongue spoke, even as my body wanted to do nothing more than sigh and bury itself deep inside her.

"Susi, I'm too far gone to do this if you aren't in love with me. I can't just fuck you. If that's all you want, you have to at least lie and make me think you love me."

"I do." Her voice broke, which broke the other half of my heart. I wanted her to mean it, so I shouldn't have invited her to lie.

"Yet not so much that you can say it out loud? What kind of plausible lie do you offer as proof?"

"I'm learning to sing the way you want me to."

At this point, she made that mysterious move again, where she overruled choice and forced me to do what I wanted to. With a condom.

I'm saving myself for marriage.

63

"Brilliant Disguise"
Jason

BEING THE SUPERIOR-TO-SOME-ASSHOLES guy that I am, I did not snivel, whine, or beg when she had to go to work. I got up and went to work myself. Besides, there's no coffee in Ian's house before nine. Whereas at the studio, even though it was only seven-thirty, Martha had hot coffee, fruit, protein bars, and hard-boiled eggs.

While I ate breakfast, I made Martha listen to the recording Susi and I had made the night before. "Just the last two songs," I said, realizing in the middle of the second that it would take some getting used to, letting others hear these sounds. If I succeeded in convincing Susi to sing live with me, we'd have to make this music in front of other people. I buried myself in email, pretending I wasn't watching Martha's reaction.

She didn't respond when I kept looking over. When the music ended, she sat back down at her own laptop to finish whatever business I had interrupted. The third time I encountered her eyes, she bent her head over a pad of paper with her pen. Then she held up the paper: 9.5.

"The point-five represents my unfamiliarity with the form. However, you don't need reassurance. You know it's good. By the way, Zak called at seven and said he won't be here until eight-thirty."

I settled down to work. We had hit on something the night before. I started singing an old Hank Williams piece and then transmuted it to something of my father's, to show Susi where the song was going. It reminded me of a piece I'd read in a thesis or lecture I borrowed from Susi's house. I found the lecture notes and copied a portion of the text into email I was sending to my select little group of Americana musicology friends, thinking to prove this deeper line about Hank Williams' influences on the Lost Sons. Also, I was thinking about the fox and the Little Prince, and accidentally clicked Send before typing the attribution for the quote I used.

My little fox sat in the sun as I crept closer and closer, and then —what? The fox turned out to be a friendly she-wolf? Where else could I go with the analogy that would make compelling lyrics? Chinese medieval poets speak of she-foxes that hide in the tall grass, waiting to suck a man's soul dry, like succubae. Definitely not those little foxes in this case. Though after thinking about onomatopoeia and the word succubus, I had to stop remembering the previous night to keep from embarrassing myself.

Before I could pull myself together to start new email to attribute the quote in the last email I sent, the instant messenger light popped on.

Chas1933: What city are you in?

Sebastian: Seattle.

Chas1933: I think that's my library you're browsing. Are you sleeping with my daughter?

What can one say in such a situation—besides 'oh shit'? I pondered that and answered, as truthfully as possible.

Sebastian: Not at this moment, sir.

Chas1933: The last one was a fool. I've been hoping it wouldn't be a pattern.

Flipping to the book plate at the front of the text, I understood that my friend Chas1933@jugum.com was Charles Neville—not the saxophone player from New Orleans, but a local music professor who wrote multiple treatises on the effect of Anglo-Celtic ballads on the music of Appalachia and the Acadia musical influences on early jazz and rock. I had embarrassed myself before a scholar I admire. Just like starting on the wrong foot with his daughter by being the incorrect Jason.

Sebastian: She has the most beautiful voice in the world.

As if blurting it aloud, I clicked Send, with no option for clicking Retrieve and therefore breaking a promise, telling the only secret about Susi that I knew and which she had made me promise to not disclose.

Chas1933: She's singing?!?

Sebastian: I wasn't supposed to tell. She's shy about it, but it's a travesty the world doesn't know her. I'd love to get her in front of an audience.

Chas1933: You can try, I suppose. Just don't let her get hurt doing it.

I took that as a mission. Zak and Ian arrived at the studio together, so I had to sign off and plug in. It was noon before I thought to wonder how someone could get hurt singing.

Or to realize that I had given my father's papers to my lover's father.

64
"Are You Really Going Out with Him?"
Susi

"THERE'S YOUR BOYFRIEND."

Randolph laid an aged, dusty file on my desk, shaking me into complete wakefulness.

Jason Taylor.

"I know." I closed my email, since it contained only bad poetry and more fictitious screeds from Dominique about how Jason stole songs and abused women.

Randolph said, "I found out from the students. They've been talking about it ever since your little fundraiser. How could you put an imposter in front of the trustees? In front of my grandparents?"

"I didn't know it. There was a mix up. Neither of us understood at the time."

"How long were you going to let the confusion go on?"

"It doesn't matter at this point, does it, Randolph?"

"Are you sleeping with him?"

"What does that have to do with anything?"

"Then you are? I thought all you cared about was teaching. For God's sake, Susi, he never even graduated from high school."

Randolph stalked out, leaving the folder on my desk. I let it sit for a long time before yielding to temptation.

The transcript stopped one quarter short of graduation. Fantastic marks in the arts and math, A-minuses in science and history. A "B" in one subject every term, usually the subject that any other student would use to skate through in order to carry enough credits: Photography, Household Economy, Health Education, Ceramics.

Then there were the letters, the ones teachers write to help students get into college. I'd spent November, December, and January writing the same kinds of letters, praising the student's talents and accomplishments, making weaknesses sound like assets. In Jason's recommendations: *Brilliant creative mind, which he chooses to apply with great force of will. Popular with classmates in spite of a tendency to be withdrawn at times. Dynamic presence in the classroom when he chooses to engage.*

I found the letter that Paul Harris wrote buried amongst the others.

> He came to us with strong recommendations from his previous teachers, but as an emancipated minor, which is usually a sign that the legal guardian has elected to put the child on the streets to live by his own wits. When he came, Jason was still recovering from his mother's death, which he responded to by burying himself in music.
>
> In spite of being abandoned by the adults in his family, Jason follows the iron-bound guidance of an inner adult that seems to serve him well, though perhaps it leads him to drive himself harder than a youth should be allowed to work. He will succeed in any music program that allows him to exercise his natural assets. He will not, however, submit to any teacher who applies lessons as a task master. But he makes a noble, courageous, and gracious sparring partner for any teacher who chooses to engage him as an equal.

Alongside these were acceptances: Cornish, Berklee, the Curtis Institute. A request from Juilliard for one more interview. Another letter that was sort of a rejection: a note that said, "I no longer attend Prescott," in a handwriting I now recognized as well as my own. Finally, a copy of a bitter letter that Hector Henderson had sent to Jason's grandfather, complaining that Jason's failure to participate in the state-wide contest for jazz ensembles had cost the school the championship. Bitterness from the same teacher who wrote recommendations that praised Jason as the leader and key talent who led the jazz ensemble in his junior year to a state championship and then on to respectable recognition at the national level.

> He let the band and the school down just to play rock-and-roll in Europe.

I'm afraid to say this aloud. I told someone I loved him when perhaps the reality is that I have no business being with him. I wasn't lying when I said it, but there were such strong influences—my chest and head filled with his music, the blandishments he uses while begging me to let down my guard, those fingers stroking his guitar. Singing is clouding my judgment.

Or something else is happening. Jason touches my lips after we sing and I fall into a fugue state, from which I cannot rouse myself until considerable time and physical distance separates us. Even now, hours later, I can feel his fingers on my lips while my whole body throbs, and the sensation threatens to pull me back into that state, so that I can't listen to my own logic or heed internal warnings that tell me this might be dangerous.

As much as I needed to talk about it with someone, he's become friends with Angelia, so I can't talk to her. I thought about calling my brother Steven, but he had discounted my concerns when I tried to talk to him about the same issues in relation to Logan: "Logan wasn't ever worthy of you. It just took that accident for you to see what everyone else knew. He wasn't on the same level as you for talent, brains, or goodness."

Maybe I don't want to talk to Steven, because I don't want to hear the same thing about Jason. Maybe I don't want to look at the same problems all over again.

Then again, perhaps it's not true this time. Before, when I thought Jason was Angelia's cousin, I thought that this man was my equal. He is beyond merely smart. He's kind and aware of others around him. Yet he's not the whiz-kid Jason Ferran. He's Jason Taylor, the high school drop-out who plays in bar bands. Who doesn't own a car or have a place to live.

Yet he has these warm, intelligent friends who care a great deal for him. He has a beautiful voice and plays his instrument with the same skill that Orpheus must have had. He's considerate. I love singing with him—it feels as satisfying as great sex, though we have had more practice singing than we've had with the other.

Still, he's a pop musician who never graduated from high school. Who in the world could be so foolish as to not take the fantastic opportunities that going to a school like Berklee would allow? Why choose to drop out of high school?

I find myself attempting to smother reprehensible feelings, because this makes me aware of my own bias, as much as I hated feeling like an outsider myself when I was at school. What in the world does a college degree prove, for that matter? Is it like kennel papers for a dog? Does it make for a better dog? Look at Randolph, who has an Ivy League degree, but didn't inherit even a modicum of noblesse oblige, much less a sensible view of life.

When I was with Logan, I worked to ignore the inequality between us, feeling guilty for my snobbishness. However, leaving school was yet another sign of Logan's lack of ambition and his immaturity. My attempt to ignore the inequality was in fact an act of condescension on my part. Since the accident, people who can still exercise their talent in the world condescend to me. It's actually pity, and there is nothing I hate worse.

Early in the morning, a tectonic shift brought us into a unison that both Jason and I seemed to be reaching for. Still, what if I am repeating the same error as with Logan, surrendering for the sake of sex to a relationship of unequal passions and unequal ambitions? What if I begin by believing I'm in love and once again have to fight back a reprehensible condescension?

Fundamentally, it shouldn't matter to me whether Jason graduated from high school. He is widely read, and nothing about him would make one think of the stereotypical drop-out in need of remedial education. It shouldn't matter to me.

However, it made me think of Logan, so it did matter.

65
"Halo Round the Moon"
Jason

ON FRIDAY NIGHTS THE band doesn't rehearse, after being in each other's armpits the rest of the week. When I went to Susi's house Friday night, after closing the studio, I could feel that she had disappeared again as soon as I kissed her hello. Looking over her shoulder, I shouldn't have been surprised to find the entire band, minus Zak, filling her living room and kitchen. Who better for her to hide behind?

"Who are you and what have you done with the woman I love?" I whispered into her hair, but everyone crowded around before she could answer. Just the way she wanted it.

She served up green curry with string beans, lover's eggplant with red pepper chips to burn our mouths, a soothing sort of fried wonton with shiitake mushrooms and water chestnuts, and swimming angel—spinach and tofu in peanut sauce, though I think Susi uses real angels. Even Ian didn't complain about the lack of animal protein, and the food was comforting, turning most everyone into drowsy, happy beasts.

Except me. I didn't get to sit by Susi. Susi didn't talk to me. Or touch me. Everyone else got to talk to Susi, so that talking and the tinkling of the table service made another kind of music. Except for me, the room was full of happy, peaceful people. It wasn't just the food, either. She had done just about everything possible in the past weeks to make every last member of the band fall in love with her. It wasn't the obvious things that I'd fallen in love with: her warmth, intelligence, kindness. The rusty angel voice. She had made some kind of personal connection with each and every one of them: fishing, teaching, baseball, movies. Cynthia had even shown Susi the effing woodshop where she spends her time when Ian drives her crazy. No one else gets to go into her woodshop, only Susi. Susi turned them into happy beasts every night with whatever she made for us to eat on break, but what brought everyone to heel was the music. Not just the tone and color and power of her voice, but that she worked her small, charming ass off with us every night. Without complaint or distraction or needing to dominate or debate.

Glinda, the good Witch of the North, who made them all forget how Jason had led them into the wilderness with the Wicked Witch of the West, was in the kitchen finishing off bowls of crème broulee with Sonny's help and a soldering torch. While they worked, Cynthia and Angelia talked about teaching. The other gentlemen of the band would have contributed to the conversation if they hadn't stuffed themselves half way to a coma on Susi's food. I listened, wanting Susi to turn and speak to me, look at me, move toward me. All night, she drifted further and further away.

Angelia said, "Yeah, it's true, we teach rich kids, plus a handful of scholarship kids who are fishes out of water like we were at Juilliard. Where we teach, several of the parents make it clear that we are servants and they are our masters."

Cynthia said, "How do you put up with that?"

"We ignore it and pay attention to the kids. It's Susi who hit on the idea of teaching ballads as the roots of rock, and it clicked with the kids. She talked the curriculum committee into letting her teach her material as double credit: literature and music. She spent hours in meetings, showing how it works when you start with "Barbry Ellen" as the text, and trace it from Britain to Appalachia, and trace Cajun zydeco back to Acadia and then all the way to Bretonne fisher villages in France."

"I figured that out on my own," Ian said. "I didn't need to go to a fancy high school to do it."

"You figured it out—almost—some time last year," Toby said.

"I want to take it further," Angelia said. "Most kids playing music don't see the string that ties them to the crusaders who carried the oud from the Levant to Europe, so it could evolved into the violin and guitar."

Susi said from the kitchen, "The folksinger girls in my class teach themselves to sing from CDs. How many of them will get a chance to try a range of vocal styles, or learn how to take care of their voices, or how to project without injury?"

Angelia said, "What if we find the next Mark O'Connor or Doug Sahm, and expose them to new influences and the ideas and techniques for how to master skills? Suppose we talk them into staying in school, which I've found is the biggest challenge with talented kids.

"Yes, it is," Ian said. "Shoot, what more painful place in the world is there besides high school? Oh yeah, jail. That's the other worst place."

"No offense, but you and Susi are both kidding yourselves," Toby said. "Arts funding has disappeared since 9-11. Because money is disappearing for music education everywhere, no one will pay you to do this."

"I disagree," Susi said gently. "I believe we can get enough to do one summer, to prove the worth of the idea. Then the funding base will grow."

Cynthia said, "You need more than just the rich bitches who want to fund impoverished violinists at Juilliard. You need to find some rich rock-and-roll bitches who wanted to help kids be great musicians."

Sonny and Susi finished setting the dessert aflame and carried the bowls to people. I got mine from Sonny. As everyone was reduced to humming and sighing over scorched sweet cream, Cynthia came to the kitchen to pour coffee, where I sat on a bar stool away from the others. Since Susi didn't want to sit by me.

Cynthia leaned on the counter, her head close to mine and her voice low as she spoke.

"Jason, have you been on the Internet today?"

"I'm trying to stop. I need the Internet surfer's equivalent of Antabuse."

"Your pseudo-brother is getting weird. He's posting more frequently, boasting wildly. It's like he's challenging you over something."

"It's just Arlo. He is ticked at me because I won't let him play roadie for us this summer." I spooned my warm pudding while we talked.

"It's not Arlo. He can't spell, and your stalker brother can."

"Maybe he uses a spellchecker."

"Forget Arlo. He's harmless. Your stalker isn't. We had the house wired today with a security alarm. Should have done it long ago."

"I'm paying friends of Sonny's to watch the house."

"You are shitting me. Why didn't you tell me?" Cynthia didn't seem as furious with me as she might have been in other circumstances.

"Does it matter?"

"I should pull the blinds upstairs. The guys in the warehouses across the alley are used to it, but I don't like flashing strangers." She licked the last of crème broulee from her spoon. "Tell Susi to get her house wired, too."

"She already has an alarm."

Toby's voice rose above the hum in the room. "I still don't get who plays which venues, Jason. Do you want me at all three?"

As I answered, I saw the surprise on Susi's face and began to fear that I hadn't planned this appropriately.

"Zak and Sonny can skip the folk scene at the museum. The rest of you need to be there. Everyone has to do the landmines benefit. We are on at seven—and you have to be in dinner jackets. Martha will have them for you when you get there. Angelia can skip the Showbox, but I hope she'll want to play. Everyone else should be there."

"What are you talking about?" Susi said.

"We're playing several benefit gigs tomorrow."

"I'm not invited?" She frowned.

"You said you didn't want people to know you were singing. These are public events."

She took a step toward me, folding her arms, ready for battle, which warmed my heart in ways you can't imagine. I'd rather she came at me straight on than fold her tent and slink off, as she seemed to be doing all evening.

"You didn't ask me, Jason. Don't I get a choice?"

"I thought you had already stated your choice."

"What if I changed my mind?"

"You are scared to be alone with me," I said, hoping the others didn't hear. She stood so close that I could touch her hair. But I didn't. "And you're scared to sing in public with us."

"That is not true."

"We don't know that. You'll change your mind again and run away. The same as you keep running away from me."

"I haven't run away."

"Do you deny that you're avoiding me?"

"I want to perform with everyone else. Let me sing with the band."

"OK, but first you have to play a morning gig with me to prove you won't fold on the entire band."

"Where?"

"Busking in the Market. Singing mountain songs. Nine o'clock."

"I'll be there."

"And I'll enjoy the pleasure of your company, if you choose to come."

I gathered my pack from where I stash it when I'm at her house.

"Where are you going?"

"Home. Maybe I'll see you in the morning."

"Why are you leaving?"

"Susi, you've been avoiding me all night. 'Fear of intimacy' is your middle name. I'm trying to be nice and not push you, since I hope you'll come back again. Let's worry about your fear of performing for now."

"I'm not afraid. Don't you want to—"

"You know what I want, Susi. If I stay any longer, I'll be on my knees, begging, in front of the audience you invited to protect you. Leaving is the only way I can preserve what little dignity I have left."

I kissed her good-night, the way I'd kiss that cousin I don't have.

66
"Stumbling through the Dark"
Susi

EVERYONE SNEAKED A LOOK at me when Jason left, which caused me to stand more erect. I don't have anything to be ashamed of. I went to the kitchen to make more coffee, where Cynthia was pouring the dregs into her cup.

"'Many fish'll bite if you got good bait,'" she said, quoting from the fishing song Ian had taught me.

"Am I supposed to satisfy your curiosity so everyone can gossip about it later?"

"You know how much the band gossips, Susi. Close to zero, I believe."

"It isn't anyone's business whether I sleep with Jason." I tried saying it to see how much bravado I had left.

"Most of us don't care whether you sleep with him—though it makes it a hell of a lot easier to be around him—as much as we care whether you'll stay with the band."

"As long as I'm invited, I'll come to rehearsal—at least, whenever my schedule allows."

"I believe that Jason's point was that there's rehearsal, and then there's the real world. You have to make a choice, Susi."

"I've made my choice. I choose to be a teacher. I'm not a performer."

"You also seem to believe that your choices only affect you. Nothing matters outside the little paradise you created in this charming cottage."

Cynthia doesn't know about subtlety. We stopped speaking at that point in the evening. Angelia and Toby couldn't be talked into staying late, which was no surprise, and at midnight Cynthia and Ian went home. Sonny finished the last of the dishes with me, being almost as meticulous as Jason is. The result of his efforts removed every trace from my house of what we had done for the past six hours.

Then Sonny left, and I was alone.

I took a shower, just to relax the tension that had built since Randolph walked into my office in the morning. Afterward I slipped naked and alone between the sheets, wanting to pass into oblivion so that I didn't need to think any longer.

The sheets touching my breasts made my nipples erect. The quilt settling down over me felt so insubstantial. It had been just one night—or a few hours early in the morning—so how could I already miss that weight pressing me into the bed, or miss that mass of male energy and heat filling the space beside me?

It had to be wrong to feel this way. I'd complained for weeks about how distracting all that testosterone was, and now I lay alone in my bed, missing it. I was alone because I had pushed him away, and not even done it subtly. Jason noticed and pushed back.

If I closed my eyes, lying in the safest place in the world (my own bed), dangerous images and sensations flooded in. Jason above me, aroused and filled with a trepidation that I had created through indecisiveness (which is more uncharacteristic of me than anything else in the last month). Jason beneath me, his beautiful face contorted in an agony of pleasure (which we had created together). Jason's hands around my wrists, holding my arms above my head, encouraging me to move against him, and then stopping to play chords on my wrist and asking if I knew what song it was ("Hymn for a Rusty Angel," that first one he wrote for me to sing).

Then I pictured again the folder Randolph laid on my desk, which roused every fear that my experience with Logan taught me.

I have to stop seeing Jason, which means I have to stop singing in the band. In the morning, I needed to carry out my obligation to perform with them for that single day, and then say goodbye to all of them before I let passion destroy the peace I had eked out for myself in the past year.

Angelia called me at seven a.m., to ask what I was wearing.

"Black," I said. "I don't know the audience. I don't know the customs. So, black."

"What should I wear? I never looked good in black. That was always reason enough to give up the symphony."

"Wear the clothes you always wear outside of school. Toby loves how you dress. Maybe his type of audience does too."

"I'm not sure."

"You'll feel more comfortable if you look like yourself."

Her second call—I have never had to hold her hand to assuage nervousness in the fifteen years I've known her—delayed my leaving, so I didn't arrive in the Market until ten minutes to nine. The clatter of early shoppers scrambling for parking and delivery trucks rumbling along the cobblestones orchestrated a cacophony of noise and confusion. That early, the air smelled of Puget Sound, though walking along the crowded street you can also smell vegetables and flowers from the truck-farmers' stalls and, of course, the smell of coffee wafted over the truck fumes.

Like most Seattle natives, I seldom enter the Market, especially on sunny weekends, except to sneak in to the Spanish Table and other specialty shops. I'd never come there to stand on a street corner by the Sanitary Market (how the language has changed since they named that structure), buffeted by busy pedestrians, the cool marine air raising goose bumps on my bare knees.

Jason already stood at the designated corner, his guitar case leaning against his leg. He smiled when I came around the corner, and I tried to read that smile—happy to see me? surprised?—but I couldn't tell what he thought. I didn't know what my own smile meant, since I hadn't followed my own advice for how to dress. Instead, I appeared in costume, because it seemed a better approach to public performance.

"Where did you get that shirt?" Jason asked. "I'm so jealous."

"At the Pendleton Rodeo when I was in high school. It was a family vacation, and I fell under the spell of the place." I'd spent half a year's allowance on an embroidered rodeo-queen shirt in black and silver, with matching belt buckle and boots. Who'd guess it survived for years, until I found it when we cleaned out my father's attic last summer.

"Will you please be careful in that skirt?"

"What's wrong with it?"

"It's perfect. Except something about it makes me want to take it off you, and I don't want others thinking the same thing. What shall we sing first?"

"'I'm Thinking Tonight of My Blue Eyes.'"

"OK. But yours are grey. I was thinking about them all last night." When it was his turn to choose, Jason named another song for me to sing while he noodled on the guitar. When I chose something for him to sing, he said, "You lead. I'll come in on harmony."

We made it through six of the songs we first sang together— and made about four dollars and some cents in change—when Ian's cousin Arlo appeared with a friend.

"Oh man, fuckin' A."

"Hello, Arlo," I said. Jason came as close to outright rudeness I had ever seen in him, not greeting either of the men.

"Man oh man. Has anyone freaking recognized you?" Arlo's voice carried across the street and down the way so that people turned to look.

"I hope not," I said, keeping my voice cool and even, though I'd spent half the night worrying about just that.

"Oh shit. My manners. Susi Neville, this is Quentin Henderson who writes for the *Seattle Buzz*. We're thinking about writing a novel together about rock-and-roll."

"Is it plot driven or character driven?" Jason asked. Without giving either of them a second to answer, he said, "We have to keep playing music if we are going to make any money."

"Fuckin' crack me up, man. Jason Taylor is playing in the freaking Pike Place Market and people walk right past. I'm taking pictures." He had his camera up and began snapping before I had time to turn my head away.

"Can it, Arlo," Jason muttered. "Just let us play music."

"All right. I'm cool. Later, man."

"'I Am a Pilgrim,'" Jason said. We began singing as Arlo and his friend walked away laughing. Arlo caught someone by the arm up the street, turned him around and pointed at us.

Whether it was Arlo's noise or that he sent friends to watch, we soon had a crowd that spread to the street, blocking traffic. A bicycle policeman came, directing people to move out of the street. Several people held video cameras or cell phones over the heads of other listeners, and everyone clapped and cheered, though Jason would not let them have their fill of clapping before he called out another song title and strummed through the lead-in chords.

Then when I most needed a drink and a break, Sonny appeared, handing me a bottle of water and positioning himself between us and people pressing too closely. Jason put his guitar away, wrapping the change we earned into the bandana that had been tied around his wrist.

"That's it, folks. We have another gig to get to."

"Will you sign this for me?"

Someone thrust paper and a Sharpie pen under Jason's nose, and he smiled. "We're playing a benefit at MOHAI this afternoon. If you come, I promise to sign after the show. Sonny?"

Some understanding between the two men caused the crowd to part, and we headed up the street.

"Where did you park, Susi?"

"Near Virginia and First Avenue. Do you want a ride?"

"Yes, please. May I take you to lunch? Susi, this isn't your car."

I explained that mine was in the shop, and then found that "taking me to lunch" meant driving him to the Museum of History and Industry—MOHAI—and walking the Chesiahud trail around Lake Union until we found a picnic table, where he shared apples, cheese, bread and a bottle of water from his pack. As he cut the apple into pieces with a pocket knife, he said, "I was mean last night, and I apologize. You must have recognized it as the adolescent defensive maneuver that it was."

"Actually, I'm sorry."

"You have nothing to apologize for, Susi. Every time you allow me close to you, I rush in and demand more. I understand that you need to proceed at a slower pace. That is, I understand it intellectually. I have a hard time modifying my behavior."

"Do you want me to explain myself better?"

"Gosh, no, Susi. Then I'd have to explain myself, which would be humiliating. Thanks for showing up today. Your being here helps me feel a lot more confident."

"Are you nervous, too? Angelia called this morning, very nervous, and she's never been nervous before a performance in her life."

"I'm not nervous about playing. I just wasn't popular the last time I played in Seattle."

"Because of your music?"

He shook his head. "When I was married, my wife called the police on me when I was shouting at her to unlock the door to my house. She told them that I had caused her untold suffering. It was a lie, and the police saw through it."

"What does that have to do with playing music today?"

"What happened—a lot of people know about it, or think they know from rumors. She hasn't taken any opportunity to tell the world it isn't true. Some of those people will be sitting in the audience to-day. Here, this afternoon, for sure. Perhaps in the later shows too."

At that moment, I owed telling him how I'd become acquainted through email with the nature of the woman to whom he'd been married. I let the opportunity pass. If we had to acknowledge what I knew about his ex, I'd owe reciprocity. The idea of Jason knowing about Logan remained intolerable to me. To live through that humiliation once had been painful. To relive it, or to see it again through Jason's eyes, seemed like more torture than I should have to bear.

"You know me, Susi. You don't believe it, do you?"

"Of course, I don't."

He sighed. "Then nothing else matters."

We went back to the museum and watched the other acts from the wings, since there wasn't much to be said for walking around Lake Union in ostrich-skin cowboy boots and a gaudy shirt.

Dan, Pete, and my friends from the Sunday bluegrass service came on stage near the end of the program and played those beautiful hymns we'd been doing together. Jason slipped out onto the stage with them, standing at the back to play guitar, half turned away from the crowd. Four songs into their performance, I found myself longing to be with them and felt no qualms at all when Dan said, "Our friend Susi Neville is here, and we're hoping she'll join us."

It was unlikely that anyone there knew me, but the etiquette of the folk crowd was such that they clapped for my entrance as if they did. We visited our favorites together, like "I'll Fly Away" and "Take Me in Your Lifeboat." The polite but eager audience applauded and greeted each new song with increasing enthusiasm.

Then Dan introduced the musicians.

"For our last song, we want to bring up a new friend who is now like a brother to us, along with our little sister Susi. Jason Taylor, come show 'em you can yodel."

Most of the audience clapped like they were supposed to. A couple of ululating calls also echoed through the auditorium. When Jason stepped to the microphone and the noise dropped, some people were hissing.

"Thanks, Dan. This is one to sing when you leave the church at night and head on down the road."

He sang "Lovesick Blues," his smoky tenor reverberating through the monitors so that it felt like it vibrated up through my boots to my very core. When Jason finished and most of the audience was clapping, Pete introduced himself and explained about the Sunday night service, inviting the audience while his hand rested on Jason's shoulder.

When the audience finished expressing appreciation for our homegrown mountain music, Pete put his arm around Jason's shoulder and mine, and invited the audience to stay to hear the Jason Taylor Band for their first performance before a live audience.

The band began with a mountain song about lost love, the kind I just don't understand.

67
"I Walk the Line"
Jason

WE DID IT. WE STEPPED in front of the most personal of audiences, and they didn't boo me off the stage. Let's ignore the fact that I hid behind Susi's very short skirt. The sweet mania of Angelia's fiddle and Toby's mandolin kept the audience from pondering the nature of my past offenses. Starting with Susi leading on mountain songs, and working our way down to the psychedelic hillbilly boogie of lower Wallingford, most people seemed to forget about what they thought of me last year. They called us back for two encores, even though we'd shifted from familiar songs to the hybrid Celtic wails in our new material.

Afterwards, plenty of people stayed to get autographs and to say, "Glad you're back." Only one person said, "I used to hear Stoneway all the time, back before you sold out," and no one spit on me.

Quentin Henderson played a mild-mannered Clark Kent, scratching notes. I didn't have to ask him what a heavy-duty indie rock fan was doing at MOHAI, because Arlo was also there, snapping pictures, an old-fashioned mini-recorder strapped to his chest, which meant someone would be downloading MP3s with Arlo's heartbeat keeping rhythm.

Angelia and Susi signed with the rest of us, and we ended up late in heading out for the landmines benefit—a benefit against mines, not for them. It was a black-tie affair where people paid a thousand bucks a ticket or bought whole tables for fifteen thousand, and then begged their friends to come and enjoy the no-host bar.

"I hate playing rooms like this," Ian said. "The sound shoots for the ceiling and then bounces back to shatter on the floor."

We had just enough time for a sound check before they shooed us out to let in the paying customers to dine on catered chicken. White sauce or green sauce, I don't remember.

"She says she doesn't want it, but then can't get enough."

Cynthia said, "Lordy, Jason, I don't want to hear about your sex life. Too much information."

"I meant singing in front of an audience. She loves it. She's fearless."

"Then maybe we can stop worrying about whether she'll tour with the band. I'm going to take a risk while I'm booking gigs and demand a no-smoking policy, without waiting to find out whether she's in the band."

We sat eating sandwiches in the dressing room they gave us at the hotel. That is, other people were eating sandwiches. I had to give the waiter fifty bucks and beg for egg salad or cheese for Susi and me. While we waited for food, Cynthia let me cry on her shoulder, meta-phorically speaking.

"What's she talking to Sonny about?" The two of them had been laughing at the other end of the room ever since they let the last waiter in.

"Fishing. It's what they always talk about." Cynthia was filing her new fire-orange nails.

"How did they get to be best friends?"

"She's best friends with everyone in the band. You're pouting, Jason. It's not a cool look on you."

Everyone decided to go for a walk or a smoke, since we had thirty minutes before we went on. As people milled around the door, the jerk-face pretty boy who drove her home in that BMW last Sunday night stood in the doorway, and I realized it was his car she had now. Susi was all over him, hugging, kissing, laughing. I would have blown my own brains out, except I don't believe in carrying personal firearms. He was prettier than I'd recognized—if Susi was an angel, then he was of a related tribe of seraphim. He seemed affable, and Susi had every effing Judas in the band shaking his hand as they walked past. Then there was just us three.

"Jason Taylor, this is my brother, Steven Neville."

That Jason is an unbalanced bozo who has a moth-to-the-flames attraction to your sister, she did not say. He could read it in my face, the way that I read recognition in the clenching of his jaw.

She said, "I'm dying for you two to meet, but I'm also dying of hunger and I have to change clothes. I'll go change, find that waiter, and then be right back." Susi ducked out, as if it were safe to leave me with her relatives.

Her big brother, for all his sophisticated élan, said, "What the hell are you doing with my sister?"

"I'm in love with her."

"She doesn't know who you are. What kind of love is that?" Steven was so much like Susi that seeing fury on that face was disconcerting.

"Could we just talk?" I sank into one of the club chairs, hoping he'd sit down too, so it would be more difficult for him to kick me in the face if he felt so inclined.

"Our father thinks she's dating a music scholar." Steven stood with his hands on his hips. "Are you lying to both of them?"

"I haven't lied to either of them."

"Don't hurt her. She's been jacked around enough in this life."

"We had a mutual misunderstanding about each other. I told her my name, but she didn't recognize it. It was a rush, finding that she liked me without knowing that I'm somebody who—"

"If she read the paper or Googled your name, she'd know who you are."

"She's been in front of audiences with me all day. She must have noticed that we aren't just some bar band. She doesn't care. Ask her."

Steven shook his head, still staring at me with the same intense grey eyes as Susi. "Play your little game if you want, but she needs to know about your drug bust."

"What drug bust?" Susi stood in the doorway, the cowgirl mini exchanged for her formal black tunic, her laughing smile exchanged for a pale, frightened mask. I looked away from Steven, who in my romantic fantasies will be my brother-in-law when Susi and I begin to live happily ever after.

"I went to jail last year, Susi. Twice. I don't tell this story because it is ugly from start to finish."

"I suppose all such stories are ugly." Susi's voice was flat when she said this, so I couldn't hear the tone or color of her feelings. "How do you know about it, Steven?"

He glared at me. "It was in the papers last year. Everyone in Seattle knows about it."

She made a dismissive gesture with her hand. "I don't read the Seattle papers. Tell me."

I said, "My uncle Beau—there hasn't been time yet to tell you much about him."

"He died. I understood that from your song about him."

"Beau took me on after I lost my mother, acting as my manager and mentor. Last year, he went out on the streets of Tacoma to buy narcotics. I came along to protect him, because I felt sure someone would fleece him or beat him."

"Your uncle was a junkie?"

"No. He was dying of stomach cancer, and his doctor didn't give him enough morphine to kill the pain. He said he wanted to shop for more, and I pretended to believe him."

"What do you mean, pretended?" Steven asked, still scowling, still wanting me to crawl in a hole and die.

"He wasn't looking for pain control. He wanted to end it. I went along because I didn't want him dying alone."

"So you were helping him commit suicide?" Steven stood ready to pin any crime on me. In spite of my fantasies about our future familial bliss, he was pissing me off such that I felt ready to meet the challenge.

"Is that what you'd call it? Until I'm in the same position, facing certain death in great pain, I can't judge whether it's morally wrong. I just didn't want Beau to be alone."

"Please tell the rest of the story." Susi offered no clues about what she thought.

"Unfortunately, I couldn't protect him. Beau scored from a dealer who was under surveillance, and we all went to jail. When I couldn't reach Karl—he's my attorney—I called my wife. But she did nothing. It was the Friday night before a three-day weekend, neither of us was carrying ID, and no one was in a hurry to find me an attorney. So I sat for days in jail until Karl came home and found my message on his answer service."

"What happened to your uncle?"

"They put us in different cells. Then Beau got so sick they took him to a hospital. He wouldn't tell anyone his name, so it wasn't until I got out and went to find him that we could get him back under the care of his own doctor. He was never fully conscious again. He died a couple of days later."

"I'm sorry," Susi said. Yet I couldn't tell if she understood. She just stared at me, as if her eyes could bore a hole into my soul.

"He would have died anyway." I have to shrug about that fact, but I have no illusions about it. "There were only two days left to hold his hand, with nothing more to say. All because my wife didn't want to find an attorney for us."

"Why would anyone do that?" Steven asked. Instead of the angry cynicism he had expressed so far, he now sounded amazed. Susi looked solemn, her one eye brow raised, questioning me.

"I don't know." This is so true that my mind whirls whenever I think about it. "She didn't like Beau's influence on me, and had developed some bizarre hatred for him. She wanted him out of the band and out of our house, though I had insisted he live with us when he fell ill."

"What about the second time you went to jail?"

"I went into a rage. I'd learned before then that my so-called wife had been holding bedroom auditions for a better partner. I couldn't swallow what happened to Beau. So I ended up arrested for domestic violence, though all I did was stand on the street and yell at her when she wouldn't let me in the house."

"You told me about that earlier."

"Afterward, I just stayed away from Seattle. I didn't see her again until a few weeks ago. All rumors to the contrary, I am not a wife beater."

She didn't speak, looking instead at Steven, as if his reaction mattered. He said, "That story matches the public record." What he didn't say aloud—the qualifying "however"—hung like a pall. He didn't like me, and he wouldn't excuse me for anything.

I said, "Susi, if you want someone to tell you what's true, Karl is inside at the benefit."

"No, I don't doubt you. I just wish I didn't know," she said. "I never wanted to know your secrets, and I still don't want you to know mine. I wish that Steven had minded his own business."

"You don't have to tell me your secrets, Susi. You can ask me anything you want to know." A bubble of hope choked my ability to say more.

She glanced at Steven, but he just shook his head and looked away. If I were to try to guess what he thought, he just wanted me to disappear off the face of the earth.

She looked back at me. "Do you use drugs?"

"No. Years ago I did enough to understand what trapped my father and then I stopped. A very long time ago."

"You used to be so well dressed, and now you don't even shave some days. You are so distracted. What happened? What do you do all day?"

"I work on music. I start at seven or eight in the morning to finish production on some older music. Then I work with Ian and the others to finish an album we have to deliver in June. At night we rehearse our back porch music with you and Angelia. After you leave, I try to solve musical problems I found during the day. What else do you want to ask, Susi?"

"Your life seems so flakey. Like living in Ian's basement. Plus all these people you owe money to everywhere."

"Flakey because I'm a musician?"

"No," she said. "I don't know anyone else so odd. Except Arlo."

Ian popped his shaved head in at the open door. "We're on in twenty minutes. They want you at the sound board now, Jason."

I touched her hand, scared out of my wits that she'd push me away. "Susi, will you still sing with us?"

"Yes, of course. I said I would."

When I left, I said goodbye but did not shake Steven's hand. That would have to wait until we were all living happily ever after.

68
"Understand Your Man"
Susi

"YOU GOING TO LET that bother you, SusiQ?"

"Hi, Sonny. I didn't know you were out here."

Sonny was handsome in a dinner jacket, almost unrecognizable except for his ponytail. His ruined teeth showed when he smiled.

"Just grabbing a smoke and taking a look-see. I shouldn't of been listening, but how the fuck could I help it? It happened just like Jason says. I was there."

"You were in jail with him?"

"He didn't do what they said he did. He is such a fucking nice guy, he could hurt himself. Pretended that whole time in the cell that he didn't recognize me." Sonny tossed the burning end of his cigarette down the alley and then took out another and lit it. "But Jason played the club scene for so long, how could I help recognizing him? Everyone in Seattle knew him. Me and my buddies did what we could, but it was a rough time. Jason worked bars long enough that throw-up didn't bother him, though he's such a freaking hand-washer, you'd think he'd flip when a couple of the guys in the cell got dope sick. Jason just had a hell of a time staying mad and trying to deal with these people at the same time."

"Was it his wife's fault he spent time in jail?"

"Yeah. I ought to send that witch some goddamn roses. If he hadn't been stuck in there, I'd be freaking dead by now. Oh shit, don't tell him I know."

"Know what?"

"He saved my fucking life. After Jason was sprung free, he got lawyers for some of us, got us into treatment. Me and Bobby Smith, we'd have fucking hosed ourselves by now if it wasn't for him. We aren't supposed to know, but I'm not stupid. No way the fucking fairy godmother was going to step in and save my ass."

"What happened to the others?"

"Bobby is around, going to meetings. Gary's dead. Mike Dee is still using, or maybe he's dead. That's pretty good, fifty percent. Pretty stupid of Jason to invest his money in junkies. Very poor return on your capital." He stopped and took a drag on his cigarette. "Though I shouldn't call myself saved. It's just a day at a time."

"My husband used. Ex, I mean. I don't have one now."

I could feel him studying me though I couldn't see anything in the dark except the glowing end of his cigarette.

"Then you know a worthless son of a bitch when you see one. And Jason ain't it. Yeah, he's been around, but his uncle kept him out of the worst of it, even living on the road most of his life like he has. Can you figure? It ends up being Beau Rufus gets him landed in jail? Can't send that sucker roses no more though, so it'll have to be the bitch bride that I thank, begging your pardon for the rough language."

He took another drag, and then looked at me. "My smoke bothers you, doesn't it? Even out here?" He tossed the cigarette far down the alley. "I'd quit to please you, but I done all the quitting I can manage in the last year."

Sonny put his arm around me and we started back in.

Randolph stood at the door, watching us, his hand jammed in the pockets of his tuxedo.

69
"Smack Dab in the Middle"
Jason

"YOU ARE DOING INCREDIBLE work, Jason."

"Hello, Ephraim. I saw you from the stage."

He wore a silk tuxedo and he came up to shake my hand, acting like he was still my friend.

"Tonight was an unexpected pleasure, amigo. I had no idea this was the direction you were headed."

"Are you here alone?" I didn't want his compliments. Ephraim is the same height as me, but has fifty pounds and ten years over me, and I hated that avuncular attitude he takes around me.

"Dominique is visiting her sister. Don't laugh like that."

"Sorry. She just isn't very original. I suppose since it worked once, she has no reason to think it wouldn't work the next time."

"I'm trying to decide if I even care." Ephraim shrugged like he didn't care, and then changed the subject. "You aren't giving Albion Records any music like that, are you? None of that funky blues, playing bottleneck guitar with a comb?"

"If you are planning to sue me, we'll have to talk with Karl present. You and I both know Dominique can't sing this."

"No. What you're giving the label is commercial and solid. You and I both know Albion wouldn't know what to do with this other material."

"What do you want, Ephraim?"

"Work with me, Jason. It's not raining in Seattle—wasn't that part of your criteria for rapprochement in our artistic relationship?"

"You are partners with my bitter witch of an ex-wife. You and I have no foundation upon which to build a relationship."

"This time next year, Dominique might be making twice as much money as you, whether or not she's visiting her sister tonight. Twenty years from now, someone will be packaging retrospectives of your work, and Dominique will be a minor footnote. I can help you, if you let me."

"You made the decision last year about who you wanted to work for, Ephraim. You chose Dominique."

"Maybe we shared the same opportunity to make faulty decisions. Maybe that's a foundation for a new relationship."

I'm great with quick come-backs on email and the phone, but not so great when the beast is staring me in the eye, daring me to sympathize. Or relent. Or sink to new depths with him. I didn't know which.

Karl came up, laying a hand on each of our shoulders.

I said, "Come to the Showbox later, both of you. There's more music that you haven't heard, Ephraim."

Karl about swallowed his tongue. "The Showbox? You didn't send a contract by me."

"We're standing in for another band that can't show. Just to close out a benefit they're doing."

"Jason, you can't do this shit without sharing the details with me. I mean, pulling this together last week was enough of a stretch. Could we just plan ahead a little, buddy?"

"Can we not talk about it in front of someone who has a great potential for being an adversary in court, Karl? You're supposed to be discrete."

Ephraim said, "I'm not going to sue you over anything, Jason. I want to help. Does this Susi person sing with your new band all the time? I need to sign her, too. Does she have an agent?"

"Call Karl, and we will talk about this Monday."

"Are you going to make me get in line with every shark who'll be calling you after this little debut? It is not a secret that you've about wrapped up your Albion Records obligation." Ephraim smiled. That superior smirk of his was bugging me.

Karl's wife slinked up, slipping her arm through his. She smiled at Ephraim and treated me, as usual, like a slimy invertebrate that crawled across her shoe. Me, the bad influence from the other side of the tracks.

"Karl, honey, it's a party. You aren't working," she purred.

"I'm always working, sweetheart. I just found out that I need to stay late tonight to take care of more business."

She said, "You're sending me home alone?"

"You're welcome to come along, but you aren't dressed for it. And I don't think you'll like the music."

She gave me death looks like Dominique used to cultivate. Ephraim managed a circumspect expression, as if he were wallpaper. She said, "But, Karl, what we talked about—"

"When we talked, I said that work came first." Karl was smiling, but his face looked like a mask.

Her lip curled with distain. "And last. Always."

She left us, which didn't bode well for Karl later that night.

"You don't have to come," I said.

"I wouldn't miss it for the world," Karl said.

"I think I'll come with you," Ephraim said.

"Oh swell," I said. "The torts-and-treaties twins are dating each other."

Karl looked thoughtful. "Your new music has the decided effect of making women not want to sleep with me. I don't remember that from before, when we were on the road together."

Ephraim said, "I know what you mean about that particular effect."

Karl motioned to someone nearby who turned out to be Warren, the admin from his office. "Can you please make sure my wife gets home safely? I can't take her, and she's enjoying the wine. Call a limo for her?"

"Right, Mr. Schwann. I'll take care of it."

"Hey, man." I shook Warren's hand. "It's nice to see you again."

He nodded to me, and then to Karl, and ducked away, leaving an opening for a ring of women who wanted autographs. I signed and chatted until Ian signaled that we were going on stage.

Karl walked back with me. "You complain about fans all the time, Jason, but then you act like the nicest guy in the world when they're in your face."

"Here, it's part of the job. I like these people when I'm at work. I just don't appreciate it when I'm not working."

Ephraim breathed behind me. "For someone like you, the world will remain a twenty-four-hour stage. You have to get used to it."

The people at the landmines benefit loved Susi. And Angelia. They didn't mind that we added a little electricity to the acoustic country set we'd done earlier at MOHAI. They liked the moody Celtic wails and the newly fuzzed out version of "Rhianna's Song" from *Woman at the Well*, with Susi singing counterpoint against my lead. No one spit on me, and Sonny proved effective in shepherding people onto and off the stage, so effective that it felt almost as comforting as when we had Beau with us, making sure everything was taken care of.

We paid a couple of Sonny's friends to schlep equipment between halls, helping out a couple of our usual guys (who are Ian's cousins, but bathe and have half a brain each), and Sonny's friends proved to be experienced and careful. Nothing got broken or left behind. No fans were treated rudely. We had time to talk to people some more, instead of having to schlep everything ourselves. I hadn't lost my temper even once by the time we were and several blocks across town at the Showbox.

Sonny had also taken to shepherding Susi. I lost contact with her between the end of the set at the hotel and the loading dock outside the Showbox. We had so little time to get ready for the next show, that I couldn't tell what I was feeling besides that uneasiness which descended whenever she wasn't right by my side.

If nagging doubts didn't appall me, I spent idle moments wondering whether my stalker was just around the corner, causing me to watch that no stranger touched my guitars. Ian accidentally stepped back into me while guys were wrestling with the equipment. We were standing around like goons, because we didn't want to muss our white dinner jackets. I didn't even notice he stepped on my foot until he spoke.

"Hey, bro. You doing all right?"

"Just spaced. Have you seen Susi?"

"Toby and Sonny have the girls inside."

"They are women, not girls," I said, reflexively.

"Yeah, sure. Hey, Jason. You aren't going to fuck it up, are you?"

"I'm trying not to, but which 'it' do you mean?"

"Susi. She's going to sing with us, isn't she? We can't lose her now."

I just looked at him, because I didn't know the answer. I didn't know how to not fuck up, and I didn't know how to keep her with us. With me.

Ian, of course, can read my face like a book, one he has read over and again. He blanched.

"Crap, Jason. You have to get this right. No one else can do it for you."

Right. I couldn't ask Martha to take care of it, or hire some of Sonny's friends, or call Karl for estoppels. Or bitch until Cynthia gave up and took care of it for me. I didn't know where to go to buy a clue.

Then I found her again, standing at the side, out of the way of equipment hassles, with that luminescent lily look that she has when wearing her black concert clothes. The wide silver belt cinching her waist showed off the bones of her hips and, even with her swimmer's shoulders, she looked small and oh so vulnerable. Then she saw me and turned on that smile she first felled me with.

So vulnerable. She could crush me with a single word. It would annihilate any ability to make it through everyday life if she said no.

70
"Iko Iko"
Susi

"HEY, SUSI. CAN YOU handle the air in here?"

"I think so. We won't be here long, will we, Jason?"

"Don't know. If they boo us off the stage, we'll be gone right away. If you stand here until it's time to sing, the ventilation should help. Here's the set list."

"I remember it. I don't need notes."

He wanted the set to begin with four songs that the crowd would recognize (even though I didn't), followed by two cover songs that, Jason said, would help people transition to the band's new work. Then I would join them.

Jason pushed my hair back, looking at my ears. "It's going to be loud. I want you to use my earphones. They don't fit you, but you won't like it without them. You'll hear what we're playing without being overwhelmed."

"If I use yours, what will you use?"

"One short night won't give me tinnitus. We will get some made for you—if you are going to keep singing with us."

His finger lingered on my earlobe after he fitted the earphones, the first gentle touch we had shared since I left his house the morning before. What had I been thinking, letting Randolph inject his nastiness into how I understood Jason?

"Please," he said, though I had to read his lips with the earphones in place, and I had forgotten what he was asking in the midst of my own regret. What I heard through the earphones came from the stage monitors. The emcee seemed to be negotiating with the crowd, announcing that the band they expected to see wouldn't appear, then playing up excitement for the replacement, and finally calling Jason's name.

The night before, he whispered, "Who are you and what have you done with my lover?" I could have said the same, as I watched Jason master that audience. He'd kept his hair tied back all day, but now it was unbound and wild. The same person who hesitated during our picnic by the lake, and who adopted a shy posture at MOHAI in the afternoon, walked out on stage at eleven o'clock and stood in a suggestive pose before the microphone. In the most seductive voice I've ever heard, he said, "Oh, Seattle, you don't know how we missed you."

He struck a long note on his guitar, pulling it up to his shoulder and turning his head in the same way he did when—when he was alone with me, in bed. As he struck a second note, the rest of the band came in with a clash of sound that sorted itself into a pattern, while the crowd contributed to the cacophony. Then the melody asserted itself. Jason began to sing, his voice muted in my earphone monitors, as if he were singing just to me.

Through all that we'd sung together, I had heard only hints of this. Since I don't know rock-and-roll, I don't know how to describe it. Tuneful rant? Rhythmic exhortation? He danced across the stage, sliding over to Ian, where they both shouted into the microphone, which was so loud through the earphones that the sound must have been overwhelming to the people in front of the stage, where that reporter friend of Arlo's stood writing notes, lost and oblivious to the throng around him. When the song finished, those people seemed to be shouting right back, filtered through the earphones as a distant roar. Jason and Ian both had huge smiles. Jason stripped off his dinner jacket, throwing it to the crowd, as he shouted, "Damn, it's good to be home!"

Then he pulled his bolo tie loose as he counted one, two, three, four, and they banged their way into another song, followed by two more. Then Sonny stepped up with Jason and they sang together, something I recognized: "I Walk the Line," because my father always played Johnny Cash when he worked in the garage or in the yard. Sonny's bass voice wasn't steady and reliable, but the wobble offset Jason's honey-smooth tenor. They followed with a Jimmie

Rodgers yodeling song, different from the modest version Jason had done earlier at the museum benefit.

While I watched from the side, Jason made love to the crowd, dancing across the stage, his shirt soaked with sweat, while he moved in ways that I associated with those two precious nights when we had—

He tore his tuxedo shirt open, stripped it off his wet torso, and threw it into the crowd, the bolo tie still swinging from his neck. "We're going to switch gears now and introduce a new singer. SusiQ, come meet Seattle."

We started with "Tio's Fury," which we'd practiced for the past month, but I hadn't heard the rich layer of texturing, with everyone on the same stage, instead of Zak down the hall and Sonny half way to the front porch. Everyone turned up loud. Holding a microphone bothered me—performing with a microphone always bothers me—and I tried not to think I was competing with the strings and percussion, just to balance it in the way that Jason had hounded us to do in rehearsal.

A slow, moody version of "Hymn for a Rusty Angel" calmed the crowd that had been restless and demanding when I first walked out. Then he introduced the next song, saying the title—"Mon Oncle, le Troubadour"—so quietly that the audience fell silent, and he played the first steel guitar chords to begin the duet with my voice. This time, it wasn't the acoustic song we'd first practiced at my house.

I watched his hands, far too conscious of his long fingers and how confidently he touched the strings. As we reached the instrumental portion of the song, we watched each other as the rest of the band took turns with virtuoso solos, with each adding to the tension that built in the course of the song. He played the single note that brought my voice back into the knit-together sounds, long bars of grievous, lonesome scat singing before the final chorus, when we wove his guitar and my voice into the final shriek of loss and pain. We both carried the final note long enough to otherwise silence the room. A deep indigo blue bloomed in my chest and filled my head.

It had been such a long, long time since I saw an audience swoon.

71
"Still I Long for Your Kiss"
Susi

BEAUTIFUL, ERSTWHILE JASON, THE modest romantic, could stand in front of strangers and play devil, hero, and lovelorn cowboy. He had no qualms about seducing women into ecstasy or driving grown men to shout out and hug their girlfriends. For the second time in thirty days, I found that I didn't know the man I'd gone to bed with.

I hardly knew the band I'd sung with almost every night in Cynthia's futon-lined parlor, trying to get the sound balanced so that no instrument overpowered another. I didn't know that we could fill a modest concert hall with a huge, round, driving sound that left people shouting for us after three encores.

The furtive Jason whom I saw duck for cover whenever we went anywhere in public was another figment of my imagination. This Jason stood for almost an hour after the show, chatting with anyone who came to ask for autographs, wondering when the band would tour, and begging for a new album.

A spiritual twin of Arlo's, if not a clone, asked Jason to sign his shirt. "Far out, man. I used to come see Stoneway all the time. Before you sold out."

"How far back do you go?" Jason asked, as if the person hadn't just insulted him.

"I've seen your shows for nine years, man."

"See that guy over there, by the girl with orange hair? He saw us play when we were in high school. He has you beat."

"No way. You guys should put out a CD of old stuff. This new stuff is cool, too. It's the middle that sucks. Good to see you back on track."

"Thanks, man." Jason shook his hand. "It means something that you'd say that. We don't want to lose your respect."

While Jason was being nice to people who insulted him, a host of women asked him to sign parts of their body or shirts, all of them hanging on his every word. Then, the house managers insisted we all needed to be out of the building so the clean-up crew could go home.

Jason caught my eye at that point.

"Hey, Susi. How you doing?" he said, stepping by my side.

"That man insulted you," I whispered, gesturing to the wild-haired gentleman bopping away from us. "Yet you smiled and shook his hand."

"No, he didn't mean any insult. He's listened to our music so much that he thinks he knows me personally. He's giving me advice because he cares." Jason smiled in a dreamy way, though maybe it was left over from how he smiled at the show. "Sonny and Karl are going to the 5 Point for breakfast. Want to come?"

"Thanks, but I think I'll just go home."

He touched my lips with his thumb. "You were fantastic, Susi. Thank you. I'm sorry I doubted you."

"Please come home with me."

I blurted it before I could guard myself against saying what I thought, just because he touched my mouth. He didn't give me a quarter of a second to reconsider.

In the car on the way home, he couldn't stop talking or leave a breath of silence for me to reconsider, or reframe, what had happened that night. "Zak was one hundred percent on. Everything I said about him is turning out to be true. And Toby! My god, could you believe it tonight? He and Angelia have something huge going between them—I don't mean about being in love, but that their music is so tight together."

He paused for a breath just as we turned onto Madrona Drive, and in that slim moment of silence, he turned fretful.

"You don't think they'll strike out on their own, do you? I mean, I'd never stop them. But lord, it feels so good, I hope they stay. And Sonny!"

This thought propelled him back into his enthusiasms.

"Do you think he'll stay with us? Or do you think he's just doing this out of charity, sort of a misguided payback?"

I said, "He doesn't seem eager to go elsewhere."

"Everyone is so good right now. I'm getting nervous about holding on to people. They have every reason to find other gigs. I couldn't blame them. I can't offer anything long term."

"Jason, it's you that makes the band good." I was stating the obvious.

"What a nice thing to say. But it's not me. It's synchronicity. Each little bit just seemed to come together at this time and this place."

"I'm grateful you invited me to join you. This was one of the most incredible nights I've ever known."

He was grinning. "You forced yourself on us. Remember?"

As I parked in the carport, he curved his hand over mine.

"I'm not forcing myself on you, Susi. You want to do this, don't you?" Which left me so confused that I couldn't think of an answer before he said, "Singing with the band, I mean. Playing with all of us."

72
"Come Together"
Jason

"WERE YOU NERVOUS?"

Susi seemed so distracted that she couldn't get the key in the lock, and I had a feeling we were headed for another train wreck. I took the key from her hand and asked again, trying not to spook her.

"If you were nervous, it didn't show."

She shook her head. "It never makes me nervous. I don't know what stage fright means, though I've seen how it makes other people ill."

I unlocked the door and held it open for her. "Then you saw what a mess I was right up to when we started playing."

I was a mess again at that moment, trying to figure out how to bridge the gulf that had opened between us since leaving my bedroom a couple of mornings earlier. The idea I had was to apply the same moxie as on stage. I crooked a finger under the silver belt that cinched her waist and pulled her toward me.

"Let's take a shower. I wanted to unhook that belt since I first saw it."

She began unbuckling mine, and my relief matched how it felt as each show started that day, when people didn't throw stones. I shrugged out of my t-shirt and then pulled her close so that I could get at the zipper of her dress, pulling it down and then tugging the dress over her head. She stood there in just a bra and those outlandish cowboy boots.

"Good lord, Susi, you don't have any underwear on."

"I haven't ever figured out what to wear with this dress so the line doesn't show through."

"You stood in front of all those people with no skivvies."

"The skirt is long. It's not as if anyone could see."

"I couldn't have sung a note if I'd known." I started to pull off my pants, not able to take my eyes off her, and then half fell over as it occurred to me. "You didn't have any underwear on for Mozart either."

"Mozart didn't care."

We made it to the shower, which we needed after the night's work, and I pulled her in with me, where the space was small enough to press us together in the way I wanted. She tried pulling that stunt on me again, touching me in ways that threatened to make me lose control, starting when she soaped my pecs and played in the hair that she'd complained about a few days before.

She took me in her hands again and soaped me half way to delirium, and then dipped down to cup and tug at my balls.

"Lord, that feels good. *'Nothing compares to you.'*"

"It's nothing you can't do yourself."

"Hmm. I don't think so."

She began kissing my nipples, rubbing her face in the soapy hair on my chest, which I couldn't do myself.

I soaped her too, starting low while she steadied herself, first with her hands on my shoulders and then twining her fingers in my hair. I moved higher, pausing with my hands on her breasts while I nuzzled the soapy sweetness of her bush, making her laugh. Then I soaped her arms and back and neck.

When I held her again, both of us dripping lather while the shower drummed against her back and splashed onto my face, she began ducking away and hiding herself. There was nowhere in the shower for her to hide, and we weren't doing anything but playing. Then I realized it was her unmade-up face she tried to hide. I turned her face toward me as she tried to slip away under my soapy hand.

"Susi, I love you. I hate that this happened to you, but it's the only face I've known. You're beautiful. Please don't hide from me."

"I don't, honestly. It makes people uncomfortable to see it."

"Not me. I think you are both brave and beautiful."

I traced my soapy thumb over the web-like veil along the left side of her face, and she shuddered, moving close to me.

"It tickles when you do that."

✳

Surfeit. People died of it in the Middle Ages.

More than enough of everything.

A sunny spring Sunday that I will remember until I die. Enough sleep. Enough food. Enough time in warm spring air to breathe and move as if the whole day were one long tai-chi form. Enough time to explore every continent, stream, mountain, and valley of a beautiful, beloved woman's body. Long hours of peace where the music was provided by the junco that scolded us for lingering on the deck with our coffee when her nest was nearby. The percussion-only compositions we invented, with the sounds of our bared bodies in collision as the major motif. The woodwinds' part was the reedy rasp of our breathing as we practiced coming together, when it didn't seem possible that consummation could feel this intensely, wildly, passionately good.

She got up after the first time and made pancakes because I was starving. If there is such a thing as afterglow, I think the light comes from a small woman in a green silk kimono, her short hair unchar-acteristically awry, flipping pancakes, singing "Angel Band" and stopping every few moments to bite the mound at the base of my thumb.

If there is taste that can be ascribed to the special permissiveness between devoted lovers, then I would say it is maple syrup and butter: the most fastidious woman in Seattle allowed me to kiss her breasts with my mouth still sticky and oily from our five a.m. feast. I will always think her breasts taste like the honey-dew of Paradise. When I hear the trite cliché of talkative women keeping satiated men from the embrace of Morpheus, I will counter with my own archetypal experience of a peaceful woman's fingers at my temples, my neck, my shoulders, pulling me with her into sleep, atomizing and becoming one with the molecules of water in a tumbling brook, drifting in the gentling breeze shooshing through the top branches of cedar trees outside the open window.

She loves me. I know she does. She feeds me, rocks me to the bottom of my battered soul, and then curls in the crook of my arm to sleep as if she has abandoned herself to safety with me.

When I awoke, I found her coolly assessing my naked body from the end of the bed.

"Your body hair no longer frightens me," she said, and then she dropped the green kimono and did some of things she does that still scare the hell out of me.

73
"Boys Want Sex in the Morning"
Susi

"*BOYS WANT SEX IN THE MORNING.*" Jason's breath brushed my ear the same way the breeze wafted over the curtains.

"Girls do too, but it's not morning."

"It's a line from a song. Uncle Bonsai."

"I don't think I know that one."

"No, you wouldn't."

"You'll need another condom."

"Yes. I've retained a certain wisdom my uncle left me. Though I'm not sure how we'll ever have children the way we're going about it."

"There isn't a plan for that."

"That's how to make things happen, Susi, by having a plan. You don't have to marry me right this minute, but we need a plan. I want to make you happy. And safe. I want to make babies with you."

"Just make me come one more time and then make breakfast. No, better just make the coffee and I'll make breakfast."

"Are you making fun of me?"

"I find the concept of you taking care of me amusing. You don't have a car or a house or anything else that grownups have. Judging from how you behave, if I didn't bring the other half of my dinner to Ian's every night, you'd starve because you're the dependent vegetarian child in a meat-eating household."

"Don't talk anymore, Susi. Ephraim rips them off. Your brother Steven wants to crush them. I can't afford you turning them blue again. Stop talking and do those nice things you do."

"Who is Ephraim?"

"He's a music industry person that I have business with. I don't want him in bed with us. Boys want sex in the morning, not a trip to the existential abyss."

"You are the one who started talking about babies. Who's leading whom to the existential abyss?"

We slept till noon, and could have slept the whole day away, as if both of us had been deprived of sleep for weeks. Jason is usually like an Irish setter that can't sit still for a moment, but Sunday he lazed around like an overfed Newfoundland dog. (I'm not afraid of all that hair as a secondary sex characteristic now, but I'm no less aware of it.) However, it was a beautiful Sunday outside, and I wanted to be in the sunshine. It took me changing into jeans and heading for the door on my own to get him up, dressed, and out for a walk. Once we were sauntering down the alley, smelling spring with the sun shining full on our faces, he was happy to be there. Ever since we left the club the night before, any little thing seemed to bring him exquisite joy. Just the look of stupefied bliss on his face made me laugh too, but then I gulped a big breath of the local blossoms and began coughing.

"Are you all right, Susi?"

"Lilacs make my throat hurt when I pass them on the street. The odor and some other essence are too strong for me. I used to love spring, but now the lilacs leave me feeling like I might cry."

The lilacs reminded me of the pain again. Which made me think that I had to tell him about it, though I still didn't want to. I'd rather take bad-tasting medicine, endure another "procedure," or dodge more phone messages from Logan. If I believed in praying for silly, selfish things, I'd pray that I never have to tell Jason how I got to be like this.

"Let's cross the street," Jason said. "If we stay out of the alleys, you won't have to walk close to a lilac."

The essence of Jason: practical solutions to existential problems.

"How about lavender?" he asked. "Or the magnolias and for-get-me-nots? Do they make you want to cry? Do we have to walk down the middle of the street?"

"No, just lilacs right now. The only lavender in bloom now is Russian sage. It doesn't have that sticky, long-distance scent of English lavenders."

"Russian sage has a sort of provocative blossom, don't you think? It reminds me of you."

I didn't answer. I think he was teasing so that I would respond with my usual naïveté. After how we had spent the night and part of the morning, I didn't feel naïve. Instead, I needed to be distracted. I wanted to ask him one more question, but I didn't want to have to tell him anything in return. He gave me permission to do both, so why should I wrack myself with guilt and doubt?

Fortunately, Jason's ebullient mood offered more than sufficient distraction. While we walked through the neighborhood and down to the lake, he pointed out minutiae as if there were meaning to behold. The bleeding hearts were in bloom. The cherry blossoms had all gone, leaving a scattered snowfall of pink-and-white tissue, pasted to the ground by the last rainfall. The dogwoods unfolded their bloom-like leaves, each tree a reverse sun rise, with the blossoms richest at the top where the tree first received morning sun, fading at the bottom where the sun might never reach.

As we waited to cross Lake Washington Boulevard, a VW convertible passed and then swung around to pull into the gravel beside us. Music blared from the car, but one of the passengers was fumbling with the controls, turning down the sound.

"Hi, Miss Neville!" It was the same four girls from Prescott who had come up to say hello after the show the night before. We had silently agreed to say nothing about how they came to be in the twenty-one-and-older part of an all-ages nightclub.

"Hello—did you meet Jason last night?"

With all the rush around the band after the show, I didn't see everyone who spoke with Jason. I'd stayed with Sonny and tried to follow Jason's instruction not to talk to the press and not to tell people my full name if I didn't want to see it in the newspapers.

"Hi, Jason!" a couple of them said in unison. They were embarrassed and ready to burst out giggling. I realized that it was because they concluded the obvious, having seen me with him at one o'clock in the morning and then again at one o'clock the following afternoon.

"I remember you," Jason said. "You made me sign your arm. But now you're wearing a long-sleeve shirt. Have you repented already?"

The girl giggled—it was Jamie Clayton, who was in my fourth-period voice class.

"No, we have to meet our parents for a Mother's Day brunch at our club house. And we're late."

They drove off giggling, their music turned up loud as soon as they peeled out of the gravel.

"Mother's Day, huh?" Jason said after they disappeared. "You are so conscientious and caring when you speak of your father and brother that I am guessing you lost your mother."

"Yes. A few years ago. Just before my accident. She had heart trouble and passed in the night."

Angling down through the grass toward the lake, we took the path close by the water, near the rushes and away from traffic on the boulevard.

"How did you lose your mother?" I asked.

"Why do you think she's lost?"

I wracked my brain. The folder Randolph dropped on my desk led me to form the idea of "orphan." Plus Jason's story from the night before.

"When you told me about your uncle last night," I said, not quite telling an outright lie. "You said he took you in when your mother died."

"She had cancer."

"Was it quick? I'm sorry—I shouldn't have asked such a stupid question. I know enough people who lost their parents that I know there are no good answers to anything."

"It's OK, Susi. Ask me anything you want. She's been gone a long time. Half the years I knew her, she spent dying. It wasn't quick.

It was a long series of hope-against-hope, with every win followed by a new defeat."

"What was she like?"

"Maybe I don't know anymore. When I was a child, she was perfection. She had a beautiful singing voice and infinite patience— she was my first music teacher. When I moved on to adolescence, she was a puzzle and a set of frustrations. I found out that she'd been a performing musician and then abandoned it. Since music was all I cared about, I pestered her about it, because I never understood her answer: 'I found bigger things in the world than music.' I just couldn't imagine what could be bigger than music."

"Did she quit to take care of you? Music doesn't always pay enough to live on."

"That must have been it. I know enough guys who abandoned the life after they had a kid or two. There was just the two of us."

We walked in silence, because I couldn't say anything meaningful. Jason whacked at the rushes by the trail with his hand.

"Dammit. It didn't need to be that way. Her family had money. My father could have helped her. She was beautiful and talented. They let her die without helping her to do anything with her talent."

One more whack of his hand roused a family of ducklings, paddling away from the bank, squeaking out pleas to their mother to wait for them.

"Don't do it, Susi. Don't let anything stop you. You're beautiful and talented. It's possible for you to have everything you ever wanted."

I turned my head so that he couldn't see that he nearly made me cry.

It wasn't possible. It was long past that time.

※

We paused amid a small riot of retriever-type dogs in ecstasy over fetching sticks from Lake Washington, because Jason wanted to point out two flickers courting on an exposed Doug-fir branch.

"Reminds me of us," he said. "The guy performs a ridiculous, arrhythmic ritual, trying to get her attention. She only looks for a second and then turns away. Which just makes him do it more— sort of like me, going to ridiculous lengths to get your attention."

The birds looked silly, forced by their hormones to act out an ancient script embedded in their DNA that made them dance together.

I said. "We have free will."

"Do we? I suppose," Jason said, speaking softly, wrapping his arms around me. "At least I don't say 'I love you' just to get you go to bed with me like that poor bird up there."

"You say it when you're already in bed with me. I thought it was a habit, like yodeling in the shower."

"Please don't laugh at me. I want you to marry me."

"Jason, please."

"I just don't understand, Susi. I know what it feels like when you let me hold you. I'm not imaging how you respond when I touch you. Explain it to me, please. Explain why I can't find you next to me every morning for the rest of my life."

"It didn't work before. I have no faith it could ever work."

"Ever?" His beautiful smoky voice cracked as he said it.

"My grandmother told me not to go to bed with anyone I wouldn't think of marrying. She gave the same advice to my mother. So I did what my mother did and married the only person I'd ever gone to bed with. Although my mother had good judgment, I don't. I can't trust the entire fabric of my life to my poor judgment."

"You can trust me. How do I convince you of that?"

"Please stop asking me to marry you."

"All right then. It goes against everything I believe in to ask this. It's a complete betrayal of my moral code to even think it, but if you won't marry me, will you live with me? I feel incomplete and half-ill when you aren't with me. We get on so well together."

"Except when you ask me to do what I can't. There are a million reasons why we can't live together. It would threaten my job, I need my privacy, Cynthia says you're impossible to live with, and—"

"What?"

"It goes against my moral code, too."

"OK, Susi. If you change your mind, tell me. I won't be changing mine. Can we go home now? I'm hungry and I want to listen to some of your father's music."

74
"Nothin' Without You"
Jason

"MY BROTHER INSISTS ON ANCHOVIES."

"I'll pass unless you want some."

"No anchovies then. The red chilies hurt my throat, so I'll take out part for me and then add the chilies for you."

After we returned to her house, Susi put us both to work making an early supper. The homely tasks of chopping garlic and pitting kalamata olives seemed to restore peace between us. We were making puttanesca, and Susi forced us to take a long time, since the bread had to bake first. It beats me when she found time to make the dough, leaving it to rise while we walked. While I was in the shower? After she had worn me into a half-conscious pile of humanoid flesh and left me to simper in her bed?

When I finished chopping the olives, she added them to the garlic and capers simmering in olive oil and butter.

"Where's a can of tomatoes, Susi? I'll open it for you."

She frowned. "If I used canned tomatoes, then it would truly be whore's spaghetti."

"Susi, such talk."

"That's what puttanesca means. It's a working girl's quick meal."

"Then why isn't it quick when you cook it? I'm starving."

"I'll chop the tomatoes. There's fresh parsley in the garden. Do you think you can recognize what to harvest?" She handed me kitchen shears and sent me out back to her garden, where I proved so adept at the hunter-gather role that I got a kiss when I returned. I did such a good job of that, and pretended to be so patient while waiting for the bread to bake, that she let me make love to her on the Mission sofa.

"She let me" is a figure of speech.

I get so lost with her in these situations that I can't keep track of who is in control. I think she trusts me enough now that she lets me start. After we quarreled on the walk—was it a quarrel?—it had taken some time to be comfortable with each other again, but I think it was me who first had the courage to touch more than fingertips.

I was kissing her, and I think my tongue found hers first. When her tongue responded, I pulled her closer and let my hands glide over her shoulder blades. Under her shirt. It was my thigh that nudged between her knees, allowing me to press up against where she had been so silky and hot that morning. She didn't resist, and I carried her over to the sofa and—I can't remember the part where her jeans came off. I was so hungry that my teeth might have played a part. She was being helpful and cooperative by unzipping my jeans, though I was still in control at that point. Between tearing open the condom and the timer announcing the baked bread, she made that move again and I wasn't in charge at all. I'm losing any faith I have that it's me who knows how to make her come five times. By the time we're done, it's me who is desperate, begging, ready to scream.

She loves me. I know she does. I can feel it in how her heart beats when my hand rests on her breast.

I just don't get it.

How can she not want it to be like this every day?

Four: Rondo

75
"Knockin' on Your Door"
Jason

WE WERE WASHING THE DISHES and seeing if there was any garlic and olive oil left on each other's lips, and I was asking whether there might be chocolate hidden anywhere in her kitchen when Ian called.

On Susi's land line. Asking for me.

"Perry Webb thinks he has your stolen guitar, Jason. He's been out of town, but tonight he was in his store looking over what his guys picked up the last couple of weeks."

"Can we get it first thing tomorrow?"

"Tonight. He invited us to come over right away."

"Is he at the shop on Roosevelt?"

"Yeah—come get me so I can ride along. Cynthia has one car and Arlo has the other."

I hung up excited, and then realized that I expected Susi would drive me over there, which brought on a severe attack of embarrassment and self-condemnation.

"What is it, Jason? You sounded so excited on the phone, but now you look confused."

"Some creep stole my Uncle Beau's guitar a month ago, but a friend maybe found it. He said we could pick it up tonight."

"What fantastic news. Let's go."

"You don't mind? I don't want to take advantage of our friendship."

"We'll both fall asleep from too much food and sun if we just hang around here."

"We have to pick up Ian on the way. When are you ever going to get your own car back, Susi? This one just doesn't look like you."

"You can't be half as frustrated about how long it's taking as I am."

It turns out we had to pick up Ian because Perry told him about a couple of other interesting instruments he had.

"Don't let Cynthia know about this," Ian said when we entered Perry's shop. "A man has to have at least one vice."

"What is Jason's vice?" Susi asked.

"Washing his hands too often and being more perfect than other people can abide."

I'm not so perfect that I can hide disappointment.

It wasn't Beau's guitar.

"Although it is a beautiful instrument," I said, when I saw my disappointment mirrored on Perry's face. I wanted to do the right thing by him, since he'd tried to be helpful. "I'll buy it from you as a replacement. I've been playing Ian's, but he is so cheap, he's charging me rent. By the note."

Ian had already settled into making love to a twelve-string Rickenbacker Deluxe someone famous played, supposedly. I won't name names; it wasn't either George Harrison or Roger McGuinn. Else, the price would have had three more zeroes beyond what Perry was asking.

"I really want this," Ian said.

"Get it."

"Cynthia will kill me."

"I'll buy it and you can pay me over time."

"She'd find out."

"Geez, Ian. Tell her it's a tax-deductible business expense."

"That didn't work the last three times."

I shook my head. "Perry, you always have great mics. I want to find one for Susi. Everything we have is for male voices. Do you have something that can handle a woman's sibilance with more grace than my gear?"

"I don't need a microphone," Susi said.

"You were uncomfortable last night with the stand-up mic at the hotel and the handheld at the club. You use your entire body to sing. So let's find something hands-free that you'll be comfortable with."

"I'm like Ian. I can't afford to spend money I don't have."

"Please let me give you a present." I could see obstinacy settling over her. "All right, Susi. I'm buying one for my own gear collection tonight. I'll have it available for any woman who comes to sing with us. Why don't you work with Perry to help make the selection? My singing isn't the best test, is it? Sibilance isn't a problem for my voice."

"It isn't for mine either," she said, with great indignation. In the end she went off with Perry to his sound room.

Ian was putting the twelve-string back on its stand, wiping away fingerprints with a soft cloth.

"I know you need money to take care of your people, Ian." I had put off for a week talking to him about business.

"Oh crap. It better not be Karl who said anything. There is such a thing as attorney-client privilege, isn't there?"

"Why didn't you say something? When I ask whether people want to tour or go into the studio with Dominique, you just say, 'Whatever you want.' I've been too focused on my hassles."

"It's my own problem. I mean, you're the one stuck married to the Dragon Woman. I was lucky enough to cash in on the sales. I played the same as I would if she wasn't there. Which she wouldn't have been if you had listened to me."

"You and Beau were both right," I said. "Though I don't know how you could recognize a poison lover when I couldn't. You've been with one woman forever. Do you have warnings about Susi?"

"Yeah. If you lose her, we will all be dicked. Don't screw up this time, jerk-face. We need her as much as you do."

"Yikes, Ephraim is in the sound room with Susi."

Ian looked down, not at the sound room. "You should talk to him."

"You knew he'd be here? You're my effing best friend. How—"

"Talk to him. I don't know the business, Jason. I always just did whatever Beau told us to do. We need someone to take Beau's place."

"Frickin' hell, Ian—"

"I'll help Susi choose a mic. Though I don't think she was even using one more than half the time on Saturday. Still, I'll help."

"Thanks. You are such a swell friend."

※

"I have been blind, Jason. I didn't see it until last night."

I scowled. Ephraim in his black leather trench coat stood in my personal space. He didn't shake my hand, though. He said, "I thought the whole problem between us came from you being pissed at Dominique, which she earned. But you're pissed at me personally, aren't you?"

"I thought you understood where I was going with *Woman at the Well*. Then you dampened Beau's bass line and Toby's mandolin. You took out the fuzz and twang. Because Dominique wanted to be mainstream. You knew better. You knew what I was trying to do."

"You left. You abandoned the project, Jason. Dominique stayed. I had to choose between you, and that time Dominique won. It's your turn this time, if you're staying and buckling down to do the work."

"What makes you think I don't have a work ethic?"

"I've heard about it. In fact, that's why I first sought you out. However, my experience to date is that you abandoned a project. I did what was right for those who stayed behind."

"I thought you were my friend." Geez, I couldn't believe I said that.

"Jason, you've been in this business a long time. You need friends, and you need people to do business for you. Don't confuse the two." He kept on me, the way Beau used to, and that ticked me off even more.

"I refuse to believe that. We did fine with Beau and other friends tending to business. The hurt didn't come until Dominique pulled us into the pool with sharks like you."

"Until two years ago, you were all broke. You had to beg radio stations to play your little homemade EPs. You had to perform three hundred nights out of each year just to buy food."

"We made enough to pay taxes and buy guitars."

"Now there's a real hallmark of success."

"It's more confusing to argue with you each time we meet, Ephraim. You say you want to help me to succeed, and then insult me at every turn. Can I go now, or do you want to explain some more about how you screwed up my music to help me?"

"Jason, I've gone to the line for you. I have other things to do, but I committed to Albion Records to stay with you through this second album, since you signed on the condition that I remain as your key man."

"You mean, I can leave Albion if you do? Screw it, Ephraim. Go do what you want and leave me free."

"It doesn't work that way. I have a commitment to the label that I must fulfill. In fact, I spent the winter arguing with my bosses that you were sunk in grief over a death in the family. I pushed out deadlines for you. I rearranged public appearances or fixed it so you could phone in interviews from Europe. I kept the whole story out of the papers as much as possible. I got everyone to buy the excuses I made without ever explaining that Beau was your last relative in the world."

"Explained to your bosses? Your boss is your father."

"Who needs artists to live up to their contracts in order to stay in business. Now, how do you and I do business together without Beau and Dominique coming between us?"

"Make her stop hassling with Karl so the divorce closes."

"All right, as much as I can make her do anything. Karl scheduled a conference for Thursday. Finish the music for her part of the new album by then. Have the complete recording masters ready by June second. We need the new CD on shelves when Stoneway goes on the road."

"And then you'll stop popping up like a gremlin everywhere I go, because we'll have no further business with each other."

"If you choose to do it that way, yes. However, I'm begging you to stay in business with me. Wherever you want to go next, I can help you succeed."

76

"Hard Hearted"
Susi

JASON AND I HAD ENOUGH time Monday morning—we went to bed early, woke early, spent only half an hour in the shower together—to dawdle over coffee before work. He was eating the last of the pumpkin empanadas, licking crumbs from his fingers in an obvious, teasing way while the Delmore Brothers sang in the background. I was doing what I'd been doing all weekend: seeking the courage to ask him one more question.

Then he cleared his throat, setting down his coffee cup so that it rattled and sloshed on its saucer.

"Susi, I've been trying to be brave enough to ask you something since Saturday night. What I'm going to ask is more important to me than anything in the world."

"We already discussed marriage. Anything more we say will make us both unhappy again."

"I promised I wouldn't bug you about that. The band has to go on the road this summer. I thought I could delay it, but we need to go for a lot of reasons. So I can't help your institute by teaching. I had meant it as a promise to you, but I have business obligations I can't escape."

"I wasn't counting on you, Jason."

"Oh." He sounded disappointed. "I wished you could. I swear this is my sole failure, and it's only because I had obligations from before we met."

"That's it? That's what you were afraid to say?"

"No. Please come with us. I thought we were just experimenting in rehearsal, but now we know the band is going somewhere important, and we can't do it without you. The band wants you. I want you."

"I have plans, Jason. You know that."

"If we have to play without you, it'll be like missing a limb. I'm scared to death that if I go on the road, you'll slip away."

"The institute takes more than thirty days out of the middle of the summer. I can't commit to anything else."

"You could start the institute in the fall. I can help then. So can Ian and Toby. What about Angelia? Is she going to choose your institute over Toby and the band?"

I hadn't thought about it, but at the moment, I couldn't let Angelia's fickle loyalties affect my decisions.

"Teaching is my life now," I said. "I can't abandon what I set out to do just to pursue the pleasure of singing. Angelia's presence isn't a required factor in my success."

"Will you at least think about it, please? I'm begging you, the way I begged you to listen to my music and sing my songs."

"Is this why you wanted to buy a microphone for me?"

"Yes."

"You have a strange knack for deceiving yourself. I don't want you to think I'll change my mind. Starting the institute this summer is too important to me."

"Don't you like to sing with us?"

"I can't go on tour with you. I can't rip up the fabric of what I'm trying to do with my life."

"Why, Susi? When I hold you, I feel every cell of your body yearn for the same thing I do. How can you not want to sing with me?"

"I need to ask you something, too. Perhaps our questions are related." However I'd planned to ask all weekend, I ended up asking in a way that felt brutal. "Where did you go to school after Prescott?"

"Oh, for crissakes." He set down his cup with a clatter and settled back on the bar stool, folding his arms in challenge. The honey-brown pleading in his eyes from a moment before clouded over to a smoldering, coffee-brown displeasure. "All over."

"Like where?"

"My Associate Arts work was done as distance learning, reading in the back of the van or holed up in a Motel 6 when we could afford it. Then I went on to do my baccalaureate and masters work on the Internet from my hotel room at Marriott State or from Starbucks U, wherever they offered a wireless connection. I did a lot of work as a visiting scholar in the great libraries on the Continent, in Great Britain, and across the U.S. I spent weeks at the library in Montreal—"

"You never finished the twelfth grade. You're a drop-out."

"The correct term is 'autodidact.' Does this matter to you?"

"Yes."

"Why? How am I deficient in either intelligence or learning? Why does it matter?'

"It matters because—"

"I can't wait to hear this. It's more than ten years past making any difference in the world. How can it matter? Oh, I know, everything went on my permanent record, and it's still following me, right? 'Mr. Taylor fails to apply his brilliance to homework he judges to be beneath him. Mr. Taylor's attendance is affected by his non-curricular activities. Mr. Taylor pissed off the choir master once again. Mr. Taylor remains our only A student with D's in deportment.'"

"It matters because it's easy to do. Anyone who understands American society knows that you graduate from high school to prove you can live by the basic rules, if nothing else."

"I don't need to prove that. I follow Dylan's basic rule: 'To live outside the law you must be honest.' I've done just fine, haven't I?"

"You let the jazz ensemble down when you left to do your own thing."

"Are those rich brats still complaining after all this time?" He stood up abruptly, knocking over the stool, and then paced as he talked, his large body filling even more of the space in my tiny house. "Not a single one of them had it in them to become professional musicians. I know what became of each one. They're insurance execs and suburban philanthropists. If I'm to blame for ending their glory days too soon, I'm sorry. But I wasn't going to make a dime at the musical equivalent of a track meet. I made enough money to live on for a year by going to Europe. And Hector Henderson never had a single effing thing he could teach me. I stayed in jazz band because I could play guitar during school hours. Susi, you cannot possibly care about this."

"I do, though."

"Just so I understand, you won't marry me or sing with me because I'm a high school drop-out?"

"I was in a marriage between unequal partners before. I won't do it again. You can't believe the pain—"

"Oh, I know about unequal relationships. I married a Berklee graduate who also thought I was a hick who needed help to get ahead in the world."

"I don't think that. Please understand—"

"That you stayed married too long to that cretinous horn-player, so now you won't have me—when you know I love you—because I didn't graduate from high school? What is that, Susi? Some advanced moral code that I'm too ill-educated to appreciate?"

"Jason, we had a great weekend. Let's not spoil it."

"OK. But you can't make love like you do, Susi, and then tell me there isn't more love now than when we began." He ran his finger down my forehead and nose, to my chin. "Even someone as ill-educated as me can see it."

The phone rang and I went to answer it, more to excuse myself from the pain of the moment than to make the phone stop ringing.

77
"Tears of Rage"
Jason

WHILE SUSI WAS TALKING on the phone in her bedroom, Ian called on my cell and told me to turn on the radio, because the deejays on the alternative station at the end of the dial were talking about the Showbox event. What a way to ruin an already destroyed morning.

"Yes, I was there," the woman deejay with the throaty voice was saying.

"You always had a thing for Jason Taylor. Do you think he beats up the new singer too?"

"He never did. That's an ugly rumor. The police dropped the charges."

"Guys with dough always get the charges dropped."

"You're just dealing in innuendo and rumor. Listen to the guy's music. He doesn't hit women. Let's go to the phones and hear from others who were there."

"Yes, hi, am I on? I was there Saturday night, and if this is where Jason Taylor is going, people who dig on *Woman at the Well* are going to crap their pants."

The woman jock said, "Yeah. I'm a fan of his, but I couldn't get into *Woman at the Well*. Way too mainstream."

"I heard them earlier Saturday at this fundraiser where I worked as a waiter. I couldn't believe it when they came on at the Showbox. At the fundraiser, they did mostly acoustic stuff, with just a little electricity. Even that beat hell out of the country diva shit he did with his wife."

"You can't say that on the radio."

"Sorry. Anyway, at the Showbox, the singer's voice just tore people up. At the start, it sounded like they were doing a quiet ballad, and she's like Margo Timmins of Cowboy Junkies, all shy and hardly looking up. When they started this hellacious guitar, mandolin, and fiddle part, she came back on vocals like a banshee on acid."

The deejay said, "Jason Taylor and Ian Griffith had already ripped everyone's head open with their guitars before she let loose."

"I've heard him play for years. He's playing and writing at a whole other level. You can hear tapes from Saturday night on the Internet. They're trading boots like crazy."

"Where's the new singer from? She's never played in Seattle before."

"Jason Taylor's blog says her name is Susi Neville, and—get this—she teaches at Prescott Prep. I bet the guys there have a hard time sitting through their classes. You can get an MP3 of one of the songs there too."

My blog? My own effing blog?

78
"Instant Karma"
Susi

"Miss Neville?"

"Yes?"

It was the principal of Prescott.

"Can you please come in early this morning for a meeting?"

"Of course. Is there anything I need to bring to be prepared?" As if I couldn't guess what this was about.

"We need to discuss your weekend activities. You know that a fundamental principle for staff is to be above reproach in all quarters of life."

"I would be happy to talk with you."

Actually, I would rather take poison and die.

I went out to say goodbye to Jason and to offer him a ride as far as Thirty-fourth Avenue, but he had already disappeared. However much discord remained between us when the telephone disrupted our discomfort, I couldn't attend to it at that moment.

At school, Randolph stood in the hallway, prepared to follow me into me into my early-morning encounter with judgment and condemnation.

"Enjoy the weekend with your drop-out boyfriend?" he breathed behind me as I knocked on the principal's office door.

79
"Box Full of Letters"
Jason

I HAVE NEVER PUT ON my pants so fast. Then I took off running across the hill to catch a bus—it's impossible to get a cab in this part of town, even though this is supposed to be a major metropolis. While I sprinted through the alleys, I called the webmaster from my cell, screaming at him.

"Stop giving people your password," Chet said calmly. "Nobody can put anything up there without your password."

"I've never given anyone the password. Take down anything dated later than the first of May. I haven't posted since then."

"The customer is always right," Chet said. "It'll be gone in the next ten minutes. But I'm telling you, it didn't get posted without your password."

Dang. As soon as I got to the studio, I spent the morning posting the information I wanted on the site, about the musical direction for the new band and the specific roots influences we were pursuing. Nothing about Susi, nothing about Angelia. I uploaded my own MP3 file, showing off the older material I had been cleaning up and another of the new band playing roots material. To calm down, I played back the tapes from the session she and I did the previous Thursday, but then I began worrying about what it did for future releases if I posted that MP3. I was in such a boil over it that I wanted to call Ephraim to ask him what the hell I'm supposed to do.

I stopped listening to the tapes and fell into a deep hole, the one that's plagued me since the debacles of the previous year, only this time I was paying five hundred dollars an hour in studio time to sit in front of my laptop and read what people said on the Internet.

It's a hole I fall into every time I go there. I want to know what people think about the music—not just the casual rap from morning deejays whose careers require them to be both controversial and placating. Not from people who called to hear themselves on the radio because they happened to be at the Showbox when we played. I wanted to know what people who cared to hear our work thought about it.

I don't know why I believed this morning, just because I was agitated, that the blogs would be any different than ever. Four women described at length how I looked in a dinner jacket and how wonderful that I took it off because of the heat. One claimed that I looked at her through all of "Rhianna's Song." A fifth caught my pick when I flipped it into the audience at the end of the Jimmie Rodgers yodel. Two guys argued about the set list, one because he intended to keep an accurate archive of the set list from every show I ever played, "for the sake of history," for crissakes, and now the two gentlemen were quarreling over whether I said the new song was called "Hymn for a Rusty Angel" or "Him and a Rustic Angel." Another woman complained that I must be lovers with the new singer and that was a bad idea, because the new singer looked like the kind of woman who'd make me fat and lazy, and a second woman said that I already looked less gaunt in the pictures from Saturday than I looked in Glasgow in January.

The pictures? The ones posted on the unofficial fan site, which included great close-ups of Ian with his shaved head and Susi looking like a trance singer from an Eighties band playing electric Kool-Aid house music. One of Susi and me at the market, singing cowboy songs in the early morning. I called Karl's office and left a message that he needed to negotiate with the unofficial site to get the pictures of Susi and Angelia pulled.

"Tell them I'll give them a personal message to post—an exclusive that they will very much like—if they'll pull those pictures."

As if I could bargain to keep material that popped on the Internet from having unintended consequences. I should know better.

Two women started a debate on the band's official blog about Ian's shaved head, one complaining it was a travesty, and the other waxing eloquent about both Ian's looks and his musical contribution to the band's new direction. This was the first post that discussed our music.

However, it didn't count because I knew it was Cynthia. She'd been doing it forever, posting messages about Ian's looks and his music, and then reading it back to him as if it weren't her.

Because Ian never reads the posts. Why can't I make myself do that?

I couldn't make myself look away as the conversations unfolded on the screen while I watched. One woman felt compelled to note that the new singer should be warned that Jason Taylor is a controlling, abusive person, while another woman (I know it's Cynthia) asserted that all the rumors were unfounded lies, that the public record shows the complaint was false. Then the discussion drifted off for a moment to an uninformed rant about how the police contribute to the silent persecution of women caught in the net of domestic abuse.

At least three guys replied, "Who cares?" and I have to make myself not answer. When I think about domestic violence, I'm ill at the notion of people seeing me as a perpetrator, as the embodiment of a far greater evil than my negligent father ever committed. The angry woman (and Cynthia) engaged with those guys over the social issues, and Jason Taylor disappeared from the current discussion for a few moments, while I slipped down the blog threads to see how people described Saturday's music.

What I most wanted to know was what people heard and how they felt about it. Not whether women appreciated how my package looked in silk trousers versus jeans. Not cute-coy discussions of whether the length of my fingers indicated anything about my privates. Not whether Ian sticking his tongue out when he concentrates indicates a penchant for oral sex. ("I'm certain it does," his most erstwhile fan replied.)

I couldn't help myself from asking.

Sebastian: Saturday night, Ian and Toby played as master musicians, and the band was in complete sync, even with so many new members added.

MarkT: We'll see. You can't tell from the MP3. It has all the problems of most board tapes—not enough bass being one problem. For me, it's too psychedelic. My favorite period was about three years ago, when the band was doing true indie country, with all original material. This new stuff is going to take some getting used to.

Everyone jumped on this "true indie country" assertion, squabbling about whether the term held any metaphysically precise meaning. Yes to Wilco, no to Ryan Adams after *Whiskeytown*. Yes to the Jayhawks, but The Replacements are just Minnesota roots rock. How to categorize Eighties West Coast rockabilly that has too much of Downey, California to be country? Could anything from the Pacific Northwest be country, alt or otherwise? Then, as my impatience grew, the squabble refocused on whether our new music could bear the indie country label, with more than one claim that no one who records for Albion Records could be labeled "indie" anything.

Then a woman posted a screed against labeling. That cheered me up.

JTgrrrl: Everyone who posted after the show missed what has happened—since Woman at the Well, Taylor's music has gone 180 degrees in another direction. I have argued before that CD was only an Albion Records interpretation of what Jason Taylor's music might sound like in an alternate universe. I don't think he produced it, in spite of what it says on the liner notes.

MarkT: You're saying they lie on the liner notes?

JTgrrrl: It says Co-produced, doesn't it? I was at the Showbox Saturday—I haven't missed a show he has done within 150 miles of where I am in the last six years, when his first album came out. What he played Saturday was both incredibly surprising—if you believe that the production of Woman at the Well was his sole work—and also completely logical if you've listened to his music over time. This is his most exciting work to date. If you don't love the board tapes from Saturday or the recent boots, you aren't going to be a Jason Taylor fan for long. I just wish they'd post the tour dates for the summer. Everyone else is posting their summer calendars this week.

So, if Susi won't marry me, maybe this woman who has seen me play a thousand times will marry me. One of the set-list curators answered back.

MarkT: So you're arguing that he went mainstream by accident? Now he's going to stay there because Albion Records will recognize that he is so good, they won't screw up his recordings anymore?

JTgrrl: No, any time Jason gets close to the brass ring, he f*cks up his chances by doing something that no record label will gamble with. I'm confident that you aren't going to hear any more of his music in elevators. Woman at the Well was his only shot at that.

Another new name logged on and sent everyone into a flurry.

LostSon2: If you don't think Jason still belongs in indie country, you haven't heard the boots from Saturday afternoon. He did Hank Williams and Ralph Stanley tunes, and SusiQ sang two Hazel Dickens and Alice Gerrard songs. I put the MP3s on the trading list, together with some outtakes from recent rehearsals.

MarkT: You have rehearsal tapes? I thought his sessions were all closed.

LostSon2: We're like brothers, so I have access. I also posted some MP3s from Saturday's sound-board tapes. But you can't hear Susi on those. Her voice is missing.

MarkT: How can her voice be missing from the sound board?

LostSon2: I think it's like how a vampire's reflection doesn't show in a mirror. She is an angel, and you have to do something special to catch her voice on tape.

MarkT: I heard her Saturday night. She's from out of this world, but I don't know about angel.

LostSon2: She is going to be the angel of indie country. She is going to be like Emmylou Harris was for Gram Parsons. Except I hope God doesn't decide to strike Jason down so young.

Frickin' hell. I yelled for Martha to find the sound-board tapes from Saturday night, and then I was on the phone to Karl, hating that the word 'estoppels' had entered my vocabulary, leaving details with Warren, who answered the phone during lunch hour. While I was shouting a While-You-Were-Out note about the idiot bastard fan freak whose heart I wanted to rip out with my teeth, Martha slipped me a note: Ephraim had a radio station manager holding on another phone line for me.

"I'm grateful that you have time for us, Mr. Taylor."

"Hi, Ray. Only the IRS calls me Mr. Taylor. Geez, I haven't talked to you since you were kind enough to let us visit in July." My throat had rasped raw from the morning's tantrums.

"It was a good session."

"How's your boy? Dylan, isn't it? He must be five by now."

"He is doing great. 'Rhianna's Song' is one of his favorites."

"No kidding? What else do five-year-olds listen to?"

"Los Lobos, Beach Boys, Beatles. Stoneway."

"You are shining me on, Ray. Tell me more tonight?"

"The show is at ten. If you want, you can come a little earlier."

"Yes. I'll bring my partner. We're happy to play if you'll have us."

The guy was effusive in his thanks, and I would make him wait until tonight to let him know that in the world of music, "partner" still meant Ian Griffith, not the mysterious angel who sang with us on Saturday.

80
"Nothing Was Delivered"
Jason

"JASON, IT'S ONE THING at my house. Don't do it at school. Stop it."

"Hi, Susi. I'm flattered that you called me. This is a first, talking to you on the phone. What is it I'm doing that I have to stop now?"

"The roses. I thought it was cute when I found them on my doorstep, though I confess I thought you did it to make me feel guilty. Do not put them in my classroom or leave them anywhere at school, however you get them inside. I can't believe you sent me more of that stupid love poetry after the conversation we had this morning. Jason? Will you please say something instead of just breathing on the phone?"

"Why do you think it's me?"

"Don't be coy. The ones on my porch first appeared the day after we started singing together. The students noticed last week when you started leaving them outside my office. I do not need the principal to notice."

"I'll make sure it stops, Susi. There's no rehearsal tonight."

"Good. I have a late meeting at school."

"Shall I come by later?"

I hate it when the sound of breathing in a phone means no. I hate it almost as much as stalkers.

I ran the mile to Ian's house to get him out of bed so we could drive over to Arlo's house to find out whether he'd posted MP3s and photos all over the Internet. That head-shot of Susi in the market had to have been one of his.

At Ian's house, effing Arlo was sitting at the breakfast table, eating oatmeal with Cynthia while she sat at her laptop doing in email.

"Shalom, bro! Did you see the bitching material I posted on your fan site? Shit, I have been up all night trying to figure out how—"

I had him against the refrigerator to hurt him the way I've dreamed of doing, while Cynthia shrieked in my ear that I'm an egg-sucking asshole.

"Hey, what a warm family scene." Ian stood in the doorway, rubbing sleep from his eyes and scratching. "Do we choose sides in this game, or is it every man for himself?"

"Jason is an asshole!" Cynthia shouted in my ear.

"Yeah, but that's not news. It's not worth yelling about," Ian said. "It's sure not worth getting out of bed for."

I couldn't stop shouting, though I was going hoarse. "Effing Arlo posted Susi's name and picture and rehearsal tapes all over the universe."

"I never!" Arlo croaked, since I had my hands around his neck.

"He just put up photos from the Saturday shows," Cynthia said. "You're being a jerk, Jason. He couldn't even post those without my help." She slapped my hands away from Arlo. "Aren't you supposed to be harassing Martha and the engineer at the studio? Go away. I have to put up with you pissing and moaning all over the house at night. Can't we have some peace during the daytime?"

Ian stretched and yawned. "I'll come along. There's nothing to do here. Does Martha have any food at the studio?"

※

Ian and I listened together to the sound-board recordings from Saturday. It beats me how my little Internet friend managed to plug into the board. Our sound tech never would have let him patch in.

Susi's voice couldn't be heard on the board tapes.

"She wasn't using a mic," Ian said.

"Yes, she was. She had it in her hand. Something happened technically."

"I think she switched it off."

"No one could project that well without a mic. She had my earphone monitors. She couldn't have heard herself sing without a mic."

"You're always right, Jason. But when we were shopping last night, Susi said she doesn't use mics except when recording."

<h1 style="text-align:center">81</h1>
<h2 style="text-align:center">"More Than I Can Do"</h2>
Jason

"GEEZ, KARL, I WAS beginning to think you gave up returning my calls."

"OK, buddy, you got me now. You aren't being the chicken-shit prima donna I thought you were."

"Gee, I'm touched."

"I read every post I could on the Internet. I think your friend is flipping. Listen: 'If he hurts this angel, God will strike him dead. I will serve as God's right hand myself if it comes to that.' There are more like that."

"Yikes."

"You need personal security."

"I won't go that way. However much *Woman at the Well* screwed up my life, I intend to still walk down the street by myself when I want to."

"Call the police."

"There is nothing they can do if there hasn't been a physical threat against me. They told me that when I filed the report on Beau's guitar."

"Be careful, Jason. I don't want to spend the next two years settling your estate. I would feel so bad about calling you chicken-shit."

"I don't mind that, but the 'prima donna' bit is offensive."

I tried to relax in the music, though I ended up following wherever Ian wanted to go for the rest of the morning, which is problematic for us, since he is never comfortable leading. He prefers to react. So it was a betrayal on my part that I had turned into a squib.

We had descended to such a state by the time Sonny came to work with Zak that Ian and the engineer were just like the statues in lower Fremont of people waiting for a bus that will never come, while I sat with my head in my hands, waiting for my brain to unfreeze.

Zak took up his drumsticks and attacked the Ludwig traps to warm up, as blissfully unaware of what was happening around him as ever.

"Can you fucking hold off?" I said, sounding far bitchier than intended.

"What's up?" Sonny asked, since he is sensitive to variables in human temperature.

Ian said, "Jason is on the rag because he thinks a bogey man is going to get his girlfriend. Is she your girlfriend this week, Jason?"

"Someone is bugging Susi?" Sonny looked startled. Then he grinned. "Besides you, I mean."

"She says I've been sending her flowers everyday—though I'm not even smart enough to think of it. This creep is coming so close that he leaves roses at her house and at school. If I call the police, they'll want to speak to her, and I don't want her to worry about it."

"I know where she lives," Sonny said. "We'll watch at the school too."

"OK, but just have your guys call the police if there's ever a problem. Don't do anything."

"Can you get cell phones for them?"

"Martha can. She can do anything. Just make sure no one bugs Susi."

I stared at my own guitar as if I couldn't recognize it. I also had to stop bugging her. It was clear from our Sunday walk in the park, from Monday breakfast, from the brusque phone call. This Little Prince was plumb out of fox bait and damn sick of practicing patience. However, there wasn't any other alternative.

82
"Ashes by Now"
Susi

AT SCHOOL, ROSEMARY HANDED me four of those pink While-You-Were-Out notes when I passed her office, and I dropped them in the trash as I entered my own office. Two from Angelia and two from Cynthia. I had returned Angelia's call once already—she had called in sick every day since Monday. She wanted to bug me about rehearsing with the band. I had about had it with email as a pernicious tool of the devil, since now Cynthia also pestered me via phone at least four times a day about not showing up for rehearsal, as if I owed her anything.

Perhaps worse, Jason's ex-wife had begun forwarding me all the email he had ever sent her. Some of the same kind of bad poetry I'd been receiving, but as if it were written backwards in a mirror for hexing, all of it mean and cruel. After reading the first couple of messages, I couldn't quite believe it of him, though I already knew that what his wife had done to him had been the basest sort of betrayal. I printed some of it, swearing that I'd just get brave and ask him, if I ever saw him again.

The principal had been explicit: my job was in jeopardy. Teachers appear at work on time (I'd never been late a day in my life until I met Jason). Teachers charged with the care of the innocent children of Prescott Prep do not sing in rock-and-roll bands that include drug users and wife beaters.

I didn't need the threat. Susi Neville does not sing in a rock-and-roll band. She knows nothing about the genre, or the life, or the people that inhabited that world. It's not her world, and their cares aren't her cares. She doesn't need to fall into a fugue state and sail off the edge of the world just because singing and satiation of appetite seem more important than a sane, rational plan of action.

I kept repeating to the principal (and to myself) that I only wanted a chance to teach and launch this summer's institute, to prove the value of the ideals in my curriculum, to give my father one more season as a teacher, to help kids who love music have a chance to learn more while playing with experienced musicians.

At three o'clock, I took the first emotional bath of the day. As I prepared once more to cajole Chastity Keller into going to Juilliard, she said breathlessly that she was pregnant and going to live with her aunt in Phoenix after graduation, but I must not tell a soul, because only the aunt knows, and it has to stay a secret, even from her parents.

"You have to tell your mother, Chastity. She'll want to help."

She looked at me in surprise. "You don't know my mother, Miss Neville. Anyway, I don't have to do anything she says. I'm eighteen now."

I have no experience or wisdom to share with her. She had kicked away all her moorings, and I didn't have a compass to lend her. What I wanted to say, I couldn't. After all, it was her life that she had made a mess of. I have wanted to shake her for the past few months—perhaps ever since she got involved with that boy who would depart in a few short weeks for Sarah Lawrence, deserting her for all time. I thought of how Jason felt about his talented mother never taking her chance. It was all I could do to keep from putting my head down on my desk and weeping for this girl.

Chastity saw the clock and grabbed her books.

"I'm rehearsing a song with the jazz band to perform at graduation. I can't let them down."

Nope, can't let the jazz band down. It's OK, though, to let God down for having given you an ocean of talent that you will let run out on the sands of Phoenix. She left me alone to think terrible thoughts, wondering if other young women who were afraid of their talents would instead have babies that tethered them to a make-do sort of life. Or if other talented women who were afraid to be alone would tether themselves to the wrong sort of man who could—

Randolph stuck his head around the corner of my door. I had come to loathe the sight of him.

"The principal wants to see you. Gwyneth Lukas is in his office."

Whom I wanted to see only a little less than I wanted an endodontic procedure without anesthesia. When I walked through the door, Gwyneth slapped me, which I hadn't experienced since high school.

Then again, this was high school.

"You bitch! You dragged that bastard into Zak's life, and now it's all ruined. After everything we planned for him."

"I'm sorry, Gwyneth. I don't understand."

"It's Zak's birthday. He celebrated it by packing all of his things into a van, to move in with one of those musicians you got him involved with. He sent a rejection to Berklee weeks ago. It's your friend who talked him into quitting."

"Jason Taylor?"

"Zak said you let him out of class for the past month to play in that band. He's out all hours with that man—a wife beater and a drug user."

"You didn't know Zak is playing in a band? How could you not know?"

The principal interrupted at this point. Up to that moment, I'd been rather proud that I hadn't let Gwyneth's hysteria affect me, and that I'd stopped myself from slapping that supercilious look from Randolph's face.

"Miss Neville, is this true—that you excused Zak from class?"

"No. I stopped reporting absences for all seniors. Most teachers have. The kids all have their acceptances. Their diplomas are waiting for them. Missed days have no effect at this point."

"Zak quit school," the principal said.

That might have been the point when my reserve weakened.

Gwyneth had gone green with fury under her makeup. "I called the foundation to inform them that the Lukas family was pulling financial support from your little scam. That's when I learned who your musician friend is. He failed the foundation's background check."

"They were false accusations. Jason Taylor has never been convicted of anything." I didn't mention that his name wasn't supposed to be on the application, because when your world falls apart, the details don't matter.

"He spent a week in jail for hard drugs. He has a convicted heroin dealer in his band. That is who you sent my child to play with."

"Miss Neville, we need to have a serious discussion."

The principal glowered. Gwyneth fumed. Randolph smirked.

I sat down and spoke as calmly as I ever had in my life.

"Let's begin. But first, that smug bastard and this newly concerned mother who hasn't got a clue what her adult son is doing with his life will not be part of our professional discussion."

83
"Everybody Has Been Burned"
Jason

YES, I WANTED TO CRY like Lear in the wilderness when Martha gave me the note.

> Couldn't wait to hear my brother's work. Don't worry. I'll be discrete.

I rocked like an over-wound metronome for long minutes, not wanting to open the box to see what wasn't in there.

The security guys Karl hired took the finished tapes from last week's work to a vault on Friday. When I called to have the tapes delivered—Dominique needed to start work this week, and she'd finally agreed to come on Friday—Karl's security brought the box back to me.

Then Martha found the note at the top of the box.

"They aren't all gone," Martha said, and I had just enough self-control to keep from deprecating her weak assurances. She was near to tears herself.

We counted the tapes and then did an inventory in the same methodical way we'd done with the older material the first day Martha came back to work with me.

Twelve tapes were missing, including the essentials. The first acoustic mind-bender that we recorded with Susi. The reworking of that song we discarded in Bergen, which I'd written for Ian, calling him brother and thanking Apollo and the goddess of music for his loyalty. Ten finished tracks that awaited only Dominique's vocals for the new album, representing over two hundred hours of studio time for Ian, Toby, Sonny, Zak, and Angelia.

No, that was a hysterical over-estimation on my part. I had tapes from earlier rehearsals. We knew how we wanted each of these songs to sound. It wouldn't take two hundred hours to find it again, but we couldn't finish by Friday when Dominique was to start recording.

"I'm calling the police," Martha said.

"Don't call Karl," I said. "There isn't anything he can do."

"Yes, he can. Karl can negotiate with the record company. It's not your fault that you'll miss the deadline."

Karl wanted to sue whoever caused it, but as Martha read the chain of custody back to me, we couldn't pin it down. The tapes sat alone with me in the studio for two hours on Friday before anyone showed to take them away. The tapes sat waiting for four hours before being signed into the vault, and sat for thirty minutes waiting for security to bring them back to the studio. Then the box sat for an hour in the studio this morning with people coming and going. Neither Martha nor I could confirm that we hadn't let the box out of our sight. By this time, Martha was crying, and only my efforts to comfort her kept me from crying myself.

The weather had started out nice that morning, but when I went for a run at noon, it turned cold as a witch's brass—heart. While I'm looking behind every bush for my stalker, five people stopped me on the street to say something about my personal life and my music. One woman thought I'd changed her life forever and another thought there ought to be a law to keep me off the public airways. So I stopped at a barber shop on Fremont Avenue and made the guy cut off all my hair. It left me looking nothing like either the concert shots on the Internet or the victim of *dementia praecox* that appeared in the *Seattle Buzz*.

Quentin, my own favorite Seattle buzzard, showed up to watch afternoon rehearsals, though I'd forgotten that I'd invited him. Ever faithful, mind-reading Martha tried to keep him diverted and out of our way. At every pause in the music, he was at me with questions about influences, up close and in my face, even if he never could manage to look me in the eye.

When it felt like the day had gone to the dogs and taken me with it, Susi came in.

84
"So Long Baby Goodbye"
Susi

I HAD TO DRIVE ALL over the city during rush hour, leaving my brother his car, getting mine back from the repair shop, and then hunting down Jason. No one was home at Ian's house, except Arlo, who gave me confusing and frustrating directions that caused me to sit through multiple lights on Stone Way and Forty-fifth. I was not calm when I arrived.

"Arlo said I would find you here."

Jason, surrounded by computers and banks of electronics, looked up in surprise from a task he seemed engrossed in with the thin, severe woman he'd been with that day he was kissing women all over north Seattle. He had cut off his hair, which made him even more dangerously handsome, which further infuriated me.

"Susi, what a surprise. Are you rehearsing with us tonight?"

"Did you advise Zak to quit school?"

"I asked him to play for me during the morning sessions. I didn't give him advice. Susi, this is Martha Cooper. She's the genie who keeps our work in order."

"He quit school because of you, Jason. I spent the afternoon arguing my way out of getting fired. I had to swear that Zak is working in a drug-free environment and that we aren't all violent drug offenders."

The Martha person said, "I'm leaving for the day, Jason. Unless you have anything else."

"No, wait, please. Look, Susi. Zak is an effing genius. Anything that gets in his way, he'll ride over it. Right now school is in his way."

"He quit school. Do you know what this means? How could you even presume to give him advice?"

"What difference does it make? His family can buy his way into any school he wants if he changes his mind. It's not as if he's boxed in, like some ghetto kid. How have I harmed him?"

"It wasn't your place to interfere."

"Susi, this isn't important right now. I have other problems. Please, could you maybe—"

"He's a gifted musician. He could have a career as a real musician."

"We're not real musicians?"

"You have talent. But a pop musician has a career span of weeks, minutes, and then it's forgotten."

"Not when they're as good as Zak. He needs to be playing here."

"I'm talking about a young man's future, and you are talking about needing a morning playmate."

"I'm talking about Zak's future, Susi. And Ian's and Toby's and Sonny's. Zak wants to be a professional musician, and he needs experience to do that. I've given him more experience in a month than Berklee could in a year."

"You also destroyed any chance for me to get funding this year."

Martha said, "Jason, I'll lock these tapes in the local vault and go."

"Wait, Martha. Susi, what do you mean?"

"Gwyneth and Freeman Lukas promised to match my grant if I kept Zak in school and talked him into going to college. She pulled her money from the matching grant today."

"Susi, you had a mercenary concern in whether he graduates. That disqualifies you from arguing whether you know what's best for him."

"You meddled where you had no right."

"I didn't meddle. When Zak asked me what to do, I told him to talk to you or his parents. You told him never to decide the future because of what someone else wants you to do."

"That was completely out of context. Where is he? I need to talk him out of quitting school. I called Berklee to ask them to ignore his refusal."

"He's staying at Toby's, but he'll be at Ian's tonight. He won't stop what he's doing. Even to save your funding."

"It's too late. You added your name to the grant as faculty, though I told you not to. Then you failed the background check with the state police. My grant is done for. There is no hope."

"Susi, if this is about money, I'll find funding for you. Leave Zak out of it. He wants to play with the band. It's his life."

"It's only pop music."

"That's not how Zak sees it. I've seen what happens to you, the more you sing. I saw how much you loved the applause, Susi. Your Juilliard crowd can't give you those thrills, can they? So why dismiss what we do because it's pop music? Do you think we don't have standards as high as your symphony buddies? Do you think we don't work as hard as your Juilliard and Berklee friends?"

"Who do you mean by 'we'?"

"I mean me. Do you think my work is inferior to what you consider good music? How about you, Susi? How hard did you work to earn the crowd's applause?"

"Are you implying that I haven't been working hard?"

"You've been enjoying yourself, but you aren't willing to go to the next level. You won't stand in front of people night after night. You want only your own pleasure. You allowed yourself one little short, sharp shock in public, and now you want to hide again."

"You think I'm lazy and cowardly?"

"I think you have great potential, and I wish you'd reach for it, like Zak is reaching for his. Can you choose the harder path in spite of how you feel about me? Or are you afraid to stand in front of an audience?"

"All this time, while saying you love me, you judged me this harshly?"

"No, not you as the person I love, Susi. But you aren't committed to the band. I have to watch out for everyone else, because I made a mistake and got us involved with a singer we couldn't trust. Right now, we can't rely on you. We love what's happening to our music, but it looks like you decided to quit."

"Like you did with the jazz ensemble."

"I decided to perform as a professional instead of playing with amateurs. You seem to want to preserve your amateur standing, while we need to advance our professional lives."

"I want to teach. I want my father to have one more season teaching."

"Are you sure you aren't teaching because you're afraid of failing as a performer? I knew those kinds of teachers when I went to school, Susi, and they were the worst. Your father doesn't want you to compromise your life that way."

"What do you know about my father?"

"Apparently more than you do."

"You arrogant—*artiste!*"

As I started to close the door, I heard Martha's voice again. "Jason, you're a nice person, but you hurt people's feelings when you get mad."

I stopped to look back. "He hasn't hurt my feelings at all. It's not as if he could."

However falsely I spoke, it allowed me to see him looking as if he'd lost his last friend, which was a small, sinful pleasure that I confess to having enjoyed for a brief moment.

That friend of Arlo's from the market, Quentin, stood in the foyer and didn't have sufficient motherwit to get out of my way. He'd cut his hair too, though the result wasn't as attractive. Perhaps it was a communicable disease attacking men in their late twenties in Seattle, causing them to chop their hair to nothing. Quentin snapped a picture as I opened the door to let him join Jason, and Jason roared in rage as the flash discharged.

85
"I Shall Be Released"
Jason

THURSDAY MORNING'S WEATHER COULD have descended on the city any season of the year—indiscriminately cold and rainy—and I didn't wear a warm enough shirt or bring a jacket for the bus ride downtown. I'd been shivering and shaking before I left Ian's house, after being up most of the night. Once I got to Karl's office, I found the coffee had cooked to the consistency and flavor of shellac, and there was nothing to eat.

It wouldn't be a good morning, and it held no promise of transmuting to a better day. While waiting for the tardy Lady D and Ephraim, Karl sat in the conference room reading aloud from Quentin's review in the *Seattle Buzz*, the one with the picture from before I cut my hair.

"'The new singer's control of phrasing and her big, big voice perfectly match Taylor's guitar and song-writing skills, helping one to forget his detour into ordinariness on *Woman at the Well*.'"

"Quentin never was a fan of Dominique's," I said.

In fact, Quentin's incisiveness cheered me momentarily, but the afore-referenced Lady D appeared in the doorway, so we managed to infuriate her even before the meeting began. Fine. It was National Whip Jason for What He Didn't Do Week. So I let Dominique lay on the cat-o-nine-tails.

"What crap did you bring me here for?" she fumed.

"Hello, Dominique. You're looking well. I'm glad you could make it back to Seattle for this meeting."

"This had better not be a waste of my time, Jason. I'm tired of playing games with you."

Karl said, "We have a final proposal here. If we can all agree, I'll file the papers today, and then you are both done with this process."

"I'm not giving up—" Dominique began.

"Anything at all," I finished for her, "since compromise is not in your vocabulary. I believe the final issues have to do with Stoneway. Here is what I suggest. We tour together, but as separate acts. Dominique can sing under the band name for this tour. After that, no one uses the Stoneway name anymore."

Dominique's eyes brightened, but right away she turned greedy again. "Then you have to open, Jason. I'm the top bill. Ephraim, tell him that I'm top bill."

Ephraim, poker-faced, didn't look at her. In fact, when I observed closely, the two of them moved as if in separate glass bubbles, not like two people who cohabited and traveled everywhere together. "Jason, I'm happy you've come around. Are you going to be difficult about the billing? What if you swap in each city?"

"Ephraim, don't agree to that."

"Jason, does the billing matter to you?" Ephraim asked.

"No, but she has to do at least half of her set as covers. My own band plays originals. Only originals."

"That might work. Her voice is better suited to other writers' songs than yours. She still needs you, Jason."

"Ephraim, why are you telling him that? I don't need him."

"No, it's the other way, Dominique. He doesn't need you. I think we can agree to all of this, except for one thing, Jason."

"Damn it, Ephraim!" she said at the same moment that I did.

"Damn it, Ephraim. I have to give on everything. You already have total surrender from me."

"Just one more thing, Jason. You have to play the Stoneway set, too. Ian and Toby can opt out, but you have to play. We still have time to find good musicians, but not enough time to recreate the Stoneway sound without you. Oh, take your head out of your hands, Jason. We agreed that it's time to get past the drama."

"I have to think about it."

"And I have to take care of business, Jason."

We stared at each other for about as long as it took God to separate the light from the dark.

Ephraim said, "Whatever you decide, we'll announce the opening act on Saturday when tickets go on sale. I think we can create enough buzz about the Jason Taylor Band to raise ticket prices a notch. Dominique, I believe you have something to say to Jason."

"I don't like it."

"That doesn't matter this time. Please tell Jason what you have to say."

"I'm sorry—I mean, I apologize for letting those rumors start and for what happened with Beau."

"Thanks a lot, Dominique. I feel so much better now."

"So, aren't you going to say it, Jason?"

"Say what?"

"That you're sorry too?"

"Dominique, I don't believe I have anything to apologize for."

"You are still a self-righteous asshole, aren't you?"

"I admit to that, Dominique. I don't see a need to apologize for it."

Karl cleared his throat. "So we're done here? Have we sorted out the difference between being in Stoneway and being married? Will you both sign these papers now, so I can file them today?"

"I don't want to be married to this fucker any longer." Dominique stabbed at the paper with her pen.

"Sweeter words you never spoke," I said. The judge would be able to read my handwriting, because I signed so carefully.

"Sixty days," Karl said. "Counting from today."

86
"Big Boss Man"
Jason

WHEN DOMINIQUE WENT TO fix her ever-perfect face in the women's room, Ephraim turned to me as if I were his best friend.

"You're doing everything right, Jason. When it's this hard and you're doing this well, you must be feeling good about it."

"Thank you." My voice broke, because it was a giant lie that I was doing well at all, and I didn't want Ephraim to know even half of it.

"Dominique wants to get on to the next thing too, so we just have to endure the next few weeks and keep it from getting bumpy."

I was spinning through the worst turbulence I had ever experienced, and Karl's office didn't have barf bags, so I just nodded.

"Listen, Jason. You have to acknowledge that I managed to get you extraordinary freedom for your work. Albion let you choose the studio. You can join the tour and still use your new band name."

"I pay for it either way, so it's big of you to let me spend my money where I want."

"You have your own engineers and technicians. I let you do the arrangements the way you want."

"Not exactly. You let me decide to give you what you want."

"I only said no once, and you expected that when you proposed songs she can't sing, just to get under her skin. You still have greater freedom than other labels would give you. If you took this same music to record in Nashville, you'd never get out of town alive."

"It's still not the music I'd be writing and playing if I didn't have to compromise with Dominique and Albion Records."

"She'll be gone from your life in sixty days. Jason. Listen, I told you I'm moving on as soon as we finish the business for this album. I'm leaving Albion Records to join my brother's label. It's an opportunity for me to help good alternative bands succeed in the market. I want you to sign with my brother's label."

"So that my money stays in your family, one way or another?"

"If you want to disparage it in that way, it won't bother me."

"How long of a leash does your brother give you?"

"Long enough to accommodate the entire range of music you played on Saturday. Even the folkie stuff you played earlier that day. If that's what you want to do."

"Do you have other musicians who want to give up the safety of a big label like Albion for your brother's little vanity project?"

"Let's see. If my brother has his own label, it's a vanity project. If you go indie and ship CDs from the back of a bus, what is that, Jason?"

"I didn't mean to be insulting," I said. "I apologize. But I intend to go my own way."

"Who is going to take care of your business?"

"I'll see to the business myself."

"You and who else? The lawyer who used to drive your bus? The ever efficient Cynthia? You don't have Beau now. Who's going to be the bad guy when you need it? Who's going to look ahead?"

"How many times do I have to say no to you, Ephraim?"

At this point, spinning in free-fall the way I was, I could still look Ephraim in the eye and see—what? He seemed almost hurt.

He said, "I heard you play last Saturday. I want you to succeed. If I'm not part of making it happen, I swear I'll die with regrets."

"What we're playing is just a logical progression of the same music you screwed up last year."

"No, it's not, Jason. You know it's more than that. Your songwriting has transformed. And your beautiful new vocalist can make angels weep. She makes me believe in angels."

"She's a guest of the band. She's not in the band."

"Screw it, Jason. I want to sign both of you. I'd work my ass off to make sure North America and all of Europe hear what true genius sounds like."

Dominique stood in the doorway, having heard who the heck knows what all.

"Are we leaving now, Ephraim?" she said. "Have you traded away enough of my assets before lunch to satisfy yourself?"

"Yes. We'll see you in the studio tomorrow, Jason. Ten more days and we're done with that and then rehearsing for the road, right, friend?"

⁂

"Sixty days and you're free, buddy." Karl rubbed his hands, pleased.

"Dominique is supposed to show up in the studio tomorrow and lay vocals down over our studio tracks."

"Yes, but you can handle her now. Ephraim is being very helpful."

"Karl, my stalker friend stole the master tapes."

"Oh shit."

"So now I have to talk Ian and Toby into playing in the studio with Dominique, because there isn't enough time to both re-record and work with her separately."

"They won't like it."

"Nope. I've posted coded pleas on my blog, begging my so-called brother to return the tapes. I'm not a big believer in luck at this point."

"Ephraim will shit himself when he hears this."

"I would prefer he didn't hear."

"There's your other work. Once you get past this."

"Sort of. Only a couple of those tapes turned up missing. Nobody will hear that work unless our mysterious friend posts tracks from those tapes on the Internet."

"Nobody will complain about working with Susi to re-record."

"No. Except she won't work with us anymore." I stopped myself from including the band. "Me, I mean. She won't work with me."

"Oh shit."

87
"Excuse Me If I Break My Own Heart Tonight"
Jason

NOBODY YELLED AT ME.

Nobody started one of those infamous fist fights that herald the end of a band.

It was still early when I told people, and I hadn't eaten. The only question came from Angelia, who had phoned in sick to that school all week so she could record with us in the studio. She wondered why I didn't tell people the night before.

"Because I hoped to wake up this morning and find out it wasn't true."

Then Sonny said it was his fault the tapes were gone, since he'd been hired to do security. "Don't pay me for the extra hours in the studio," he said. "I blew it."

"No, it didn't happen on the territory you are covering, man. It just happened."

Ian said, "We know what we're playing, so it won't be like last year," but the whole time he was staring at the floor and not at me.

Angelia and Toby spent a lot of time just looking at each other, and finally Toby said, "I'll be here in the morning. I know you can't control the Dragon Woman, so we'll have to just fake our way through it."

"Just so we get to play the new music afterwards with Susi," Ian said, still watching the floor.

Zak and Sonny were both silent.

I said, "We are touring as two bands, with separate sets. We'll be playing originals as the Jason Taylor Band. I'm hoping you will all come along for that. The label is putting together musicians as Stoneway to support Dominique. I'll be playing the Stoneway sets. Anyone else want to share that half of the gig?"

They all left me sucking wind, until Sonny said, "I need the bread. I can't be fussy."

"Me, too," Ian the floor-man said.

"I don't," Toby said. And Angelia's instrument was never part of the songs for Dominique.

"Thanks, Toby. I understand. And I apologize for asking you this late."

"It's bearable because we still get to play with Susi," Ian said. "That's worth paying a toll to the devil."

"She doesn't want to sing pop music," I said, as calmly as I could.

"I'll talk to her," Angelia said, simultaneously with Cynthia and Sonny.

I shook my head, because I couldn't say no out loud.

Ian said, "So we'll just do the backporch stuff with her, huh? A mostly acoustic set? That's cool. We can make the twang and fuzz work almost as well without—oh crap."

Ian can read my face. For that skill, he didn't need an effing high school diploma either.

I made it through that rehearsal. I'd be a liar if I didn't say it was Ian who led us back to the music, starting with a rage piece I wrote when I first learned that Uncle Beau was ill. We were recording each instrument on separate tracks, of course, so it will be easy to cut out how badly I played and replace it later. Everyone else knew how to stay professional, doing their best the entire time.

Afterward, Zak came up to say how stoked he was that I respected him enough to invite him on the road.

"Hey man, I think you should call home, though. I hear your mother was pretty upset yesterday about you quitting school." Which screwed up Susi's life and my hopes, I didn't say.

Zak blinked. "I moved out of the house two weeks ago. She just now noticed? It must have sunk in when Sonny and I moved the Hammond B3 out of the basement."

At home in the evening, it was only Ian and me, picking at the same material we had worked on last winter, as if we had to check that the music still linked us so that harmony will occur on cue, no matter what.

"Think I'll go to bed early," Ian said after we had picked the music to pieces. "Are we starting at eight tomorrow?"

"Not until ten. I have prep to do."

"Cynthia could talk to her, Jason."

"No."

"Or Angelia."

"No. When I have a better handle on this work with Dominique, I'll talk to her again. She came in right after I found out about the tapes, mad at me because Zak quit school, and I sort of went berserk on her. Lord, I need to get a grip."

"Yeah, maybe a little. Jason, it's better if you just ignore what your stalker friend is doing now."

"Ignore that our tapes are gone? How can I do that?"

"I mean ignore what he's saying about Susi. You know, the bit he's been hammering on the blogs for the last couple of days, about how Ephraim is hitting on your girlfriend after stealing your wife, because you don't know how to take care of your women. We all know it's just B.S."

88
"Till I Get It Right"
Jason

I FORCED MYSELF TO not look. It was the week's sole moral victory on my part. I turned on my laptop. I logged on, but I didn't go cruising anywhere that would make me mad. Or crazy. I finished the notes for the next meeting with Ephraim and Dominique, giving her every last thing she needed to prepare for the session. Then I tried to relax by just cruising other blogs to find diverting information—not music blogs, but news and art and people's general craziness preserved for all time through the glory of the World Wide Web. Or at least as long as they paid their Internet service provider bills.

Nothing engaged me enough to either pacify my agitation or divert my attention from the anxiety gnawing at my insides. I checked a couple of my private lists and traded bland news about old musicians, their influences, and their legacy. After about twenty minutes of proving to my Internet friends that I was more intelligent than a doorstop, Chas popped an instant message.

Chas1933: Steven told me who you are.

Sebastian: I hope you don't take my artifice as a personal insult. The only place where I can be myself right now is with my friends on the Internet.

Chas1933: After poking around on Google, I can see the pressure you're under. Susi would understand if you tell her.

Sebastian: We aren't exactly in communication now. Steven will be relieved, I'm sure.

Chas1933: For myself, I'm sorry to hear it. I wanted to ask you some questions about the Lost Sons material you got me access to.

Sebastian: I'll try, but I confess that I haven't studied up much myself.

Chas1933: Guess I'll ask the hardest question first. Why won't you acknowledge in public who your father is?

Sebastian: Of course you'd start with the most brutal question. So you believe the rumors on the Internet?

Chas1933: It's in the source material.

Sebastian: Somewhere along the line I came to hate Jesse Rufus as an irresponsible bastard who hurt people. I don't want to be like him, and I don't want people to think of me and Jesse Rufus in the context of music, which is hard to achieve, since my voice sounds like his. Or in the context of life, which is easy if I don't say anything about who my father is.

Chas1933: It isn't because you aren't sure which brother is actually your father?

※

Chas1933: Are you there? Did my last message get lost?

Sebastian: I'm here. I'm trying to think what to type in the little box. I never once in my life considered it a possibility.

Chas1933: Even after seeing ten years' worth of correspondence between your mother and Beau? Now I'm stuck between a rock and the hard place you're in. I want to publish what I'm finding—about how Beau and Jesse worked together on music and lyrics. Everyone has assumed that Jesse wrote the lyrics, but with these letters, it is clear that Beau wrote poetry to your mother that pre-dates similar material in their songs. I can't point to my data, though, if you don't want the world to see it.

Sebastian: I have to confess right now that I'm hurting. I don't know how to think.

Chas1933: Perhaps you should start by reading some of their letters. It's pretty powerful stuff.

Sebastian: Do you have anything electronic I can look at?

Chas1933: I'm mailing attachments to you right now. Want to read and then talk about it in the morning?

It was freezing cold in the basement. Cynthia had turned the main heat off because it was supposed to be spring and she doesn't like sleeping in warm rooms. I tried to read lying in bed with the laptop, a blanket pulled over my head.

My mother was in love with Beau.

She stopped singing in the band and wouldn't go on tour with them, because Jesse came onto her while she was secretly in love with Beau. For all I can tell, I'm the result of a one-time date-rape.

She never told Jesse. From the scant evidence of the few letters Chas forwarded, Beau wrote to her for years and came back to visit when I was five. And wasn't I a big surprise? He fell in love with her and then kept coming back again and again over all those years, until she wasn't there to come back to anymore.

After I threw up, I wept.

Well, what would you do? How much machismo—or machisma—would a person have to have in order to not hurl and weep?

300

I needed to talk it over with someone, and it was too close to midnight to go looking for Chas1933.

※

"Did Beau ever say anything to you about my mother?"

Ian lay in bed watching dieselpunk videos yet again.

"I could build that," he said.

Cynthia shook her head. "No, honey. Your hands aren't allowed near metal lathes." She was idly rubbing his shaved head while reading an Inspector Montalban story.

"Ian, tell me what you heard: My mom? Beau?"

Ian started channel-surfing before answering. "Did Beau ever say anything at all? He was the quintessential silent bass player. The most he ever said at any one time was when he ragged us for dicking around and being late to a gig. Or to tell a waitress how he wanted his eggs. Or if he had to go after a booking agent who was screwing us out of money."

"I mean personally. Did he talk about my mom?"

Cynthia looked up. "Beau said she was an angel whom God caused to suffer for no reason."

"When did he say that?"

"I don't know. You guys were rehearsing 'Rhianna's Song,' and I made a comment that no woman could be as pure as the woman in the song, and Beau said she was an angel. Et cetera. Jason, sweetheart?"

"Yeah?"

"We're in bed. Even though we aren't doing anything at the moment, could you leave us the fuck alone?"

※

Huddled in my borrowed basement room, I switched off instant messaging and couldn't bring myself to check my email. How much weirdness can I stand to have delivered to my own bedroom?

Where do you go for relevant information with which to frame thought? Tolstoy's MyUniquelyFuckedUpFamily.com? Is there a search result from Google or KartOO or Bing that will help a person

301

in a situation like this? How do you even determine what to type in the search query?

"What if your father date-raped your mother and your uncle picked up the pieces."

"What did your lost family think when they were alive."

"How to understand why your mother—"

What do I type here? There isn't any joke to make. She died when I was fifteen, and she spent the three years before that getting ready to go, so I think she was a saint. She is not here now to explain it to me, and she didn't leave me with a guide to the inside of her mind. Uncle Beau, who left me a complete map for how to deal with work and everyday life, didn't leave a note explaining that—what? It wasn't me he did all that for—trying to keep me in school, then traveling with me all those years while Ian and I were living on the road and learning to play music. We were infants then, and we never would have survived if Beau hadn't stuck with us. I thought all this time that he did it to make up for his brother having abandoned us, but it appears Jesse never knew about me. Beau took care of me because he loved my mother. Inordinately. Incessantly. Incandescently.

As a fourteen-year-old, I sat in lower Wallingford listening for hidden meanings that my father might have buried for me in his songs. I didn't know I was listening to poetry that the man sitting at our worn kitchen table had spawned for the woman who poured him a cup of coffee and asked if he had kept himself well since last they met. The same man sat next to me in the van we took to gigs, teaching me flat-picking country and bottleneck blues, traveling chords and Reverend Gary Davis fingerstyle technique, and DADGAD tuning for Celtic melodies. The whole while he loved my mother above everything in life—and why in hell did I never wonder what he was doing playing bass in a juvenile bar band if he could teach me all of that?

Frickin' hell, you are supposed to figure out you aren't the center of the effing world when you're what—twelve? Why am I so stunned that these people had other motivations and other passions?

In my heart of hearts, I don't think this sense of upset comes from finding out I wasn't the motivating focus for these two dear people. It is learning that my mother and Beau had this huge burning thing at the center of their lives. And they didn't let me in.

I wanted to write to Chas and say, "Tell me where you live so I can come read all those letters. Right now." I wanted to run there. I wanted to touch the papers and see the envelopes. I wanted to know what it looked like when Uncle Beau poured his heart out on paper and cultivated the seeds of a song. I wanted to read every word he sent my mother and what she wrote back. For years now, since she has been dead for almost as long as I knew her in life, I thought it the saddest thing that she didn't have a true love, just our lonely little life in lower Wallingford. I was wrong, because somewhere in there they shared joy together. Even if they didn't invite me to that party, I wanted to read what it looked like between them.

There was no chance I'd find any answers floating around in the giant bit bucket of the Internet. Without thinking it through, I swapped jeans for running clothes and ran across town to Susi's house. On a night like tonight, she would have to let me in. There isn't another person in the world I could talk to about this.

89
"Talk to Me"
Susi

"HELLO, MISS NEVILLE. DO you remember me from the other night?"

"Of course, Mr. Vance."

"Do you know who I am?"

"No, other than your name and that I have seen you with Jason. I heard that you said kind things about my work the other night."

"I'm a business agent for the label Jason records with."

"Please come in. May I offer you something to drink?"

"Thank you, no. I want to get straight to the point. I want Jason to continue working with me, and I'm desperate for help to persuade him. Jason is not making the best business decisions on his own."

"Are you suggesting that I give Jason advice? I am certain that would not work well."

"Miss Neville, I hope that you might encourage him to listen to me. We both have his best interests at heart."

"Why choose me? I have only just met him."

"I know who you are, Miss Neville. Does Jason?"

"He knows who I am in my present life," I said. That's enough.

"You're recording highly original music with him."

"We just call it backporch music, Mr. Vance."

"What have you learned from working with him?"

"He is a brilliant composer and arranger. He's perhaps the most talented director of performing musicians that I've ever met."

"Can you appreciate, then, why I want to see him succeed?"

"Yes, but I don't know you, except that Jason wasn't happy when he spoke of you."

"I can tell you what Jason would say about me. He'd describe me as the man guiding his career until I ran off with his wife."

"Is that true? It sounds melodramatic."

"The nouns are correct, but the verbs don't reveal the time sequence properly. His wife ran off—but not with me. Jason also ran off. Alone. While I was picking up the pieces, I ended up with his former wife."

"You must appreciate that I'm not in a position to speak about Jason when he's not here. If he feels betrayed—"

"Then you feel compelled to take his side."

"Both my personal experience and every story I've heard have led me to think that his ex-wife isn't a nice person."

"She isn't." He seemed thoughtful. "How could you have personal experience with her?"

"She writes me email every day, explaining how awful Jason is and how he will betray me."

"That's not true about Jason. Miss Neville, I don't want to talk about Dominique. Please help me convince Jason to sign with my record label."

"That is not any of my business," I said. "Anyway, I thought he was already recording."

"His contract ends with this album. I want to keep him with me."

"Even if I were inclined to interfere with his business, I couldn't do that, Mr. Vance. I have a little knowledge of your world. Artists can't own their own work, even when you don't want to package and promote it for them anymore. You want to shape artists into pre-defined molds. Jason could never fit."

"Jason is brilliant enough to break the rules, with the right guide."

"That would be you?"

"Can't you help me, Miss Neville? If I signed you to record, that would bring him to my label."

"Sign me? I'm a teacher. I'm no longer a professional singer. I couldn't do that just to help coerce Jason into anything he might not want."

"You aren't going to sing and record with Jason?"

"We were just playing around. It doesn't have a future for me."

"Then I should say goodnight, Ms. Neville. I can see that I've made you uncomfortable. I'm sorry."

"It was nice to meet you. May I tell Jason you spoke with me?"

"Yes. Honesty is the only way to proceed with a person as incapable of deceit as Jason."

90
"I Just Wanted to See You So Bad"
Jason

IT WAS PLENTY LATE at night by the time I made it to Leschi, even with hopping a bus for part of the way, which raised my anxiety level. Although it took me across more miles faster than my feet could manage, I had to sit still while it moved my body through space and time.

Ephraim's gun-metal grey BMW turned onto the arterial just as I stood on the corner opposite the street light, waiting to walk up the empty alley to her house.

"Susi, it's Jason."

I knocked on the door, not knowing why I ever expected that she'd welcome me in, listen to my grief, tell me what to think. A trodden red rose lay in the shadows of her front step, indicating that my would-be brother had again crept too close.

She didn't answer, though her car sat in the garage. And Ephraim—damn his eyes—had been to visit just a moment before.

Ephraim. I lost it.

"Come on, Susi. Let me in. Talk to me."

The lights were on, and the sound of Skip James leaked from the cracks of the doors and windows.

"Susi! Dammit, let me in. You let that bastard Ephraim in. Don't fuck with my mind right now—"

An arm came around my neck, so tight it hurt, and a pair of hands ripped my arms back at the elbows, immobilizing me. As I sputtered to speak, my assailant tossed me half way across the alley and then pressed me up against the neighbor's retaining wall.

Two figures bounced in the shadows, one tall and the other small. The small one kept pressing too hard at my throat.

"Get your hands off me," I croaked.

"Don't fuck with the lady. Leave her be."

"What? I'm the guy paying you."

"Yeah, sure. Joe, check to make sure he doesn't have a weapon."

"Don't touch me!" I not only used the bad mother word, I shouted it. Then I called their mothers worse names.

The smaller man ignored what I was saying, and the volume at which I was saying it, while he ran his hands down my running shorts, where nothing could be hidden. "He's OK, Joe." So they were both named Joe.

"Yeah, I'm OK. Now leave me the hell alone and let me talk to her."

"Whoa, buddy. We're walking down the alley right now, away from here. Together."

"The cell phones in your pockets belong to me. You're supposed to call the police if someone comes. Without hassles. Call now. Or call Sonny."

"Sonny is working his night job."

"Then we agree that you and I both know Sonny. Call the effing police if you aren't calling Sonny. I'm not leaving without talking to her."

While little Joe #1 was calling, and big Joe #2 was in my face, keeping me immobilized against the retaining wall, a patrol car rounded the corner into the alley, its blue lights flashing. I was happy to see them, because we could end the current détente.

Except I hate it when the one policeman gets out of the patrol car with his hands on his service revolver, and the other just stands in his open door, talking into the radio.

"Evening, gentlemen. The neighbors are unhappy with the noise you have been raising."

I jerked away from Joe #2, and the cop had his revolver out.

"Please put your hands behind your head."

I complied, knowing full well that arguing was not in my best interest. "I was reaching for my ID."

"Can you do that carefully, using your left hand?"

"It's in my sock."

"Who wants to explain the problem here?"

"This guy is bothering our friend," Joe #1 volunteered. They offered their ID in a graceful, experienced manner.

"Miss Neville is a friend of mine, and I want to speak with her."

"The noise complaint makes all this commotion sound less innocent, Mister—" He checked my ID. "Mr. Taylor. Is this you?"

"No, it isn't," Joe #2 said. "Jason Taylor has long hair."

"I cut my effing hair. I'm Jason Taylor, dammit."

The cop said, "I think that's easy to see, even though the picture shows long hair."

Joe #1 said, "Oh shit, man. We are so sorry."

A second patrol car came down the alley from the other direction, the blue strobe casting everyone in alternate shadow and skeletal glow. When this car parked, Officer Page stepped out of the passenger side, his hand resting on his service revolver.

"Good evening, Officer." I looked at Office Page as I spoke, hoping he'd recognize me, fighting the guilty sense that I wanted to glance away. The two Joes explained themselves again—they just happened to be taking a short-cut through the alley, but the lady who lived there was a friend, and any gentleman would want to interfere in such a situation, since I was pounding on her door and shouting.

"I only raised my voice to be heard. In case she's listening to music or on the phone and can't hear me."

"If the lady doesn't want to speak to you, you can't stand on the street shouting at her." It must have been an official script, because Officer Page argued the same way the year before, when I wanted my voice to penetrate to Dominique on the third-floor condo. "I'm sure you don't want the pain of charges pressed against you, Mr. Taylor."

"Can't you just knock on the door and ask her? She doesn't want me to go away."

"Here she is. Sorry for the disturbance, ma'am. Mr. Taylor says you don't want him to go away. Is this true?"

She was standing there in a silk shirt and linen trousers, looking small and delicate, and exhausted.

"Yes. I'm sorry for the bother, officers."

"Are you sure you're safe, ma'am?"

"I'm not going to hurt her!" I sputtered. "I wouldn't. I couldn't."

"Please calm down, Mr. Taylor. If she wants to invite you inside, we'll leave you. But if you continue this way, I'll have to ask you downtown to discuss the meaning of disturbing the peace."

She invited me in.

I wish she'd sent me downtown with Officer Page.

91
"It's All Over Now, Baby Blue"
Jason

WHEN I CAME INSIDE, I didn't know what to do with myself. Where to sit or how to stand and be comfortable. After my tantrum on the street, I was too aware of how much larger I am than she is. I came there to find comfort and found that instead I presented a threat.

I sat on a bar stool at her kitchen counter while she turned on water to make tea, a familiar gesture I now recognized as what she does to calm herself. Under the soft, indirect light in the kitchen, she seemed to be another source of illumination, faintly glowing. She turned her calm, perfectly made-up face to me, and I wanted to cry out that I knew how much pain and passion she masked, and how much I had hoped never to add to that pain. Or perhaps I just plain wanted to cry.

She said, "Ephraim Vance came by to ask me to persuade you to do business with him. If you have any idea that his visit meant anything else, you are very wrong."

"I'm sorry."

"He's very complimentary to you. I refused to help him, because it seemed disloyal. However, I don't understand what he wants."

"He wants me to sign with his label."

"Why does he feel so strongly about it?"

"He likes our music."

"That's not enough explanation."

"My music made his company millions of dollars last year. He wants me to do that every year."

I waited for the repercussion, the reactions that would transform our relationship forever. Shock and anger. Recriminations for hiding it from her, though it was she who had insisted repeatedly that we keep our individual secrets. A new-found interest in my wealth.

Nope. Instead, she said, "He's offering you the opportunity to excel in your particular world of music, and you choose to do less?"

"I want to excel. But I want to make my own music. I want to own the music I make. It is not worth money to do less than that, Susi."

"It must be nice to have the option of achieving your dreams and the privilege of being able to quibble over compromises at the same time."

"You jumped onto Ephraim's team pretty quickly. You don't understand how controlling record labels are."

"No?" She raised her eyebrow in question. "However, I do know what it means to be denied the opportunity to pursue a dream. I lost mine once. I begged God. I offered to make a deal with the devil, but neither God nor the devil chose to intercede. I wish I had your problems."

"If your dream was to sing, you can still achieve that, Susi. You heard how people responded last week: they love you. It is just a matter of you choosing the right material."

"The right material? You mean just sing your pop songs?"

"Why are you such a snob about the music we play? You put Zak down for wanting just that. Is it because you think that's all high-school drop-outs can achieve?"

"All right, yes, Jason. I think pop music is an idle way to pass time. A series of lightweight fads. It's not something that serious people do."

"Yet you want to teach roots music. What do you think that is, other than the last generation's pop music fad? If you sing with us, will you be too déclassé? Compared to what? Billie Holiday? Maybelle Carter?"

"I do not choose to stand up in front of people and perform. It's not part of my life. I have become a teacher, and that's where my future lies."

"Susi, however displeased you are with me, you can't walk away from your talent. You can't choose the lower path."

"Teaching is lower than performing? And you call me a snob?"

"I don't mean in general. I mean for you. Susi, you are so powerful a singer, so incredible, you can't—"

"You can't presume to decide what's best for me."

"Someone has to. You can't do what my mother did—settle for less, muddle through life without people knowing what God gave you. That's what I came over here to talk to you about tonight. I learned things about my mother and my uncle that left me confused. I feel worse about that because of all the misunderstandings between us, Susi."

"We aren't going to share secrets tonight. We aren't going to talk about what you think I should do with my life based on what your mother did. Or didn't do."

"You say it's just pop music and you don't want to perform. But if you choose to do the work, you could have the same effect on audiences as any of the great singers. The same as—"

It occurred to me where I had last experienced the same kind of power as Susi had. I flung open her music cabinet searching for it.

"Listen to this. It's disciplined, brilliant music, the kind snobs approve of. I swear when you sang Saturday, it had the same effect on people."

I slipped the disc in and punched through cuts to get where I wanted, trying to remember *Turandot* well enough to judge where that song would be. Liù the slave girl, singing about her devoted love to the secret prince, willing to die for him.

"I heard this in Seattle two years ago, and it's the same level of intensity that you are capable of."

Tu che di gel sei cinta.

I had the volume too high, so that Liù's lament filled the room, the singer's notes burning through my chest. I closed my eyes, and the impact of the singer's lustrous voice turned the world blue behind my closed eyes. The singer who rendered Liù's essence through song had the same breath control and power as Susi, the same absolute control of phrasing. Each note filled the holes in my soul in a human voice so familiar—

I opened my eyes to find Susi watching me. I strangled on my own words.

"Susi, this is you."

Only the color and timbre had been destroyed. Or altered. Transformed into the rusty angel's voice that I knew. She had said that she didn't care about the web of scarring on her face, for that destruction was insignificant compared to what she'd truly lost. I hadn't listened closely enough to hear what she was saying.

"It's the best role I had in the U.S. They liked me much better in Europe, directors and audiences both. That's over now. Yet I do not want to be condescended to about whether I know how to work hard."

"Oh god, Susi—"

"Back then, I also thought that hard work alone would take me to the next level. When I listen now, with all my ambitions removed, I don't I hear it—true greatness, I mean. I would have been disappointed when my ambition couldn't make up for deficient talent. We will never know now, and there is no use thinking about it."

She switched off the music. Because she's the bravest woman I'd ever met, she held my gaze as she told the secrets she'd been refusing to share.

"One night I lost the chance to find out what I could be. The fire Logan started—he was smoking cocaine when I came home unexpectedly. The fire ruined any chance of work for me, and destroyed everything else that he hadn't already wasted or sold. I'd left our finances to Logan because I was too busy working. My bills didn't run out before my health insurance did. My dad mortgaged this house to—oh, never mind. Everything here is Dad's, since I ended up with nothing."

"I am so sorry. If I had known—"

"I didn't tell you, because I'm sick to death of pity. I wanted to get to know you without pity being part of the relationship."

"All this time, when I have been praising your voice, it must have felt like I was sticking daggers in you."

"It doesn't matter."

"Yes, it does. I said I'd never hurt a woman, and yet I hurt you out of my own arrogance. I'm humbled by your suffering."

"I think it would be best if we didn't see each other. I need to take care of my own business, and I have let myself drift into your world far too long, just because I'm physically attracted to you."

"No, Susi. Please don't."

"You already knew I stayed married when I shouldn't have. I stayed married for sex, not love. I can't believe that the strong attraction I feel now is a healthy impulse. It is just what led me once before to lie to myself, to make bad choices, to destroy my future.

"You're letting the past rule your future. I'm not that man. You can't say goodbye. You can't walk away."

"Yes, I can. I have to. We're unsuited to each other's worlds. Because of you, I jeopardized my job and all the work I've done to replace my old dreams. It's too much to risk just to go to bed with you."

"I'm begging you, Susi. Separate how you feel about me from singing with the band. You can't prefer being alone to singing."

"You need to go now."

"But the music—"

"I'm sure you'll find another woman to sing for you. Please go."

All the will power that I use to move through the world dissolved.

"OK. I won't force myself on you again. But, Susi, I know your voice. I understand it, the beautiful way it is now. If you won't be with me, I can still write songs that are perfect for you to sing."

"Please go. Take your shirt and toothbrush away. And take this. I don't want this sordid stuff in my life. Tell your ex-wife to leave me alone, please."

She thrust an envelope into my hands, piled the other things in my arms, and pushed me out into the cold night.

Where a Seattle City patrol car cruised down the alley.

92

"Goin' Down This Road Feeling Bad"
Jason

I COULDN'T FACE MY cave at Ian's, so I went to Glo's Diner and ordered a plate of eggs amidst Seattle people in flannels and black jeans kicking off the morning. While I ate, I read the contents of the envelop Susi shoved into my hands. It wasn't the illuminating love poetry Chas found in Beau's letters to my mother. It didn't provide answers to existential questions about life in an unpredictable universe.

However, it did explain why Dominique hated me and despised Beau, and why Susi thinks I'm an ill-educated heathen.

My erstwhile fake brother, the stalker, had sent Dominique pages of screed, beginning just after the nightmarish fortnight during which her infidelities had been thrust in my face while I was trying to confront how undisciplined and contrary she proved to be in the studio. The same week that Beau came back from the doctor with a short-term death sentence. The dates of the letters were simultaneous with the deeper changes in Dominique that I experienced, when she became not just difficult but malicious. The things my stalker wrote to her—tagged with phrases like "As Beau says," or "Even Ian can see," or "Toby has always said"—would have turned a saint against all of us, but especially against me. The most evil of thoughts were attributed to Beau in those emails.

Dominique has no hope of becoming a candidate for sainthood, but I would never have said such things to her. No one in the band had ever voiced such outrageous thoughts. At least, not until my days as a guest in the Pierce County Jail, and then after *Woman at the Well.*

My stalker brother agrees with me that Susi is a saint and that where she walks, the avatars rain blessings. He's been telling her so in daily emails, repeating words from songs I'd written years before or stealing bad poetry from untalented songwriters who—

I shouldn't criticize other songwriters because their taste doesn't match my own. However, Susi didn't know enough about the last thirty years' popular music to recognize any of the plagiarisms, and my stalker had done as he did with Dominique: he pretended to be me. I pulled my cell phone out a half dozen times while I read, wanting to call Susi to say that I didn't write this maudlin tripe. That I'm so sorry she thought I could write such cruel, demeaning insults as Dominique had received.

Officer Page came into the diner, when the scum had dried on my second plate of eggs and hash browns that I'd ordered as rent for my table. He signaled to his partner that he'd catch up and then dropped into a chair at my table.

"Hello, Officer."

"Good morning, Mr. Taylor."

The scene from earlier, and the pile of screed on the table in front of me, added up to a very poor story.

"I'm embarrassed."

"It wasn't your fault the first time, Mr. Taylor, and I sort of understand what happened tonight. But you can't let your feelings get you into trouble."

"I know. I screwed up."

"We stretched procedure, letting you stay. That's why we came back by a few times."

"Thanks. I appreciate you caring for her safety."

"I won't ask if you made peace, since you wouldn't be sitting here if you had. What are you going to do?"

"Beats me. I wrote one song that I thought made her fall in love with me. I guess I should try writing another."

"You can't make a person love you. That's what my wife says anyway."

"Can I use that line in a song? Will your wife sue me?"

He laughed. "Naw, she was lying anyway. She went out of her way to make me fall in love with her, and she tries it again every year or two."

"I wish I had that wife."

"Mine is taken. You'll have to get your own."

Karl is always at work by seven-thirty, and so I met him at the elevator on his way up from the parking garage. We ate breakfast bars while the coffee brewed. When he offered to pour, I managed to hold my cup out, hardly shaking, acting like life could go on as it always had.

"I need you—"

"No lover in the world has said those words to me as often as you have, Jason."

"I'm not in great shape this morning, Karl. We'll have to take this slowly. I'm about to see Ephraim and cave on every last thing. Before that, you need to do the paperwork to donate all the royalties for songs I share with Dominique."

"Not the Musicians' Aid trick again."

"No, I did a bad thing—it didn't start as bad, but it had unforeseen and unpleasant consequences—and I owe restitution."

"Someone is about to sue you?"

"It is not that kind of obligation, Karl. You have all the papers for Susi's Troubadours Institute. That's the entity getting the royalties. Steven Neville is the financial administrator, so please do all the work with him."

"You'll end up like that guy from Credence, with no right to play your own songs without paying royalties."

"John Fogerty. I'm selling the rights to the Lost Sons catalog to Charles Neville. Can you do that paperwork this morning?"

"I can't believe the old guy has that kind of money."

"It costs him one dollar. If he hasn't got it, please lend it to him."

"Damn it, Jason. I can't let you do this. You're giving away both your income and your assets."

"I can make more money. Yet I have no idea how else to take care of my obligations. I don't want anything back from Chas except Beau's personal correspondence. Can you work out with Chas to get facsimiles made so I can have the originals?"

"You finally saw what's in those letters?"

"Yes, I did. And yes, I should have listened to you. And I should have listened to Ephraim. Can you come to the meeting with Ephraim? I need you there, and I don't want to move the meeting."

"Will you listen to me about protection from your stalker, too? Did you see what he posted last night?"

Karl handed me a folder thick with print-outs.

LostSon2: My brother should die for what he did to that angel. Humiliation and pain should be his, as he deals them to others.

"Yikes."

"There's more."

LostSon2: The angel of death, having passed over, will leave no evil son alive. As the Lord visited unto Jesse, so shall the angel of death visit until his son for the evil he has done.

"Are these on my blog or the fan site? Are they out there still?"

"They were on your site, but the webmaster took them down. I called Cynthia early this morning, so she's serving as majordomo, not letting anything post that doesn't look right. I called and asked the fan site to do the same. They seem willing to work with you."

"They're all good guys, so I'm not surprised. I better write pieces for both sites. Should I placate him? Or what?"

"I have a call into a guy from the Seattle Police to get advice. I don't think you should do anything until we hear what the best action to take might be."

The receptionist came in just then. "Karl, he's here."

"Wouldn't you know, the one day he's on time. I'll be right there. Jason, can you excuse me for a minute?"

I was too agitated to say yes, but I managed to nod and then to amuse myself while Karl was gone by reading the Troubadours Institute folder on his desk. He had researched all the officers of the nonprofit—Angelia, Steven, Susi. He had unearthed a photo of Susi as the slave Liù. A close-up, so you could see how breathtakingly beautiful she had been, with a thick, luxurious mane of honey-blond hair, her grey eyes softer, her gaze more muted than piercing.

"You knew," I said when Karl came back.

"Their social security numbers were in the papers you sent over. I was more than idly curious about where your money was about to disappear."

He sat down at his desk, his face in his hands. "Damn, I fucking hate that. I'm not cut out to be part of the ruling class."

"Karl, what's wrong?"

"I had to fire somebody. Wish I could fix it, but I can't run a social service agency and a law office at the same time. I just hate being the bad guy with my own people."

"Yeah, it bites big time. I fired a drummer last week."

"The work the guy left is a mess. It'll take a week to straighten it out."

"Do you need Martha back? She has everything so organized at the studio that I could use a different temp for a while."

"Yes, indeed I do. Dammit, I hate being the boss. I feel like closing this whole shop down. Maybe I should give up law and be your guitar tech. Except my wife already is about to quit me."

"You were lousy at that job. We had a whole season of broken-string dramas in every set. You have been much more useful handling my business. Please be there when I meet Ephraim at ten."

"Anything else you want me to give away first? Perhaps your nuts encased in solid brass?"

"No. Can I use your shower and sleep on your sofa until then?"

"Your girlfriend didn't let you get any sleep last night?"

"There is no girlfriend. It was a figment of my over-active imagination. There is no new singer in the band. There is no—"

"What happened?"

"Isn't it obvious? I'm an effing asshole."

"True. Can you cite concrete details?"

"I'm the most self-righteous fool ever made since God first breathed life into a lump of clay."

"Go sleep while I do your paper work."

93
"Lonelier Than This"
Jason

"Before we start with business, Dominique, I want to offer you the humblest of apologies."

"It is about time."

"First, I didn't write these." I laid down the sheaf of travesties I'd carried away from Susi's house. "These came from the same stalker who's plaguing me. I apologize for them only because some fan's misplaced loyalty subjected you to this vileness."

Ephraim said, "I told you it couldn't be Jason."

Dominique didn't look up. Since I had to get past judging her on thin evidence, I went on with the main course for breakfast: pure crow.

"What I want to apologize for is my own awfulness to you, Dominique. We have artistic differences, with dissimilar goals and ambitions. I'm so careful to never judge any other musicians in public, and yet in private I castigated your ambition, your work ethic, and your talent in ways I had no right to. I was wrong to judge you, and worse, to do it in ways that hurt you. I won't ask your forgiveness because I don't deserve it."

I don't know that I expected a particular reaction. Perhaps complete condemnation would have been preferable, for then we could return to our habitual mean-spirited sparing. She offered no reaction at all. She just stared at me for a moment and then looked out the window. This promised to be the warmest, most intimate working relationship I'd have for the coming summer. I took a breath and finished what I had to do.

"I am agreeing to do what Ephraim asks, to the best of my abilities," I said. Karl let out a hissing sigh, which meant he didn't like this. "To start, I'll do the production work Ephraim wants, and I'll do the twenty-two cities as part of Stoneway. Ian will work with me, along with the bass player and drummer who have been rehearsing the new music. If we start now, and if you have other good musicians selected, we can rehearse enough by the end of June to give people their money's worth."

Dominique still wasn't speaking, but Ephraim had been burning holes in me with his eyes this whole time. Ephraim said, "Thanks, Jason. We'll start work this afternoon if you're ready."

"Yes. I brought along a CD with most of the material, and a new outline of how the album will work. If you're ready to discuss it."

Ephraim nodded. Dominique, for all I could tell, was mad that I left her with nothing to be mad about.

"My work has gone in such a different direction since *Woman at the Well* that it's been hard to determine how to bridge two worlds while giving you honest music that works for Dominique's voice."

Ephraim read my outline, without reacting.

"I'm proposing a two-CD set that creates a 'he said, she said' story with the music. On one, Dominique does these six new songs. Ian and I will back her, in the style and musical range suitable to her voice. The other half of the "she said" CD will be cover songs she's already recorded. After listening to the demos that Ephraim gave me last week, I believe that I can add a guitar line to ensure continuity with the six originals."

"I only have to do six songs with you?" Dominique said at last.

"That's the idea, yes."

"What are you doing on the other disc?" she asked, wariness ringing in her voice.

"The same six songs in the way Ian and I play them, in that style you disparage as cowpunk. The other songs are reworked live music from when you first started singing with the band. That includes two songs from *Woman at the Well*, played the way I intended them. With lots of Beau Rufus's bass line, but without your vocals."

She sputtered. "Those songs belong to—"

"On both CDs, every song was written within the time for when you claim to be my co-writer, Dominique. No matter what style we choose to play the music, you still make money."

Ephraim shushed her. "Let's hear what you have."

I put the first CD in Karl's player, to play Side 1 Track 1 of the proposed *She Said* side, but without vocals. I could hear every minute adjustment we had made to get that sound. Play it the way we like it, then tone down, slow down, re-pace everything so it would sound like a Clear Channel radio hit. Perfect in its own kind of way, but not a way that suits my taste. It felt like the work of an idiot savant: careful re-creation of precise notes and rhythm, played in a world where real feeling doesn't exist.

"That's easy to sing," Dominique said. She sang a few lines, having bothered to learn the lyrics and music I'd sent her. "It sounds nice."

Then we listened to Side 2 Track 1 of my *He Said* version. I'd written this song a year ago, so it shouldn't have any of the sound we'd been practicing lately. We recorded it only last week, jamming hard before we restrained ourselves to create the tracks for Dominique to sing over. The difference to me was like cadaver versus living flesh. You could hear that living musicians played this music, and they loved it. When the vocals came in, it was that weird mix of my tenor versus Sonny's rocky bass which we'd discovered when kidding around with old Johnny Cash tunes. I always hear my voice as too sweet and high, because it buzzes that way in my head. On tape, with Sonny's voice amping up the vocals, it kicked the song into a separate galaxy far, far away from Side 1.

"The song means something else this way," Karl said, puzzled.

I played half of Side 1 Track 2, and then stopped it to play Side 2 Track 2, where Toby's mandolin threatened to peel paint and Ian's guitar interrupted to peel your eyeballs. I smiled, thinking of what a damn good time they had the day we recorded that. As I started to replace Side 1, to play the next track, Ephraim held up his hand.

"That is sufficient."

"Are you satisfied, Ephraim? If you don't send me back to the beginning, we can be done on June second."

Ephraim was shaking his head, which had a physical effect on me. Like being kicked in the gut and having to choke back a need to vomit. "The delivery clause in your contract mandates 'technically satisfactory' and 'commercially satisfactory.'"

"Don't look for another way to screw me, Ephraim. This is a demo. You know the final masters will be as technically satisfactory as possible without God Himself serving as engineer. You asked me to do production, so you must want my definition of perfection. You will get it."

"Your lack of modesty shocks and amazes me, Jason."

"Don't hit me on the 'commercially satisfactory' clause. I don't like mainstream, but I know what it's supposed to sound like. This is a faithful creation of what makes up nine out of ten songs on Billboard. Just because I don't want to do it doesn't mean I can't. If I wanted to play whore for you, I could give you six more just like these, but—"

"I don't want more," Ephraim said. "I don't even want this half dozen."

"But they're good!" Dominique said.

I was contemplating cold-blooded murder, which Karl must have seen because he stood and settled his hand heavily on my shoulder.

Ephraim said, "I spent the past week with the marketing studies the label did against the videos and audience reactions to the last album. I read every review and comment I could find on the Internet since last Saturday. I don't think it would be good for Stoneway to repeat the toned-down sound I mistakenly introduced in *Woman at the Well*."

"What do you want, Ephraim?"

"People want to hear your music the way you like to play it. Albion Records wants the *He Said* half, but not the *She Said*."

"You bastard!" Dominique hissed. For once, she got it faster than me.

"Relax, Dominique. If you want to work with Albion Records, you have already laid down an entire album. I'll arrange for you to work with another A&R man and producer. You won't have to work with me."

She used the bad mother word.

Ephraim was still shaking his head. "Let's separate business from everything else, Dominique. You can't ride with Stoneway to get what you want. It is not good for Albion Records if people become confused about whether they are buying Jason's work or your voice."

She started to speak but Ephraim once more stopped her. He spoke quietly, the way people do to command absolute attention.

"You can call Eric in the A&R group to finish the work we started this winter. Or you can go party with your new friends at Commodore Records. Whichever you prefer. Meanwhile, I have business to discuss with Jason."

I tried counting how often in the past twenty-four hours that my sense of reality proved to be one hundred eighty degrees out of plumb.

Dominique stood, smiling in the way that used to scare me. "Is it true what they say? Your new bitch girlfriend is replacing me?"

"Please don't call names," I said, not venturing into the rest— that Susi isn't my girlfriend and she isn't performing with us. I didn't have to say anything, because Ephraim (of all people) said:

"As of right now, there are no bitches performing with Jason Taylor."

94

"We Gotta Go On Meeting Like This"
Jason

WHEN SHE CLOSED THE DOOR—slamming it for what I hoped was the last time that I would hear—Karl burst out in dismay.

"No offense to your joyous reunion, but how the hell can you get back in bed with Ephraim?"

Ephraim and I stared at each other, feeling out what this might be.

"I gave Ephraim a hint about the phone bill, since I figured that I'm not the only naïve guy in the world. Is that about right, Ephraim?"

He nodded. "Unlike you, Jason, I rather expected that she'd entertain other bed partners. I can accept that."

"Oh, yuck."

"When you're my age, Jason, fidelity might look different to you."

"Nope, I don't think so. We aren't wired the same. I believe I'll still draw the same firm line."

"In my case, I draw the line on a partner sleeping with other recording companies. However, I don't believe that Dominique's last scouting trip resulted in everything she desired. I'm sure that granting her freedom from the contract won't please her the way it would please Jason if I'd flipped the other way and let him off the hook."

"Um—" I felt like hugging him. It seemed like a long time since there had been anything good news.

"We're digressing from our discussion of your work, Jason. Rumor has it that you are working your ass off, cleaning up your live work. Show me what else you have."

I took a breath, gathering the courage to begin. Karl put his hand on my shoulder again, which buoyed me. I put three more CDs on the table.

"There is a long CD of older material, live and studio, from before I met Dominique. It's clean and ready to release, or will be in just a few more days. No one owns rights to any of the songs except me, Ian for two instrumentals, and Beau for the tracks where we covered Lost Sons' material. This music beats anyone else's garage band anywhere. It is not too alternative, so it will appeal to more than a handful of interested listeners. Stoneway's new audience from *Woman at the Well* will like it as much as our old fans. The live work will earn money for the new label. That will be the last of any new work by Stoneway. As we agreed yesterday, after this summer's tour, there is no Stoneway."

I managed to mean it, and found I was ready to say goodbye to Stoneway, since no one else would be taking the name.

"What about the Jason Taylor Band?"

"We have this other collection—we call it backporch music— that a reasonable number of people will want to hear. It is mostly acoustic, and it is either old-time mountain music or songs of mine."

Ephraim nodded. "If this was where you're stopping, I'd warn you against it, but I heard you play last week, so I want to know what's on this one." He tapped the edge of the final CD.

"It's the next logical step after the *He Said* material."

"What we heard at the Showbox last week?"

"And beyond. I need two more tracks. The others are done and set. I have the songs. We just haven't finished the arrangements."

"Susanna Childs sings on all of them?"

"Five of them," I said. "Not the final two. She's a guest of the band. She is not a member."

Karl let out a breath again, as if he'd been kicked. Ephraim, still playing poker with me, just nodded.

"This is goodness," he said. "Are you bringing this as an artist who wants to sign with my brother's label, or are these chits for resigning with Albion Records? Mind you, Albion will make you take your backporch music and peddle it on the Internet, and my brother's label won't take you without all three discs."

"Karl knows what I want because I asked him to make overtures. As soon as Albion Records accepts *He Said*, I want to sign with Rama Jam." I named a label that, like Subpop and Hightone, works for artists and does right by them. "Rama Jam has done an excellent job of figuring out an Internet business model."

Ephraim laughed. "I'm surprised you know the term 'business model,' Jason. Have you talked with my brother personally?"

"Listen to me. I don't want to shop around. I don't want to be romanced by your fellow sharks. I'm going to focus on Rama Jam, because I like how they do business."

"Rama Jam is my brother's label."

Yikes.

"Ephraim—"

"You couldn't know. He hates my father—his stepfather—so he never mentions it. Will you work with me? Why don't you consider coming to Rama as an investor, too? That's where I'm putting all the money you made for me."

"Partner with you?"

"You are a better judge of others' talent than most A&R guys in the trenches, when you let your guard down and speak your opinion out loud."

"Jason's capital is tied up, for the most part," Karl said. "Though I wish I knew who I was negotiating with about what right now."

Ephraim watched as I tried to find firm ground. "Partner with the label," I repeated, stupidly.

"What can you bring besides this material? Your royalties? You have the Lost Sons catalog, which I know my brother lusts after. Re-issuing that catalog could be lucrative, with the right promotion."

"I don't have the catalog anymore."

"Oh screw, Jason. Who did you sell to? Is it too late?"

"Susi's father has it." It made me smile to think about it. "You know, Chas Neville is the perfect person to work with. He's smart and informed. He's been chasing down rights to other old material as a hobby."

"What about your royalties from *Woman at the Well*?"

"I gave the songwriting royalties over to an institute that trains young musicians in roots music."

"Your girlfriend's gig?"

"She is, unfortunately, not my girlfriend, but yes. Her nonprofit holds my share in future earnings."

Karl had his head in his hands, but Ephraim was laughing. "Dominique is going to love auditing royalty statements. This will be a thorn in her side for the next twenty-five years. Who do we contact to start negotiating for the Lost Sons catalog?"

"Probably Chas himself."

"Do you want to do this, Jason? Can you work with me?"

I held out my hand to shake Ephraim's, like grownups do.

"You've been right all along," I said. "I want the Jason Taylor Band to succeed in every way possible. A small crowd of devoted fans won't be enough. I need partners I can trust, and I can't shop for that among strangers. I realized this morning that you and Karl are the only people I know well enough to trust."

"When did you decide to trust me?" Ephraim said.

"Ian made me listen. And Susi."

"What did Susi say?"

"Besides goodbye? She said you were trying to keep me from hurting myself, the same as you've been saying. As things go right now, that sounds about perfect. Also, I finally heard what you were saying, that you tried to take care of business when I lost it over Beau. I was a basket case for most of last year, and everything I have in the world right now I owe to you and Karl for taking care of my business."

Karl laid a yellow pad on the table. "Shall I take notes and prepare an agreement? Do you need to bring in an attorney, Ephraim?"

"I am an attorney. How do you think I survived this long, swimming with you sharks?" Ephraim said. "Why don't we go to lunch and beat out details while we eat? Are you really Jason's business manager? What do you know about the business?"

Karl said, "I hope there's a cram course at night school so I can catch up on the details. When I last managed anything for the band, it was as roadie ten years ago."

"That is too modest. Karl helped Beau get back the rights to the Lost Sons catalog," I said. "That experience is worth a lot to us. The way I see it, there are two kinds of work to discuss: the band and the label. For my interests, I would like Karl to represent the band and Ephraim the label. Is that a good starting place?"

When the three of us stepped into the elevator, Karl—damn his eyes—said, "So if Ephraim is going to be your partner, are you going to tell him about the stolen tapes while he's still the Albion rep?"

Watching Ephraim blink, and having mastered false bravado that morning, I said, "Since we don't have to spend the next two weeks recording with Dominique, there is no reason why he should be concerned about what it takes us to deliver the final masters."

I smiled at Ephraim for the first time in over a year, and he decided not to have a coronary.

We spent almost three hours at lunch, sitting in a sports bar on Lake Union, with TV news blaring in the background. They could make veggie burgers, which is another benefit of living in Seattle again. Just when the time came to meet Ian and the others at Temple Bell, the local news showed close-ups of Dominique in plastic hand-cuffs, with Quentin Henderson making sure his face got on camera.

95
"Concrete and Barbed Wire"
Susi

I DIDN'T SLEEP AT ALL.

I know I did the right thing in closing the door on Jason. Yet the right thing should make it possible to put one's head on a pillow, close one's eyes, and drift off to the land of Nod. I re-read every-thing I had scribbled in my mental health journal, which was like reading a precise history of self-deceit. As humiliating as it was to review, I could at least take comfort in knowing that there was a modest sort of integrity I could claim: I only lied to myself.

I went running at dawn, pounding pavement, hoping that it would pound out of me whatever had taken away my self-assur-ance. I came back throbbing from the run, but never emptied my mind. Showering, dressing for work, making my lunch—it was all too mechanical to be diverting.

The truth flashed before me every moment: I'd tried to venture into the world, but I had done so in a cowardly, half-hearted way. However much I might privately decry Jason's arrogant wrong-headedness, I had hurt him.

Since my boss had made it clear that my every action would be watched, I vowed to perform each act with scrupulous attention to all the rules, both overt and covert. My attendance sheets would be one hundred percent accurate, though I'm sure that in the final weeks of school, I'd be the only member of the faculty still doing that to the seniors. All student papers would come back marked in detail the day after being turned in for grading. Every class would follow the day's lesson plan rigidly, with no time out for detours of thought or inspiration. An observer would be able to walk into my classroom at any moment and find a model classroom of calm decorum and the orderly progression of tuition. An atmosphere in which no learning could possibly be taking place.

"Everyone read about you and Jason Taylor on the Internet," Jamie Clayton said after fourth-period voice class. "We have a bet that the principal can't stand that you're more famous and important than he is. So we're supporting what you're doing, Miss Neville. We know what's happening."

I did not take comfort in that.

Asking what the Internet said about me was more than I could do. Looking for myself? The idea was out of the question. I had to believe that if it were bad, my brother Steven would tell me, since he lives on the Internet. Wasn't the Internet the well-spring of hideous rumors? I hear them from students all the time:

You can give yourself CPR by coughing during a heart attack.

J.F.K. standing in Berlin claimed to be a jelly donut.

The rock formation on Mars is a model of a human face made by extraterrestrials.

Ironing your mail will kill anthrax spores.

Perhaps ironing my email would kill the spores of hatred and vexation that I received every day. I didn't need to browse the Internet for bad news, for I had Randolph to appear just at the start of lunch period.

"I'm so sorry, Susi." He looked like someone died. "The foundation has rejected your grant."

"I'm sure you're really broken up about it, Randolph." Of all things, this was not a surprise. Rather than an announcement of a death, it was only a statement that the internment was complete. Alas! Poor Yorick, and all the rest of the graveyard scene.

"Susi, you didn't used to be so cynical. Your new friends have not been a good influence."

"I don't have new friends. All I have is teaching, Randolph. It's my entire life."

"If you're coming back to the real world, Susi, you know that I'm always right here for you."

"The real world?" Perhaps it was lack of sleep, but the idea of Randolph representing the real world struck me as ludicrous. I laughed aloud.

"Shall we have lunch together, Susi?" He ignored my outburst, but he has always ignored anything to do with the real world that I live in. Or wanted to live in.

"No, thank you. I brought my lunch. I'm going to get it from my car and eat it in the courtyard with the students."

"I'll walk out with you."

"That is so thoughtful." It wasn't his fault. Still, I wanted to rake my nails across his flesh anyway. I took the faxed rejection letter from his hand, folded it into a square and tucked it into my pocket with my car keys.

In the courtyard, a local news station was filming an interview with several students and Hector Henderson, so the whole area was clogged with students. Even the ones usually out smoking behind the gym were there.

"It's the jazz band," Randolph said. "Prescott fielded state champions for the first time in ten years."

I tried to spot among his students which of them were the leaders who, like Jason, had pulled or pushed the rest of them to a championship. I couldn't quite tell. Jeremy Simpson stood among the students, talking into the TV microphone, but the reporter could have selected him because he was the best looking member of the jazz band. That sad-sack newspaper friend of Arlo's stood with the other reporters, taking notes. Chastity Keller hung at the far edge of the knot of students, the blankest possible expression on her face, blank enough to frighten me.

"You!"

A hand on my shoulder half spun me around.

"You bitch!" A hand slapped me before I saw who it was. For the second time in a murderously long week. "I don't care if you fuck my bastard husband, but don't you dare fuck with my boy-friend. I still need him. You cannot take everything I've worked for!"

When the sting subsided enough that I could see, it was a tall, auburn-haired Fury who must be Jason's wife. She was one of the most beautiful people I'd ever seen, but she was also more stunningly angry than should be possible for a human. What else could I see? The thrilled faces of three dozen students turned on us, with a camera in the midst.

"Let's step away from here," I pleaded, wrenching away and sprinting for the parking lot. Surely the burden of the camera set-up would delay their following, if indeed a mere cat fight interested Channel Four News.

"Come back, you little bitch!"

I stopped where she'd parked her car—students at this school also drive Porsches, but they weren't allowed to park them in the faculty/guest lot. Hers ticked, cooling alongside my modest Corolla. That pretty much described the baseline differences between us. She was like a thoroughbred racehorse against my Welsh pony. One absurd thought crossed my mind as she came toward me: How could Jason choose me? Then the next thought: But he did.

"He chose me," I said aloud, though I shouldn't have. This angry person needed pacification.

"You lying bitch! You made Ephraim throw me out. I need one more album with the band. You're stealing my place. Why would he choose a nobody like you?"

"Several good reasons," Angelia said. "For one, she can sing."

Angelia stood with Cynthia and Arlo at her side, and for once I took comfort in Cynthia's girl-with-a-razor-in-her-shoe demeanor.

Dominique sniffed at Angelia. "Who are you? You're nobody, too."

"I'm in the band. You're not."

Cynthia said, "On one side we have you, playing bitch goddess. On the other, the band is playing music. The two don't exist in the same universe."

Behind us, the cameraman and Arlo's newspaper friend had emerged from the courtyard, and the principal and Hector Henderson loped alongside, arguing against the change of focus.

"I'm leaving," I said. "No good can come of this fracas."

I had my car key in my hand, prepared to do just what I said, when Dominique advanced on Cynthia and I found myself tossed aside in the clash between the two battling goddesses. As I fell, my key raked down the side of her car.

Dominique shrieked as the camera focused on us. "You bitch! You fucking bitch!"

"Not very original," Cynthia remarked. "Those aren't lyrics that Stoneway could ever use. Perhaps you could join a punk band. Though as Ryan Adams pointed out, you'd have to be able to sing."

Just as Dominique chose to slap Cynthia, who could hold her own, blue lights flashed. A Seattle patrol car whipped into the lot.

While the officers approached, Zak walked up from the other side, looking around before recognizing us. He exchanged a hippie-like handshake with Arlo, who repeated his usual spacey greetings.

"I thought you were playing music, man."

Zak said, "Jason canceled the morning session. We aren't playing until later. Maybe you can give me a ride back."

Randolph stepped up, moving into the bullying posture he used with the boys when he prepared to administer discipline. "You no longer have business here, Mr. Lukas. You withdrew from school, which makes your presence here trespassing."

"I came to empty my effing locker. You were always the king of assholes, Randolph. It is the one true thing my mother said."

"I don't have to tolerate such language from you, young man."

"There isn't a person standing here who can't recognize a flaming asshole when the light from the flame is shining right in their faces."

A murmur rippled through the students, like the famous Wave cheer.

"People here can't speak up, but I can." Zak turned to the crowd of students. "Seize the day, like you learned in Miss Neville's class. Declare freedom from the tyranny of assholes!"

"Officer, we'd like you to remove these trespassers from the school. It is distracting and dangerous to our students."

"Oh stuff it, Randolph," I said. "The police aren't going to get you out of this. Zak, can you please leave? I don't need your mother raining hellfire down on me again."

Once I spoke, attention turned back on me.

Dominique said, "Arrest her! She vandalized my car."

"She fell," Cynthia said, "because your big butt pushed her."

Dominique didn't have a big bottom at all, but it was an obscenity-free insult, and some hideous devil called forth joy in me, because that line might make it on the evening news, unlike anything else that had been said so far.

A second squad car came, and the four officers divided us up, asking each of us for identification.

The officer questioning me stood close by, looking at the picture on my school identity badge, asking if there was anything with my address inside the car. While I fetched papers from inside my car, Arlo and Zak looked in the back window—standing far too close to the officer who had already asked them twice to step back.

"Frickin' hell, Susi, that's the box of Jason's stolen tapes."

Zak gestured at a box in the backseat, which I know wasn't there when I parked the car. I was distracted, because Zak had taken to using Jason's pet expletive.

"Susi has the stolen tapes?" Angelia said.

"What tapes?" I asked, but the policeman had already focused on the word "stolen," and the whole conversation took a left turn.

"Ma'am, I need you to unlock all the doors and open the trunk."

"I didn't steal anything." I bent my head to open the door for him. "Oh, it isn't locked."

Cynthia said, "She couldn't steal anything. She pretends to be a goody-goody type, but she's just chicken-shit."

"I am not," I said.

"You're scared of Jason."

"I am not."

"Ladies, can it," one of the officers demanded. A third was taking a guitar case from the trunk of my car.

"Hello!" he said. "This is that guy's guitar that Lee Page was all over us to help find. Look, it says Beau Rufus on the case."

The officer at my elbow said, "Ma'am, I'm going to have to ask you to step over to the squad car with me."

"She didn't steal it," Zak said. "I put it in there when we were rehearsing at her house. Weeks ago."

"Then if you'll both step over here, please."

"She vandalized my car," Dominique said, after staying quiet for several moments.

"Take a leap at the moon, Dominique," Cynthia said. "Call your insurance agent. Maybe he can also find you a spot in a half-rate band, one that auditions for free snatch instead of talent."

Dominique slapped her, hard enough that Cynthia fell back against one of the officers, who toppled too, landing at the feet of the cameraman, who panned down and then back to the rest of us.

"How could Jason Taylor ever sleep with you, you silly twit?" I knew I'd weep later for having said it aloud.

"Fuckin' A," Arlo said.

96
"In My Hour of Darkness"
Jason

MARTHA CALLED MY CELL phone to say the police asked me to come recover my lost property. It would take a poet instead of a songwriter to come up with such a twisted metaphor.

When we got there, Dominique had already paid bail and left. Ian arrived when we did, and we found Arlo, wanting to tell us what happened.

"What the hell were you doing there, Arlo?" I hadn't had my fill of pounding Arlo or satisfied myself that he wasn't the source of all havoc in my life.

"Peace, man. I love you like my own brother, if I had one."

"Screw that. What were you doing there?"

"I was eating breakfast with Cynthia when she read a post on your fan site, saying Dominique would kill Susi when she found out Stoneway had replaced her in the band."

"Good lord."

"Then a guy called the house to say Dominique was looking for Susi and he worried for Susi's well-being."

"Who?"

"I don't know. I didn't talk to him. Cynthia said it had to be your stalker guy. So we went to go find Susi to help—"

"Oh shit, man, just don't. There's no fucking way in the world you could do anything that would help."

"Fuckin' A, man. You don't have to act like I'm some asshole."

He was right. For the next catastrophe of the day, I had to admit it. And apologize once more.

Karl helped Ian free Cynthia, but Susi would have nothing to do with his offer to help her. Ian took both Cynthia and Arlo home, which kept me from wringing his cousin's neck for lack of anyone better to attack. While Karl and I tried to figure how to help Susi, Zak came down the hall with his mother and a guy whose suit and briefcase screamed "attorney." Zak stopped to shake my hand, though I was quaking too much to get a grip.

"Sorry we missed work this afternoon. We're playing tomorrow morning, right? Eight o'clock?" he asked, as if nothing had happened and we weren't standing in the hallway of the effing city jail.

"Not till Monday, man. Everyone needs a break."

Gwyneth had adopted the most hostile posture possible for a woman of her station in life. Her long nails clawed at the sleeves of her sweater as she folded her arms and tapped her foot, which showed the great restraint that her manners taught her, for she wanted to scratch my eyes out.

"Let's go, Zak."

"You can go, Mother. I'll get a ride to Toby's."

"You should come home."

"Thanks, but I'm living at Toby's now."

"I blame you." Gwyneth turned on me, tapping a nail on my chest. "You are the jerk who caused all this."

"It's all a misunderstanding," I said.

"Zak isn't going to college because he wants to play music with drug addicts and wife beaters. You call that a misunderstanding? It's your fault."

"Mom, forget it. I wouldn't go, even if I hadn't met Jason."

"You asshole." She got me on the sternum with a stabbing nail.

"Stop. You're just embarrassing yourself, Mom." Zak jammed his hands in his pockets and walked down the hall and out the door.

Her attorney hustled her away, and my own attorney shrugged and allowed as to how he ought to go home, too, since there wasn't squat he could do here, while at home he could at least fight with his wife.

That left me alone in the hallway with an older man who leaned on his cane, having had the opportunity to enjoy the floor show we offered. Glasses thick as the proverbial cola bottles and a Karl Marx beard that any old lefty would be proud of, he regarded me with more than idle curiosity, until it struck me who he was.

"You must be Chas Neville," I offered my hand, hoping against hope he would take it, relieved as hell when he did. "I'm the one who caused this. My name is—"

"Jason Taylor. I thought that might be you."

"I'm so sorry for this."

"From what I heard, you didn't cause it and couldn't have prevented it. Except maybe she wouldn't have to deal with that crew out there if it weren't for you." He motioned to where the press waited to pounce.

"I told her last night that we were more than a bar band. We got sidetracked when I learned what she'd been hiding from me."

"She doesn't ever talk about what happened."

"It was excruciating to learn. I've been harassing her to sing in public. I confess, I thought her reticence was a kind of cowardice that she should overcome. What a self-righteous fool I was."

"It's good you got her out. Steven told me about it. I'd like to have heard her that night, though I suppose I'll get a lot more chances. When are you playing live again?"

"I don't think she'll speak to me after this."

"She might need to be righteous for a little while. She's just like her mother that way. You can't blame me for that."

"I want to marry her. I've been begging her since we met, but she wouldn't consider it seriously because she thought I was a broke guitarist from a bar band. Now she thinks—oh lord."

"She'll come around. Did you sleep with her?"

"I—yes, sir. I did. I—"

"Spare me the details. But if she slept with you, she'll marry you. She's like her mother that way, too. I always said it limits her options and reduces new chances for self-knowledge, but she won't listen to me."

"I don't know how I'm going to explain myself to her."

"When I looked for you on the Google, to see what Susi had gotten herself into, I found that you've had quite a mess on your hands for a considerable while now."

"I'm mortified, sir."

"No reason to be. Reading all of your history in one sitting gives me a different perspective than you had while living through it. Pretty brave of you, leaving your old blogs up after your wife had pretty much done you in. The only part I don't understand is how a guy as smart as you could be so naïve about a woman. Of course, I'm assuming that the part about wife-beating isn't true."

"It isn't."

"Didn't think it could be after I listened to your music."

"I'm having a rather odd moment with this, sir. I've lived the last few years of my life on the Internet, but I didn't expect my girlfriend's father to browse my archives."

"This arthritis keeps me from moving around, but the Internet keeps me from being shut out from the world. That's how I found you before Susi did. I listened to several of the bootleg recordings. I didn't care much for that one CD, but I got Silver Platters to send me your albums from before you met that woman. I liked those fine."

"Thank you."

"You sound so much like Jesse Rufus. Only better practiced. More disciplined. Shoot, I must have I upset you with that question last night."

"As I said, I hadn't considered it until you asked, but I've been thinking about it every spare moment since. It's Jesse. I'm sure of it. I've replayed in my mind every gesture between my mother and Beau Rufus, every word they ever said to me. I'm sure it's Jesse."

"I didn't find anything in those papers that would indicate Jesse ever knew."

"It doesn't matter. Beau did more for me than Jesse ever could have."

"That new boot that's all over the Internet, with all that wailing grief. That song is about Beau Rufus?"

"Yes. It's Susi's voice."

He stopped at that and stared at the floor, and in that fleeting moment, I tried to imagine how he and Steven would hear the echoes of Liù wailing in the new music. Then Chas shook his head and came back from his brief reverie, wiping one eye.

"I read all your lyrics and the guitar tabs on your fan sites. I'm betting you correct people when they get the tabs wrong."

"I feel rather exposed."

"Can't say I drew any conclusions that others wouldn't. I see a self-made man who overcame considerable obstacles. I see a man who spent years teaching himself what he couldn't learn in school. I hear a great musician who has a lot to offer the world."

"Thank you. It means a great deal that you would say that."

"And I think I see a good boy who's been in a lot of pain."

Chas curved his hand around mine, like you do when you're trying to show a certain fingering on a guitar.

"Lots of men have been through worse, and done better than I managed." I was choking on the lump in my throat.

"From what I've read you have plenty to complain about—watched your last relative die in pain, that woman has humiliated you in public for months, people you've never met hate you for things you didn't do. That are morally repugnant to you." Chas sucked at his moustache, thinking. "Then there's the fact that I can read all about your pain on the Internet."

"I'm past feeling sorry for myself," I said, gritting my teeth so hard that my jaw ached. "There's nothing I can do about it."

"You already did. I want to hear more of the music you made from it."

For the first time in the whole nightmare, I lost it. Chas was polite enough not to say anything when his hand got wet or when it took me several minutes to quit shaking. He put his hand on my shoulder when it was too obvious that I couldn't choke it back enough to speak.

He said, "Steven will take Susi home and stay with her tonight. Why don't you help me get back to my place and stick around for a while? I don't get about so good, and I could use some company."

"I don't drive. I don't have a car."

"You've got that there cell phone. Call us a cab."

97
"A Fool Such As I"
Susi

WHEN YOU DON'T SLEEP, the best thing is a run, the week's long run, not some three-mile jog.

It was going to be a sunny day—it had started with fog over Lake Washington—and since it would be the first day of the rest of my life, it needed to start in the garden. There needed to be hard physical work that required a great deal of concentration.

Waiting for the sun to break through and find my garden, I set to screening rocks out of that patch I wanted to reclaim for flowers. Or maybe trailing-vines like pumpkins. Or cucumbers. I think there might be sufficient sunshine through the season to allow cucumbers to ripen.

Or melons. Melons would be a fine fruit to harvest.

"You forgot gloves, SusiQ."

Sonny sat on the deck, swinging his legs over the edge, watching me. He was right about the gloves, but I wasn't in the mood for advice.

"Blisters are good for you," I said.

"Yeah, especially when you wipe good old dirt in them. Best balm for the soul in the world." He wasn't smoking.

I didn't answer, just heaved another shovel full of glacial till into the screen I used to sift out the rocks.

"Takes your mind off the pain in your soul," he said.

I stuck the shovel into the ground, and stomped it in with my boot heel so that it would stand on its own.

"Do not," I said evenly, "give me another lecture about Jason and true love. It infringes on the bounds of friendship."

"I got nothing to say about Jason," Sonny said.

"Good."

I screened rocks, stopping for gloves because shoveling is one kind of blister, but mechanically rubbing rocks through a screen really requires a leather second skin. Sonny whistled "Angel Band" while I worked.

"What if—"

"I'm done with existential questions," I said, not looking up. "What if people minded their own business, and left me out of their dramas?"

The sun had peeked through the clouds at last, so Sonny now cast a shadow. He nodded his head at my last question.

I screened soil in blessed silence, and then fetched my shovel again. Stomp, hoist soil, drop into the screen. Free soil from scree.

"What if you never sang in public again?"

"That's been the plan for two years," I said.

"No lovers?"

"I have a family. And friends."

"What if you shrank your world so there was only you?" he asked. "No directors. No collaborators. No audience. Nothing greater than what you do yourself. Alone. Like I was before Jason brought me back."

I didn't answer.

"No band?" he said. "You didn't have a band before, did you, SusiQ? In your other life? You didn't even know what being in a band meant then, did you? Back when you were a diva."

I didn't look up for several minutes. When I did, Sonny was gone.

98
"Badlands"
Jason

"I TALKED TO HER last night, Jason. I offered her generous compensation."

"What the hell, Karl? Why were you even speaking to her? You said you were going home."

"I ran into your Susi in the courthouse when she was on her way out. I was backing the press off so you wouldn't have to deal with them. After the hassle, it seemed like a good time to ask her to not sue you."

"Just great. Her first conversation is with my attorney instead of me. I cannot express my gratitude."

"That sounds disingenuous, Jason. Seriously, you should be grateful. Anyway, she says she won't sue. She won't sign anything that has your name on it for any purpose in the world."

"So you called to tell me this to cheer me up?"

"Yes, actually. I'm honing a highly professional skill that specializes in pacifying your ex-lovers, since I already invested in asbestos underwear. For a nice guy, you sure know how to piss girls off."

"It's a special talent. So why am I supposed to cheer up?"

"She said she never wants to see or hear you again."

"Yeah, I'm happy now, Karl."

"She said, 'Hear you.' Get it? I said to her, 'So you don't want to hear from him?' And she said—"

"Spare me."

"She went into a rage. She said, 'I don't want to hear his voice. I don't want to hear his guitar. I don't want to hear him breathing by my ear. I don't want to see his hands. I don't want to see him walking across the room, smiling at me. I don't want to sing his music again. Ever again.' Then she started crying."

"No, she didn't. She never cries. Nothing makes her cry. Except that time I turned out not to be Angelia's cousin. That night with Mozart. And the first time—"

"She didn't start crying right away. It wasn't until Sonny said—"

"Sonny was there? What was Sonny doing there?"

"Waiting for her to get out of jail, I guess. He went off with Susi and her brother. She didn't start crying until Sonny said, 'Never is a long time, SusiQ. Does it start right now?'"

"OK, you made her mad. You made her cry. You have nothing over what I'm capable of. I'm still the master at creating utter despair around me."

"Don't you get it, you jerk? She's in love with you. She doesn't care about anything but you."

※

"Come on, Susi. Don't make me stand out here and yell until the cops come."

Something dropped and she screamed, but she didn't answer. I had called all morning, but first there was no answer. Then there was a busy signal for the last hour. I wanted to warn her I was coming, as she had once asked. However, I couldn't wait any longer.

"We'll only get through this by talking about it. I'm standing here in front of God and everybody admitting that we have to talk."

After several hideous long moments, while I listened to her talking to herself, she said distinctly, "Stop pounding on my door."

"Come on, Susi. I'm just a musician."

"Please go away."

Her voice cracked at the high end from stress. That my wanting to talk with her created such distress was intolerable. Darting around the garage to the path behind her house, I swung myself onto her deck and then just stood by the open door. She looked at me from behind her kitchen counter, her eyebrow lifted in surprise. And—dammit—dismay. It was if she was afraid of me.

"Susi, at least let me tell you that I didn't send those letters to you. Or to Dominique."

She shook her head, looking down. She leaned on the counter as if in abject misery. Her posture, the stress in her voice, the whole scene roiled my insides, and I took a breath to find enough courage or recklessness to proceed. Knowing I had hurt her felt like a knife in my heart.

"Susi, there's this loony guy, a nut who follows me. He thinks he's my brother. He pretends to be me. He wrote those letters. I'm not the stupid, mean-spirited half-wit you think I am."

I stepped from the deck through the door.

"Please talk to me, Susi. I can't live with—"

As I reached out my hand to her, something cold and hard pressed up against my neck. A scratched and bleeding hand grabbed my forearm.

"Please don't hurt him," Susi said.

"But Jason hurt you, Miss Neville."

I knew the voice, though it was pitched near to tears.

"Warren?"

He stood in front of me so that at last I gazed into my shadow. He wasn't doing any too well. Though he still dressed like me, it had been a couple of days since he'd put on those clothes. The waxy, grey pallor of his skin seemed ghastly, and his eyes darted wildly as I spoke.

"Hey, buddy. It's me. Come on, Warren, we're friends. What's up?"

"Friends? You liar. I know what you think of me now. You said on the phone you hate me. You want me to die."

"Hey, guy. I didn't know it was you. I thought it was a stranger trying to spook me." As I took a step, he moved closer to me, the knife unsteady in his hand. I could feel sweat break out, running down my neck, prickling across my forehead. Thirty seconds in the room, and I'd never been so effing scared in my life. "I don't think that about you, Warren."

"You made me get fired. Now I don't have anywhere to go and I can't be your brother anymore." His voice was pitched in pain and hysteria so that it cut as badly as his knife could.

"Let's go talk to Karl. He'll know what we should do."

"God will slay Karl right after he slays you, Jason. You are both scions of the same devil."

At this, Susi made the slightest sound of dismay. I tried to see her, as much as the pressure on my neck would let me turn. As lily-white as she was, it wasn't paralyzing fear that marked her face. Her eyes darted as if trying to make a plan. I didn't want her to move from where she stood.

"Please help me out here, Warren. I'm worried about Susi. We should let her go outside while we talk."

"You are going to screw her over, like you did all the others. Susi isn't like the others."

"No, she is not like anyone else, Warren." He must have been able to hear my heart pounding.

"You shouldn't talk to her. You shouldn't be in the same room with her." His voice sounded like it was bleeding at the edges.

"I love her, Warren, and she loves me. Tell him, Susi. Tell Warren you love me. He's not going to hurt anyone. He's just scared. Isn't that right, Warren?"

"I'm not scared of you. Dominique made you evil. You used to be a good guy, Jason. You were a great guy. Then you made love to an evil woman. It made you evil too. I don't want evil to touch Susi."

Susi swallowed, trying to speak. "Jason isn't evil, Warren."

"You're an angel. You can't see evil, Miss Neville."

ANNIE PEARSON

"Warren, let's make sure Susi is safe. We both care about her, so please let her go outside while we talk."

"You don't care about her, Jason. You just drive her crazy. Like you drive me crazy."

"I do care about her, Warren, more than you can imagine."

"You said mean things to her. You made her cry. She was crying all night. It made me so crazy, I couldn't think what to do. Now you won't go away and leave her alone."

She spoke softly. "Warren, Jason didn't do anything mean to me."

"I heard you fighting. He yelled at you the other night when you wouldn't let him in. I heard you crying this morning."

"We just have—artistic differences. Isn't that right, Jason?"

"Yeah, Warren. She knows better than me, and I wouldn't listen. I'm listening to you right now. What do you want, Warren?"

"I just want to hear her sing. Without you around to make her unhappy. You make her so unhappy."

"No, Warren, he doesn't. If you want to hear me sing—"

She began to sing "Angel Band," her voice high and piercingly clear.

> "Oh, come come Angel Band
> Come and around me stand
> Oh bear me away
> On your snow white wings
> To my immortal home."

In the middle of the chorus, the knife eased away from my neck and he stepped back.

"I can't stand it. You hate me. You all hate me. Susi hates me."

Warren was turning the knife on himself, and I lunged to stop him just as Sonny stepped in the doorway and put a chokehold on him. We were so close that Warren fell toward me, and I collapsed with him, pinioning the poor guy.

"Had a cop do that to me one time," Sonny said. "Swore I would never let that happen again."

"Geez, Sonny. What do we do now?"

"You keep sitting on him. He is too frail to take my weight, but we had best hold him down. SusiQ, take Jason's phone and call 911."

"How does it work? OK, I turned it on. Where's the dial tone?"

"For crissakes, Susi, punch the numbers and press Talk."

"You don't have to criticize, Jason."

"I'm sorry."

"Hello, this is Susanna Neville at 4305 Leschi Place. There is a disturbed man who entered my house uninvited." She sounded as calm and sensible as she ever did. "He was threatening suicide. My friends have subdued him, but we need the police. Yes, I'll stay on the line. He is unconscious, but he's breathing fine. I don't think he's injured. To find Leschi Place, they should drive south on Thirty-Fourth Avenue and turn east on Denny." She paused. "How could they be?"

Holding the phone away, she said, "The neighbors complained about Jason and the noise, so the police are already on the way. Isn't that nice?"

She directed the cops to her door, managed the scene, answered questions, and listened as I answered the ones she didn't know. Then she sent them all away again, and we restored order in her house, so there was no trace of what had happened. When it was all quiet, Sonny kissed her on top of the head and said, "See you, SusiQ."

Then she turned to me, after having confessed that she loved me in an effort to save me from being killed.

"You ruined my life."

99
"Changed the Locks"
Susi

"THEY FIRED ME, JASON. They ordered me to stay off school property and not to have contact with any students."

"I'm sorry. I never intended—"

"Now I have no way to make a living, and my dreams of the music institute are nothing but ashes. Gwyneth has her attorney taking action against me because of Zak."

"Karl can take care of those problems if—"

"My neighbors have called the police six times, because either the press or those thugs you paid to watch my house keep trespassing on their property. Their attorney called me, just before your good friend Warren interrupted."

"Karl will talk with them to—"

"Your wife has harassed me by email for weeks. Your damn wife—to whom you are still married, all the while you've been begging me to marry you. Is she moving in here, or do I move in with her? Or do we all live with you in Ian's basement?"

"That's almost solved. It's just a matter of time—"

"You blamed her for everything that happened in the last year, instead of taking charge of your own destiny. What is that about? What does Ephraim have to do to prove that you can have everything you want? You just need to take responsibility for making it happen."

"Actually, we worked that out so—"

"Then your wacko stalker destroyed what little peace I could find in my own home. If you'd told me who you really were, I'd expect that sort of person in your wake. It's not as if I haven't dealt with it more than once myself. The creep who menaced me in Turin was much worse than your friend Warren. That one managed to bleed all over my dressing room. If you had only told me."

"I wanted to know—"

"You said you loved me, but then your attorney tries to keep me from suing you. Why would I ever care how much money you have or want a penny of it?"

"I didn't tell Karl to—"

"I have been subjected to more humiliation across all the local news media than a human should have to endure. My brother told me what they said on that stupid radio program. I can't walk out in public unnoticed."

"I didn't mean to—"

"If I had a dog, it'd be dead by now from what you didn't mean to do."

"What dog?"

"You said you wanted to take care of me. Like how mafia hit men take care of people? Is there more of my life you want to take care of?"

"We still need to have kids together. I'm hoping you'll tour with us this summer. You pretty much need to decide about the touring part today. Or Monday. Otherwise, we can't use your name to sell tickets."

"Are you insane? Do you need professional help? You ruined my life."

"I won't be half as crazed if you'd just agree to tour. You can start your institute in the fall, since you'll have plenty of your own money by then."

"My own money?"

"What you earn touring. Plus your institute has my portion of songwriting royalties from *Woman at the Well*. If it goes the way I plan, you should also have an advance from our new recordings before fall."

"Goes the way you plan? The way you plan for anything, you make the fiddling grasshopper look like Solomon in all his wisdom and glory."

"At least I'm good at taking action. If I hadn't come to see you today, who knows what would have happened."

"If you had gone home, your stalker would have just followed you there instead of bothering me. Oh, I forgot. You don't have a home. Then, at least it would have been Cynthia dealing with that poor man instead of me."

"I'm not sure about that. I think he fell in love with you and came here just like I did."

"It isn't love. It's an obsession like people have, fixating on an unachievable object to make up for their own inadequacies."

"Look, I feel bad about it too. But I didn't cause it. Karl and I will make sure Warren gets the professional help he needs."

"I wasn't referring to your stalker."

"OK, Susi, stop. I'm sorry you lost your old life. I didn't intend that to happen. But everyone knows you should be singing. You can teach any time. Except when we're touring. Then you have to be with me."

"How could I ever let my professional life get involved with yours? You raise havoc all around you."

"Yet it always turns out all right. Ask Ian. He has let me take care of business for him for years."

"Jason, you live at Ian's house. Your uncle Beau ran your business for the past ten years. Your attorney sends someone over to brush your teeth in the morning. You have a small army of people who take care of you. You can't take care of anything more complicated than making sure you have bus fare in your pocket."

"That isn't true. Who said that?"

"Ian told me this morning, when he called to ask me to please forget that you are such a jerk. Almost everybody else called to say the same thing, to ask me to see the bigger picture."

"And?"

"I don't want to be with someone just because of sexual attraction."

"You're with me because we belong together. Because we have interesting work to do together. Because being apart from each other now would be too lonely to endure. The sex is just a bonus."

"Maybe to you. But it's what keeps my heart beating at night."

"OK, if we have to have sex to keep your heart beating, I can live with that. You can still do whatever you want the rest of the time. I would never dream of telling you what to do, Susi."

"That's totally false. You are a complete dictator in rehearsal."

"That isn't personal. And we don't rehearse all the time."

"I wanted the rest of my life to be free of monomaniacal music directors and paparazzi and living out of suitcases. I'd have to change my whole life to be with you."

"It is a great life, except it used to get lonely. I hope we can end that part. Susi, I know you love me. Karl told me. He said you cried."

"I did not cry."

"There were witnesses."

※

I tried to tell him, that when I thought about us never singing together again, the idea left me ill, barely able to breathe.

At that moment, Jason touched me.

He put his hand on mine, and when I looked down, I couldn't remember what it was that had always disturbed me about his touch, because it was just his long, slender fingers grazing the back of my hand, the same way he touches the strings on my father's Martin.

"Susi, what's wrong? Say something."

He touched my lips in that way he does, causing me to shiver.

"Susi?"

"I love you. That's all."

100
"Passionate Kisses"
Jason

WHEN YOU HAVE BEEN as scared as you've ever been in your life without time to feel the jolt of adrenalin until it's all over, when you have had to acknowledge that you inadvertently but irreversibly altered the life of the person you love most, and when you have spent forty-eight hours discovering that nothing in your life is as it seems, then there isn't a possible transition into eroticism. It is true that when both of you find your fingers still tingling from fear, you want to touch each other. Yet arousal and sexual response aren't as important, or even noticeable, as other things.

Not as important, for example, as discovering that in the daylight, her grey eyes have tiny gold flecks that seem to shine light from inside her soul. Or that the side of her lips with the tiny scars is so sensitive and has to be touched in a special way. After a month of idiotic blindness, when you realize that the athletic body you admire is shaped by nature and discipline to be one of the finest vocal instruments in the world, you want to touch it differently. It requires more than a few moments of devotion to acknowledge how the divine can manifest itself in human form.

When you lay your hand over another person's beating heart, and when you know that the human being in your arms loves you passionately, and that person isn't going away, doesn't want to be anywhere else but right there in your arms, then it isn't eroticism that causes you to cry out or sigh. Replete isn't how you feel at the end, but rather through every moment, with every breath. There is no actual point of climax for either of you, when the moment you first touch is the culmination and it carries on, unconnected to any ascending intensity or need for release.

It carries you both into a shared world where touch forges bonds that nothing can break, until you are both strong enough again to move more than inches away from each other, sure your heart will keep beating if you can't feel her heart under your hand.

After biological necessity drove me from our shared bed, being the only power that could overcome such powerful spiritual and emotional bonding, I returned from the bathroom with the complete, divine understanding that the rhythms of our lives had merged. Susi only nodded when I explained, but then to prove my point, she went to the kitchen to make food before I could say I was starving.

※

"Don't start, Jason."

"I didn't. I said a week ago I wouldn't. Anyway, I don't need to say anything. You have believed in your heart that our souls are already married, ever since you first went to bed with me. Your father said you were that way."

"How do you know my father?"

"We have been corresponding by email for a few years. What is that smell? I'm so famished."

"This is an unbelievable coincidence—about my father, I mean. You, however, with amazing consistency, are always hungry."

"You have to believe in coincidence, Susi, even if you don't believe in fate. Otherwise, what were you doing in Neumo's looking for a Jason at the exact same moment that I needed to fall in love with you?"

"The idea of you and my father discussing me is too nerve-wracking. I can't ponder any other existential questions."

"We didn't start talking about you until yesterday. Before then, music was all we had in common. Though he figured out a couple of weeks ago that you were sleeping with me. If you can call it sleeping. I don't think I've a good night's sleep since I met you. It's cornbread, isn't it?"

"My father knows? Oh lord, he must think—"

"That's how he tricked your mother into marrying him, by getting her to go to bed with him. If I had known you were that way from the beginning, it would have saved me a lot of worry."

"I'm what way?"

"You have to marry every man you go to bed with."

"That is not true."

"I'm just going by what you said and what your father confirmed. If you slept with people you didn't marry but your father doesn't know about it, I suppose you could tell him. For my part,

I don't want to know. I want to believe that I have the long-term exclusive rights to your heart."

"Please just shut up." She seemed to be about ready to serve the food, because she slammed a couple of pots on the stovetop and then banged plates down on the counter.

"But, Susi, he bet me the first hundred dollars he earns that you would marry me. Personally, I think it is offensive to bet on women. However, I'm betting that I'll lose and he is betting that I'll win, so it seems morally OK. Or at least, it's not too much in the grey area of relative values."

"What hundred dollars?"

"The first money that comes from the record company advance. Chas bought the catalog of Lost Sons music. Huevos rancheros? Did you put jalapeños in mine?"

"Yes, and *queso añejo*. Is Dad buying old music over the Internet?"

"Sort of. Anyway, I'm thinking that we could get his lectures out in several alternate forms faster than the advance will pay out. So he'll make money off his own work, rather than just off his investment. Do we get butter with the cornbread?"

"You know the butter is in the refrigerator. You can stop eating for thirty seconds to get it yourself. Dad will lose the bet because there is still an enormous chance that I'll murder you before I ever marry you. Please slow down and tell me what you're talking about."

"Martha has found a transcriber and an archivist who'll begin working with Chas on Monday, so we can capture his lectures and notes. Martha is great. She can find anything. I'm surprised she didn't find my guitar before you did. Anyway, Arlo will drive him anywhere he wants to go for his research."

"Arlo? It is not like you to talk with your mouth full."

"I have a lot to say and I'm starving. Arlo came back after he took Ian and Cynthia home last night to give us a ride to your father's place. It turns out Arlo has a chauffeur's license and, amazingly, an immaculate driving record. Plus, Arlo can do all the taping of Chas's lectures, since he has so much experience illegally recording concerts. Arlo has it in his head that he can make videos, and we can publish them online and as DVDs. Why do you keep putting your hands in my hair, Susi?"

"Because it's so beautiful now that it's short. I can't help myself."

"If I'd known, I would have cut it a month ago. I can't pay attention to my food if you keep doing that."

"Sorry."

"Anyway, Chas isn't sure about video, because he thinks he'd have to get spiffed up too much. But your dad is pretty charismatic. I think the camera might like him. Whatever he and Arlo decide, I voted for moving the transcripts to the Internet as quickly as possible. I think they should publish weekly, both video and transcription."

"I don't know what to say."

"Can you just say yes to touring with us, and we can talk about the other stuff later? Ian and Toby and everyone else—they can't take the suspense much longer. Come with me now—I have to do a radio interview this evening. You can sing with me."

"On the radio?"

"Is that compromising? Is it because of the microphones? I swear I won't make you use one live unless you want to, but on the radio, you need electricity."

"After what happened yesterday, they'll ask embarrassing questions."

"Nope. My old pal Quentin is doing the interview, and he knows questions about you are off limits. Come on, it'll be fun. Afterward, you can have a late supper with me at Chas's place. He and I have business to discuss. Of course, you and I will have to bring the food."

"Why don't I call my brother Steven, and he can join us?"

"Um, I don't know if I'm comfortable with that yet."

"I don't know if I'm comfortable with you and Dad becoming best buddies. Oh god, you already are, aren't you? You should wipe that butter off your lips."

"Come help me, Susi."

"No. Your tongue and lips burn from jalapeños."

"It's not jalapeños."

101

"Straight A's in Love"
Jason

ARLO GOT A SECOND SUMMER job, living in Karl's house as caretaker while Karl sells it and waits for his own divorce to be final. We are buying it, because the first floor is perfect for low-mobility individuals like Chas, and the basement is just waiting to become a studio, though Cynthia argues that I'm paying for the house a second time.

Hiring Arlo was the first sign that Karl decided to take risks again. He vowed as to how it wasn't a serious risk when he sold his practice to a friend and signed on to learn the music business from Ephraim. That change is just an adventure, he said, not a risk. He kept Martha as his only employee, though she's working out of her own apartment with just a phone, high-speed Internet, and fax (for contracts) until we all get back to town. Whenever Karl joins us on the road, I get a great deal of pleasure from watching him struggle with the opportunities for casual sex that he's offered just because he's with the band. He's still saying no, but he doesn't think it's humorous now. To sublimate, he too got a chauffeur's license so he can drive the bus like in the old days—he says it gives him time to think about things.

Zak moved his stuff into Ian's basement when I moved out, although I don't know how Cynthia can complain about me and then take on a teen-age drummer. On the road, Sonny watches out for Zak, since everyone voted me the World's Worst Mentor, which I don't think is fair, and I don't think Cynthia should get to vote if she's only with the band half the time. It works out well though, because Sonny doesn't want to be places that eighteen-year-olds can't go. Zak still isn't returning to school in the fall—but hey, this isn't an old-school MGM musical where everyone makes the proper choices for the bourgeois status quo in the end.

In fact, what they don't tell you in the rom-coms is that for every day of casual deceit, it takes ten days of protesting innocence and promising faithfulness and positing a probable future to gain the trust that you need for a genuine relationship. Not that I minded talking all night, every night. Or biting my lip to keep from saying,

'You deceived me, too.' I'll never say it, because I got a happy ending that I didn't deserve.

On the other hand, Angelia and Toby are pregnant, which leaves me insanely jealous, since Susi and I are still working on that plan. We reached consensus with each other. Now we are just negotiating with fate, if you believe in that as a force in the universe. I'm not willing to trust anything more to fate, even though it's taken me this far.

We are going back to the studio in October—I want to do an acoustical set of just Susi and me singing Beau's songs—and then to Europe for most of the winter, which Susi says is good because she prefers Europe in the rain. Before we left town for the summer, Zak and I passed the GED test, so I proved that I'm as good as any high school graduate. However, Susi pretended like she didn't find that amusing. She insists now that the only schooling I need is a vocal coach, to make sure I don't hurt my voice.

For her own education, Susi has undertaken a summer-school remedial course in the history of rock-and-roll, and she accepted me as a tutor. She's one of the rare women in the world who first met Bruce's music through *Nebraska*. It provided a context to help her understand what happened to music between the Great Depression and when the time-travel machine dropped her in my lap. She jumped straight from intellectually comparing Hank Williams and Bruce Springsteen songs—"Mansion on the Hill"—into a seemingly physical fondness for *Darkness at the Edge of Town*. Sonny tried to introduce her to Black Flag, The Clash, and related influences, but she turned scholarly.

"How can a band be the progenitor of anarchical, non-commercial rock and then have a retrospective compilation that's a best seller?" she asked. "I don't understand."

Which baffled Sonny. He continued with his historical review, only to have her ask the same questions about grunge. Lest we forget that she's a different sort of girl, she announced early in her new adventure that she prefers Steve Earle to Bruce. "Because I identify more with Mr. Earle's lyrics," she said. Which leaves me uncomfortable. If I don't stop her, we have to listen to *El Corazón* over and over on the bus.

It would drive me to drink, except I tried getting drunk again at our wedding in August, and I pretty much didn't enjoy the last part of it, even if I didn't throw up. Also, I haven't finished learning to drive yet. Zak got his license back when he turned eighteen, and he's teaching me, but we need Ian to rent the car in each town when we want to practice driving, since Ian is the only one among the three of us that has both a credit card and a driver's license. Then Ian has to drive the car off the rental lot and around the corner, where he gets out and waits until we come back for him. He says there's a limit to which elements of his life he's willing to trust to my hands.

The part I like best is when we roll down the windows, turn the radio up loud, and let the wind blow through while the white lines zip by and Zak beats a rhythm on the dash board.

It reminds me of a song.

About the Author

ANNIE PEARSON lives and writes in Seattle. In addition to the *Rain City Incidents* series, she also writes the *Accidental Heretics* adventure series (as E.A. Stewart).

The *Rain City Incidents* series focuses on life in contemporary Seattle, among people whose work drives their hearts' desires, often in conflict with other love affairs.

Annie Pearson posts about writing and eclectic project planning at www.anniepearson.com.

Acknowledgments

We support musicians, who inspire and add value to everyday life, by paying for their music. The chapter titles and lyric references in *Nine Volt Heart* are intended to help readers find songwriters who have influenced contemporary music. The lyrics are the property of their respective owners:

"Nine Volt Heart" lyrics by Dave Alvin and Rod Hodges, © 2004, Blue Horn Toad Music, BMI; Blowout Music, ASCAP.

"A Fool Such As I," lyrics by William Trader

"A World Out of Time," lyrics by Henry Kaiser and David Lindley

"Absolutely Sweet Marie," lyrics by Bob Dylan

"All that Heaven Will Allow," lyrics by Bruce Springsteen

"All the Right Reasons," lyrics by Gary Michael Louris

"American Music," lyrics by Gordon James Gano

"Angel Band" (traditional)

"Are You Really Going Out with Him?" lyrics by David Ian Jackson

"Ashes by Now," lyrics by Rodney Crowell

"Badlands," lyrics by Bruce Springsteen

"Big Boss Man," lyrics by Lee Hazlewood and Martin Cooper

"Box Full of Letters," lyrics by Jeff Tweedy

"Box of Rain," lyrics by Robert Hunter and Phil Lesh

"Boys Want Sex in the Morning," Andrew Ratshin

"Brilliant Disguise," lyrics by Bruce Springsteen

"Call Him Up and Tell Him What You Want," from "Jesus on the Mainline" (traditional)

"Can't find my own way back home," lyrics by Steve Winwood

"Can't Hardly Wait," lyrics by Paul Westerberg

"Carry That Weight," lyrics by John Lennon and Paul McCartney

"Chains of This Town," lyrics by Chuck Mead

"Changed the Locks," lyrics by Lucinda Williams

"Christine's Tune (Devil In Disguise)," lyrics by Gram Parsons and Chris Hillman

"Come Together," lyrics by John Lennon and Paul McCartney

"Concrete and Barbed Wire," lyrics by Lucinda Williams

"Cynthia," lyrics by Allen Toussaint

"Dark As a Dungeon," lyrics by Merle Travis

"Everybody Has Been Burned," lyrics by David Crosby

"Everyone's in Love with You," lyrics by Steve Earle

"Excuse Me If I Break My Own Heart Tonight," lyrics by Ryan Adams

"Fearless Heart," lyrics by Steve Earle

"Fishin' Blues," lyrics by Henry Thomas (Taj Mahal)

"Flesh and Blood," lyrics by John R. Cash and Glen Ballard

"Fool's Paradise," lyrics by Dave Alvin

"Frying Pan," lyrics by John Prine

"Get Rhythm," lyrics by John R Cash

"Give Back the Key to My Heart," lyrics by Doug Sahm

"Go Slow Down," lyrics by Samuel Llanas and Kurt Neumann

"Goin' Down This Road Feeling Bad," lyrics by Delaney Bramlett

"Halo Round the Moon," lyrics by Steve Earle

"Hard Hearted," lyrics by Grant Sabin

"Hard Times Come Again No More," lyrics by Stephen Foster

"Hey, Mister, That's Me up on the Jukebox," lyrics by James Taylor

"Hometown Blues," lyrics by Steve Earle

"I Ain't Broken but I'm Badly Bent," lyrics by Del Reeves

"I Ain't Ever Satisfied," lyrics by Steve Earle

"I Gotta Know," lyrics by Thelma Blackmon

"(I Heard That) Lonesome Whistle," lyrics by Hank Williams Sr.

"I Just Wanted to See You So Bad," lyrics by Lucinda Williams

"I Lost It," lyrics by Lucinda Williams

"I Must Be Somebody Else You've Known," lyrics by Merle Haggard

"I Shall Be Released," lyrics by Bob Dylan

"I Walk the Line," lyrics by John R Cash

"I'll Fly Away," lyrics by Albert E. Brumley

"I'm Gonna Sit on the Porch and Pick on My Old Guitar," lyrics by John R Cash

"If Money Talks," lyrics by Jason Ringenberg (Jason & the Scorchers)

"If You Knew Susie (Like I Know Susie)," lyrics by Buddy G. DeSylva and Joseph Meyer

"Iko Iko (Jock-A-Mo)," lyrics by James "Sugar Boy" Crawford

"In My Hour of Darkness," lyrics by Emmy Lou Harris and Gram Parsons

"Instant Karma," lyrics by John Lennon

"It's All Over Now, Baby Blue," lyrics by Bob Dylan

"Knockin' on Your Door" (traditional)

"Last Blue Yodel," lyrics by Jimmie Rodgers

"Little Honey," lyrics by Dave Alvin and John Dommensen

"Lonelier Than This," lyrics by Steve Earle

"Lovesick Blues," lyrics by Irving Mills and Cliff Friend

"Mama's Opry," lyrics by Iris DeMent

"Maybe I'm Amazed," lyrics by Paul McCartney

"Mean Woman Blues," lyrics by John Lee Hooker

"Money Honey," lyrics by Jesse Stone

"More Than I Can Do," lyrics by Steve Earle

"My Old Friend the Blues," lyrics by Steve Earle

"No Surrender," lyrics by Bruce Springsteen

"Nothin' without You," lyrics by Steve Earle

"Nothing Compares to You," lyrics by Prince

"Nothing Was Delivered," lyrics by Bob Dylan

"Out of the Blue," lyrics by Neil Young

"Passionate Kisses," lyrics by Lucinda Williams

"Playing in the Band," lyrics by Robert Hunter and Bob Weir

"Price to Pay," lyrics by Lucinda Williams

"Right in Time," lyrics by Lucinda Williams

"Ring of Fire," lyrics by June Carter and Merle Kilgore

"Rip It Up," lyrics by Robert Blackwell and John Marascalco

"Send Lawyers, Guns, and Money," lyrics by Warren Zevon

"Shake My Mother's Hand for Me" (traditional)

"Shame on the Moon," lyrics by Rodney J. Crowell

"She Said She Loved Me (But She Lied)," lyrics by Jimmy Thibodeaux

"She's About a Mover," lyrics by Doug Sahm

"Shop It Around," lyrics by Jason Ringenberg

"Slippin' and Slidin'," by Little Richard, Edwin Bocage (Eddie Bo), Al Collins, and James Smith

"Smack Dab in the Middle," lyrics by Charles Calhoun

"So Long Baby Goodbye," lyrics by Dave Alvin

"Something About What Happens When We Talk," lyrics by Lucinda Williams

"Still I Long for Your Kiss," lyrics by Lucinda Williams and Duane Jarvis

"Straight A's in Love," lyrics by John R Cash

"Stumbling through the Dark," lyrics by Gary Louris and Matthew Sweet

"Take Out Some Insurance," lyrics by Ralph Kinsey and Jesse Stone

"Talk to Me," lyrics by Kurt D. Cobain

"Tears of Rage," lyrics by Bob Dylan and Richard Manuel

"That High Lonesome Sound," lyrics by Peter Rowan

"That's Not the Issue," lyrics by Jeffrey Scott Tweedy

"That's Why God Made You," lyrics by Tim Ferguson

"The Cause of It All," lyrics by Roy Orbison

"The Night's Too Long," lyrics by Lucinda Williams

"The Weight," lyrics by Robbie Robertson

"Tickin' Bomb," lyrics by Shovels and Rope (Cary Ann Hearst and Michael Trent)

"Till I Get It Right," lyrics by Larry Henley and Red Lane

"Tougher Than the Rest," lyrics by Bruce Springsteen

"Un Bel Di," libretto by Luigi Illica and Giuseppe Giacosa

"Understand Your Man," lyrics by John R Cash

"Wake Up, Little Susi," lyrics by Boudleaux Bryant and Felice Bryant

"Way Over Yonder in the Minor Key," lyrics by Billy Bragg and Woody Guthrie

"We Can Talk," lyrics by Richard Manuel

"We Gotta Go On Meeting Like This," lyrics by Rodney Crowell and Larry Willoughby

"Where Shall I Go?" (traditional)

"Wild Card," lyrics by Buddy Miller and Julie Miller

"You and Me and the Sea between Us," album by The Teds

"You Can't Always Get What You Want," lyrics by Mick Jagger and Keith Richards

"You're Still Standing There," lyrics by Steve Earle

From Jūgum Press

RAIN CITY INCIDENTS SERIES by Annie Pearson
When bad things happen to quirky people under grey skies

Artemis in the Desert
Eliot Arden, a Seattle artisan, and Sean Frederick Wentworth, the steampunk manga artist, undertake the same motorcycle journey they traveled ten years before. But this time, dreams and desires might just heat up like red slickrock in the sun. Or is that fire sparked by a 900cc bike sliding sideways down a backcountry highway?

The Grrrl of Limberlost
A murder in a Seattle coffee house. A murder on a decaying boat dock on Puget Sound. Samsara Byron, the security expert, insists this has nothing to do with her. She's heroically fending off an attack on the world's cyber infrastructure—if she could only get a cell signal.

ACCIDENTAL HERETICS SERIES by E.A. Stewart
Lost in the Languedoc Crusade

Bone-mend and Salt (Book 1)
Fight or beg for mercy when enemies turn an unjust war against you? Three ruined crusaders battle conspiracy and disaster while trapped in the new war against the Cathar heresy. Swords and grit must defend against deceit.

Trebuchets in the Garden (Book 2)
How do you prepare for the dawn of the Inquisition? Three embattled crusaders seek justice and respite amidst terror, siege, and conspiracy—as zealots prepare to ignite the next heretics' pyre.

ECLECTIC FICTION

Bad Reputation by Ajax Bell
A close-up portrait of pre-AIDS Seattle that illuminates dark corners, where homeless kids cluster for safety near the revitalized Pike Place Market. *Bad Reputation* contrasts the deeply personal need for friendship with the universal dilemma: people aren't always what they seem.

www.jugumpress.net